DATE DUE

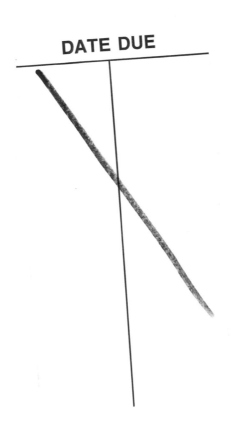

we

are

all

that's

left

we

are

all

that's

left

Carrie Arcos

Philomel Books

Also by Carrie Arcos

Crazy Messy Beautiful

PHILOMEL BOOKS
an imprint of Penguin Random House LLC
375 Hudson Street, New York, NY 10014

Copyright © 2018 by Carrie Arcos.
Penguin supports copyright. Copyright fuels creativity, encourages diverse
voices, promotes free speech, and creates a vibrant culture. Thank you for buying
an authorized edition of this book and for complying with copyright laws by
not reproducing, scanning, or distributing any part of it in any form without
permission. You are supporting writers and allowing Penguin to continue to
publish books for every reader.

Philomel Books is a registered trademark of Penguin Random House LLC.

Library of Congress Cataloging-in-Publication Data
Names: Arcos, Carrie, author. | Title: We are all that's left / Carrie Arcos.
Other titles: We are all that is left | Description: New York, NY : Philomel Books,
[2018] | Summary: Told in two voices, Nadja grows up in war-torn Bosnia in the
1990s and, in the present, refuses to discuss her youth with her daughter, Zara,
until both are traumatized by a terrorist attack in Rhode Island. | Identifiers:
LCCN 2017040313 | ISBN 9780399175541 (hardcover) | ISBN 9780698198630
(e-book) | Subjects: | CYAC: Mothers and daughters—Fiction. | Post-traumatic
stress disorder—Fiction. | Terrorism—Fiction. | Yugoslav War, 1991–1995—
Fiction. | Bosnian Americans—Fiction. | Photography—Fiction. | Faith—Fiction. |
Bosnia and Herzegovina—History—1992—Fiction.
Classification: LCC PZ7.A67755 We 2018 | DDC [Fic]—dc23
LC record available at https://lccn.loc.gov/2017040313
Printed in the United States of America.
ISBN 9780399175541
1 3 5 7 9 10 8 6 4 2

Edited by Liza Kaplan.   Design by Jennifer Chung.
Text set in Adobe Garamond Pro.
This is a work of fiction. Names, characters, places, and incidents either are the
product of the author's imagination or are used fictitiously, and any resemblance
to actual persons, living or dead, businesses, companies, events, or locales is
entirely coincidental.

to my children

may you always be
a voice of faith,
hope
and love

Don't turn your head.
      Keep looking at the bandaged place.

      That's where the light enters you.

                                        —*Rumi*

THE RIVER DRINA begins in the mountains, between the villages of Šćepan Polje in Montenegro and Hum in Bosnia and Herzegovina. It unfurls like an emerald-green ribbon, bending and twisting, carving its bed from limestone, creating a natural border between Serbia and Bosnia and Herzegovina in several places. Eventually it reaches the village Višegrad, where the majestic white stone bridge stands with its eleven large, sweeping arches. Though over four hundred years have passed, the bridge still gives tribute to the might of the civil engineering and artistry of the Ottoman Empire, but most of all, to the power of a single vision.

It began as a gift, a way to try and link two shores of people separated by faith. The idea was that if people could find a way to meet one another, they would see that one side of the bank was not that different from the other side. They would understand that God was not contained by ideologies or empires or peoples. They would know hope.

Today the bridge is peaceful, quiet. A boat passes underneath with a father and son going fishing. Tourists sit on the stone sofa in the middle, taking pictures, enjoying the weather and the view. Friends sip strong Turkish coffee in the café, on the bank, in the shade of the trees and a single willow. The bridge is indifferent to them and to the others who have crossed over and under. But it bears witness.

And if you stand under it long enough, if you run your hand along the cold stone, it will tell you stories. It will make you weep.

July 1

ANY NEW ENGLANDER worth their salt will tell you that real clam chowder is made with a thin broth and a splash of milk. It's not the thick, creamy stuff that chain restaurants serve, where you can stick a fork in and watch it stand for days. At least, that's what Dad has always told me.

"Here, Z, taste this," Dad says, and holds out a spoonful to me.

"Perfect," I say, already knowing before I taste it that it will be.

Dad makes the best chowder. That's *chowda* if you are a real New Englander, which Dad is. Born and raised in Fall River, Massachusetts, in the Portuguese section of town, though he's only half Portuguese, on his dad's side. On days like these, when he is home and cooking, he likes to think of himself as another Emeril Lagasse, one of Fall River's biggest claims to fame. Dad is not Emeril, though his accent is similar. Most days, Dad's an orthopedic surgeon over at Rhode Island Hospital in Providence. But some days, like today, he puts on his white apron with the big lobster on the front and plays chef.

I take a picture of him stirring the pot because I like when he's in this mood. It also reminds me of one of my favorite pictures from when I was little—it's framed and hanging on my bedroom wall. I'm standing on a stool next to Dad in front of the kitchen sink. Both of us are wearing aprons. I have tiny pigtails. And Dad's turning to the side, looking down at me and laughing. I'm smiling, huge, up at his face. I'm not sure if I remember it—I was probably only around three—but I remember the feeling. The fun I used to have in the kitchen with him. How he'd let me make a mess and not care, unlike Mom, who freaks about messes.

These days I'm so busy, it's been a while since I've had the chance to cook with him.

"Dad, we should make chicken cacciatore some night this week," I say, knowing it's one of his favorites.

He looks at me with surprise. "I thought you didn't eat chicken."

"Dad, come on. I started eating meat again last month." After watching a documentary in school about how chickens are raised for slaughter, a group of us decided to become vegetarians. I lasted the longest, but gave it up when I smelled bacon cooking. I figure meat in moderation is okay, and that seems like a good compromise.

"All right! My daughter has finally returned."

I stick out my tongue at him and put in my earbuds. At the dining room table, I give my computer screen my attention again. He's making it difficult for me to concentrate on my edits. I've got a new batch of photos I took of some friends as we were walking around Providence a couple days ago. Mostly it's just them being silly. Audrey and Sibyl lying on the ground, their limbs at crazy angles. More at the food truck with us eating, and tons of shots of walking. I basically take photos of anything that interests me. But there were a few that I thought were promising. Like the one where Audrey and Sibyl are running and the image is blurry. I can play with that one. There's also the couple I took of Max and Natasha. I like the shots where they didn't realize I was photographing them. They feel the most authentic. The photos that are posed are good too. They just don't feel as genuine to me.

I probably take at least a hundred photos a day. I've always got my camera on me, ready for whatever I want to document. Anytime I do anything or think *I want to remember this moment*, I take the picture. It's also why I love to look at my old photo albums. The ones where I'm a baby or pictures of my grandparents or Dad when he was little. It's so gratifying to notice the details, the moments in time forever captured.

When I look at photos, I can literally remember the smell of the room or how something tasted or even how my hand felt in someone else's. Photography is like time travel. I know I want to pursue it full-time. Maybe be a portrait photographer, but not like the ones you go to Sears for. Unique or artistic portraits. Ones that show the personality or essence of a person. Or even a fashion photographer so I could blend the two. I don't know. I'm still figuring it out.

For now, I'm working on the shot where Max had pulled Natasha in for a kiss. It's a great close-up. Her eyes are actually a little open because she wasn't expecting it. Max's hands are on the sides of her shoulders. Both of their mouths are open, and Max looks like he's going to eat Natasha's face. It's awesome, one I'll definitely post for Blur, this online group for young female photographers that I'm a part of.

I feel a presence behind me and hear mumbling. My right earbud gets pulled out.

"Hey!"

"What's this?" Mom says. She points to the picture of Max and Natasha. "What kind of pictures are you taking?"

"Mom, relax."

"Don't say relax. These are inappropriate."

"What? Come on, Mom. They're just kissing." I close the computer, not wanting her to see the others that she'd probably freak out about even more, especially the ones with Natasha in only a bra. Not because I think they're indecent, but because I don't need more drama.

"Why would you photograph that?"

"It's not a big deal."

"I don't think God would approve."

Mom only pulls the God card out when she's trying to make me feel guilty, playing Him like He's some grump-faced old man. Like this past Halloween, when she snooped on my laptop and found photos from the slasher-themed shoot I did. I don't normally do staged photo sessions—I much prefer to capture people in real moments—but my friend Luka was into horror makeup, and it was so cool, with cut necks and bulging eyes, bodies piled on top of one another and straggling limbs. Mom said it was disturbing to God to take such photos. And then she told me she was just seventeen the first time she saw a dead body.

I had stopped arguing then. I waited for her to tell me about it. Surprised that she was actually bringing up something from her past and the war. But she just stared at the bodies in the photograph.

"Death is not art," she said, and walked away.

I had stared at her back, feeling hot anger and confusing shame. She had, still has, the ability to evoke both in me for reasons I don't understand, and I end up stoking those coals for hours after.

But I have no guilt when it comes to God and art. This time, I don't give my mom the satisfaction of having the last word.

"Well, I think God would approve. God's the ultimate artist, after all. He made the human body. The Earth. The galaxies. I think He can handle some kissing. Dad, will you tell her?"

Dad gets it. He's the one who supports my photography. He bought me my first camera two years ago, while Mom just complained about the cost.

But Mom sends him one of her looks, and he simply raises his eyebrows, takes a taste of his soup. I swear, Mom has him so whipped, it's ridiculous. I know what'll happen later. Later, he and I will talk, and he'll tell me I have to try to understand where Mom is coming from. That she grew up in a different culture. That she's more traditional and has been through a lot, blah, blah, blah.

I'm tempted to take her picture right now. Her green eyes are all wide. Her perfectly penciled-in brows accentuating her indignation. Her hands on her hips. Her mouth tight like a razor. Show her what she looks like. Then maybe she'll see herself like I do. Completely unreasonable.

"Zara, I have told you. We have rules for the photographs. No risky pictures."

Mom and her rules. You can't approach art with a bunch of rules, like how she says I need to fold the laundry by folding shirts into thirds with the sleeves tucked in, right over left. How I need to clean the bathroom with specific wipes for the counter and different ones for the tub. Or brush my teeth for a full minute.

"This is *my* art, Mom."

She points to the computer. "That looks like soft porn, not art."

"It's not porn." I stand up, laptop underneath my arm, and walk away from the dining room table. I pass Benny, my younger brother, who's just come up from his room, probably to see what the commotion is about.

"And the word is *risqué*, not *risky*!" I yell right before I slam my bedroom door.

I throw my computer on the bed and feel like crying. But I don't. I've been in this spot so many times with her. What's the point of crying about it? She's never going to change.

I just wish for once she wouldn't react. That she would make an effort to try to understand that I'm not just taking pictures. I'm creating art. I wish she would try to understand where I'm coming from.

I'm going to get in trouble with Dad for what I yelled. I know how sensitive Mom is about her English. On the surface, Mom seems American enough, but it's the small things that betray her. Like how she drops her articles. Or how she still hasn't mastered the hard *g* sound of English. Sometimes she fudges idioms, like "it's raining cats and dogs" becomes "it's raining the dogs and cats."

When I was little, she used to speak to me in Bosnian. There's this song I have a hazy recollection of, like the lingering scent of someone's perfume after she's left the room. But at some point, Mom stopped speaking it altogether, refused to do it when I asked. She would give some excuse, like she was tired or that she couldn't remember the words. But it was her primary language for the first nineteen years of her life. How could she forget it?

Now I only hear Bosnian when she's dreaming. She talks in her sleep, and it's always in the soft musical lilt of her first language. I've often listened for her Bosnian words, curious about their meaning. That is, until the dream turns into the nightmare she's been having for as long as I can remember. The one that makes her scream.

In the safety of my room, I can work on my photo without anyone's judgment. But I don't feel like doing any more work. Mom has totally messed up my creative flow. And I don't want to stay in my room the rest of the night either. They'll give me space, I know. Dad will think I need time to cool off and reflect, and Mom will think I owe her an apology, so neither of them will check on me for a while, if at all.

I throw on a sweatshirt, stuff my phone in my back pocket and sling my camera over my shoulder. Then I open my window and climb outside.

Baker's Beach is almost abandoned by the time I get there, just thirty minutes before sunset. The lot is empty. I park and head to the right for the sand dunes. Since I'm not going swimming or in need of a chair, I bypass number 223, the little bathhouse that my dad's side of the family has rented since before he was born.

I climb the hill and survey the dunes. They ramble along for miles like a long run-on sentence. These dunes were my playground as a kid. My friends and I would run and jump off the massive hills, or we'd tumble down, getting sand all over us like we were donuts rolling in sugar.

The air is cool and salty, a welcome reprieve from the typical humidity and heat earlier in the day. The cool air will also keep the horseflies away. Better photo conditions overall.

I look through the lens of my camera. There's nothing I like from this vantage point, so I walk deeper into the dunes.

I'm alone.

That might scare me in a different environment, but I've been coming to this beach forever. Besides, it's private, so there are never random people hanging around. Tonight, I like the desolation of it. The feeling that I'm the only one in the world.

On top of another sand hill, I look down at the shoreline and see that I'm not as alone as I thought. There are a handful of people sitting on chairs. They're probably staying to watch the sunset.

I snap some pictures of them in the distance and keep walking.

The sweeping view of the ocean and dunes presents itself before me like a painting, like there's intentionality in the mixing of the colors from deep blue to fluorescent to yellow and orange as the sun lowers. I take a deep breath and relax. I can't help but get swept up in the moment, like it is a holy one. Or what I imagine going to church is supposed to feel like.

I've been to church and a mosque, too—multiple times. Both left me feeling disappointed. Like they were trying to capture something wild and give it a name and a place and a time.

Dad is Catholic, and Mom is Muslim, but they're not exactly devout; both my parents only attend their respective places of worship on religious holidays. We'll go to midnight mass on Christmas and sometimes to mosque for prayers during Ramadan. Still, we do have a Quran in the house, tucked away on the third shelf of a bookcase, directly next to the Bible. I've read pieces of both, trying to understand God in the pages. But it's all pretty dense.

My parents have a healthy respect for each other's beliefs, but religion isn't something we talk about. It's like my parents think it's too private a thing. I've only seen Mom pray a couple of times, and always through a crack in her bedroom door. On her knees, alone, like she's keeping a secret. It doesn't really feel like something I can ask her about.

At least they've never tried to force either religion on me. It's a good thing, too, because the two religions are difficult to integrate. There's no middle ground between them, other than simply believing that God exists. Both are a maze of dogma and practices that I don't completely understand. Throw in the thousands of years of both sides trying to kill the other, and, well, let's just say neither one has done a great job of winning me over.

But it doesn't mean that I'm not a spiritual person. I believe in God, but it's not like I pray or have this intimate relationship with Him or anything. I just know that I feel close to something when I create. Like there's this godly force I'm interacting with that's bigger than just me.

I watch the glory taking place in the sky. It's so beautiful. To me, God lives in sunrises and sunsets. It's in the middle where I'd like to catch more glimpses of Him.

"You got some great ones," Audrey tells me later at her house after I show her my photographs.

"Yeah? I won't really know until I develop them."

"Look at this. Is this real?" She's focused on one where it almost looks like I created it in Photoshop. The colors in the sky are so vibrant as they stretch above the dunes, making the sand look like sienna whipped cream.

I nod. "And I haven't even messed with it yet." I'm thinking of adding greens to the sky, playing around with the tone.

"I think you should take our senior pictures. Forget going through the school and their crappy company with the lame backdrops. I bet you'd make tons of money."

"Tempting, but portraits are kind of a different thing."

"Yeah. A thing that people would pay for."

I don't tell Audrey that straight portraits rarely capture the emotion I look for in a photo.

Her mom, Rebecca, pokes her head into the room. "You girls want some ice cream?"

"Sure, Mom," Audrey says.

"Great! Come and get it."

Audrey moans and rolls her eyes, but we get up and follow Rebecca to the freezer.

I'm always amazed by the ease of Audrey's relationship with her mom. Their conversations trail and loop along without any tension or hidden subtext you might wander into like an invisible minefield. They shop together, get pedicures and seem to genuinely like each other. It's completely different from me and my mom. If I had to categorize our relationship, *it's complicated* wouldn't even suffice. More like *it's nonexistent.*

Rebecca talks to me like I'm a normal person. She doesn't make me feel like I'm constantly disappointing her. Or that I can't be myself. That I'm not organized enough or sweet enough or just not enough, period. A couple weeks ago, I told my mom that I wished she could be more like Rebecca. I wanted to hurt her, but Mom only stared at me and walked away. Sometimes her indifference is worse than the anger.

Audrey hands me the scooper. I pack two vanilla scoops. Rebecca passes me the caramel syrup.

"After ice cream, you should probably make a packing list?" Rebecca says it more like a question than a command. My mom would have given an order. "Tomorrow we can run to the store for anything you need and last-minute party supplies."

"Ugh," Audrey groans. "There is that."

"Less attitude, please," Rebecca says. It surprises me a little how sharp her tone is. But secretly, I'm glad. It makes me feel better that despite how it looks sometimes, not everything's perfect with the two of them.

"Fine," Audrey says, pouting. She takes her long black hair and quickly ties it up on her head in a bun, something she does when she's irritated.

Audrey is leaving for her dad's in a couple of days, right after the Fourth of July party her mom always throws. She goes for a whole month every summer. I call it the *month of gloom.*

We take our bowls of ice cream back into Audrey's room.

"Don't be sad," she tells me, probably because of the look on my face. "It'll go by like that," and she snaps her fingers.

"Oh, wait." I turn around and look. "Is it August already?"

"Besides," she says, ignoring my sarcasm, "you'll be busy with your photography class. Think of me, I'll be the one babysitting two kids by the pool." She's not too thrilled about having to spend that much time with the three-year-old twins her dad has from his second marriage.

"True," I say. And she does have a point. At least Benny is a pretty cool kid. I tried to hate him at first. I had a good thing going being the only child; I didn't want a little brother at ten. I'm pretty sure I asked for a puppy. But he turned out to be a surprise in a good way.

I know he's my mom's favorite, which kind of stings, but the truth is he's my favorite too.

"Plus I'll have better weather, food and the ocean."

"Brat," she says.

Instead of packing, Audrey and I stage photos of us eating. My favorite is the one where she peeks over the rim of the bowl at the camera. She looks like she's about to do something that's going to get her in trouble. I ask Rebecca to take a couple of us together. And then I get a few in of Audrey and Rebecca.

"Pass. Pass." Audrey looks through the pictures. "No. Ooh, this one. And the other one with my mom." Audrey picks a photo of us trying to give our best serious model faces, but it's so ridiculously bad. We look like sad children. I love it too.

"Crap," I say. "I almost forgot my 365 shot."

365 is a yearlong self-portrait project I started last October with the other members of Blur. We post the pictures on our individual pages and then give each other feedback. At first, I tried to work within a specific theme, but it was too difficult to keep up. Now I try not to overthink it and just go with whatever I'm feeling in the moment. The results have been both surprising and disappointing. But the point is to challenge yourself and learn. I had planned to take one at home after dinner tonight, but as usual, the drama with my mom took over.

"Want me to take it?" Audrey asks.

"Nah. That wouldn't be a real self-portrait. I just need to think."

I walk around her house, searching for what, I'm not sure. I go out the front door. The light is on, so there are a healthy number of insects hovering by it. I get an idea. Audrey stands in for me as I set up the shot. I set the timer and then take Audrey's place.

"Creepy," she says as we look at the result.

I'm staring at the camera, but most of my face is in shadow, and the light is skewed and full of slightly blurred insects. There's a larger mosquito type thing with long, droopy legs in the foreground. It's not the best, but it'll do for today.

I tell Audrey I'll see her on the Fourth, hop in the car and head home.

· · · · ·

I park the car on the side of the road, avoiding the gray gravel driveway. I think Dad had the stones installed purposefully for my teenage years, so he could hear me coming and going.

The lights are on in the front. I glance at the time and see it's after ten.

I tiptoe across the grass so I can enter back through my bedroom window.

Rounding the corner, I see Mom sitting at the kitchen table, smoking. If I could go closer, I'm sure her usual scent—a mix of coffee and cheap perfume—would be gone.

She brings the cigarette to her mouth, takes a drag and exhales a long plume into the air. After, she sips from a wineglass. Cigarettes and wine. Mom only smokes when she's really upset.

I take her photo and look at it. From this angle, or maybe it's the moonlight, she looks so young. Like she's only just a kid.

July 2

THE NEXT MORNING, after the sound of Dad leaving for work wakes me earlier than I'd like, I stumble down the hallway and plop myself next to Benny on the couch. He's watching his favorite cartoon. It's the adventures of two larvae, which is gross and silly, but I like being with him. I pull some of the blanket up over my legs, and he snuggles into my side.

He laughs at the yellow larva farting and using the gas to propel himself forward like a race car.

This show is seriously messed up.

"Benny, breakfast is ready," Mom says from the kitchen.

He jumps up and sits at the kitchen table. My stomach stirs at the smell of scrambled eggs, so I follow him and do the same. Mom sets down a plate, and Benny eats noisily, eyes still locked on the TV.

I know she sees me, but Mom turns and walks back to the counter. She doesn't say good morning or offer me breakfast. So *that's* what kind of day it's going to be. Not a yelling-at-me-in-anger kind, but the silent treatment. Dad says it's a coping mechanism from whatever trauma she experienced in her past.

I say it's her weapon of choice.

This morning her silence is full of gibes that hurl themselves at me with full force—

I'm disappointed in you.

I don't like you.

You are not the daughter I wanted.

Why can't you be more like Benny?

I've learned to deflect them by pretending they come to me on thin slips of paper. I crumple them up into small balls and eat them.

The kettle issues a sharp wail, signaling it's done. Mom's making coffee the Bosnian way. She measures three spoonfuls of ground coffee into the small copper-plated pot with a long neck, called a *džezva*. She pours in half of the boiling water from the kettle on the stove and stirs it. Next she puts the *džezva* on the burner. Once that boils and rises to create a thick foam, she turns off the heat. Then she pours the hot water on top of the boiled coffee. She stirs it again and sets it on a tray next to a sugar cube and one small cup.

The one cup is significant. Normally she would offer me some. But not this morning because I've obviously pissed her off and she wants me to know just how much. Drinking coffee together is the one ritual Mom and I have. Dad can't stand coffee, and Benny is too little. When I was young, I remember watching her prepare it and begging her to let me have some. She finally let me at twelve, and even though the taste was more bitter than I thought it would be, I pretended that I loved it. It was something we shared, something special. Over time I grew to like the taste, and of course, sugar made it better. But mostly I liked that it was ours.

Today it becomes her way to persecute me. I don't let her win. I get up and grab some cereal from the cupboard. As I pour it, Mom sits next to Benny.

"Mom, which is your favorite?" Benny asks her.

"What?"

"Red or yellow?"

She looks over at the screen.

"Yellow."

"Mine too."

"Zara?"

"Red," I say.

"Hey, did you know that Zack watches it too? Can I have a playdate with Zack today, Mom?"

"Maybe after swim lessons."

"Did you know I'm learning to dive? It's not that hard. Well, it was scary at first, but now I go in without making the biggest splash. It's all about the splash." Benny starts cracking up at something happening on the screen.

The whole time, Mom acts like I'm not even at the table. I don't know how long she's going to last, but I know she can go a full forty-eight hours—so can I—and I have too much work to do to let her stifle my creative energy today. That's what all of this negativity is, a creative suck.

I decide to get it over with.

"Mom, I'm sorry for what I said last night."

She doesn't look at me, but she says, "Okay." Then she stands up and gets me a cup of coffee. When she sits again and passes it to me across the table, I know we've made a truce. I bite down on the sugar cube, which has lost a little of its sweetness, and take my bowl and cup to the couch.

From the kitchen, I hear Benny say, "Mom, are you going to watch me swim?"

"Of course."

"But sometimes you leave."

"This time I'll stay."

"Good. Remember when I did the belly flop?"

He laughs and then she laughs, and it's like they're in perfect harmony.

I feel something like loneliness and hurt creep across the floorboards toward me. But I shove the spoon into my mouth and stuff it all down.

Later, I show up to my first class of the summer photography program I'm doing with Mr. Singh, a famous local photographer. I haven't had much formal training, so I thought it would be a good idea to learn from a professional, and Mr. Singh has an excellent reputation as a teacher. But it wasn't as simple as just signing up for the class. We actually had to apply and get accepted. For the application, I had to submit a portfolio, which I agonized over for weeks. I had never applied for anything like it before. Fortunately, the Blur girls helped me select which photos to include.

When I was accepted, I freaked out. Dad made a big deal about it too, buying me a new lens for my camera. Even Mom congratulated me.

I look around the room, trying to size up the other students.

Of course, I can't tell their ability based on outward appearance, but I can judge confidence. The place is oozing with it, along with a bored indifference, which masks an anxiety I recognize.

To my left, a girl bites her nails.

Mr. Singh begins by showing an image on the large screen up at the front. It's a woman in red standing in the middle of many tents in what looks like some kind of refugee camp. He asks us to tell the story.

"Story?" a boy behind me asks.

"Yes. What is the story this picture tells?"

We're all quiet until a girl in the front row says, "It's a story about a girl all alone, abandoned by her family. She has endured great hardship, but there is something that suggests she is rising above her circumstances. That's why her red dress is whipping up. Her back's to us because she's facing her future. She's actually getting ready to leave the refugee camp and make a life for herself."

"Good," Mr. Singh says. "Anything else?"

"Or, she's an alien," a boy to my left says. I follow the gaze of others as they turn to look at him.

Mr. Singh raises his eyebrows. "How so?"

"She's on Mars and walking through her city after it has been decimated by a sandstorm. She's on her way to search for the wind god, who can lead her to where the water is."

Mr. Singh points his finger at the photo where there is an empty jug at her feet.

"Interesting, um . . ."

"Javier."

"Javier. Anyone else?"

No one can top Javier. I could try, but I'm not usually one for speaking up in class.

"Okay, then. This course is going to focus on photography as storytelling. There's single-frame storytelling, like what we've tried to read in this image. Then there is the photo essay, multiple-photo stories. We'll be working on both. During the course, we'll discuss story techniques in general—what makes a viewer linger. What makes a viewer ask questions? Is it lighting? Composition? Long exposure? Motion? The 'rule of thirds'? Edges? Leading lines? As you work, you must ask yourself, what do I want the viewer to feel? To see? Before the end of class I'll go over some equipment recommendations. But for now, let's look at another photo."

This time it's a picture of a long pier leading into a still lake. On the edge of the frame are a pair of feet.

As with the previous photograph, the class discusses what the story could be. We move on to another photo and then another. Mr. Singh starts pointing out the technical details as we continue, explaining what the photographer did to get the image, and what she could possibly be trying to say with it.

I've filled four pages of notes before class is even finished.

For the last fifteen minutes of class, Mr. Singh walks the room and looks at the photos we have brought with us today. I chose one of the photos I'd been working on when Mom and I got in the fight. It's Audrey and Sibyl running down the street toward the camera.

"Very good, Zara. What would you say the story is?"

I stare at the picture. Audrey is looking straight at the viewer, her mouth open in the middle of a laugh or a breath, while Sibyl's face is turned, looking away from her. Her hair is covering the side of her face. I heightened the blur around their feet and their arms so it almost looks like they're not even touching the ground.

"I'm not sure . . . maybe something about having fun with friends." My voice, nervous, comes out scratchy like the texture of the light in the photo. "I was more caught up in the moment. They just look really happy."

He only nods, doesn't say anything more and moves to view the person's work behind me. Fun with friends? Lame. I look at my picture again and see something that could be in anyone's social media account. I should have used the one that got Mom all freaked out. At least it would have caught his attention.

When Mr. Singh's had a chance to look at everyone's photos, he tells us that we have two assignments. The first is to work on a single-frame story due next week. At the end of the course we will also have to turn in a series of ten photos for our multi-photo story.

"There's a photography exhibit going on in Boston that you may want to arrange to attend. It's actually called *Narrative*, perfect for our class." He writes the link to the exhibit on the board for us to take down. Half the class takes a picture of it with their phones. I write it in my notes. "In the meantime, look for the stories around you. What stories do you already find yourself in? Maybe start there. Good luck!"

I get out of there pretty quickly. All kinds of ideas are

swimming in my head. I've just got to catch one and then I'll be on my way.

When I pull up to the house, Benny is outside on his scooter. He's not wearing his helmet, so his dark curly hair shakes and bobs as he moves.

After I park and exit the car, I begin shooting some photos.

"Zara! Look." He jumps off a tiny ramp Dad got for him at the start of summer. *Click. Click.*

"Awesome, Benny. Do it again."

He does and I take a ton of pictures, trying to get the sequence.

"Did you get it? Did you get me?"

"Yeah."

"I want to see."

He ditches the scooter and runs up to me. I bend and show him the pictures.

"Oh yeah. Cool. Look at how I'm jumping. Bam." He strikes a pose with his leg up in the air like I captured him.

"Hey, want to do a real photo shoot with me?" I ask.

"But I'm playing."

"You can keep playing, I'll just follow you around."

He shrugs. "Sure. I won't do anything weird, though."

I laugh. "No weird. Just be normal."

I take photo after photo of Benny doing all the things he usually does, like playing with toys and eating snacks, drinking milk, playing video games. I know I don't need that many, only ten. But you really need to take a lot in order to get the jewel.

Even with all my shots, though, I'm not sure what story I'm trying to tell.

Then I decide to stage some. Maybe I could call the series *Boy* or *Childhood*. I take a series of photos of Benny strumming his ukulele. The next shot I set up is him holding my old dolls. It takes a little bit of negotiating to get him to do this, but an offer to buy him a toy the next time we go to the mall does the trick. He makes me promise to take him tomorrow so I won't forget.

A little while later, Dad gets home from work and pokes his head in my room to see what I'm up to.

"What's this?" he says when he sees Benny. Benny is wearing an old dress of mine and playing with action figures that I've set up like a tea party. I've also smudged red lipstick on his mouth, making it smear on both sides so you can't tell if he's frowning or smiling. On his head is a Red Sox hat.

"Zara says I have to."

"Benny," I say. "Traitor."

"Hey, bud, why don't you jump in the shower. Get cleaned up and then we can build that new Lego set together."

He jumps up, almost rips off the dress and runs out of the room.

"Thanks, Dad," I say sarcastically.

He comes in and sits on the edge of my bed.

"Do I want to know what's been going on in here?"

"It's just a project for my new class. I'm exploring the concept of boyhood."

"Okay, well, just don't torture the kid."

I roll my eyes. "He's fine, Dad."

"So, how was the class?"

Dad is stalling. I know he wants to talk to me about Mom.

"Great," I say. And wait for what's coming.

"So . . . we should talk about what happened last night with your mom."

Like I said.

"Dad, you know she was overreacting. She just makes me so angry. She never tries to understand my work."

Dad can't argue with that. Ever since I started taking photography seriously a couple years ago, Mom acts like she's not interested. She's always telling me to put my camera away. The only time she even comments on my photos is to express disapproval.

"I understand you were upset, but your mom just has a different way of looking at things," he says.

"She called my photo pornographic. Do *you* think that's what I'm doing? Shooting pornos?"

Dad gets a little flustered at the word, rubbing the back of his neck with his hand. "No, Z, of course not."

"So how do you think that makes me feel?"

"Pretty bad."

I settle a little into the pillow behind me. "Yeah. Exactly."

"But how do you think your mom feels?"

"I know exactly how she feels. She hates what I do."

Dad sighs. "Or she may feel like you don't like her, or that she's losing you, and that scares her."

I look at him like he's crazy. "Mom is not scared of me. She's the one who's scary."

"I didn't say *you* scare her. Look, I know it's not easy, but you know, she's had to overcome things that most people never have to."

And here it comes. The speech about how I should try to be more understanding.

"Sometimes people who go through the kind of trauma your mom experienced get affected in all kinds of ways. Now, it doesn't mean that bad behavior is acceptable, and that a person isn't responsible for their actions, but it does mean we can try a little harder to show empathy. Your mom has dealt with a lot, and she's worked really hard. Sometimes we have deep wounds, and when they get poked or scratched, we lash out. The lashing out usually happens to the people we love the most."

"Well, she must really love me, then," I say.

He laughs. "You have no idea."

When I was little, I used to follow Mom around, a little duckling, just to be near her. Part of it was instinctive; she was my mom and I wanted to be close to her. Just like any kid. But the other part was bigger—I wanted to know her so I could understand where I came from. With Dad, it was easy. I could tell that I got my love of trying different foods from him, my eye for clean lines, my insistence on doing something over and over again until I got it right. But with Mom, I could never find an opening. She only gave so much of herself; most of it she kept somewhere else. Somewhere boxed up, out of my reach.

After a while I stopped searching, stopped looking for the secret and not-so-secret doors. I also closed my own. Now we are two houses alongside each other. A long fence built between. There was that poem we read in English class last year, something about good fences making good neighbors. But I wonder: what do good fences do to mothers and daughters?

In seventh grade, I was assigned a project where I had to do a profile on my parents. Dad was more than happy to answer all of my questions about growing up in Fall River, Massachusetts, his family, how hard he worked in medical school. But Mom, she didn't want to do it, and the more I pressed her, the angrier she became. Dad told me it was painful for Mom to talk about her past because she lost her whole family in the war in Bosnia.

I hadn't even known she'd been in a war.

If I had been in a war, I wouldn't keep it a secret. But for Mom, it was like her life was divided—before the war, and after. For her, there was no looking back. She never even called herself Bosnian. She was American.

I've researched the Bosnian War on my own and from what I've been able to piece together, former Yugoslavia started to break up in the early '90s after the end of communism. Yugoslavia comprised six different socialist republics, which each sought independence in the early 1990s. Serb leaders in Bosnia feared a Muslim-controlled Bosnian state, so the Bosnian Serbs began a campaign to eliminate every non-Serb in Bosnia, focusing mainly on driving out and killing Bosnian Muslims. The policy was called ethnic cleansing.

What still makes it really confusing to me is that the people of former Yugoslavia were all Slavic in origin, so they all kind of looked the same. But there were many years of bad blood politically, and unresolved conflict between the three main ethnic and religious groups: Serbs (Orthodox Christians), Croats (Catholics), and Bosniaks (Muslims). Old hatreds and fears drove much of what was behind the fighting.

I was shocked to read about the killings, the rapes, the death camps. I watched footage of snipers picking off civilians in broad daylight on a city street. Bombs dropping from planes. Buildings exploding and on fire. It was as if I was reading about World War II, not something that happened only twenty-five years ago.

And I couldn't believe my mom had been a part of it.

The Bosnian War lasted almost four years and was pretty brutal. Something like one hundred thousand people were killed, fifty thousand women were raped and countless were injured. Afterward, leaders of the Serbian military were hunted down and charged with war crimes, including genocide, since they had strategically attacked and eliminated Bosnian Muslim men, women and children.

Because Mom's Muslim, her whole family was targeted, and she had to flee to Sarajevo. After that, she came to the States as a refugee. I'm not really sure what went down, though, because she never talks about it. I only know the very basics.

I know she's Muslim in name, but aside from observing Ramadan and Bajram (which is like a small Christmas), she's barely religious. Dad refers to Mom as Muslim-lite. She believes in God but doesn't follow a prayer calendar or observe Islamic laws and traditions. I can't say I mind. I don't think I'd like having to wear a hijab all the time. Even though I do think some of them are pretty.

I used to catch Mom staring off sometimes, and I'd ask her about her past and the war. She'd wave my questions away like they were nasty swallows, stay silent or leave the room. Or, if she was in a good mood, she'd change the subject, switch focus, ask about my day at school instead. But it always came across like she was trying to keep things from me. A few years ago the silence crept in between us and never left. Now it's always there. A quiet, deafening protest forged and nurtured by each of us for different reasons.

And when Dad bought me my camera, things between us grew worse. Something about the sound of the shutter bothered my mom. Or the lens pointing in her direction. Maybe both, I don't know. She never liked having her picture taken, even though she was always camera ready. Her perfect face painted on first thing every morning. But whenever I tried to take her picture, she'd turn. Or make an excuse. Or just walk away.

I don't ask to take her picture anymore.

I've tried to find old photos of Mom, but there are no pictures of her before age twenty—when she first came to the United States. It's like she didn't exist before arriving here. Those early photos I took were my attempt to will her into being. Into a person, and a past, I could access. I'd study her face, try to dissect my own from the prints.

Everyone who meets us says we look so much alike. As far as I can see, we share the same sea-green eyes, that's it.

Not that it would matter if we did look more alike. Green eyes or not, we have nothing in common.

July 3

THE NEXT MORNING, Benny and I join Mom on a trip to the farmers market. Even though the air is so thick with heat you could cut a knife through it, the warmth is not enough to thaw the usual cool front that still hangs somewhere between Mom and me. Dad suggested I go as a peace offering, help her with the shopping. I'm here, all right, but I'm not sure peace or help is part of the equation.

At one of the stands, a couple of yellow jackets hover, drawn by the pungent smell of overly ripe peaches. Mom doesn't seem to notice them. Her hand rests first on one lopsided peach, then on another, taking so much time, choosing as if her life depends on it. I stare at the yellow-and-black bodies, ready to run away if they head for me.

Mom picks up a peach that is bruised and caved in on one side. I turn and shake my head, both disapproving of her choice and as an attempt to relieve the nausea I feel from the smell and the heat combined. It's so hot out already.

Mom asks the vendor how much.

They are a dollar each.

Mom says she'll take five. Five dollars for rotting flesh. I don't get her at all.

She gives one to Benny, who immediately takes a bite. The juices run down the corners of his mouth like melting butter. I hold up my hand to stop her from offering me one.

As we move down the line, I take pictures. Some are of people. Most are of food. I'm thinking I'll call this series *The Farmers Market*. Not a very original title, but effective.

We keep going until Mom stops in front of baskets of multi-colored heirloom tomatoes. I zoom in on and snap a few shots of a green tomato, beautifully white striped like a zebra. Mom talks with the vendor and then she's laughing at something he says. Before she can react, I get a few in of her too. I check them and am surprised that I got more than a blurry profile. Most of my photos of her are indistinguishable. She could be any woman with bangs and shoulder-length layered brown hair.

"You want my photo?" the vendor asks.

As an answer, I start taking some of him. He has no problem being my subject. He even poses, tipping his baseball cap in my direction.

It's only been a couple of seconds, but Mom says, "Zara, others are waiting."

There's no one behind us, but I drop the camera and follow, determined not to get into it with her. Again.

Mom's like that girl who's always following the rules and worried about getting in trouble. I bet she never took risks, never did anything crazy.

I feel sweat running down my back, so I find a sliver of shade from a small blue umbrella and stand there. Today it feels like the tropics, or what I imagine the tropics would feel like since I've never been. It's probably mid 80s with 100 percent humidity. Hopefully I'll get some good photos to make the trip worth it, since Mom clearly doesn't care that I'm here.

Benny pulls on my shirt, ungluing it from my back. His hands are all sticky and gross. They leave a stain. But he points at something up ahead and across the way. I follow his finger to see what he's looking at.

"You can get me candy instead of a toy," he says.

"Later," I say. "You know Mom's system."

"Yeah," he says, but his eyes remain on the homemade candies on the other side.

Mom's system looks like this: we walk up one side of the market all the way to the end and then turn around and go down the whole other side. There is no crisscrossing allowed, no changing of lines. No varying from Mom's way of doing things, just like with everything else.

And then there are all the weird things you shouldn't do at all, like drink cold water or sit too close to the TV or sit on concrete.

One day last year, I was sitting on a concrete slab out front when she picked me up from school.

"Hi, Mom," I said once I was in the car.

"Don't sit on concrete like that again," she said. "It'll make your ovaries freeze."

I stared at her openmouthed and then put in my earbuds.

The sick thing is I don't sit on concrete anymore. I don't even want to use my ovaries yet, and I'm already worried about freezing them.

. . . . .

At the strawberry stand, the vendor holds out a toothpick with a piece of fruit attached. I take a bite and nod to my mom.

"These are amazing."

"Yes, but expensive."

I look at her like she's got to be kidding because she just paid five dollars for the worst peaches ever and now she's balking at three dollars for a pound of strawberries.

For probably the thousandth time, I think about how I don't understand my mother.

"Mom, really. These would be great at Audrey's party. Everyone loves strawberries. I could cut them up and add cream. Pour it over some pound cake. Perfect dessert." Dad would approve of my culinary suggestion.

"Okay. One basket."

It's a small victory, but I relish it.

"Come, Zara," Mom says. "Watch your brother."

"Yes, Mom."

Benny and I follow her up the line, eating samples along the way. At some point, he takes my hand.

The candy's coming up on the other side. Benny sees it too. He sighs.

Maybe it's the sigh or the way he's watching the candy, but I decide to hell with Mom's weird system.

"Mom, I'm getting Benny candy."

"Zara—" she starts to say, but I keep walking. Just because she's neurotic and probably OCD doesn't mean I have to be. I don't have to be anything like her.

I'm not.

Right as we reach the candy stand, there's a huge boom that reverberates through my whole body. I don't even realize I've been picked up and hurled into the air by some unseen force until, suddenly, I hit the ground, hard. My lungs gasp for air. I cough and cough. I can't breathe. I roll over. The side of my face comes apart. My hands fly up to my ears, protecting them from what feels like screwdrivers pounding into both.

I open my eyes, but they instantly sting and water. I shut them tight.

Benny.

He was standing right next to me.

My head is a deadweight, but I still try to lift it. My eyes are burning. Everything is filmy, so I reach out and search the ground for my brother. I stretch my fingers as far as they can go. I find my camera. But no Benny.

I try to say his name, but my jaw is so tight, like it's been wired shut. My whole skeleton feels like metal. Each time I move, there's a jolt through my body. Then the ringing starts—high-pitched—along with a throbbing in my head.

I keep searching for what feels like forever, until finally, my hands find a small body.

"Benny," I manage through clenched teeth. "Are you okay?"

"I think so," he whimpers. "Zara?"

"I'm here."

His hands grab for me.

"What was that?"

"I don't know."

My back is on fire, like a murder of crows is ripping into

it with tiny sharp beaks. I reach around to touch it, and there is something hard jutting out of my skin. I pull out a small piece of glass from underneath my shoulder blade and stare at it, wondering how that got there. Did I somehow fall on broken glass?

I start to register the noises and the images. All around us, people are crying and dazed. Smashed vegetables and fruit litter the ground between the aisles. It looks like some kind of war zone, like some scene you'd see in a foreign country on the news.

I grab my camera. It seems to be working, so I start taking pictures, using the lens like a telescope. It's hard to see through the smoky haze.

"Mom?" Benny calls. "Mom?"

I lower the lens and stumble across to where we last saw her. My feet trip over a man lying facedown.

He doesn't move.

I don't even apologize as I crawl over him. I accidentally step on his leg, but I get no reaction because it's no longer attached to his body. I keep going.

"Mom?" I shout.

My mother is not here.

My shoe leaves a bloody print on the asphalt like a stamp. I move slowly through the thick smoke, sweetened by all the splattered fruit. To the right, a man pushes the insides of another's stomach back into the cavern of his body. I can't keep the contents of mine in either.

I lean over and throw up all over a pile of unrecognizable debris.

This is some type of horror movie. I force myself to keep walking.

I reach where I remember the vegetable stand to be, but it's now just a pile of battered trash.

My mother is not here.

I look down and see a severed clenched fist and feel the bile rise again. But then I recognize a yellow shoe on the ground. Her yellow ballet slipper that I hate, but which she wears all the time. I pick it up, cradle it to my chest. It's smudged with dirt.

And then I see the matching one. It's underneath a wooden plank, and next to it is a bare foot. The foot is bare because I hold the shoe the foot is supposed to be wearing.

Benny is suddenly by my side, and I'm about to tell him to stop crying, that it'll be okay, when something deep within me claws its way out and I'm screaming.

I'm screaming and screaming, and holding my mother's shoe.

1992
Spring
Višegrad
Bosnia and Herzegovina (BiH)

NADJA STOOD WHERE Marko told her and tried not to move in the cold. She watched her breath become a ghost and float away to haunt someone else. Behind her, the bridge rose, solid and ancient and empty. The bridge that was so famous, people from all over came to see it and take pictures, much like Marko was making her do now. It was still so early that most sane people were warm in their beds or maybe just now waking. But Marko had wanted to capture her with the sunrise.

"Okay. Okay. This is perfect. Yeah, so, just look at the water."

Nadja stared at the Drina flowing swiftly to the left of her. The river was normally an emerald green, but now it looked blackish. The early dawn masked its beautiful jade color. If she believed in old tales, she might think that creatures lurked in its depths.

The shutter of Marko's camera, a quick *click, click, click,* stamped the air like a seagull's prints on sand—all thin and singular in the morning quiet—while a breath of a breeze stirred through a willow's leaves, sounding like rain.

He posed her several times as the sun rose steadily. For the last one he had her look straight into the camera.

"Got it!" he said. He walked up and held her and kissed her nose. "You're so cold."

"What do you expect?" Nadja said. "It's freezing."

"I'm sorry, but I really wanted to do this."

She reached up and brushed aside some of the long dark hair that stuck out of his gray beanie and fell into his eyes.

"It's all right. I can suffer for your art."

Marko kissed her again. His lips traveled along her jawline, and he whispered, "Thank you," in her ear, tickling her.

She laughed. "Just make me look good."

"Impossible not to."

They walked over to a café to get coffee and some breakfast. They talked about her piano studies, his photography, how he wanted to document specific moments in time. They argued about Nirvana. He was a fan. She not so much. She said she preferred New Kids on the Block, but only to get an eye roll from him. U2 was a safe choice. They both liked the band. Marko had bought her a tape of *Achtung Baby* for Christmas. She'd already played it so much, the ribbon had gotten tangled. He'd had to show her how to use a pencil to rewind it.

They didn't talk about what had happened when her family fled to Goražde, another city only about forty minutes away, in the middle of the night a couple of weeks ago. They didn't mention the Četnik soldiers that had showed up and still walked the streets even after Nadja's family returned a few days later. They didn't talk about him being Serb and her being Bosniak and how that somehow mattered now. Before, they had always simply been Bosnian. They no longer spoke of Croatia, the Dubrovnik being in ruins, the fact that Marko would turn eighteen in two months and would be drafted into the JNA (Yugoslav People's Army) like all other boys his age. They didn't talk about the things his father said about her.

"Oliver," Marko said. His eyes narrowed over the lid of his small coffee cup, measuring her response.

"Oliver," Nadja said in agreement.

Oliver was a Croatian singer very popular in Bosnia and Herzegovina, especially Sarajevo. Sarajevo, the city they both wanted to escape to. The plan was she would attend the university next year and then he would join her the following year. To leave their tiny town that had few prospects. To chase down a life that they couldn't have here. Nadja would need to go on scholarship and was getting ready to apply for one.

Everything would be different in Sarajevo.

Nadja took a bite of her *lokumi* and couldn't help but frown. Her mom's pastries were much better.

She felt someone watching her and glanced to her right. It was Mr. Radić. She was about to smile in greeting, but he glared at her. She quickly dropped her eyes. His look made her feel like she was some rotten thing he had just eaten and needed to spit out. Nadja thought that he probably had a rough night of drinking and was here sobering up. Her family knew he was a widower and a drunk because he was their neighbor. Four years ago they had helped him with the funeral arrangements for his wife because he didn't have the money. Sometimes her mom brought him baked bread. They had always been good neighbors. Mom said that's what you do in the hard times. You help each other.

"Hey, where'd you go?" Marko asked her.

He lit a cigarette, took a drag and passed it to her. She did the same. A thick plume of smoke now danced between them.

"I'm here," she said, and passed the cigarette back to him. But her mind still lingered a bit on the old man.

"What do you think?"

"About what?"

"I knew you weren't listening."

"I'm sorry. I was distracted."

Marko glanced at her neighbor.

"You don't have to be afraid. I'm with you."

She smiled faintly because he meant it.

"Let's get out of here," Marko said.

Marko paid their bill, and they left the café. They walked arm in arm all the way up the narrow one-lane road back to her house. Their boots crunched on the patches of old snow that hadn't melted yet. It was the start of spring, but winter held on tight.

In front of her house, Marko kissed her quickly, just in case her parents were watching through a window.

"This is for you," he said, and handed her a mixtape.

"Thanks," she said, reading *Songs for Nadja II* scrawled across the yellow masking tape.

"This one is more Nadja centric," he said. "Maybe you'll like it better than the last."

"I loved the last one."

Marko smiled, kissed her on the mouth again and left.

Nadja watched him round the corner, then she opened her front door and deposited her boots, hung up her jacket by the door. She walked over to the fireplace, where there was a fire already going.

"How was Marko?" said Benjamin, Nadja's ten-year-old brother, from the couch, followed by kissing noises.

"Shut up, Benjamin!"

"Ooh, Marko. I love you."

Nadja stormed out of the living room. Not for the first time did she wish she were an only child. Her mom and dad were at the kitchen table smoking and drinking coffee. They watched the news on the small TV.

"Do you want some breakfast?" her mom asked, not looking away from the video clips of destroyed buildings and fires. The drama happening in what felt like another world to Nadja.

"I already ate."

"And how is Marko?" her dad asked.

"Fine."

He studied her face, searching for something more. He didn't find it, so he turned back to the TV.

"Serbs are talking war, revolution," her dad said.

"I don't believe it," said her mom. "Only *papci* listen to this talk."

"Not anymore. I hear them whispering behind my back at work. Remember last week? I was sent home early." Nadja's father worked as a teacher at the high school she attended. Sometimes it was a drag for her to have her dad there, but other times, when she needed a pass, it worked in her favor.

He leaned forward, his left hand waving around as he spoke, revealing the exasperation behind his words. "What do they think?

We are part of a secret plan? We are jihadists? We don't even go to mosque! We eat pork. We are terrible Muslims." He pointed his finger. "This will get worse before it gets better. Maybe we should have stayed in Goražde." He looked at Nadja. "What does Marko say? Does his father tell him anything?"

Marko's father worked in government. Ever since Nadja had overheard him telling Marko to "be careful with the Muslim girl," she noticed that Marko only saw her whenever his family wasn't around.

"We don't talk about these things," Nadja said.

Her father stared at her. "This is all people are talking about." He turned his attention back to the screen. The image had begun to wobble. He reached for the left antenna and maneuvered it until the picture cleared.

Nadja didn't want to talk about war or Croats or Serbs or Četniks or Bosniaks or anything else. It confused her, but mostly it worried her that she saw fear in her father's eyes.

She went to her room, removed her red flannel and threw it on her bed. Then she popped the tape Marko had given her into the portable black radio on her dresser. As she pushed the big black Play button, a slow love song came on. She imagined dancing to this song with Marko at the school formal coming up.

Nadja grabbed some tweezers from the top of her dresser, where she kept a bunch of necklaces and bracelets. She plucked some stray hairs underneath her brow while she sang along to the song. Her English wasn't the best, even after studying it for years in school. But she knew most of the words to the American pop songs.

"Rush, rush . . . Hurry, hurry, lover, come to me . . ."

One day she planned to go to America. Maybe study music there. She hoped Marko would go with her. They would travel to New York and walk all around the city. She imagined the photos he'd take of her there. How she would take the subway and live in an apartment and have an exciting life compared to the one in Višegrad.

Nadja wondered what Marko was doing now and if she'd see him later today.

Through her open window, she saw her neighbor Mr. Radić walking down the street. She hid behind the curtain so he wouldn't see her. And she didn't fail to notice as he stopped in front of her house, spat and continued walking past.

What have we ever done to him? she wondered.

But the more she thought about it, she realized he had never been a nice man.

July 3

THE TV HANGING in the corner of the room plays footage from somewhere in Idaho, then it switches to California, then Texas. The reporter explains how the attacks were strategic, hitting Americans where we wouldn't expect it. On the third of July instead of the fourth. In shopping centers and strip malls, grocery stores—farmers markets. The targets were small, precise, exposing our vulnerabilities.

The hospital is packed with survivors, relatives of the victims, doctors and nurses. I stare at the footage of a farmers market in a small Rhode Island town. I watch like I am simply a spectator, like I didn't just live through the bombing.

When I first arrived at the hospital, a thick swarm of reporters had buzzed and pestered me.

How do you feel? What was it like? Do you have a few words for people?

They shoved microphones in front of me, but my mouth was clamped shut, still sore from the blast. Even now, my jaw is heavy, with the constant taste of metal in my mouth.

Police officers, more than I've ever seen before, huddle together outside. I should tell them to spread out. They're an easier target when they're together like that. Besides, what protection can they offer me now? They're only human flesh, which, after this morning, I know is the easiest thing to pummel and maim.

I feel bile rise as I think of the open stomach and the man holding the intestines in his hand. I wonder if it was the large or small one. How do you tell the difference?

"Zara?"

Dad says my name softly, like he used to when I was a little kid. I tear up and unhinge my jaw. "Hey, Dad."

He places his hand on my shoulder. Even though his touch is light, it sends pain down my whole right side. He looks exhausted. The last time I saw him was hours ago.

When Benny and I arrived at the ER of the hospital where Dad works, I glimpsed a slight wince of concern before he masked his face with professionalism. There had already been a number of ambulances to arrive before ours, including the one that Mom rode in, unresponsive and with a weak pulse. But still breathing. Once we got there, everyone was yelling and running, but to me they looked like people on fast forward, sped up one minute and then somehow slowed down the next.

Benny had a big cut on his leg and a few surface-level scrapes on his arms, knees and forehead, but Dad was worried about him enduring any additional trauma just by being in the hospital, so Dad's sister, my aunt Evelyn, came to get him pretty quickly. I, however, needed sixty-seven stitches in my back, thanks to the glass and nails that exploded from the pipe bomb. But there were so many people in much worse shape than me.

I'd seen and overheard words like *missing limb*, *critical condition*, *blood transfusion*. It was enough to know that some shrapnel in the back was hardly anything in terms of life and death. I barely even felt the nurse pull out the glass, nails and pieces of metal. Dad said I was in shock.

It's been hours, and still, I barely feel anything.

He leads me in and out of clusters of people. Some are like me, freshly wounded. Others are family or friends. Even though it's overcrowded, there's a nervous quiet. Everyone watches the TV. Everyone waits as if the worst is yet to come.

Once we're inside an exam room, Dad carefully examines the stitches and dressing on my back.

"Looks good. Really good. Shouldn't even leave a big scar." The last part he means as a comfort, but I know he's not telling the truth. Of course I'll have a big scar. How could I go through something like this and not?

He examines my face next, carefully removing the white bandage to look at the damage underneath. My arms are also scraped up, but nothing bad enough to require stitches.

"How's Mom?" I ask when he's done.

"She's . . . Would you like to see her?"

I stand and wince. It's like I've had the most intense workout. My whole body is sore. I've also got the worst headache, small needles piercing behind my eyes, even with the pain medication the nurse gave me earlier.

I carry what few belongings I have with me—my camera and Mom's left shoe—and follow Dad to room 311 in the intensive care wing.

I enter behind him and stop.

Mom is in a white bed. Her eyes are closed. There are tubes coming out of her arms. She's hooked up to one of those oxygen nose things. A machine pumps every twenty seconds. I know because I've already counted to forty, standing there, staring at her.

Someone has cleaned her face, wiped all of the dirt and blood from the wound on her head. But she would be upset to have us looking at her. That she is exposed this way, without her hair or makeup done. Her face is undefined, naked. I look away.

Dad checks her vitals and holds her hand and bends and kisses her and whispers something close to her ear.

I am still in the doorway. He motions me over.

"She had some internal bleeding, but we were able to stop that. Lacerations to the chest and legs." Dad speaks to me in clinical language like she's a patient and not Mom. But she's not his patient. She's his wife. She's— "She suffered serious head trauma, so she had cranial surgery to relieve the pressure."

The words *head trauma* contain no emotion, reveal no hint of who the woman with the shaved head lying in the bed is.

I nod, mimicking his bedside manner—don't appear upset; smile, keep your eyes on the patient.

"They said she was found underneath a structure. It could have been that collapse or maybe some other debris that knocked into her." He notices what I'm holding for the first time. "Is that her shoe?"

"Yes."

He turns from me then, but not before I see the anguish in

his eyes. He brings his hand up to his mouth to stifle a sound, but I hear the sharp intake of breath. If Dad loses it, I think I will freak.

"When will she wake up?" I ask.

He clears his throat. "That's what we're waiting on. She's currently in a coma."

It's not exactly an answer to my question, but I remain quiet. I sit down in the chair next to Mom, suddenly feeling exhausted.

"You can hold her hand. It might help."

I haven't held Mom's hand in years. I can't even remember the last time. Was it crossing a street? I stare at one of them. I used to think they were so pretty. Now her fingers are swollen; her nails are bruised deep purple. There is dirt underneath them.

"You can speak to her too, if you want."

"She can hear us?"

"I don't know, but it helps if you speak to her. In case she's listening."

He checks his phone.

"Zara," he says, his eyes on the screen, "will you be okay here?"

"Yeah, sure."

He kisses me on the head.

"I love you, Z."

"Love you too, Dad."

"We'll get through this. Your mom"—his voice cracks a tiny bit, and my eyes water because I've never heard uncertainty in his voice before—"your mom is a fighter. The bravest person I've ever known. She hasn't gone through all that she has . . . for this," he says. "Courage, Z."

He leaves me alone with my mother.

I listen to the machine click. I listen to her breathe.

I've never really thought of Mom as brave. I know she survived a war and came here from a refugee camp in Eastern Europe, but she's always seemed more anxious, more tightly controlled than courageous. Still, it must have taken a lot to start over. She met my dad two years after she arrived in the States. He was in his first year of residency when she walked into the ER with a broken arm. After he set it, he asked her out.

Now Mom's arm lies battered and uncovered next to me. I touch her hand, surprised to find how soft it is.

"Mom?" I say. "Can you hear me?"

I wait for a response, but there's nothing except the slight movement of eyeballs flitting behind the lids like they've been doing since I stepped into the room.

I don't know what else to say.

My mouth is dry. My back and legs are sore, but nothing like they'll probably feel in the morning. I sit there as Mom's chest rises and falls, and I wait.

Minutes pass, and my breaths come faster. I try to slow them down, but I can't. I feel myself giving in to the fear. Fear because of what's happened. Fear because sitting next to her now doesn't feel that different from being in the presence of her silence. She's probably taking so long to wake up to punish me.

But then it hits me—

She could really not wake up. She could be gone forever. Even though I have wished her horrible fates both under my breath and in my own head, suddenly, the reality of my mom dying chokes me. I would never have the chance to know her. I'd never know where I came from.

And she wouldn't know me.

She doesn't know me.

I finally think of something to say to her.

"Don't you die on me," I whisper.

And I hold her hand like I imagine a dutiful daughter would.

1992
Spring
Višegrad
BiH

NADJA EXHALED, ADDING her own plume of smoke to the already hazy living room. Uma, her best friend since the age of seven when they met in class, sat next to her on the couch. On the other side of Uma sat her parents. Nadja's parents occupied two separate chairs across from the couch. Nadja held Uma's hand and played with the green-and-purple rope bracelet she wore. The power was still out. Thick yellow candles on the coffee and side tables cast large shadows on the walls that moved like apparitions every time someone shifted in their seats. They listened to the radio, hunched over, leaning closer, as if proximity to the device would give them more answers. Benjamin, the only one not smoking, drew superhero characters from his comics in his notebook. Nadja recognized one as Wolverine. She shook her head. She couldn't get into comics. She preferred words to pictures. And not even superheroes could help them now.

There was fighting in the north and talk of villages being burned. Even Sarajevo had experienced violence. At a protest in the city, there had been a woman shot dead in the street.

Nadja's dad tried another channel. This one spewed propaganda about how Muslims were organizing. How they couldn't be trusted. The voice warned about Muslim neighbors hiding guns and planning to kill everyone. Serbs needed to band together against a possible jihad. The voice called for a holy war to protect Greater Serbia.

Nadja's dad turned the radio off.

She wondered who the voice was talking about and if she needed to be afraid of such Muslims. The Muslim faces staring back at Nadja in the room looked just as confused and afraid as she was.

"We shouldn't have come back," her dad said.

It had been only a couple weeks ago that tanks and Serbian paramilitaries and blasts like thunder engulfed their small town. Bags were quickly packed and then they were running, dodging bullets, heading for the car. They passed others doing the same. They escaped to Goražde, only thirty-nine kilometers upriver from their town. They spent seven days there, all in one small room of another family kind enough to help them. The residents of Goražde had been welcoming, offering help, turning their sports center into a processing center for those fleeing Foča and Višegrad.

Resistance fighters, just regular civilians from Višegrad and other nearby villages, had taken control of the power station and dam that served the whole region. Murat Šabanović, the leader of the rebels, had threatened to blow it up, wanting to flood and destroy Višegrad instead of turning it over to the Serbs' control. Shelling began, and this was what led people to flee. Murat didn't have the explosives, but he did pull the turbines, setting the Drina free. The flood damaged many homes and buildings in Višegrad.

Thankfully, Nadja's own home was on high ground, up on the hill, so it had survived without detriment.

After five days, Serbs came to Goražde and told the people who had fled to come back. Told them all Muslims would be safe. The JNA, specifically the Užice Corps, had freed Višegrad from the Serbian paramilitaries. They would reopen schools, stores and cafés. Everything would go back to normal. The power plant and dam that had been the object of the fight had been secured by the Serbs. Nadja's family came back to find some flood damage and a couple of buildings shot up, but otherwise things did go back to normal. But still the Četniks remained and roamed. Thousands had set up camp in the area. Nadja's family tried ignoring the now open contempt with which some people treated them, people like Mr. Radić, teachers her dad worked with, the mailman and some of Nadja's mother's customers, who stopped buying her jewelry.

"We were foolish to trust the JNA." Nadja's father, his broad shoulders hunched over, sounded bitter and tired. She worried at his tone.

"But they are here to keep peace," Uma's father said.

"They are pulling out. Besides, the JNA is in the hands of the Serbs. They are leaving us to the Četniks." The men with long, dirty hair and beards who patrolled the town all hours of the day.

Nadja's mother took her husband's hand, watching his face intently. He lowered his voice, as if it were wrong to speak freely in his own house. "Why do they make us sign a loyalty oath? Why have they confiscated all Muslim weapons? Not only guns, anything. Kitchen knives? What is that telling us? We have nothing to defend ourselves with. We are sitting ducks. Some of my

Serb colleagues have left, and many are acting strange, like they know something. It is not coincidence. We are leaving at the end of the week for certain."

Nadja and Uma exchanged looks but remained silent. Uma's hand tightened around hers. Nadja wondered about Marko. She hadn't seen him in days, and she was worried about what that meant.

"Where will you go?" Uma's father asked.

"I don't know. Sarajevo, I think. It will be safer in a big city. I have a friend there from college who is willing to house us until I can find transport out of the country."

"I heard they are not letting Bosniaks leave by car," Uma's mom said.

"We will journey on foot, then. I must protect my family."

"You should join us," Nadja's mother said.

"But we have lived here all our lives," Uma's mother said. "Why should we have to go? What will happen to our home? There is nothing for us in Sarajevo or any part of the world. It won't get as bad here as you think."

"You think Karadžić and his animals will stop?" Nadja's dad said. "They call us *balije*." He waved his arm. "No one would say such a derogatory remark to me before. You will see. Only Serbs will be allowed to remain. It is fascism all over again. No more Tito. No more Yugoslavia. Nothing to stand in the way of old hate." He stood up and paced in front of them. "We will be caught here. Your home may not last another shelling. It has stopped now, but who knows if or when it'll begin again? And what about the burned homes already? We are right next to Serbia.

What makes us think we will be safe here? Our history? Our population? With this"—he pointed at the radio—"being broadcast all the time? We leave. If I am wrong?" He shrugged. "So what? We are inconvenienced for a time. If I am right . . ."

Silence answered him.

Nadja didn't want to leave Marko. Maybe her dad was exaggerating things. Why would anyone want to hurt them? They were not soldiers in an army. They were just a regular family. But she couldn't deny the holes she saw outside the buildings, the crater in the street she'd had to walk around on their return from Goražde. The one that looked like a bear had clawed its way through the town.

Nadja and Uma hugged each other longer than usual at the door. They hugged like it was the last time.

"I'm afraid," Uma said in her ear.

"Don't be," Nadja said. "You will see, this will all be resolved. We'll be back in school and complaining about it in a few days."

Uma pulled away, tears in her eyes. "I never thought I'd say I miss school."

"Me neither." Nadja touched Uma's ear, the small silver third piercing she had gotten recently. "Looks good."

"Yeah?"

"Yeah."

Uma and her parents opened the front door, and her dad looked down both sides of the street. It was a quiet, clear night with the power still out. You could see some candles flickering in windows. The mood was ominous, like something was coming, though nothing was there. If the darkness had something to tell them, some knowledge of deceit or death, it remained silent.

"God be with you," Nadja's father said, and then he closed the door.

Up in her room, Nadja packed a bag of essentials. That's what her mother had told her—only take essentials. *This is so stupid,* Nadja thought. *What are essentials?* Marko, he was essential. The way he touched her, the way he looked at her, the way he made her whole body feel like it was alive. Maybe he could come with them? How could she make him fit in her bag?

She removed the mixtape from inside her cassette player and put it in the small open suitcase on her bed. She carefully folded each item before putting it in her case: panties, bras, jeans and shirts, sweaters, a sweatshirt, socks. She pulled some photos from an album and enclosed them in a letter-sized envelope along with her identification papers. The small stuffed bear on the bed was the last to go in. She shoved the case under her bed.

Tap. Tap. Tap.

She froze at the sound on her window.

Tap. Tap. Tap.

She opened the curtain. Marko.

She put her finger to her lips and helped him climb inside. He held her and sat on her bed. His hands cupped her face, and he kissed her.

"We are leaving," she said after pulling away to breathe.

"When?"

"The end of the week. I have a suitcase packed."

"Where will you go?" he asked.

"Sarajevo. My dad has a friend there."

"Good. I was coming to tell you to go. You need to get somewhere safe."

"What happened?" She searched his eyes and saw the fear.

"I have heard things. It's crazy. I . . . Look, my dad has been called to duty. He says I will be too." He grabbed her arm and looked deep into her eyes. "Tell your dad to leave tomorrow."

"You're scaring me."

He dropped her arm. "I don't know if I'll be able to protect you, don't you see? I . . ." He kissed her, hard, too hard. She pushed him away.

"Protect me from what?"

"They want all the Muslims *gone*."

She felt a sudden shiver in her body from the way he stressed *gone*. Did the *they* include Marko? And what did he mean by *gone*? Maybe her father hadn't been exaggerating after all.

Marko knelt down on the floor and held Nadja's body to his, burying his face in her stomach.

"Marko . . ."

He looked up at her, his eyes dark as pebbles. "I love you. The world is going mad, but I want you to know I love you. That is the truth."

He got up and climbed out the window. She watched as he went, his figure hunched over, hands in his pockets, quickly walking away from her down the narrow street.

July 3

DAD HELPS ME out of the car, leading me by the elbow up the walkway to our house. My camera is slung over his arm. Aunt Evelyn opens the door.

"Zara, honey." She hugs me too tight, and I shrink a little from her touch because of the pain. I'm still wearing the hospital gown open at the back. I didn't want to have to put a shirt on over the wounds.

"Oh, your back! I'm so sorry. Here, let me help you." She takes over Dad's hold on my arm and leads me to the couch. Then she hugs my dad, pulls back and searches his bloodshot eyes.

"How's Nadja?" she says.

"We don't know anything new," he says. "It's still early."

Aunt Evelyn reaches out and places her hand on his arm. "What can I do?"

Dad sets down the camera, puts his hands on his hips and looks around as if the answer is to be found somewhere in the living room.

"Can you stay the night? I need to get back, but I want to make sure Z and Benny are okay."

I want to tell Dad to stay, that it would make me feel better to have him here, but I know he can't bear not being with Mom in case something changes.

"Sure. Sure," she says. "Whatever you need."

Dad goes to his room, while Aunt Evelyn gets me a glass of water. When he comes back, he gives me a hug and kisses the top of my head. "I love you. Try and get some rest," he says. And just like that, he's gone.

Aunt Evelyn smiles while I slowly drink the water. She's nice, the kind of aunt who always remembers to send birthday presents, but she and I aren't exactly close. She's pretty busy with her own stuff, so we don't see her that often, even though she only lives about thirty minutes away. The last time we spent any significant time together was when she broke up with her fiancé. She spent the night, and Mom made coffee and sat with her for hours. I hadn't known what to say because she was crying a lot. Mom seemed to know exactly what to do.

Mom, who is now in a coma in the hospital. It doesn't seem real.

"Where's Benny?" I ask, placing the empty glass in her outstretched hand.

"He's asleep," Aunt Evelyn says. "Poor kid was really shaken up."

"Yeah, I bet." I stand up and feel woozy. Now that the shock and medication have worn off a little, and the adrenaline has left, the pain is intense. A wave of nausea hits me. I walk down the hallway and crack open the door to Benny's room.

He's sleeping on his stomach with his foot sticking out of the covers and hanging over the side. I creep in quietly and place my hand on his face. He looks peaceful. You'd never know that he almost died earlier today.

"Love you, Benny," I whisper.

He doesn't stir. I leave.

When I come back to the living room, Aunt Evelyn is waiting for me.

"Can I help you with anything?" she asks.

"I think I'm just going to wash up and go to sleep."

"Are you sure you don't need help?"

She takes a step toward me, but I hold up my hand. "I can do it."

I'm not allowed to get my wounds or stitches wet for a full forty-eight hours, so I take a washcloth and wash slowly, carefully. But as delicate as I try to be, the fabric feels like sandpaper, scraping, bruising, revisiting sites of my body's trauma all over again.

Afterward I put on a gray cotton skirt and the loosest tank top I have. I take one of the pills Dad left for me. I try to find a comfortable sitting position, but I can't. So I lie in my bed on my side. Audrey texts that she'll call me in a bit. We've been texting since I was in the hospital. My phone has been going crazy with texts and calls from all kinds of people. Somehow, word got out. I don't have the strength to answer everyone, but I've sent a few texts out to my real friends, like Sibyl and Natasha, and let Audrey take care of the rest.

My head is now throbbing, and I hope the pain medication I just took will kick in soon. Anything to dull my senses, to put out the fire on my back and the ache in my bones.

I turn over on my stomach and click on the TV. Every channel is focused on the bombings. The headline ISIS CLAIMING RESPONSIBILITY IN JULY 3 ATTACKS ACROSS U.S. crawls across the bottom of the screen. The number of casualties has risen from the initial eighteen to thirty-six. There's footage of people running for cover. The smoky haziness after. Children crying. Why do they always show children crying? When a reporter interviews a woman who lost her sister, I change the channel. I need a distraction, something that doesn't require me to think. I search until I find *The Princess Bride*. Classic.

Then there's a knock on my door.

"Yeah?"

Aunt Evelyn opens it. She's already in her pink pj top and bottoms. Her brown hair in a high ponytail. She looks like she could pass for my sister instead of Dad's.

"You left this downstairs." She places my camera on my desk.

"Oh. Thanks." I can see the smudgy lens, the dent on the side, the dirty strap from here. It looks too heavy to hold.

"You okay?"

"Yeah, I'm just going to watch this until I fall asleep."

She nods. "I'll be in the guest room if you need me."

"Okay," I say. She closes the door.

My phone rings. It's Audrey.

"Hey," I answer.

"Hey. How are you doing?" She says it in this too soft, too sweet, overly concerned way that makes me upset.

"I'm alive."

"Want me to come over?"

I don't really know what I want. Part of me wants her here. The other part wants to hide from everyone. So I say, "Maybe tomorrow."

"Okay. How's your mom?"

I sigh. "Still in a coma. My dad's at the hospital now."

"Holy shit, Zara. I can't believe it. I mean, if you had been right next to her, then . . ." Her voice breaks a little, and she's crying.

I know I should feel sad too, but right now, I don't feel anything.

"It's just so crazy," she says. "What did we do? Why would someone want to kill people like that? I don't understand it. Did you know Christine was there with her family too?"

"I didn't, no."

Christine is an amazing tennis player, like, on her way to Wimbledon. But she's more Audrey's friend than mine.

I wonder if anyone else I know was at the market. I don't remember seeing anyone, but the details are fuzzy; it's hard to remember much of anything. Anything except those damn yellow shoes.

"Yeah, she was hurt too, but I don't know the details. I'm just so glad you're okay," Audrey is saying. "Oh my gosh, I completely forgot, how's Benny?"

"He's fine. Sleeping." And I'm suddenly so tired that, as much as I love Audrey, I don't feel like talking to her right now. "Actually, it's really late. I should probably . . . go." My brain's fighting to find the words.

"Okay. My mom is going to make you guys some food for

a few days. And she wants me to make sure you know you can come here too. If you want to. And I'm not leaving for my dad's until next week. I told him I need to be here for you. So I'm around if you need anything."

My eyes water. "Thanks."

"Of course. You're my best friend. Love you, Z."

"Bye," I say.

By the time Buttercup pushes the Dread Pirate Roberts down the big hill and she hears the familiar refrain, "As you wish . . ." and realizes he is actually her long-lost love, Westley, I am overtaken by a sudden wave of nausea. I almost don't make it to the bathroom. I throw up everything until my nose and throat are burning. Then I flush the toilet and lie down on the floor. But soon I feel another attack coming on, and I'm dry heaving into the toilet.

A pair of hands pulls my hair back off my face.

"Zara, poor baby," Aunt Evelyn says.

She helps me to my feet. I take the small cup of mouthwash she places in my hands and rinse out my mouth.

"Come on. Let me help you get back in bed."

I walk with Aunt Evelyn down the hall and into my room. The last thing I remember is her humming something and playing with my hair.

July 4

I WAKE UP in the dark. The clock on my nightstand reads 3:15. That must mean in the morning. I move slowly because everything hurts. The gauze covering my wound sticks to my back like a wet towel. I wince as I free it from the dried blood, or maybe it's pus from the wounds on my back. When I sit up, my head spins. Whatever Dad left for me to take was powerful stuff. My throat is raw from throwing up.

I check my phone, and there's a text from Dad saying for me to call if I need to. I text him instead because it's so late and he may be sleeping.

A text immediately returns to me.

Glad you got some sleep. Sitting here with Mom. No change, but we are confident about her recovery. You feeling okay? Take one of the painkillers if it is too much, but make sure you eat something first.

No kidding, I say.

Rest easy. Be home soon. Love you.

I walk to my parents' room, quietly. The bed hasn't been made. Mom would never leave her room like this: half the covers on the floor, dirty clothes in a pile by the bed, drawers slightly open with their contents peeking out. In his hurry, Dad must have frantically packed a bag.

Something about the messy sheets, the way they stare at me, defying my mom's cleanliness, bothers me. I make the bed, even though every movement is accompanied by pain. I place all her little pillows in a row, exactly how she does it every morning. I also pick up the clothes and shut the drawers. I sit down on the bed and look around the room. Better.

The jewelry box on her dresser catches my eye. A couple of her necklaces are sticking out like someone was riffling through it. Maybe Dad was searching for something. I can't imagine Mom leaving them that way. I get up and begin putting the pieces back inside. One of them is my favorite necklace of hers, a choker with black stones—the one she never lets me wear. I start to put it on, but I catch my reflection in the mirror. There are cuts and scrapes and a large bruise that's formed on my right temple. I lift the bandage.

That can't be my face.

I touch my skin lightly. My upper cheek is all swollen and red with a large gash. I must have done a face-plant while falling. Fuzzy images return to me, a severed leg, Benny coughing and looking up at me, Mom lying unconscious, a child crying . . . I push them away. I don't want to think about that right now.

I leave the mirror and open my parents' closet, step into Mom's side. All her clothes are neatly hung and organized. Her shoes all perfect in their racks. I don't know what I'm looking for exactly. Maybe something beyond the cleanliness and order. Something that might tell me who she is.

There are several boxes way up on the highest shelf of the closet. I grab a chair and stand on it. The pain in my shoulders and back is intense, but I struggle through and carefully pull one down. The first box is full of sweaters, clothes for the winter. I put it down and look through another one, moving slowly. This one has paperwork in it, some forms and bills. I open another, and there are tons of soaps and bath oils. It's a little hard to manage, and my back is killing me, but I shove that box aside and notice a small, pretty red one deep in the closet. There's a thread tied around a knob on the lid, so I unwind it and lift it off gently. I sit with the box on the bed.

A small brown bear lies on his back looking up at me. He's dirty and smells like ash. Underneath him are papers. Many sheets of lined paper like from a college-ruled notebook. The tabs have been picked off. They look like letters, I think, with a salutation at the top of the page—*Draga Mama, Dragi Benjamin, Dragi Marko,* etc. and Mom's name at the bottom. I pull one out and try to read it, but it's in Bosnian. They all appear to be in Bosnian.

What I spy underneath the letters makes my breath catch. There are dozens of old photographs. My heart races, but I flip through them slowly, careful with the edges, studying the faces. In many of them the only person I recognize is my mom. They must be pictures of her family—of my grandparents and uncle. I've never seen these people before.

Mom is so young. Her hair is long, all one length and without bangs, not the layered look she has now. In one photo, she and her parents and brother are standing together on a bridge with what looks like a river underneath and a little town on both sides of the hills. Mom doesn't look happy to be there; I know her irritated face. I smile, seeing it already there when she was a teenager.

There's another photo with her and a boy sitting together. His arm is around her. I turn it over and read *Nadja and Marko '92*. Mom would have been about sixteen or seventeen. The guy she's with is really cute—medium-length dark, shaggy hair, that '90s grunge kind of style. He's got deep brown eyes. I wonder who he is.

Behind that is another photo of my mom; she looks about the same age as in the last one. The shot is of her standing in front of a large bridge. I think it's the same one from the family photo. There's a river to one side of her. On the bank is a single weeping willow just slightly out of focus. Her mouth is wide open in the middle of a laugh. Her hands are reaching toward the camera, like she's trying to tell the person who is taking the photo to stop. She's wearing a red scarf and beanie. She looks so happy. *Nadja '92 Love Marko* is scrawled on the back.

I feel like I've just discovered the greatest treasure, and it makes me both sad and angry. I hold the photo of a family I never knew. How could she keep them from us? Since I'll never meet them, I would have loved to at least know what my grandparents looked like. I stare at them. Mom looks like her dad, but she's the same height as her mom. Her mom is pretty, with brown hair swept up on top of her head. It looks like the photo was taken on a warm day. They're all in T-shirts and jeans. Mom's brother, my uncle, is making a goofy face, like he's purposely messing up the photo. It's totally something Benny would do.

I want to ask Mom about them, about where she grew up, about her life before the war. But now . . . what if I don't get the chance?

I study the picture some more. I try to pull out a smell or sound or texture, but I can't. All I get is a feeling of immense loss that surprises me with its intensity. After all, I never knew them.

I keep searching through the box, and I find prayer beads, a small bottle filled with some dirt. There's also a silver necklace with a glass heart at the end. Inside is a dried petal of some kind. What is it about these items that made them special enough to keep?

There's a Superman comic, too, the pages worn like it's been read over and over. Last, hiding underneath the comic, is a small sketchbook whose cover has drawings of superheroes like Spider-Man and the Hulk. It says *Imovina Benjamin—Ne dirajte!* and inside it's filled with more drawings. Some heroes I recognize, many I don't. I flip to the end, where there are sketches of men with shaggy hair and beards holding guns. I close it, suddenly afraid and unsure if I should be looking at all these things.

I knew Benny was named after Mom's brother, Benjamin, but seeing something he owned, something he created, makes him come alive in a whole new way. Did they call him Benny too?

The name suddenly becomes infused with greater meaning. The whole box does. If my Benny had died in the bombing, would I have kept artifacts from his life? His action figures? The Lego TIE Fighter he just finished building? Photos from my shoot of him the other day?

What if those pictures were the last I took of him? They seem so inauthentic now. Some imposter's desperate attempt to make art. I'll delete them later.

I put everything back where it was, place the lid on top, and walk over to the closet, ready to return the box to the back of Mom's shelf, when I notice something on the bottom. A tiny little latch. I pull on it gently, and a secret compartment opens. Many precisely folded bills come tumbling out. I count the cash—two thousand five hundred dollars. Why is she keeping all this money hidden?

Why does anyone hide cash? What is she planning? Or did she steal it?

I don't know what to think, but I feel uneasy somehow.

I refold the cash and put it back where I found it, tying the ribbon around the outside exactly like my mom had it. Then I place the box on the top shelf of the closet.

My head is spinning. I feel like I've just peeked over the cliff of some great abyss I didn't know existed, and I don't know if I want to venture into it.

It's all too exhausting to deal with, so I pull back the freshly made covers of my parents' bed and slowly sink underneath. The sheets smell like my mom, like the perfume she wears. I try to go back to sleep, but every time I close my eyes, the few images

I can recall from the farmers market—the ones I keep trying to block out—parade behind my eyelids. The severed leg. The blood. My mother being pulled, lifeless, from underneath the rubble. Benny's terrified face. The little girl crying on the news.

The longer I lie here, the stronger the images grow, so I get up and walk to the kitchen. I'm nervous that if I don't eat, I'll get sick again. But I'm also nervous that if I do eat, I'll get sick. My stomach growls. There's Chinese food leftovers in the fridge, but I don't feel like eating them, so I decide to make some blueberry waffles. I tie Dad's apron around my waist and get to work, which basically means I just measure some waffle mix, pour it into a bowl, add water and stir. I add the blueberries after the mixture has set in the waffle maker, just like Dad showed me, and close the lid.

While I'm waiting for the waffle to be done, the front door opens and Dad walks in. He leans one arm on the wall while he removes his shoes, his head resting in the crook of his arm, unaware that I'm watching him. He looks even more tired than before.

"Hi, Dad," I say, worried what emotion he'll let show on his face if he thinks he's alone.

"Oh, Zara," he says, startled. "You're still up?"

I shrug. "Couldn't sleep. You want some waffles?"

"Yes, actually. That sounds really good."

He walks to the liquor cabinet and pours himself some vodka and tonic in a small clear glass and then joins me in the kitchen. He sits at the table, sipping his drink.

"How are you feeling? How's your back?"

I don't tell him about my reaction to the pain meds. I don't want to give him something else to worry about.

"I'll live."

"Let me check your face." He peeks underneath the bandage and pulls away, giving me a sad smile. I feel my heart crack.

"Why don't you keep it covered for now until it heals some more."

The light turns red, a sign that the waffle is done. I open it up and see a perfectly cooked waffle. I set it on a plate, grab the syrup and put both in front of Dad.

"Thank you. Mmm. Whoever taught you how to make waffles? He's the best."

"Ha."

I prepare another waffle for myself and watch for the red light.

"How's Mom?" I ask.

A small sigh. "The same."

"So, what does that mean?"

"It means her body needs more time to recover. She's going to be okay."

He takes a drink. I stare at the waffle maker.

"She's going to be okay," he says again. But I'm not sure if he says it for his benefit or mine.

After a few minutes, the light turns red. Another perfect, crisp brown waffle. I put it on a plate and join Dad at the table.

He reaches over and places his hand on mine, and we hold hands while we eat.

I consider telling him about the small red box I found in Mom's closet. But what if he doesn't know about it? Would he be upset to learn that she's kept whole parts of herself hidden from him too? Even so, Dad knows more about Mom than anyone. I know the basics from when I did that school project, but this feels more urgent. I need to know more. And if there's anyone who can tell me what I need to know, it's him.

"Dad, what happened to Mom in the war?"

He breathes in deeply. "I've told you."

"Not really. Just bits and pieces. Please?"

He finishes his drink.

"Please."

He sighs. "I don't know everything. She's mainly spoken about her time in Sarajevo. When she lived there and it was under siege."

"How did that happen again?"

"What—the siege?"

"Yeah."

"Well, it's complicated. But basically, Sarajevo is located in a deep valley, and the Bosnian-Serb-controlled army surrounded the city. They wouldn't let anyone in or out. It would be like if our military suddenly cut off Rhode Island from the rest of the country."

I nod like I can imagine it, even though I can't.

"Sarajevo didn't have electricity, water, gas. No food. At the same time, they were continually shelled, bombed and shot at. It was very dangerous. Even though the United Nations was there. Mom called them the Useless Nations, among other things." He smiles.

"What about before Sarajevo?" I ask. The photo of her family comes to the front of my mind. "Like where she grew up?"

"Well, she's from Višegrad, a town in eastern Bosnia, near the border of Serbia."

"Did she tell you what happened in Višegrad?"

He shakes his head. "Not in detail. I only know that she lost her whole family."

"It's crazy. Just because they were Muslim?"

"I know. It would be like if you were out walking around in Providence and someone asked what your name was, and then just by your last name, you could be taken away and put in a concentration camp or killed. Zara Machado would make you Portuguese, a Catholic, so if the government turned against Catholics, you would be seen as a threat."

I can hardly wrap my head around what he's saying.

"The Bosnian Muslims from the villages, like where your mom came from, had it the worst. If you were lucky, you got kicked out of your home and put on a bus or a train, or loaded into cattle cars or the back of a truck, and taken out of the country. If you weren't so lucky, you were killed."

"But I just don't understand how that could happen. How could people just take someone away and kill them?"

"People fear what they don't understand. And that same fear and lack of understanding make people do terrible things to one another."

I think of the bombing I just survived. The fact that I live in a world where people bomb farmers markets. It's not the first time I've heard of a terrorist attack happening in America; it's just the first time I've experienced it firsthand.

"So is that what those terrorists want for us? To kill us just because we're American?" I imagine the guy who planted the bombs in the market. Did he think he was fighting a war? Maybe that God wanted him to do it? I shudder. What kind of God would ask that?

Dad takes my hand again.

"Zara, the world we live in is broken. And . . ." His eyes fill with tears. "As your dad, all I want to do is protect you from it, but I can't. You don't know how helpless that makes me feel."

Seeing my dad cry makes me want to cry. It also makes me scared. I need him to stop crying. He's the strong one. If he falls apart, what chance do I have?

"I'm okay, Dad," I say. I squeeze his hand. "Just . . . Can you tell me more? Like, how did Mom get to Sarajevo?" I ask.

He rubs his eyes. "She's never told me the full story. I only know she was one of the many refugees who escaped to Sarajevo, and a family who knew her father took her in. She lived with them for two years until she was smuggled out through a Red Cross convoy."

"She was smuggled out in a car?"

Dad nods slowly. "She was. And from there she lived in a camp in Germany for a year. Then she won a lottery that gave her passage to the US. I met her two years later."

"At the hospital, right? When she broke her arm?" I ask this to encourage him to tell the story, even though this is the part I know.

"Yeah. Well, it wasn't a true break, just a hairline fracture. When I saw her, she was sitting so erect and staring straight ahead. It must have been very painful, but you'd never know it. I was a resident and nervous, but not from lack of ability, of course."

"Of course," I say.

"She was just so beautiful. And stoic. And those eyes. Pretty, green and defiant. I stumbled through her exam like an idiot. I walked her out of the hospital and asked her if she wanted to have lunch with me."

"And?"

"And now I'm looking into those same eyes of our daughter."

"Can I see the picture?"

Dad gives a small smile and reaches into his back pocket for his wallet. He pulls out a photo that has been cut to fit inside one of the plastic flaps. It's one of the only photos of them from when he and Mom were dating.

They're at Baker's, down near the water. There are bathhouses in the distance behind them. Mom's wearing a cute blue bikini top; the photo is cut off above the waist. Her hair is in a ponytail, and her head is thrown back mid-laugh. She's really laughing, hard, at something. Dad's next to her in a pair of swim trunks, and he's laughing too, but looking at her.

I used to ask Dad to see it all the time. It's one of my favorites. One of the few glimpses of Mom as she used to be, captured when she was young. I would stare at this picture and try to get into the moment. I'd absorb all the details. The colors. The sand caked to the side of her arm. Dad's goatee, which seems hilarious in its '90s grunge vibe; I've only known him clean shaven. His hair down past his ears. The bracelets on Mom's arm. The other people sitting on towels and chairs around them. Everything about the picture is oriented toward her.

My eyes tear, but I blink them away. She looks so happy. I would have given anything to be there with them. To know her when she was still capable of feeling such joy.

"She's going to be okay," Dad says, misunderstanding my emotion.

"Yeah," I say, wondering what my mom was thinking in the photo, what it was that could have made her so happy. Wondering what has changed since.

1992
Spring
Višegrad
BiH

THAT MORNING, NADJA was up before her parents. She hadn't slept well, worrying about whether she should tell her dad about what Marko had said. But she would be punished for having a boy alone in her room. She stood and shivered in the chill and headed for the kitchen. The heat wasn't on because there was something wrong with the electricity again.

She put on her gloves before opening the stove door and placing some wood inside to get it going. With no electricity, the only heat they had came from the fireplace in the living room and the woodstove, which her mom always used to complain about, but now came in handy.

Her parents soon awoke and they had some leftover vegetable soup and bread from last night. They were all quiet.

Benjamin had his sketchbook with him at the table. Nadja saw he'd added a long-haired bearded Četnik to the page. The sleeve of the man's jacket bore the patch with their emblem—a skull, a double-headed eagle and crossed swords. Superman stood over him and pointed in one direction as if to say, *Go! You are not wanted here.*

"Good drawing," Nadja said, surprised at how lifelike the Četnik looked.

Her father took the book. He flipped through it. "Benjamin. No more of these, okay?" He tore out the one with the Četnik, opened the stove and threw the page in the fire.

"But I just got him to where he looked right!" Benjamin said.

"We don't want anything that could make us look like we're troublemakers."

"It was just a drawing," Benjamin said.

"There is no more *just* anything. Benjamin, Nadja, come here."

Nadja and Benjamin walked to where their father stood by the stove. He placed his hands on both of their shoulders. "Did you pack the one bag like we asked?"

They nodded.

"Good. We are leaving tonight."

"Tonight?" Nadja said, immediately worried that she wouldn't be able to say good-bye to Marko. And he had acted so strange last night.

Nadja's mom looked around the kitchen. "Only one bag. All of our albums, my mother's dishes—"

"Bring one photo album, one dish," her dad said. "The rest will wait for us until we return." But there was doubt in his voice. Nadja wondered if her mother heard it too.

Her mother took a slow turn, as if she were trying to memorize the room.

Her father opened his arms for all of them, and they had a big family hug. He bent and kissed Nadja's mom.

"Yuck," Benjamin said, and they all laughed.

"Off to work," he said, and he gave Benjamin and Nadja an extra hug.

"Why?" Nadja asked. "If we are leaving, it doesn't matter."

"We need it all to look normal. You must act normal. Do not say good-bye to anyone. Understand? Nadja? Benjamin? I'm serious. You cannot tell Marko or Uma or anyone."

"Yes," said Benjamin.

"I understand," said Nadja. "Are we really going to walk all the way to Goražde again?"

"If we have to. If the main roads are blocked with checkpoints, it's better to stay off them."

"What will they do if they check us?" Benjamin said.

Nadja noticed the look that passed from her mother to her father.

"Detain us while we fill out the right paperwork," her father said. "It will take forever. It's better to leave on our own and get to Sarajevo, to Amir's house, as fast as we can. Think of it like a family camping trip."

"Can we fish?" Benjamin asked, perking up at the idea.

"Yes, of course. We will fish," her father said. "We may even catch something. It will be an adventure."

As Nadja's father spoke, he glanced at her mother, at the door, at the clock on the wall like he was already running from something.

"I like adventures," Benjamin said.

"It's supposed to rain," said Nadja.

Their mother walked their father to the door and kissed him. With the door closed behind her, she leaned on it and said, "Well, they say Sarajevo has the best *ćevapi.*"

Benjamin laughed. Nadja smiled.

They knew she hated *ćevapi.*

. . . . .

After bathing, Nadja stood in front of her bedroom mirror and applied blue eye shadow, black liner and mascara. She was putting in her hoop earrings when she heard something that sounded like gunfire. She froze, thinking maybe she'd imagined it.

No.

There it was again. A quick staccato. Three shots. Maybe five.

She ran to the living room, where her mother stood, her arms around Benjamin's neck like a noose. The front door opened, and suddenly her father ran through it, slamming and locking it behind him.

"Soldiers! Down the street." He was out of breath. "Coming up here. Everyone in the bedroom. Quick." He led them to Benjamin's bedroom, which was the farthest from the front door, and shut and locked them inside. Terror throbbed in Nadja's heart and brain as she huddled next to her parents against the back wall, afraid to even breathe.

A couple of minutes later, there was loud banging on the front door. Nadja pressed her body into the side of her father. With a huge thud, the door crashed open, like it had been kicked through. Loud footsteps stomped around, followed by crashing and things being knocked over. They could also hear muffled voices. Someone tried to open the bedroom door, the only thing keeping Nadja's family out of sight, and then banged on it. Within minutes, the door was kicked in. Nadja's father positioned himself in front of his family, trying to shield the three of them with his body.

A man wearing a balaclava and dressed in a black military

uniform with the Četnik insignia on the upper arm shouted at them to get out.

He pointed an assault rifle at them.

"Move now or I'll kill you!"

"Don't shoot!" her father said. "We will come. Don't shoot." He held up his hands, and behind him, Nadja, her mother and brother did the same.

Nadja's father went first. Then Nadja's mother, then Nadja and Benjamin, too, were each grabbed and pushed facedown to the floor. There were two other men dressed as paramilitaries and wearing balaclavas in the house, looking through everything. Another came out of her parents' bedroom with a handful of jewelry, her mother's creations.

The one who had found Nadja and her family, the one with blond hair, read from a small notebook he held in his hand. "Who is Musanović?"

"Me. I am," her father said.

He turned and asked the man who suddenly hovered in the broken doorway of the house, "Is that true?"

Mr. Radić. Their neighbor. He nodded, his eyes large and bulging. "Yes, he is the Muslim pig."

"Anyone else here in this house?" the soldier asked.

"No, no, only my family."

"Out," the soldier said, motioning Nadja's father toward the door with his gun.

"What is wrong? What did I do?"

Another soldier exited her parents' room holding a gun. "Found this."

"Illegally housing weapons."

"That's not mine," her father said.

The soldier standing next to him hit Nadja's father with the butt of his gun. He fell to the floor.

"No!" Nadja's mother screamed out.

Blood oozed from a small cut at the top of his hairline. Nadja started crying.

The man kicked her father in the side twice. "Get up."

Her father stumbled to his feet, holding his head. The blood ran between his fingers like red paint.

"You too," the soldier said, motioning to Benjamin, who still lay facedown on the ground.

"He is only a boy," Nadja's father said. "Come here, Benjamin."

Benjamin got up and stood next to his father. He was crying now, looking back at his mother and Nadja as he and his father were walked through the front door.

"Where are you taking them?" Nadja's mother asked, crawling toward them, slowly making her way to her feet. "Why? What has happened? They are nothing to you."

"For questioning," the blond said. He pointed his gun at her. "Would you like to be taken to questioning too?"

"It will be all right," Nadja's father said. "Be strong, Maja, Nadja. It will be all right." He kept repeating the words as the soldiers led them away.

"I love you!" her mother shouted. "I love you!"

Her mother waited until the men were out the front door before she leapt to her feet. Nadja gathered herself and chased after her.

Outside, men and boys lined the middle of the small, narrow street. They were mostly neighbors, people Nadja had seen her whole life. Nadja's father and brother were sent to join the back of the line. Cries of "why?" ran up and down the street from the women forced to stay behind.

Nadja recognized one of the men in uniform as her former teacher and her father's colleague who taught a couple of doors down from him at the high school. She almost called out to him, but the look he gave her was one of complete loathing.

Hadn't they all gone swimming together last summer? Weren't there talks of doing that again? Something about him helping her with a recommendation letter for school in Sarajevo?

Wait, Nadja tried to say. *What's happening? Why isn't anyone doing anything?* But she could hardly open her mouth. Fear flooded her body, rooting it to the ground. Shame and fear. A fear so cold and sick that she trembled.

Nadja and her mother watched helplessly as the men and boys were led to a truck and told to get into the back.

"Be orderly about it! Hurry up!"

One of the men stepped out of line. "What right do you have to do this? What have I done? Where are you taking—"

A soldier knocked him down and hit him repeatedly in the head with the end of the rifle until the man lay still.

Nadja stared at the blood oozing out from the wound at the base of the man's skull. She could see bits of his brain exposed from the open flap of skin. There was wailing now from the women standing by. The soldiers started shouting, telling them to get back to their homes.

"Please," a woman begged, holding on to a boy. "Please. He is my only son."

The largest soldier, with dirty long brown hair, approached her and hit her across the face with his palm. She fell to the ground but still held on to the leg of her son. The soldier aimed his gun and shot her in the head.

At the shot, Nadja felt her body go numb. It was like she was in a dream and everything had slowed down. She saw people moving and talking, but she couldn't hear them or understand what they were saying.

Somewhere a woman was dying in the road.

Somewhere the blood trickled in a pencil-thin line and dribbled into the grass border at the edge of the street.

Somewhere the cries became untranslatable moans.

Nadja closed her eyes and tried to wake up. This wasn't real. She was in a nightmare. Soon she would wake up and be in her room. She would wake up, and everything would be okay again.

Nadja opened her eyes and watched as the men and boys were loaded onto the bed of the truck. Her father and Benjamin stood in the back because there was no room to sit. Normally she'd be irritated at Benjamin's tears because he could be such a baby sometimes. But now he seemed so brave. She saw her friend Jusuf then, just a little to the left of them. He held his football. He was wearing pajamas and had the strangest expression on his face. He seemed to be looking at Nadja but not looking at her at the same time.

She wanted to call to her family. She wanted to tell Benjamin she loved him. Tell her father. But she couldn't speak. She couldn't cry out. She could only watch. Her father held up his free hand. He was telling her something. *Wait. Wait,* she thought. *Wait! I need to hear what he's saying.*

"Wait," she croaked out.

But the truck was already moving. Already taking her father and brother away from her.

"Wait!" she screamed.

The truck rounded the bend, traveling downhill toward the center of town slowly because of its load. She stood with all the others left behind and watched until she could no longer see them.

Nadja sank to the ground, hysterical. Her mother stood next to her, screaming as well. Calling to her husband, to God, to anyone who would listen.

"Shut up!" a soldier said. "Everyone back to your homes before I shoot you again. You are lucky it's not up to me. If it were, I would shoot you all today and then come back and shoot you again tomorrow!"

A soldier touched the top of Nadja's head. "You're pretty even when you cry," he said.

"Nadja." Her mother yanked her arm, dragging her away from the soldier and back to their house. Until today, he had been the man who worked at the post office.

She dragged Nadja past Mr. Radić, who stood in the middle of the street. He was saying something, but Nadja couldn't hear. She stared at his mouth, open like a grave.

July 4

"ZARA."

I feel a presence standing over me.

"Zara?"

I open my eyes. *Benny.* He looks so scared. I scoot over, carefully, trying not to twist in a way that will aggravate the stitches in my back, and make room for him in my bed. He lies down next to me.

"Zara," he says, "are you okay?"

"I'm just really tired." I don't tell him that I haven't slept for more than minutes at a time since the attack. That every time I try, the images are there, underneath my eyelids. I'm afraid to dream, afraid of nightmares.

"Does your face hurt?" he asks.

Yes.

"Not really," I say. "How about you? You feel okay?"

He holds up his leg that has a bandage on it. "I'm okay. Just this. And this. And this." He shows me all the marks on his skin that aren't covered up.

I examine all of them. "Not too bad."

"Can I see under your bandage?" he asks.

"Um, maybe later."

Benny looks disappointed, but he doesn't press it.

"Is Mom going to die?"

"No," I say. "No, she's going to be fine." I have no choice but to lie to Benny. He wouldn't be able to process the uncertainty of her condition. I can barely process it myself.

"Do you think that man who lost his leg died?" he asks.

I picture myself stepping on it, feel the oddness of it under my foot, and the bile rises. "I don't know."

"There was a lot of blood," he says.

"Yeah."

We're both quiet for a moment. Then Benny says something so softly, I almost miss it. "I'm glad you didn't die."

I pull him in and squeeze him tight. "Me too, Benny," I say. I run my fingers through his curls. "Want to watch a show?"

In answer, he sits up, grabs the remote and turns on the TV. I glance at the clock. It's nine thirty in the morning. At this time yesterday, we were flying through the air. My back was being pummeled by shrapnel. Mom was being buried by a produce stand.

Memories of the bombing come at me in a rush—the screaming, the dust, the smell of flesh burning, the severed hand in a closed fist, the blood a deep river in my ears. I hold Benny close, afraid I'll sink under it all.

We lie there for a while, each of us dozing in and out of restless sleep, until the doorbell rings. It's a little after eleven.

I open the door, and Audrey and her mom stand there with

bags and bags of food. Dad is back at the hospital, so Aunt Evelyn helps Rebecca put things away in the kitchen.

It's a nice gesture, but all I can think about is how Mom wouldn't like people to be doing this—opening cupboards, drawers, moving things around, taking stock of our possessions as if it were the most natural thing in the world and not at all invasive.

But Mom isn't here. She's in the hospital. In a coma.

Instead, Audrey, Sibyl and Natasha are here. We're sitting in the backyard because Audrey's mom thought it would be a good idea if I got some vitamin D. The look on my friends' faces is one of concern. I pretend not to notice as their eyes keep darting to my wounds. Good thing my cheek is still covered. They're all dressed in cute shorts and tops, while I'm in a baggy shirt and leggings, even though it feels like a hundred degrees outside. I haven't brushed my hair since yesterday.

"What else do you need, Zara?" Audrey asks.

On the outdoor table are all kinds of things that I love—chocolate, Dr Pepper and Pirate's Booty. But I haven't touched a thing since they got here.

I shrug. "I don't know." Suddenly the light is too harsh. I want to go back to bed. "I can't believe your mom canceled the party."

Audrey looks at me. "Are you serious? Of course she did. This has rocked our whole town. The whole country. It seems weird to celebrate now."

"Everyone's scared," Sibyl says. "Like it was just the first wave of attack or something." She takes a sip of her water.

"I know. My mom didn't even want me to come over here,"

Natasha says. "She's barely let me out of the house since it happened."

"It's crazy," Sibyl says. "I can't believe you were there, Zara. That you were hurt." Her eyes water. "And your mom. Like, how long do they think she'll be in a coma?"

Audrey shoots Sibyl a look.

"It's okay if you don't want to talk about it," Natasha says.

But the three of them look at me and almost lean forward, like I've got the best piece of gossip for them.

"Um, it was bad. Just bad. After the explosion, there were bodies . . ." My heart races, and I feel a pain behind my eyes. I squeeze them shut to try and get rid of it. "Actually, I don't totally remember." This is not true. I see the haze. Smell the burning. Suddenly, my fingers hurt. I notice they're a little scratched up. An image flashes in my brain—I'm tearing at a broken structure, at wood and metal. Some of it so hot, my fingers get burned. I frantically dig, trying to lift the pieces off the body that lies underneath. My mother's body.

I stare at my hands.

"It's all right," Audrey says. "We're just glad you're okay, Zara."

I don't know if I'm okay. All I know is I'm alive.

"Do you think I've gotten enough vitamin D?" I ask.

Audrey laughs. "Probably."

I get up slowly. My whole body aches. I can feel the skin around my stitches pull when I move. My back is swollen and itches terribly. It takes every ounce of restraint to keep from reaching behind to scratch. My cheek itches too.

"Here, let me help you," Audrey says, and I let her lead me inside.

We pass Benny on the couch playing on his iPad.

"Hey, Benny," Sibyl says.

"Hey," he says, not even looking up from his game. Mom wouldn't allow him to be on a device like that, especially on a sunny day. She'd tell him to get off and go play outside.

"Benny," I say. "Benny."

He looks up.

"Just fifteen more minutes, okay?" I say, and then cringe. I sound just like her.

"Okay," he says, and refocuses on the screen.

We get to my room, and Audrey helps me onto my bed. When I'm settled, the three of them stand there, looking at me. I'm not sure what to do. We've never been in this position before. With me being almost maimed from a terrorist bombing. Usually we're out taking photos, or at the mall or movies, or hanging at Natasha's house because she has a pool.

Sibyl picks up my camera. "Did you have this with you?" She turns it around in her hand and notices the place where it's dented now. "Oh no, is it broken?"

Is it? It's weird that I don't know.

"You have pictures?" Natasha asks.

"Um, I don't remember," I say. I really don't want to talk about this.

Audrey and Natasha crowd Sibyl on each side and look at the LCD display together. I curl up on my side. I close my eyes. They're quiet for what feels like forever.

"Zara, you should see these," Audrey says.

"Hey, guys, I'm actually pretty tired," I say.

"Oh. We should go, then." Audrey gets up first.

"Love you, Z," says Sibyl. She begins to get emotional again, which is so Sibyl, but I can't deal with it now.

One by one, they touch my arm as if they're at some funeral procession.

They leave my room and close the door. I stare at my camera, still in the spot where they left it, on my bed, near my feet. I make no move to pick it up.

After I hear the front door close, I get up and go to the bathroom. I stand in front of the mirror. No wonder they looked so concerned. Even with the bandage on, I can see the surrounding bruising is beginning to turn colors, and the scrapes don't look good. It's time to assess the full extent of the damage.

The bandage hurts to remove because I go too slow. Once it's off, I see—the pus from the major cut has dried and is now all yellow and orange crust. There's fresh blood from where the wound stuck to the bandage, too; I must have injured it all over again by ripping it off, even going as slowly as I did.

Gross.

I take a warm washcloth and press it to the side, gradually cleaning away all the gunk. When I'm finished, I can see it looks like I skidded across asphalt on my upper cheek. I don't even remember falling on it. My arms are scraped up, too; what hit the ground first? There must have been a lot of gravel and debris flying around during and after the explosion. Maybe some rocks flew at my face? It's hard for me to get a clear picture of what actually happened.

There's a knock at the door.

"Yeah?"

"Zara, you okay in there?"

"Mm-hmm," I say. I know Aunt Evelyn is concerned about me, but I wish she would ask a different question.

I apply a thick coat of A and E ointment. On the side it says *use to prevent scarring.*

I gently rub the gel across my face and up to my temple, where smaller scratches make it look like I was just the victim of a kitten or maybe a hamster attack.

I step back to examine my face again, and it's now a shiny, angry red. My eyes well a little. I'm pretty sure I'll have some kind of scar, no matter what the tube says. That time I fell off my bike and scraped up the side of my leg wasn't even this bad, and I still have a patch of skin on my upper thigh that is darker than the rest of my leg. The evidence of my fall noticeable even to the untrained eye.

I grimace again, and my face morphs into something worse. The mirror wobbles like in a carnival funhouse. The damaged side of my face droops. Blood runs down.

I close my eyes. Open.

My regular jacked-up face stares back at me. Barely an improvement.

I take off my shirt, but it's very difficult because of the stitches. They pull and tug on my skin every time I move. I try to get a good look at my back in the mirror, but it's hard to twist far enough around. I'm supposed to apply the ointment to my back as well, but I can't get the whole area. I'll have to ask Aunt Evelyn to help me with it later.

I open the door, looking up and down the hallway to make sure Aunt Evelyn isn't standing out there, waiting. She isn't. I go to my room and grab my camera. It feels bulky and awkward in my hands, like I've forgotten how to use it. I run my fingers across the dent, notice the scratches. The lens is dirty, but undamaged.

I return to the bathroom and place the camera on the edge of the sink, set the timer and stand with my back in front of it. I have to adjust the angle a bit before I get a full image. When I examine the photo, I can see that the sutures cross the whole of my back in three uneven lines, as if I am being patchworked back together. Like some experiment, something brought back from the dead like Frankenstein's monster. *Wound repair* is what the nurse had called it.

It doesn't look repaired.

It looks like the largest wound I've ever seen.

It's disgusting.

I'm disgusting.

There's another knock at the door.

"I'm fine!" I call out before she can ask.

I stare at my face in the mirror. Tears streak and burn the cuts on one side.

I'm fine.

July 5

DAD REMAINS POSITIVE for me, but I don't have to be a doctor to know that it's never a good thing when someone doesn't wake up from a coma in over forty-eight hours. So he jumps into action with a plan. Aunt Evelyn is going to stay with us until Gramma and Vovo get here from Florida—another indication that Mom's condition is more serious than he's letting on.

For now, Aunt Evelyn remains at the house with Benny while I head to the hospital with Dad.

I sit forward in the small wooden chair in Mom's room.

Nothing has changed, except her face is now bruised on the same side as mine. Her eyes still look swollen. If she could open them, she'd look like a raccoon. Dad said that's to be expected because of the blow to the head. I notice she has metal staples toward the back of her head on the right side where they shaved her hair and operated. They're covered with a type of jelly. To prevent scarring? To keep them from falling out? Whatever the reason, it's not pretty.

If I had stayed with Mom instead of taking Benny over to

the candy stand, that could be me lying in the bed. I get a chill thinking about it.

"You cold?" Dad asks. He's holding Mom's hand, but he must know that it's pointless. Can she even feel anything? Besides, Mom isn't much of a hand holder to begin with. Except for maybe Benny, but that doesn't count. He's still little.

Mom's eyes move underneath their lids like she can hear my thoughts.

I lean back, but wince when my back hits the chair.

"Any idea when I can get my stitches removed?"

"Well, your back will need to heal a bit more first. But don't worry. They won't be in forever. Make sure you apply the ointment when you can. Anytime you remember. I can help you. Aunt Evelyn too. The first five days, especially. And now that it's been a couple days, you'll want to let your cheek breathe a bit. Keep the bandage off for a while."

"Oh, yeah, and walk around like a freak? No thank you."

"You are not a freak, Z. Anyone will know you've been in . . . an accident."

Dad kisses me on the top of my head. Then he leaves to check in on some of his patients.

Mom and I are alone.

Now that it's just the two of us, maybe I can try to talk to her. "Mom, I found your secret stash. It's okay, I won't tell Dad or anyone about the money." I feel awkward talking to her in this state, but I press through. "I was thinking, though, if . . . when you wake up . . . maybe you could tell me about some of the other stuff. Like who the people are in the photos. Maybe we could start there."

Mom lies there listening, or not listening, I don't know.

The machine breathes with her.

"If you can hear me, maybe you could give me a sign. Like, move a finger or something."

I watch her intently. Nothing moves but her eyes underneath the lids. Her hands don't twitch. Her mouth doesn't open or curve upward.

Our usual silence fills the room. Even now, it's like she's punishing me. It's too much. Suddenly, I can't hold in what I've been wondering ever since I saw the photo of her and my dad.

"I've done the math, you know. You were pregnant with me, and that's why you married Dad." The bite in my voice cuts through the quiet. It's kind of freeing to speak so directly to her. "So you must have thought about it. Getting rid of me. Right?"

Silence. Eye movement.

I feel awful. How is it possible to be so mad and sad and mixed up all at the same time? I don't know what else to do, so I close my eyes and take deep breaths. If I were someone who prayed, now would be a good time to do so. Even though I never have before, I wonder if God would hear me if I tried talking to Him now. I don't know. But it's worth a shot.

"God, I know you're really busy, but please, help my mom. Please don't let her die." I hope He's listening.

I leave my mom's room and wander the hall. There's nothing more depressing than hanging out at a hospital. The aesthetic of the place is the worst—sterile, white and sanitized. Almost everyone is sick. There's a stifling amount of inertia because most people are just sitting and waiting.

No one wants to be here.

Especially me.

I feel guilty leaving Mom's room, like there's this unspoken expectation that I should be sitting with her 24/7, but I just can't. I can't take the sound of her machine. I can't take the way Dad checks in on me and smiles and tries to act like everything is going to be okay. Everything isn't okay already, and if she dies . . . well, then I don't even want to think about that.

But mostly I can't stand to look at my mother, because I can't look at her without feeling like I'm looking at a stranger. Why does she feel the need to keep so much of her life—and herself— hidden away? Hidden as though it were her history, and hers alone. And now she's just lying there.

I look up the latest news on my phone to find out if there's any new information about the bombings. Nothing yet on who the individual suspects are, but there are new details about ISIS claiming responsibility.

I feel sick.

I don't know where to go, but I can't stay here.

I take the elevator to the ground floor. When the doors open, it's loud. There's a group of people clustered near the entrance to the hospital. Some look like reporters, others like people visiting. I don't want to have to deal with people, so I turn and walk down the hall instead.

I keep walking the halls of the hospital, anything to get away from the crowd, until I realize I'm completely turned around. When I come to the nearest set of signs, I see I'm in another wing. On the right, I notice a sign that says CHAPEL. At least I know that will be safe and quiet.

Once I'm in the doorway, I'm taken with all the bright colors of the stained glass surrounding me on the walls and the ceiling.

I step inside, but hesitate when I see there is another person here, sitting in the front row. He doesn't turn around when I enter. I sit down in the back row on the opposite side of the guy and try to be as quiet as possible.

The artistry on the ceiling is really intricate. I don't have much to compare it to, but it's better than I would have expected to find in a hospital chapel, anyway. I don't know if it's all the color or what, but just sitting here is nice. I feel a bit calmer.

When my neck starts to ache because I've been looking up at the ceiling for too long, I lower my gaze and try not to stare at the back of the guy in front of me. He's hunched over and hasn't moved since I entered the room. I assume he's praying? I wish he'd finish soon, because I'd really like to be alone.

He shifts in his seat, and I put my head down, pretend I haven't been staring at him for the last five minutes. I feel his gaze on me, so I close my eyes like I'm praying. And then I actually do pray. *God, please help my mom.* I use the same words I said earlier, because maybe if I say the same prayer multiple times, God will know I mean it, and take it more seriously. Only this time I add, *And please help me too.*

Since my prayer lasts about three seconds, I'm not sure what else I should do. The guy is facing forward, head down again, and I'm feeling anxious with him here. I shift in my seat, and my phone falls to the ground.

He turns around in his seat and stares at me.

"Oh," I say. "Sorry." Then I notice that I'm speaking too

loudly. "Sorry," I say again in a whisper. "I didn't mean to disturb you."

"What?" he asks, and then removes the earbuds I didn't notice before.

"I didn't mean to disturb you," I say again. "It's just so pretty in here."

"No worries," he says, and smiles. He looks up at the ceiling. "This is the best part."

"Yes," I say, following his gaze.

"I'm Joseph," he says.

"Zara."

He smiles wide, and it lights up his whole face. He's wearing a red shirt and two necklaces with some kind of charm at the end of each. He looks like he's probably around my age.

"You visiting someone?" he asks.

"My mom. You?"

"Grandmother."

I nod.

"Looks like you had something happen too?" He touches the side of his face to indicate the scrapes on my own.

My hands fly up to my face, and I'm suddenly self-conscious. I had forgotten for a moment that a huge white bandage still covers my cheek.

"Oh, yeah. I was at the farmers market." Even from where Joseph sits, he can probably see the tracks of red that climb up to my temple.

"Wow," he says, traces of the previous smile now gone and replaced with genuine concern.

"Yeah. Wow."

"And your mom, was she there too?"

"Yeah. She was hurt pretty bad. She's been in a coma since the bombing. My dad, he's a doctor here, he keeps telling me that she's going to be okay. But how can we know, you know? She might never wake up." I shrug, and it pulls at the stitches on my back. I wince, but if Joseph notices, he doesn't say anything. I don't know why, but it feels so easy to talk to this complete stranger. Maybe it's being in a chapel.

"My grandmother survived the 2010 earthquake in Haiti. She lost her sister and two cousins. Now she's here with cancer."

"I'm sorry."

"Thank you. This morning she told me that she's fine with dying. That if it's God's will, then it is His will."

Something about that logic bothers me. "It seems odd to think that God would want someone to die."

He shrugs. "I don't think she means it like how you might be thinking. She's not saying God is planning on taking her life. We're all going to die sometime. I think she just means that she knows her life is in God's hands and if her time is now, then she trusts God has a reason for that."

"And is that what you believe?" I ask. "That everything's in God's hands?"

He smiles. "That's a complicated question."

I wonder what my mom would say if she heard me talking about God in this way. Would she be surprised? Did she think it was God's will when her whole family was killed? Or that we survived a bombing? Were the bad things that happened to us really God's will? That makes it sound like God is out to get us. That He doesn't care. People do bad things all the time, like the bomber. How can acts of violence, terrorism, be God's will?

Joseph stands up and moves closer to me so that now there's only one row separating us. He's black, and his hair is styled with a slight fade and medium-length 'fro twisted on most of the ends. He rests his hands on the back of his seat. I notice his fingers are long; he wears a couple of silver rings of varying sizes on both hands and a leather band on one of his wrists. There's something engraved on it, but I can't make out what it says.

"I think it's normal for us to look for answers after terrible things happen," he says. "To try to make sense of it all."

Is that what I'm trying to do? So far I haven't been able to make sense of any of it.

"Last year," he continues, "a friend of mine died. One day he's shooting hoops with me, the next day, he's dead." He stops speaking and begins playing with the leather strap around his wrist.

"Oh, I'm sorry," I say.

He shakes his head. "I started thinking about life and what I believe. Like, take my grandmother. She has seen terrible things happen in her lifetime, but she still has this strong faith in God. Why? Is it just to make her feel better? Or is there some deeper meaning?" He holds up the black journal he has on his lap. "I started writing down questions, and then I went in pursuit of the answers."

"What do you mean?"

"Well, I started with religion, to see how they answered the questions. I began with the big ones: Judaism, Christianity,

Islam. Kind of crazy how they all come from the same story."

"Um, yeah . . ." I say slowly.

"You know—Abraham? The story in Genesis, the first book of the Bible or the Torah."

I stare at him sideways, suddenly wary. I didn't come in here to be given a lecture on religion. Of course I find the one religious weirdo.

"Interesting," I say, not wanting to be rude. I look over my shoulder at the door, suddenly hoping maybe someone else will come in.

"Check it out," he continues. "Abraham had two sons— with his wife, Sarah, and his wife's servant, Hagar. Ishmael, Hagar's son, was taken to Mecca and became a prophet and an ancestor of Muhammad. Isaac, Sarah's boy, became the father of the Israelites and the ancestor of Jesus." He leans back. "So you *could* say we've been watching one big family feud play out across generations."

I stare at him. Is this guy for real?

When I've finally found my voice again, I say, "Yeah, well, as someone who was just caught in the crossfire, I don't really see it that way."

"Right. I'm sorry. Of course not. I don't mean to be insensitive. I . . . sometimes I just have this habit of saying too much. My mom always points it out. Whenever I get excited about something. Or I'm nervous or whatever . . ." His voice trails off.

I stare at the ground. Suddenly I feel like crying, and I regret coming inside the chapel. I hate that it feels like I can't get ahold of my emotions.

I stand up to leave, but Joseph stands too and keeps talking to me.

"I've just always been curious about God. Who He is. How to know Him. And sometimes it seems crazy to believe that there even is a God, but people from every culture, in every time, have believed, so there's gotta be something to it, right? The more I learn, the more questions I have. Look." He opens his journal to show me what's inside. The page is full of words and sketches and musings. I read through a few of them and look at others. Like— *If there is a God, why can't we see Him?* And *Why does He allow bad things to happen to good people? Why is there suffering?* Some of the same questions I've had.

"Is your family religious?" I ask, a little curious now.

"Yeah. They're mainly Christian, so they think it's a little weird what I'm doing. My dad's afraid that I'm going to shave my head and go be a monk or something."

"Why?"

"Right now I'm studying Buddhism."

"Oh."

He sighs. "You think I'm crazy, right?"

"I don't know you enough to make that judgment, but I'm currently leaning toward eccentric."

He chuckles. "Fair enough. I'll take that over crazy."

So maybe he isn't a weirdo. Maybe he's just a guy searching for meaning.

"Okay, so tell me, what do Buddhists believe?" I'm genuinely curious now—about Buddhism, and about Joseph. I've never met anyone who studied so many religions. Most of my friends believe what they do because it's what their parents believe in. It's more tradition than belief, more of an obligation than an inspired choice. Or else they're like me and somewhere in the middle, undecided.

"Well, I'm still discovering," he says, "but the First Truth is that all life is suffering."

"Yeah, I think I got that memo."

Joseph gives me a small smile.

"Do they explain why?" I ask.

He shakes his head. "Why is a futile question, because there is no answer to that. It's about accepting the First Truth so that we can move forward and live each day one at a time."

I think I understand him, so I nod. "So, being in the moment and staying positive?"

"Sort of. It's more like practicing mindfulness, searching for wisdom, approaching all life with compassion and ultimately freeing oneself from the burden of a life of suffering."

"Well, it seems like the only way to do that would be to die," I say dryly.

If Joseph is put off by my sarcasm, he doesn't show it. "There is a dying to self that's involved." He shows me a diagram in his book. "Again, I'm just learning about the Eightfold Path and Nirvana and all of it, but I'm really digging some of it. I even started wearing this." He fingers the band on his wrist. I read the word *Mindfulness*. "It's to remind me to focus my thoughts and to try to understand the intention behind my actions."

Suddenly there's a loud noise outside in the hall. I duck down behind the chair, covering my head with my arms. My heart rate and breathing quicken. I squeeze my eyes shut, but I see the body parts, the dust hovering in the air. I hear a person screaming.

"It's okay. It's okay," a voice says. "I think someone just dropped something."

I open my eyes, and a body is kneeling next to me. Joseph.

"Just breathe," he says.

I'm confused about where I am, but I try to breathe in through my nose, out through my mouth. It takes a few moments, but then I look around and see that I'm in the hospital chapel. When I realize I just freaked out over some random noise, I feel my face burn with embarrassment.

Slowly, I stand up. My breathing isn't as ragged, but my heart's still racing. For a moment, it felt like I was back at the farmers market all over again.

"Maybe I should get someone. A nurse. Or—"

"No, I'm fine."

Joseph stands there looking at me and then looking at the entrance. He seems unsure of what to do.

I take a deep breath. "Really, I'm okay."

I walk on shaky legs past him without saying good-bye, and I don't stop until I'm out of the hospital and around a corner, where I lean over and throw up. I wipe my mouth with the back of my hand and try to muster enough strength to walk all the way back to my mom's room, where she remains unchanged, where there are more questions than answers and where all life is truly suffering.

1993
Winter
Sarajevo
BiH

NADJA PLACED THE black headphones that had been hanging around her neck over her ears. She pressed Play on the Walkman in her pocket, even though the batteries had died a long time ago. The music still filled her head, a memorized track on loop. She made her back as flat as she could against the side of the mangled building, knowing, bullet-hole-ridden or not, it would offer her the most protection. The part of Sarajevo she was in had been cleared of most anything else. All of the trees that used to line the streets had been cut down and used for firewood. Most of the stumps dug up as well as the siege continued deep into winter without electricity. A couple of cars with their insides removed sat parked nearby. Their seats, engines, anything that could be considered useful stolen.

Nadja smelled the snow in the air, but there wasn't a cloud in the sky, only her breath as it pushed through the thick wool scarf that covered her face.

She set down the two plastic jugs of water she'd been carrying. Dalila sauntered over from the building across the street, out in the open, like she was impervious to the violence surrounding the area, surrounding *them*.

"Don't be stupid," Nadja said when Dalila got to her side.

"Come on, they've been quiet all morning. Look." Dalila stepped out from the cover of the building. She walked around. She shook her skinny booty in the direction of the Serb front line.

A woman on the third floor of the apartment building poked her head around the opaque plastic covering of a window, like she was peeking out of a shower. "Crazy girl. You want to get killed!"

Dalila yelled, "Good morning!"

The woman waved her away, but Dalila just kept dancing. The woman's head disappeared behind the plastic.

"Dalila," Nadja whispered.

"Fine." She stomped back over to where Nadja hid. "Let's go."

They bent and picked up the water jugs and walked close to the perimeter of the buildings up the steep hill toward their house. When it was still quiet, they moved toward the middle of the street. As they climbed past a small red Fiat with the top crushed and a door missing, the sound of gunfire pop-pop-popped through the air. The girls ducked and darted back to the cover of the doorway of the nearest building. The water sloshed and spilled from their jugs. Nadja's heart raced as she noted the bullet holes scarring the sides of the red wooden door like pockmarks.

"Bastards!" Dalila yelled.

A spray of bullets answered her. Their sharp sound echoing off the gray buildings.

Nadja sank to the ground and closed her eyes. Her muscles burned. Her shoulders were sore from carrying the water so many blocks already. She rubbed her hands together. They were freezing even through the gloves. She stuck them underneath her armpits to try and warm them.

Dalila sat down too. "Bastards," she said again. This time in a whisper.

Nadja pointed. Across the street, the warning *Pazi Snajper*— "Danger Sniper"—had been painted in jagged black lines on the side of a building that had had its roof blown off. Dalila laughed and then Nadja laughed and then they were laughing so hard, Nadja's side hurt. Even though her stomach was constantly hurting from hunger, this hurt felt good.

It triggered a memory of her and Uma laughing and running. They were ten and had just pulled a prank on Ivan, a boy in their class. They hid behind the school, huddled together in the grass, trying not to laugh, but laughing all the more because Ivan's face was so mad when he opened the bag and saw nothing was inside of it. Nadja almost smiled at the memory.

Uma.

The last time Nadja had seen her best friend was that night in her house. What had happened to Uma? Did she get out of Višegrad? Nadja buried the image, the thoughts, like she did all the others that came to her. The names. The faces. The questions and worries. Easier to stuff them all into a tiny space deep within her than to let them out to consume her.

Over the months since arriving in Sarajevo, Nadja had transformed herself. Her body was now built of boxes, steel ones, locked and heavy; she was surprised she could walk and not sink into the ground. Not be swept away from the memories of that night, with the boxes labeled BRIDGE and DRINA. The keys she kept hidden from her own self.

This was how she survived, how she would survive.

Nadja touched Dalila's knee where the rip in her jeans was getting wider. Dalila looked so small in her black coat and red scarf pulled tight around her. Her narrow face somehow sharper in the gray beanie. Small strands of dark brown hair peeked out of the sides. Nadja wondered what Dalila had looked like before the war. Dalila said she'd had a great figure. She said she would walk the street and make the boys' heads turn. Now Nadja noted Dalila could barely fill out her bras. How must Dalila see her? Was she as skinny?

"Ready?" Dalila asked.

"Yep."

They picked up the jugs and darted from doorway to doorway. Every few minutes, the gunfire would start. Sometimes Nadja saw it ripping up the asphalt in tiny dust clouds. But either the snipers couldn't see them or they were just playing. Nadja thought it was the latter. If they really wanted it to, no matter how fast they ran or where they sheltered, the bullet would find its mark.

As Nadja and Dalila made their way up the road, there was a man in a thick brown coat and a woman in a blue one doing the same—coming down on the same side of the road. The girls waited in one doorway, a beautiful brown wooden one with two round iron knockers, while the man and woman stood in the next doorway up ahead. They would have to go one at a time. The man said something to the girls, but they couldn't hear him over the gunfire.

"You go first," Dalila said.

Nadja started running, but so did the man and woman. Somehow there had been a breakdown in communicating who would go first. When they met in the middle, Nadja had to swerve to avoid knocking into them. The bullets whizzed, and one of the water jugs she was carrying shattered. Nadja stopped and tried to save some of the water, but it emptied quickly, running back down the hill they'd just climbed.

She turned toward where she thought the sniper might be hiding. She pulled down her scarf, freeing her mouth. "Do you know how long it took me to get that? How many hours I stood in line? Just do it already!" She stood there defiant, not even noticing Dalila already running toward her.

"Nadja, move." Dalila shoved her with her shoulder because her hands were full with the jugs.

In the next doorway, Nadja tried not to cry. She thought about going back to the water station to try and get more, but she didn't have anything to put it in and she knew by now that the little water there would already be disbursed. They had stood for three hours waiting and had been at the end of the line when they'd received their water ration.

"It's okay." Dalila patted her back. "I don't need to bathe for another week."

Nadja wiped the sides of her eyes where the tears had started to mix and sting with her sweat. She felt one of her headaches coming on.

"No, you stink," Nadja said.

"You hear that?" Dalila yelled toward the snipers. "That's how we'll get you out of here. We'll all be so stinky, the stench will fly up to where you hide and kill you!" Dalila held up her arms as if to expose her armpits. "Get a good whiff of that!"

Nadja raised her arms too. The girls were answered with a couple of bullets ricocheting off the side of the building. Dust flew off the side, clouding the air around them like tiny billows of gray smoke.

"I don't think they like your plan," said Nadja.

Dalila shrugged.

"Fucking snipers," they both said.

July 6

IN THE MORNING, I wake up gasping for air. The nightmare lingers, and I see a dark shape move at the foot of my bed. I close my eyes, count to five and open them.

The shape is gone.

I'm alone in my room.

I'm not at the farmers market. I'm not running. My body is not on fire. I'm not screaming. No one is screaming. There is no explosion.

I'm safe.

My door creaks open. I close my eyes, pretend to be asleep. I sense someone looking at me, but the door closes just as I'm about to see who it is.

Now that it's been a few days, I'm finally allowed to shower, so I get up and turn on the faucet. My back feels like it's on fire as the water pounds into it. After I get out, I carefully redress my cheek and go spend time with Benny. Dad doesn't think it's a good idea for him to go back to the hospital. I agree. I'm not even sure if it's such a good idea for me.

Benny asks me to show him the pictures I took of him on his scooter. We scroll through them on my laptop. It's weird to look at these now. The world was a different place then.

"Let's get some more cool shots," he says. "You can catch me in the air. Like this." He stands on the couch and jumps off, kicking his leg out.

I smile but make no effort to grab my camera. I think it's somewhere in my room, which feels way too far away. "Maybe later. I'm tired." And I'm struck by the fact that I haven't taken a picture in days. Just the idea of even picking up my camera now seems exhausting. I feel my eyes well.

What is wrong with me?

"Ready, Z?" Dad calls.

I blink back the tears before they can fall. "Yeah," I say.

Then I hug Benny good-bye, wave to Aunt Evelyn and leave with my dad to go see Mom.

Shortly after arriving at the hospital, two police officers ask to speak with me. I don't know what I could tell them that they probably don't already know, but Dad signs the paper they put in front of him and gives them permission to question me in his absence. I don't want to do this. I want him to stay. But before I can even speak, Dad explains how he needs to get back to work. His patients need him.

He's not fooling me.

I know it's his way of dealing with what's happening with Mom—throwing himself into work, never stopping, because if he stops, he'll have to feel.

What about how I feel? And Benny? Does Dad honestly think his patients need him more than we do?

I glance at the officers. We're in one of the doctors' offices, a woman who works in pediatrics. Children's crayon drawings line the walls in white frames. I feel a heat creep up my spine, adding to the continual pain I'm in.

"Thank you for talking with us, Zara," the female officer says to me.

As if I had a choice.

We sit in three chairs, kind of in a triangle. Across from me, hanging on display, is a stick figure with long hair riding an elephant. There's a small table in the room pushed up against the wall. Two coffee cups and two water bottles adorn it.

"Would you like something to drink?" she asks.

"No."

I glance at the door, making sure it's still open. It is. Even so, my heart races. This was not a good idea.

"First of all, how are you doing?" She leans toward me, concern in her eyes.

"Okay."

"I can't imagine the ordeal you've been through," the male officer says.

"No." The woman shakes her head. "Are you sure we can't get you anything?"

I relax a little in my chair. "Maybe I'll take a water."

She hands me a bottle. I open it and see that my hands are shaking. Some of the water spills down the side of my mouth as I take a drink.

"First off, my name is Steve, and this is Mona. We're questioning everyone we can who was at the farmers market when the explosion happened," Steve says. "Would it be okay if we record this?"

"Um, I guess."

He takes out a small device, presses Record, and sets it on the table.

"Can you take us through what you remember?" Mona asks.

I tell them about the morning, starting with when we arrived at the north end of the market. Where my mom parked and the direction we walked. I tell them what I saw, which was a normal day at the farmers market. There were people walking around, talking, shopping. I try to go back through the experience slowly, as if I am moving through a movie frame by frame. Stopping to examine each moment.

There were the tomatoes and the vendor with the hat. What is his name? I've seen him many times before. He's always at the market. Why can't I remember his name? And then we were walking again, I think. Looking at . . . other things. My brain feels fuzzy, almost like it's got these tangles and webs now that it didn't have before.

"I don't remember," I mumble.

"You don't remember what happened after that?"

"No, wait, I think Benny wanted . . . um . . . something."

"Like what?" Steve asks.

I stare at him. "I don't know . . . he wanted . . ."

What did he want? A toy? No, there aren't any toys at the market.

"You must have been terribly frightened," Mona says.

But my mind is with Benny. We were on the ground. He was scared. His hand felt so light in mine. And it was sticky, I think. His hand was sticky with something.

Mona pulls out a detailed drawing of the farmers market.

Every stand is labeled. There are purple X's and marks scattered throughout, a code I can't read. "Can you point to the spot on the map where you found your mother?"

I trace my finger along our path and leave it in front of the stand I think we were near when we split up for some reason. I can't remember why we split up.

"Thank you," Mona says. She makes a mark with her pencil. "And you and your brother were . . ."

My finger hovers above the map. I don't know where to place it. I'm not exactly sure where we were. At least a couple of tents down and across from Mom? But really, what does it matter now where Benny and I were standing when the bomb went off? This questioning is making me tired and annoyed, and I'm ready for it to be over. I place my finger four tents down from where I found Mom just to hurry it up.

Another mark.

"I know this is difficult," Steve says. "You're doing a great job, Zara. We have just a couple more questions, if that's okay?"

I sigh. "Fine."

"Did anything stand out to you that morning?" he asks.

"What do you mean?"

"Thinking back now and given what you know happened, did you notice anything that seemed unusual? Any people that seemed out of the ordinary?"

I try to remember, but most of the morning is still foggy. Why did we even go to the farmers market? Mom was buying something. What? Apples? Some kind of fruit? I close my eyes and try to think.

"It's okay," says Mona. "Take your time."

A wave of nausea comes over me then as I suddenly remember the super-sweet smell of gross, rotting peaches.

"Peaches," I say.

"What about peaches?"

"She bought rotting peaches. My mom. It was disgusting."

Mona and Steve look at each other. "Was there someone odd by the peaches?" he asks.

"I don't know. I'm not sure what you mean by odd."

"Like anyone who was acting strange or who looked suspicious? Maybe someone who looked—"

"Like a terrorist?" I finish. "Do you mean did I see any men who looked like they were Middle Eastern?"

"Did you?" asks Steve.

"Not that I remember, no."

"Terrorists can look like anyone," says Mona.

This is starting to make me uncomfortable. I can feel my temples throb. A migraine is coming on. I glance back at the door, and it seems to have narrowed. Like someone has inched it closer to closing. I shouldn't be here. I should be with my brother or my dad or anywhere but here.

"How is your mother doing?" Mona asks.

I shift in my seat. "She's still in critical condition."

"Has anyone from her mosque come to visit? Her imam, maybe?"

"What? She doesn't have a mosque," I say, confused.

"Oh, I thought she went to . . ." Mona checks her notes and says the name of a mosque in our area.

"Maybe once or twice a year," I say. "During Ramadan. But she doesn't, like, go on a regular basis or anything." How do they know the name of Mom's mosque?

"Have any of her Muslim friends come to visit the house before? Anyone recently?"

"Her Muslim friends?"

"Yeah."

I stare hard at Mona. "Are you trying to imply that my mom had something to do with this?"

"No, of course not. We're simply trying to get as much information as possible." She leans forward, invading my space, but I don't back away from her. "People died. Good people. Innocent people. Many others were wounded. Some will never walk again. It's our job to get to the truth of how this happened, who orchestrated it."

"My mom isn't even religious. But the last I heard, America is a free country and we're all free to practice any religion."

"Zara, I think you might have misunderst—"

"No!" I don't let her finish. "You're suggesting that because my mom is Muslim, she might have ties to terrorists? That she could be one herself? Do you think *I'm* a terrorist too?"

"It's okay, Zara," says Steve. "We're all very tired and on edge. We know you and your family had nothing to do with this. Would your mom be lying in a coma if she did?"

I can't help it, my eyes water. I feel my face flush with embarrassment at my tears and anger at what they're suggesting. The wound on my cheek burns under the bandage.

Yeah, sure, my mom fits the profile. Refugee. Muslim. Kind of a loner. *Terrorist.* They've checked all the boxes.

This is bullshit. My dad will be furious when he hears what they said. I stand to leave.

"Listen, if you think of anything else that might be useful to our investigation, please contact me." Steve hands me his card. I fold it in half and stuff it in my pocket. "Anything. Anything at all."

I leave the small room and walk down the hospital corridor, feeling beat-up. Again. Everything hurts, inside and out.

How could they even insinuate that Mom was some religious fanatic who would not only blow up people, but almost kill herself, her own children? It's absurd.

But then I remember the box and the money. I head straight for the elevators.

There's no way Mom is a terrorist. I know she didn't have anything to do with the bombing. But why did she have all that cash hidden? Was she planning something?

The elevator door slides open, and I step inside.

When I get to my mom's room, I linger in the doorway. Looking at her now, lying there, you'd never know she's capable of keeping so many secrets, and I'm struck again by the force of it all. I think about the bomber. Did he have a family? Did they know what he was plotting? Or was he good at keeping secrets too?

There's so much we don't know about other people, even those we're related to by blood. It's even crazier to realize how people of the same family can be so completely different.

And not for the first time, I think, *Who are you really, Mom?* as the oxygen machine clicks on.

AFTER SEVERAL MORE blocks uphill, darting from doorway to doorway, Nadja and Dalila made it to the once-bustling center of Bjelave, one of the neighborhoods in Sarajevo.

Empty.

No open market. No one selling anything. The old dry fountain, which used to always run fresh mountain water available for drinking, mocked them as they passed. Down a couple more streets, they turned right and found the door they wanted—a green splintered one—on the opposite side of the main entrance of the house.

The smells of ash, human BO and mold met them as they descended. Once inside, they removed their large black boots and left them by the door with other pairs of shoes on a rack. They kept their coats on because the basement was freezing. It was set up with a sleeping area composed of mattresses taken from the bedrooms upstairs and piles of blankets that Ramiza, Dalila's mom, made them fold every morning. According to her, even in a basement, they weren't going to live like animals.

In the far corner, Amir, Dalila's father and an old friend of Nadja's father, had set up a makeshift aluminum stove. He built shelves and tore one of the cabinets out of the kitchen for Ramiza to be able to store items. Throughout the basement, flames flickered from the tin cans of vegetable oil they used as candles—the only light because sandbags covered the single window. The window that allowed them to see the street, and allowed others to see in.

Amir sat on the couch that he and Faris, Dalila's brother, had brought down to the basement when the shelling got so bad that it looked like they would have to dig in for the winter. That was earlier, when everyone said the war wouldn't last past fall. Now they said it couldn't last into spring.

The room was a little warmer than upstairs because of the heat that came from the stove. A haze of smoke hovered in the air from the cigarettes and whatever else was burning. Probably the closet doors from the fourth bedroom upstairs. Amir had decided they would begin with the bedrooms on the upper floors before working their way down, using whatever they could for firewood.

"Back, Mom," Dalila said to Ramiza, who knelt at the stove.

"Thank goodness. No trouble?" She held out her hand for the jugs.

"Some snipers, but they were just playing with us," Dalila said.

"I lost a jug. I'm sorry, Ramiza," Nadja said, and set her single jug next to the stove. She removed her headphones from her ears and let them rest around her neck like usual.

"Were either of you hurt?" Ramiza said, pulling Dalila close.

"No," said Dalila.

But still Ramiza examined Dalila's body for any wounds

or scratches. She did the same with Nadja, even though Nadja strained a little at the touch.

"Fucking snipers," Amir said from the couch. He unwrapped a pack of Drinas—the brand of cigarettes everyone smoked—read the inside of the paper and snorted. "Nothing good this time. Advertisement for Yugos."

Amir was a handsome man with dark but graying unkempt hair and a beard. One side of his glasses was held together with silver masking tape from when they were knocked off his face four weeks ago. He had been at the hospital, where he worked, when a shell hit the side of the building. He'd been thrown across the hall.

His bad leg was propped up on a pillow, injured from a bullet wound fighting on the front lines last year.

When the Serb-controlled JNA surrounded Sarajevo and started attacking its citizens, Amir had been one of the first men to dig through an old box, find his grandfather's WWI pistol and head off to fight. He had never even fired a gun. In the early days of the siege, men from each neighborhood in Sarajevo volunteered and fought, sometimes with only a handful of bullets. They weren't soldiers. They were ordinary men, like Amir. Fathers protecting their families. Even though Amir now walked with a limp and suffered from the searing pain of sciatica all the way down his right side, there was a fierce pride when he spoke of those first days. Today his son fought in his place.

Most days Amir sat on the couch, his brown trench coat wrapped tightly around him, refusing to talk about what he had seen. Sometimes he raged at the world, especially the West and

"Bill Fucking Clinton," who, in his opinion, had left Sarajevo citizens to be slowly exterminated like they were nothing more than cockroaches. He worked at the hospital as an anesthesiologist in forty-eight-hour shifts. He spoke even less of what happened there.

Before the war, Nadja would have looked to the adults around her for answers. Now they seemed just as dazed and bewildered as she was. As the war dragged on, they burrowed themselves into the basement and the side of the hill like they were already in a tomb.

When she'd first come to them, they had pressed her for answers, but Nadja couldn't speak. She didn't talk for two months. Dalila took her hand and led her from place to place like she was a little child, and not eighteen. When she finally spoke, the first word Nadja said was *Why?*

Now she didn't think there were answers to the *why*. The *why* that raged across Sarajevo. The wringing of hands up to the sky, why? Why was this happening to them? Why didn't anyone stop it? What had they done?

All Nadja knew was the human heart contained great depths. Before the war, she would have talked about the deep capacity for love. She'd had no idea how wrong, how naive she had been. Now she knew the heart held a darkness that could swallow up the whole world.

Amir struggled with the transistor radio in his hands, trying to get it to work. It had been broken for a couple of days. When Faris was away at the front, they listened to the radio all the time.

It was their only way of knowing what might be happening with him.

It had been almost two months, and there had been no word of Faris. The unspoken worry took up the rest of the space in the basement, making it overcrowded and at times suffocating. Nadja and Dalila looked for every opportunity to escape, even if it meant going for a water run. The fact that it meant putting their lives in danger meant nothing to them. Their lives were always in danger. Simply living was dangerous.

Nadja joined Dalila on the floor next to the stove. They removed their gloves and tried to warm their hands with the little heat there was. Nadja ignored the ache behind her right eye, a light headache, hoping that if she did, it would just go away. She didn't want to get one of her migraines.

"I'm sorry again about the jug," Nadja said.

"It's only water. We can get more later," Ramiza said, patting Nadja on the shoulder. She poured some from one of the jugs into a large pot and heated it on the stove.

"Want me to make coffee?" Nadja asked, already getting up.

"Sure, love," Ramiza said.

No one mentioned that the coffee beans were actually lentils. They hadn't had real coffee for over a month. Nadja used a teaspoon of oil, careful not to go over because she didn't want to waste it. She fried the lentils, blackening them. Soon the misleading smell of steak filled the small basement space.

Nadja pressed a hand into her stomach. She was hungry. She was always hungry and always thinking about food. And no matter how often she told herself not to think about it, she kept thinking about it. Sometimes she and Dalila would play a game. They would talk about all the food they would eat when the war ended. The feast they would prepare. In the string of limitless hours of boredom, they would pore over the pages of a cookbook Dalila had saved from becoming firewood. Marking and underlining and taking notes. Reading the pictures of food like they were actually consuming them. Sometimes they drew pictures of the food.

When Nadja finished roasting the lentils, she ground them by hand in the small grinder. Then she poured the hot water over the lentils and served the coffee in small cups. Everyone took one. No one said it tasted like muddy water and nothing like coffee.

"Let's see, what do we have to eat?" Ramiza played along and acted like she was perusing a large cupboard of food. There were only two MRE bars left, along with a bag of beans, some flour and rice. They had been eating beans and rice for months. "Beans? Rice?"

Amir grunted from the couch. He picked up his copy of the *Oslobođenje*, Sarajevo's daily newspaper, and read it. Every now and then swearing under his breath, calling politicians *kriminalci*. Nadja couldn't help but agree; they were criminals, allowing for the situation to become like this.

Ramiza gave the girls the last of the MRE bars from the Americans. Nadja read the date on hers: *1967*. What ingredients could last more than twenty-five years? She didn't even notice the taste anymore. At least this meant that another week had passed and tomorrow Nadja and Dalila could be on the lookout for a Red Cross truck carrying more food.

"You need a haircut," Ramiza said to Amir.

"I'll make an appointment. Dalila, you free tomorrow morning?"

"Let me check my schedule." Dalila mocked opening a planner. "No, pretty booked. But I can see you now."

"Good." He put out his cigarette in the full ashtray that rested on the arm of the couch.

Dalila stood up and got some scissors from a box with first aid equipment. Her father hobbled over to a smaller chair, which he pulled close to the stove. Dalila first combed his hair and then started cutting it dry.

For a few moments there was only the sound of Ramiza preparing beans for a later meal and Dalila's cutting. Nadja studied Dalila's technique.

"Maybe I could give it a try?" Nadja said.

"Dad?" Dalila asked.

He answered yes with a flick of his hand.

"Okay, so you do it in sections and then pull it up, but be careful not to cut too much. You want to make it even."

Nadja copied what she had watched Dalila do many times. She concentrated and tried to cut it as evenly as possible, combing and pulling up just enough hair. Amir's hair was straight, so it was not difficult to see the lines. When she finished, she stepped back, and Dalila and Ramiza inspected the cut. Dalila noted a section where it was uneven, so Nadja fixed it.

"Want to see, Dad?" Dalila said, hunting for a mirror.

"No, it's okay," Amir said, running his hands over his head. "It's fine. Thank you, Nadja."

"You're welcome."

"You should trim his beard too," Ramiza said. "He looks like one of those drunk Četniks." Ramiza spat the word.

"Is that a thing to say to your husband?"

"I always tell the truth."

"The truth. Now, that's a shifty companion," Amir said, and returned to the couch. He picked up the radio and began taking it apart again, trying to understand the nature of the problem.

"Nadja, take some water and bathe," Ramiza said. "Use a little perfume too." Then she said what she always said. "We may live like animals, but we don't have to smell like them all the time."

Nadja grabbed a change of clothes out of a small suitcase from her section of the room. She took the plastic bowl of water Ramiza handed her. She climbed up the stairs, opened the door, noting the chill right away, walked around to the front of the house and opened the front door. She passed the living room with a large Turkish rug in the center and only a chair. A small kitchen with a table and a *heklanje* spread across it, the fine lace now more yellow than white, like the plastic yellow flowers in the vase in the middle. The bathroom was down the hall. She went inside and shut the door behind her.

Setting the bowl down in the sink, Nadja first dipped a toothbrush into the water and brushed her teeth with a little bit of baking soda. She removed her Walkman, coat, sweater and shirt, and stood naked from the waist up in front of the mirror. Her body shook. She knew she was skinny, but seeing her ribs peek out shocked her. In only a year and a half, she had lost any womanly curves she'd had and now looked like a photo of a girl suffering from anorexia that she had seen in a class at school.

Thinking of school made her think of her old teachers and friends, which made her think of home and her family and . . . She gripped the sides of the sink. The wave of emotion came on suddenly, like a mortar attack. The memory itself like bombs dropping from the sky. But there was nowhere for her to run and hide. She closed her eyes and breathed deeply, pushing away the feelings. Driving them back with the numbness she wore like a *potkošulja* underneath her clothes. It didn't last long, maybe a minute, but she was afraid if she indulged the feelings any longer, she would go mad from them.

She would be like the woman who lost her son in the shelling three weeks ago. He had been playing with his friends outside in a small patch of grass, stiff from frost. The day was beautifully clear. Nadja remembered because she had moved a sandbag to the side and stared up at the sky from the window. She watched the kids, a little jealous that they seemed so happy. One moment the boy kicked a ball. The next moment his body flew through the air like he was a stuffed animal. Adults collected his body and rushed the parts to the hospital. The woman never left his side. Nadja had overheard Amir tell Ramiza that the woman was being force-fed. He also said maybe they shouldn't waste precious resources on her. Because she had no will to live, she was like one already dead.

Nadja shook her head free of such thoughts. She looked at her green eyes in the mirror. She was not dead. No, she was not dead. But the dead clung to her. They lived inside of her.

With a blue washcloth from a doorless cupboard, she took a tiny bit of soap, dipped it into the water and rubbed soap on the wet cloth. She washed her face and neck. Her arms and armpits. Her stomach and breasts. Doing it quickly because it was so cold. Not cold enough for her to freeze to death, but enough for her skin to burn.

After bathing the top half of her body, Nadja rinsed the cloth in the water, wringing out the dirty water in the sink. She wet her short brown hair so that it was a little damp and washed it over the tub. Careful to use as little water as possible, she rinsed the soap from her hair as best she could.

Once her hair was clean, Nadja put on a clean long-sleeve shirt and sweater. She then removed her jeans and the long underwear she wore underneath and began to wash the lower part of her body.

When she was finished, she put on a pair of jeans that were a faded light denim and seemed two sizes too big for her, although they were the size she wore last year, or maybe it was even more recently than that. Nadja couldn't recall. Time was no longer measured for her in such clear increments. How long had she been in Sarajevo? It could have been days. It could have been three lifetimes.

Nadja belted the jeans tight at the waist so they wouldn't fall down. She piled on two sweaters and a coat—the last of her clean clothes. She placed her dirty clothes in a hamper in the bathroom. Tomorrow she and Dalila would wash them with Ramiza and hang them on the line at the side of the house.

Nadja grimaced at her reflection. Ghost girl. That's who she was now.

In a small basket on the bathroom sink was a bunch of

makeup. She applied some blush, which accented her cheekbones, making them angular and sharp, as if she were constantly pursing her lips together. She added black liner to the bottom and top of her lids before applying mascara. She also dabbed a small amount of perfume behind her ears.

She brushed out her wet hair, noticing that she was losing more of it in the brush than usual. She wondered if she would have bald patches like the girl down the street. Maybe she should shave it again. Or maybe she'd have Dalila cut it for her, since it had grown out and was now a little past her jawline. Nadja would have loved to style it, but the blow dryer and curling iron were useless. The water and electricity had been off for months, and there was no telling when they would be turned back on again. Maybe Amir would be able to siphon the electricity away from the nearby hospital again soon, but Nadja doubted she could convince him to do it for something trivial like her hair.

Nadja left the bathroom, taking only the empty plastic bowl with her. Instead of going back to the basement, she went to the living room, bare except for the piano.

Not long after Nadja had arrived to Dalila's family, they'd had to move from their own home over on the opposite side of Sarajevo. Because of all the bombing, it was getting too dangerous not to have a basement of their own. At first, they spent every night sleeping in the basement of a school with a bunch of other families and individuals. When more refugees from the east, as well as other parts of the country, started pouring in and it became too crowded, Amir found this abandoned home. The original family must have left when the war started.

Dalila's family and Nadja moved in, happy to discover that most of the belongings were still there. Clothes, cooking supplies, books, tools in a shed, and a baby grand piano.

They were respectful of the personal items. The family photos left on the wall were removed from the wood frames and kept in a pile in the large bedroom on the second floor. The empty frames were one of the first things they used for firewood. Nadja was glad when Ramiza removed all the photos from the wall. She couldn't bear them looking at her, especially the three children. It was easier to use their things, sleep in their beds, without their watchful gaze.

Now, in the second winter of the siege, most of what could be easily burned had long since fed the small makeshift stove Amir built for Ramiza. The family had spared the piano when they discovered that Nadja played.

Nadja walked over to the beautiful instrument. She trailed her hand across the keys before sitting down on the bench. She shook out her hands and blew into them, trying to warm them up. Then she put her headphones back on and started quietly playing a slow melody that turned into something more complicated. It wasn't a piece she had learned by sight or by study, but one that came to her now. She played by ear and by note, but she enjoyed playing more when she could just create and follow the music wherever it took her. Today it took her to images of mountains of varying shades of green.

When the song ended, someone clapped behind her. She turned sharply in her seat, ready to run or attack.

A young man in a faded green military jacket stood in the

living room. By habit, Nadja eyed the door and the windows, planning her escape route. But a moment later, she recognized him and let a whisper escape her lips. "Faris."

Dalila's brother looked similar to when Nadja had last seen him two months ago, though a dirtier, more tired version. His sandy brown hair now fell to his neck, and he had a new scar above his left eye.

"Sorry. I didn't want to disturb you."

"Amir and Ramiza will be so happy you're back!" She started to get up.

"Just a sec. Can you play some more?"

"But don't you want—"

"A few more minutes' waiting won't bother them."

He sat down on the floor and leaned back against the wall next to the piano, laying his rifle next to him. He lit a cigarette and closed his eyes.

Nadja resumed, and when she finished the song, Faris asked for one more.

"It's cold," she said, her breath a steady fog in front of her.

"It's always cold," said Faris.

She played again, something in a minor key, something almost haunting. Or maybe it was just the acoustics of the empty home. The notes echoed throughout the rooms, chasing old ghosts.

As the last note sounded, Faris held out his cigarette to Nadja. She took a puff and handed it back to him.

"I should have learned to play," he said.

"It's not too late."

"Maybe," he said.

"How was the front?"

"Oh, the same. They fire. We fire. We are not so far from them, so sometimes at night they call out to us, insult our mothers, tell us to surrender. We tell them to fuck off. Yesterday, one of them called my name. He and I went to the same school. He asked about this guy we both knew. I told him Skander died a month ago. He yelled, 'Too bad.' And then the bullets started flying." Faris stared off like he was still somewhere on the front.

"We have water. You should wash," Nadja said, taking in the creases in his neck that were dark, lined with dirt.

"Yes. I must smell."

"We all smell," she said. The truth was she was getting used to the smell.

After . . . after she left Višegrad and before she came to live with them, Nadja had survived in cramped quarters with other refugees from different parts of eastern Bosnia, until she was smuggled into Sarajevo. She thought she'd never want to smell again. She never knew human beings could smell worse than animals. There were smells she knew she'd never forget, like blood. And fear. Fear smelled like sweat and urine and ugly. The worst kind of ugly. Sometimes she'd smell cooking from one of the cafés that was still open and remember her mother. Nadja had wondered then if she could do something to get rid of her sense of smell.

"Do you know smell is actually the first thing that attracts us to each other? I always thought it was legs or, you know . . ." Faris chuckled.

Nadja played a D chord, but in her mind, she buried her face in Marko's neck, nuzzling, searching for his smell. What was that cologne he wore? And again, she wondered, wished that there was a part of her brain she could stick a knife in to drive out the sense—and the memory.

"A sniper almost got me today," she said. Changing the subject to redirect her thoughts.

"Where?"

"Coming back from getting water."

Faris nodded and finished his cigarette, putting it out on the wooden floor. "Fucking snipers."

Nadja stood up and held out her hand. Faris grabbed it, and she pulled him to his feet. They walked outside and then down the stairs to the basement and were met with cries of "Faris!"

Dalila ran right to him. He picked her up in a big bear hug. Ramiza was next, followed by Amir, who smacked him a couple of times on the back before giving him a hard embrace.

Ramiza offered him a cup of lentil coffee.

"Mom, throw that away." Faris produced a sack of coffee beans from under his coat.

"Oh! Where'd you get this?"

"Someone handed it to me when I was walking home, thanking me for my service."

"As they should," she said. She wiped her tears and immediately rinsed out the grinder, then started measuring the new beans.

"Most of the time, it is a cup of tea, coffee, something hot. Today, a whole bag of beans. I've also got some other things."

Faris emptied his pockets on the couch next to Amir—a few packs of cigarettes wrapped in white. "A little less than last month. Compliments of BiH." On the other side of the wrapping, Nadja knew, would be some kind of text, an advertisement for shoes or the label to a box of detergent, maybe even a clipping for a movie. It was always a surprise.

The smell of real coffee soon cut through everything else. Nadja breathed it deeply, smiling despite herself. Thankful now for the sense. Was there anything better than the smell of strong coffee?

Ramiza gave them each a small cup. "Sorry I don't have any sugar," she said, nervous with excitement at Faris being home. It was like having an important guest.

By candlelight they sipped coffee, and smoked, and listened to Faris explain the battle at the front. He gave elusive details, mostly generalities, as if to spare them. Nadja knew he would speak to Amir in private, low whispers later. The most specific was the story he had told Nadja upstairs. The fighting wasn't getting any closer to ending.

"We need better weapons," he said. "It's a joke."

"What about the tunnel?" Amir asked.

Underneath the airport, there was a secret tunnel that ran from Dobrinja and came out in Butmir. Both entrances were heavily guarded. It was kept secret from the Serbs. The tunnel was built so supplies and aid could be smuggled into the city. But it also provided a covert way out and in. It took two hours to walk it, stooped over and wearing a mask because of the low ceiling and poor air quality.

"Even though it's hard, it's still better than running across the tarmac. Too many people still get killed trying to do so."

Nadja knew how dangerous it was firsthand. She remembered trembling with fear and dropping down in the grass, crawling on hands and knees as the man in front of her pressed his fingers to his lips. "When I tell you to run, run," he said to her. She was with another woman and her young daughter. They were just one group out of four who were trying to cross the airport into Sarajevo. The problem was the Serbs had a direct view of the tarmac and shot at anything that moved. The airport was also controlled by the United Nations (United Nothing), and if the UN caught you, they would arrest you. Or they would return you to Sarajevo, thinking that you were trying to escape. It was fine for those wanting to get in, like Nadja. But for those wanting to get out, it was a problem. No one was allowed to leave Sarajevo, but refugees from other cities fled there in the beginning of the war. Many thought it would be safer in Sarajevo or, like Nadja, had people there to help them.

Nadja had made it across the tarmac. The woman hadn't. The last Nadja saw was the woman lying on the grass with her eyes staring open. Her daughter sat next to her. The man pulled Nadja along as the lights from the UN truck found the crying girl. This is what had allowed them to make it. The woman's death had been the perfect distraction. Nadja had felt nothing as she left them.

As they enjoyed Faris's return, outside the shells came in spurts. After a relatively light day of shelling, the night turned heavy. It was as if the enemy was pummeling them with big fists across the valley. Other times the army that surrounded them was a cat and just toyed with the civilians, picking them off one by one. Playing with its prey.

They ate a small dinner of beans and rice that Ramiza had fried up with oil. Dessert was a kind of cake made without sugar, eggs or milk that Ramiza learned from another woman in the neighborhood who had learned from someone else. It was a recipe passed around and around. It didn't really taste like cake, but no one complained.

Nadja watched the family like she watched most things now—with reserve. It was in moments like these, the four of them all together, sharing family stories and intimacies, that she knew she wasn't really a part of their family. She had been added on like an appendage, but she could be easily severed. She sat on her mattress and pulled her legs up to her chest, making herself as small as she could.

By 21:00, everyone was lying in their own makeshift bed. Nadja and Dalila were back to back, sharing the mattress, not only out of a sisterly friendship, but out of necessity. They had started sleeping this way at the onset of winter and agreed to continue. Their bodies gave more warmth when they were together.

Nadja took longer than the others to fall asleep. She was still nursing a headache. She could tell by their breathing who was up and who wasn't.

In the end, she wasn't sure whose body gave in first: hers or Faris's.

She wondered what he was afraid to see in his dreams that kept him awake. She already knew her own demons.

In the morning, Nadja woke, tired. Her breath thick in front of her. Dalila and Faris were still asleep, but Ramiza and Amir were up, trying to light a fire. Amir cursed and cursed as if the words were an incantation that would bring heat and flame.

Nadja went to the small window, the only one with glass that remained, pushed aside a sandbag and saw white.

Snow.

DAD SLAMS HIS hand on the steering wheel.

"That's appalling," he says. He's fuming because I told him about my interview with the police officers. "I really can't believe that. *Dammit.* I should have been there."

Yeah, you should have, I think. I rub my temple. I feel a headache coming on, and it seems like it's going to be a bad one.

"Did you get their names?"

I pull Officer Steve's card out of my pocket, now all bent at the edges. "The guy gave me his card."

I'm careful not to sit back against the car seat. My back still aches, and there's no way I'm taking any more of those painkillers. Not even Tylenol. In some twisted way, part of me wants to feel the pain. Because when people ask me how I'm feeling, I'll have something to tell them.

"Good," Dad says, snatching the business card from me. "I'll be calling him up. You're not to talk with anyone else, media, officers, whoever, unless I'm present, okay?"

I look over at Dad. Is he serious? "It's not like I ever wanted to talk to them in the first place. You're the one who left me with them alone."

I feel his eyes on me, but I'm already facing front.

"I know," he says. Pause. "I'm sorry. I know we're both just doing our best here. There's no manual for any of this. But don't worry about those officers. Our lawyer will handle this."

"We have a lawyer?"

"We do now." His jaw is set like his hands on the wheel, hard and tense. "I've got to get gas and then we'll head straight home." He pulls into a gas station. "You hungry? I can pick up something."

"Not really."

"Okay. Me neither."

He parks the car next to the available pump. I notice some commotion near the front door of the convenience station and point.

"Great," Dad says sarcastically. "What now?"

Two men surround a third. Even though our car windows are up, I can hear the raised voices. I roll down the window. I can't make out everything they're saying, but I catch enough to know it's something about protecting our country and how Muslims hate us and are trying to kill us. The second guy says how do they know he's not one of them, one of the people who tried to blow us up? The man they think is Muslim backs away from the other two, but they don't let him pass. The bigger one strikes him in the face. Then there's another hit, and he's pushed. He falls to the ground. It all happens so quickly. The man on the ground covers his head and gets into a fetal position as they kick and beat him.

"Call the police," Dad says. He opens his door, but points at me. "Stay in the car!"

He runs over and yells, "Hey!"

"Dad!" I shout after him. I don't want him to get involved. What if they turn on him?

I dial 911.

The voice answers on the third ring. "This is 911. What is your emergency?"

"Um, there's a fight." My voice is shaking. "Two men against one. They're beating him pretty badly." I tell her where we are. She says an officer will be here in five minutes.

Five minutes? That's too long. I open my door.

Dad shouts at the men, but they don't stop. He grabs the bigger one from behind and pulls him off the downed man. The attendant runs out of the store at that moment with a bat, followed by a woman who has a spray bottle in her hand. The guy swings at them, but he doesn't even come close because Dad has him in a head hold.

"Get off me!" the guy yells.

"Not until you calm down." Dad pushes him to the ground with his knee in his back. I had no idea Dad knew how to do that. The guy struggles, but he can't get out of my dad's hold.

The woman sprays something at the first guy, who screams that his eyes are burning. It must be pepper spray.

"All right. All right," the guy my dad's holding says.

Dad releases him, and the man shouts a few obscenities, but Dad positions himself in front of the man they attacked.

"Zara?" he calls to me.

"Five minutes," I yell.

"Police," Dad says, out of breath.

The two guys run to their car, with the blinded one now crying out about how he can't see. If I had my camera, I could get a beautiful, clear shot of the license plate. But my camera is at home. And by the time my fingers stop trembling and I remember I can use my phone, they've already sped away.

Dad bends down and begins helping the man on the ground. There's so much blood on the concrete. My head is spinning.

"Zara, my pack and blanket," he yells.

I hear him. But I can't move. My eyes are locked on the man who was badly beaten.

"Zara!"

The man on the ground moans. Blood oozes from the side of his head. The images that, until now, have only come to me in bits and pieces begin flooding back. All the bodies. All the blood. All the screaming and crying. *Where's Benny? Isn't he supposed to be with me?* And then I look over to where Mom is supposed to be, but she's not there either. Everything is fuzzy. I can't catch my breath. The wound on my cheek aches.

Someone calls my name. I turn around and wonder why I'm in a gas station parking lot.

"Zara," Dad calls again, bringing me back to this moment. "My bag, please. Now!"

Suddenly I'm unfrozen and running toward the car. I get the blanket and Dad's medical bag from the trunk—the one that he always has on him in case of emergencies—and run over. I give him the bag. Dad hands me a wallet to look through while he makes a call to the hospital, asking for an ambulance right away.

The license in the wallet says Matthew Patel. There's also a

Providence College ID with the same name. Bank card. Credit card. *Patel.* I'm pretty sure that's Indian. I show Dad. He nods, then places the blanket underneath the man's head. He's checking the man's injuries and using whatever he has to help him. The station attendant and woman are still nearby, and other bystanders are now crowding around too.

Police sirens sound in the distance.

"Matthew?" Dad says. "Matthew, I'm a doctor."

Matthew says something. Dad doesn't catch it the first time, so he bends closer.

"What was that?"

"Matt," he says.

"Matt," Dad repeats. "You have a concussion. Some broken ribs and mild contusions on your face and body, but I don't think much more beyond that."

"Not even Muslim," he says.

What are we becoming?

"We'll stay with you until the ambulance comes," Dad says. He holds the man's hand. "Is there anyone we can contact for you?"

"My parents," he says, and Dad finds them on Matt's phone.

Matt closes his eyes, and tears run down his face.

The police sirens that had been building now pierce the air as a car pulls into the lot.

"Is he going to be okay?" the woman with the pepper spray asks.

Dad nods. "I think so. I should probably call his parents."

Will he be okay? He will live, if that's what she means. But who knows if he will be okay. How does this man recover from being jumped in a gas station parking lot? How will he ever be able to walk around and not watch his back? How will I?

The world crumbles around me. The ground shakes, rolls. Everyone is running, screaming. The air thick with smoke and dust. I can barely breathe.

AFTER DAD DRIVES me home, he stays with us for the rest of the evening instead of going right back to the hospital. He and Aunt Evelyn sit outside on the patio, drinking beer. I'm still shaky from what happened at the gas station. I read on my phone that attacks have been happening all over. I feel so bad for that guy, Matt. I wonder if he's still in the hospital, if I'll see him there tomorrow.

I find Benny in his room, drawing in his sketchbook at his desk. Benny loves to draw. He especially likes to create characters from different dimensions and worlds. Tonight, his drawing looks familiar. I peer over his shoulder.

He's drawn the farmers market. He's sketched people running and body parts. Pools of blood. But there is a large figure in the middle who looks like he's trying to help someone up.

"Benny, who's that?" I ask him.

"That's you."

"Me?"

"Yeah. I'm not finished with the hair," he says as he begins to draw long hair on his comic version of me.

"What's she, I mean, what am I doing?"

"You're rescuing us. That's me you're helping up after the bomb went off. And then, see . . ." He points to the candy stand, surprisingly untouched in his drawing.

"And . . ." He flips the page. "Here. This is where we find Mom and help her."

He's drawn a mound of rubble and a shoe sticking out. I feel light-headed.

"You remember all of that, Benny?"

"Yeah."

He turns back to the page he was on and continues to sketch me.

"I wish Mom was home," he says. "I miss her."

"Me too," I say, and my eyes well with tears, because I mean it.

Later I sit with Mom's box. I feel guilty, like I'm doing something she wouldn't approve. Like I'm prying into a space she keeps just for herself. But things have changed. It's been four days. I know the chance of her coming out of this gets smaller with every minute that passes. Now isn't the time to care about her privacy or rules. This might be the only way I have of ever really getting to know her.

I study the photos, especially the one of her by the bridge. Whoever took the photo obviously has an eye. I find the one of her and the boy and put the two photos side by side. They look like they were taken on the same day; their clothes and location are the same. I turn it over and read their names again: *Nadja and Marko '92.* Maybe this guy was her boyfriend. Whoever he is, the photo hasn't aged too well being trapped in a box. The corners are worn too. I wonder how many times Mom stared at it. The shot reminds me of something.

I get up and rummage through the bottom drawer of my dresser. I find the photo album underneath my sweaters, right where I stuffed it—months ago. I almost threw the whole thing out, but in the end, I decided to keep it.

The album is labeled *Mike and Zara*. Mike, my first and only boyfriend, now ex. I don't go slowly through the pictures. I'm not in one of my sadistic nostalgic moods that I sometimes indulge in. And it's not like I only save evidence of the good moments either. If I truly am about capturing all the little pieces of life, then these are a part of my story. I don't want to erase Mike from it, even if he was kind of a jerk in the end. Besides, if I ever have a daughter someday, I want her to be able to look at them and laugh at our styles, like I do with Dad and his eighties outfits.

If I have a daughter, I'll answer any question she has about me. I won't keep things from her. I won't be like my mom.

I quickly find the picture I'm looking for. Mike and I are side by side, looking up into the camera. He's taking the selfie. It's practically the same pose as my mom and her guy's.

Classic. Timeless boyfriend-girlfriend shot. It's strange—sure, this photo is from another time and place, but it doesn't really seem that different from today and the pictures I take with my friends.

The pictures I *used* to take.

How many days has it been now? I've barely even held my camera. I'm so behind on my 365 project, maybe I'll just abandon it altogether.

I keep looking at Mom and this guy Marko, and I wonder why she kept this photo. Nostalgia? Or did she love him? I suddenly feel that thing in my throat, like I'm going to cry. If Mom were here, maybe I could ask her about it. Maybe she would pat a spot beside her on the bed and tell me everything. She'd make some coffee. Maybe she'd finally let me in.

Maybe not.

I put the photo aside and look again at some of the other things in the box, like the pages of writing.

I pick up one and stare at the words in Bosnian. I could wait for her to wake up and then ask her about them.

If.

If she wakes up. The tiny word catches in my throat.

I could try to translate them on my own. It might not be perfect, but at least I'd get an idea. I download a translation app and take a picture of one of the pages. In a few moments, it translates the Bosnian into English for me. It's an awkward translation, so it takes me some time to rewrite the words so it makes sense in English.

Today we are trapped in the basement again. Too dangerous to go outside. They pound us from the air, trying to exterminate us. They should flood this place if they want us rats to die. I'm so hungry all the time. I wish I were dead. I think about it. The ways I could do it. I never tell D.

The rest of the translation is too difficult for me to make out the meaning. This will never work for all of the letters.

I read her words again. *I wish I were dead. I think about it. The ways I could do it.*

Did Mom ever take it one step further? Did she ever try to kill herself? The thought makes me shiver and sends a wave of pain up my back.

I've never felt so hopeless that I wanted to end my life. Not even now, when things are the worst they've ever been.

I put the phone down and hold the photo of my mom again. This time it feels heavier in my hands. I wonder who D is. I wonder where Mom was sitting when she wrote that letter. I lift the paper again and smell it. It smells old, like opening the door to a room that's been shut for far too long. It smells nothing like my mother.

1993
Winter
Sarajevo
BiH

NADJA STOPPED WRITING and reached for the small shard of colored glass, turning it over in her gloved hands. She'd seen it on the side of the road a few days ago and kept it. Her mother had always called such discoveries treasures. Some of her best jewelry pieces came from broken glass. Her favorite piece was a necklace with a silver chain and a heart made from glass with petals inside. She had always seen the beauty that came from the broken. Now Nadja struggled to do the same.

Amir snored loudly on the opposite side of the room. Nadja put on her headphones. She imagined there was music to drown out the sound. Her father had snored, but she couldn't remember the exact sound. Just a faint feeling that he had. Even now, she couldn't be so sure.

She removed the glove on her left hand and touched the razor-sharp side of the pale green glass, letting her finger teeter on the edge. Like her life, it could go either way. She pressed until her fingertip bubbled with blood. She brought it to her mouth and tasted it. She could do it. End it now.

The door opened above, and Faris's eyes found hers in the candlelight. He put his fingers to his lips and motioned for her to come. She blew out the candle she wrote by, folded the paper and hid it and the glass underneath her pillow. Then she shook Dalila awake next to her. They got up and tiptoed out of the womb of the basement and followed Faris out of the house.

"It's freezing!" Dalila said as soon as they were a couple of homes down.

"Here," Faris said. He gave the two girls a cigarette. "This'll warm you up."

Dalila grunted, but she took a puff and passed it to Nadja, who did the same. It didn't make her warmer, but seeing the small ember gave the illusion of heat.

They kept close to the buildings, but there was no darting tonight. By some miracle, there was no shelling, only the syncopated gunfire coming sporadically from the distant hills. Maybe the enemy knew that some days, like Christmas, were too sacred for killing. They had the cover of night on their side, too, though Nadja knew that snipers had special goggles. Faris said you could practically count the hairs on someone's head through those things. The image was stunningly close and real and personal. So real, he said you could maybe even see the color of the eyes. Nadja wondered how many snipers noted that hers were green.

"Got a new joke for you," Faris said as they walked.

"No Mujo and Suljo ones, please," Dalila said. Mujo and Suljo were joke characters popular more with Dalila's parents' generation than theirs. Nadja nodded in agreement.

"I said a new one. Okay, so these two guys are walking and talking. One of them puts his cigarette behind his ear to save for later. They start crossing the Latinska Bridge when a sniper starts shooting at them. The guy with the cigarette gets hit on the side of his head, and his ear falls to the ground. He stops and frantically searches the ground. His friend tells him, 'Get under cover! Don't be stupid! You've got two ears!' And the injured guy replies, 'I don't give a shit about the ear, I'm looking for the cigarette!'"

Faris laughed aloud.

Dalila groaned. "Everyone has heard that one already."

"Not me," Nadja said, and chuckled.

"Yes. The other day in school. That kid with the bad breath told it."

Nadja shrugged, not remembering. She struggled to concentrate in the makeshift school that met in a basement a couple times a week. The teachers mostly volunteered because there was no money to pay them. The mothers took turns guarding, sitting outside the door on chairs they dragged from their homes.

"You love me. Say it." Faris nudged Dalila so she tripped a little and put his arm around her.

Nadja felt like she was an intruder on an intimate moment, until Faris pulled her in too. They walked that way down the narrow hill, like they were stumbling home from a party and not putting their lives in danger.

As they descended into the graveyard of the city, Nadja felt as if she were slumbering and this were a dream. The valley of Sarajevo's old town, Baščaršija, lay to the left below them. Across was the other side of the valley, where the enemy watched or slept. The homes still standing rose on both sides like two- and three-story tombs with red-tiled roofs. Everything was gray except for those rooftops.

The week-old snow and ice crunched beneath their shoes. Nadja's boots were a size and a half too big, so she wore two pairs of socks, one with holes in the heels. But still she had to hold on with her toes every time she stepped so they wouldn't fall off.

The sky hung above, so full of stars, looking like it might burst upon them. She felt big and small at the same time, letting the potential of the night meet her.

As they left their neighborhood behind, they stopped speaking, knowing they took a risk being out past the ten o'clock curfew imposed by the Bosnian government. Finally, after walking in the cold for many kilometers, they arrived at the church. There was a silent line of people snaking out the door. Nadja didn't recognize the faces because they were in a different part of the city. The danger of being outside meant that people primarily stayed within their neighborhoods. Her usual range of motion was so small—basically a kilometer radius around the house that included a few neighbors, the basement school, the hospital, a water station and, when the UN truck came by, humanitarian aid. Nadja still hadn't had a real chance to explore the city.

Mirela, Faris's girlfriend, found them in line. Faris kissed her and then she gave Nadja and Dalila a hug. He took Mirela's hand as they moved forward into the building.

Inside the church basement, it was standing room only, shoulder to shoulder, warmer than outside. Every time someone moved, shadows crept up the candlelit walls. It was a secret midnight mass that somehow many people knew about. An unofficial act of resistance. They were all there as Sarajevans first and Muslim, Croat, Serb, Jew second.

A violin player and a double bass player played a song from Handel's *Messiah*. Nadja recognized it. Her music teacher had given her the songbook when she turned thirteen. She didn't remember the words—something about comforting people. It seemed fitting now.

After the music, the priest led the people through the rituals of mass. Nadja was familiar with the rhythm of the service because she'd gone to midnight mass a couple of times with her family and their neighbors. One of her dad's coworkers had been Catholic, and they had spent many Christmases with his family. Though they were not Catholic, it was common to celebrate other religions' festivals. She had always loved Christmas, with all the lights and the presents and the baby Jesus.

Nadja listened to the story of Jesus's birth. Of Joseph and Mary. Mary, who wasn't much younger at the time than her. The priest explained how Jesus was born into a difficult, oppressive time, much like how they were living now. In those days, the people were subject to the Roman Empire and lived in poverty and suffering. In fact, the priest said, Mary and Joseph were kind of like many of the people in Sarajevo—refugees, rejected, with no place to call home. But in the midst of all the pain of the world, God chose to meet the pain with a sacrifice of His own. The gift of His son. His gift was love.

"There is no safe place for love," said the priest. "Love only travels into dangerous places. And look at us lucky ones here, in the most dangerous place of all."

He got some small laughs at that one.

"The only way through suffering is love. Love will define us.

Not what happens around us or what happens to us. We must not let hatred destroy us. Many of us are broken, but love will put us back together. The light of the world has come. His name is Jesus, and no darkness will snuff Him out."

Nadja wished his words were true. But the darkness had destroyed all that she loved. Dalila reached for her hand. Nadja felt guilty that she had allowed some love in, almost like she was betraying her family's memory. But she held Dalila's hand because she wanted to believe.

At this time, people were instructed to hold up the small candles they had brought with them. Normally, a candle would have been given, but these were not normal times.

The priest lit a candle in the front row. Nadja watched as the light began to grow, first in one small line and then in a wave that flooded back to where she was standing.

Dalila unpocketed her candle, and she and Nadja held it together.

A small choir of five people faced the crowd and led them in the singing. As they sang, their breath rose in front of them like a visual piece of the music. Nadja watched the candlelight flicker every time her breath hit it. Even though she knew the words, Nadja didn't sing. She couldn't. It was like her voice had been stolen. So she closed her eyes and tried to let the music penetrate the part of her that she knew was dead. Maybe it could be healed. Maybe *she* could be healed by this love that the priest talked about.

Though she doubted she would ever know love again.

The music swirled around and inside of her, traveling in her blood, pumping through her veins, returning to the source: her broken heart. As the chorus swelled, Nadja held her breath, waiting for new life.

She found that she was still broken. Nothing healed. No miracle performed. But . . . she was no longer a barren wasteland, no longer the way she was when she'd first arrived to Dalila's family. Something grew now in the cracks. No matter how she felt about it, she would continue on. Nadja lived. She was not dead. She didn't know why. But she had been spared when others hadn't.

She stood with all the others in a crowded room. She couldn't deny the hope that came from standing together, looking to God together. They were still here. They were survivors. She had survived.

It was like being in a room full of fallen stars. And they were beautiful.

At the end of the service, the mood was lighter than it was when people entered. The ancient story of Jesus was more than just a symbol of hope tonight.

People milled about, hugging and kissing and wishing one another a merry Christmas. She even heard a few say, "*Essalamu alejkum.*" Peace be upon you.

Outside they waited for Faris as he said good-bye to Mirela.

Dalila sighed as she watched them slip away behind another building. "I'm going to die a virgin. Fucking war." She smoked the last cigarette she had in her pocket.

"Dalila. Nadja." Mrs. Vinković, an older woman who lived a couple blocks down the other side of their hill, approached them. "You're not here alone, are you?"

"No, with Faris," Dalila said.

Mrs. Vinković breathed in deeply. "Beautiful night." She played with the prayer beads in her hands. "My grandmother's," she explained, noticing Nadja looking at them. "Never was much for praying before the war," she said. "Now I pray. It helps. Are you coming next week, Nadja? My piano is old and lonely."

Mrs. Vinković's piano was lovely. Nadja hadn't played on a nicer one. Somehow it was still in tune. Mrs. Vinković kept it clean, free of dust. Once a week, Nadja usually visited and played for her and a couple of other women on the street.

"I will."

She leaned forward. "I may even have payment for you. Maybe some sweets. A package arrived from my sister in Germany." Mrs. Vinković brought her fingers to her lips. "Don't tell anyone. Merry Christmas, girls. God be with you." She patted Nadja's shoulder as she walked into the night.

Crack.

The sound whipped through the air. Startling them all. The whistle following it.

Everyone ducked and ran. Hands over their heads, as if that could protect them from the sniper's bullet. But Nadja just stood there. Someone grabbed her, threw her against the safety of the building. Faris's body, thick and tense, covering her. A couple more shots echoed, making it difficult to tell where the sniper lay in wait. Maybe it was two snipers.

The beads were on the ground next to the open hand. Nadja darted out and grabbed them. She wrapped them tightly around her wrist.

"What are you doing?" Faris yelled at her. "We have to go."

He pulled her with him and Dalila as they ran away from the building. Away from Mrs. Vinković's body, lying still in the dirty remnants of snow as the blood began pooling from the wound in her chest.

In the morning, Dalila woke Nadja and led her outside to the entrance of the house. The smell of something baking hit Nadja as soon as she opened the front door. She joined the rest of the family in the kitchen, huddled around the stove. Ramiza had made *kiflice*. It was a simple crescent that could be made from flour, oil and powdered milk—their typical UN rations. Normally it would be stuffed with cheese or have some kind of jelly. Nadja bit into the warm one Ramiza gave her. She didn't even miss the cheese. It was nice to be in the kitchen. The stove, though it didn't heat the whole house, provided enough warmth so they didn't have to wear their jackets or gloves. The sun was out and shone through the plastic tarp covering the windows.

There was no sound of gunfire or shelling outside. Faris thought there must be a ceasefire this morning, since it was Christmas Day. Amir didn't trust it; the Serbs followed the Orthodox calendar, and technically their Christmas was a couple of weeks after December 25. He kept looking outside, waiting for the bombs to start falling.

"Okay, so time for presents," Ramiza said.

"What?" Dalila asked. She looked at Amir, who raised his arms and shoulders like he didn't know what Ramiza meant. But he gave a little smile too, like he was in on it all along.

Ramiza removed three small parcels from a drawer in the kitchen and handed one each to Dalila, Nadja and Faris.

"I thought we didn't have money for gifts!" Dalila said.

"It's not a big deal," Ramiza said. She turned back to the stove, focusing on the pot of boiling water. "Not even a proper Christmas."

Each gift was wrapped in a new scarf that looked like it had been made by Ramiza's friend who lived a few houses away. Dalila's bundle contained a romance novel, lip gloss and a new toothbrush and paste.

Dalila smiled. "Thanks, Mom! Dad!"

Faris's scarf contained a new pair of gloves, a pack of Drinas and a toothbrush and paste. He wrapped the green scarf around his neck, declaring it was the best scarf he owned.

Nadja opened hers, and her legs went numb. The comic was used. The edges curved as if the previous owner had stuffed the book in his back pocket. It was an *X-Men*, Volume II. She recognized it immediately as one Benjamin used to read. She ran her hands over the cover showing Cyclops blasting something off the page with his eyes. Wolverine, in red, waited below him. There was also a Superman comic, one that looked a little older, a little worse for wear. A pair of thick gray socks tumbled to the floor. Nadja couldn't even bend to pick them up.

"I noticed you needed new socks, Nadja, and Amir mentioned the comic books. I hope you like them."

Nadja couldn't speak. She nodded and held the books to her chest. Months ago, she and Amir had gone to the market, back when they had a meager amount of money to spend and cigarettes to barter with. There was a store with a basket full of old comic books. Nadja had stared at them, picked one up and smelled it. While Amir shopped, she read them. He must have noticed.

Amir put his hand on Nadja's shoulder and squeezed it.

"These are great, Mom, Dad," Faris said, already wearing his new gloves. "Perfect for when I'm back with the guys."

He hugged Ramiza and Amir.

Nadja still couldn't speak.

"So, I've got something too." Faris ran outside, down to the basement, and came back in with a bag. "Nothing's wrapped, but, you know . . . So this is, like, for everyone." He removed the items and placed them on the kitchen table: five eggs, two oranges, three bananas, sugar, two cucumbers and three toma-toes. Ramiza's and Amir's eyes went wide.

"Where did you get such things?" Ramiza said.

"Oh, I have my ways." Faris's eyes sparkled.

Ramiza's hands fell softly on the eggs. "We haven't seen eggs in . . . I can't remember when."

"Faris, how?" Amir asked him.

"I may have given an interview or two to some British journalists."

Amir grunted, but he kept quiet. Normally he would have ranted about how the journalists are like addicts, their drugs being war and misery. He might have said, *What good has all of their reporting done other than reveal to the Bosnian people that they have no value in the eyes of the world?*

Nadja opened the first page of *X-Men*. The panels were just like she remembered.

"I didn't know you were into comics," Dalila said.

Nadja shrugged.

"We can switch when I'm done with this if you want." Dalila held up her book, some romance novel set in Paris.

"Okay."

"Oh, and here. Nadja, I got these for you." Faris tossed her a pack of batteries.

She almost fumbled the catch. She stared at the batteries in her hand. Faris just ruffled the top of her head like he sometimes did to Dalila.

Nadja had nothing to give them. Nothing to give the family that had taken her in. She suddenly felt the pain of that. Of being the burden, the orphaned girl who could only take and take and never give back. Worried that she might cry, Nadja rose from the floor and did the one thing she could do. She sat at the slightly out-of-tune piano and played for an hour. Her only gift.

Later, after they had eaten and cleaned up and visited with neighbors, wishing them a merry Christmas, they descended into the protection of the basement because the enemy had started shelling again as soon as the sun set. After one got so close the whole house shook above them, Nadja put the batteries into her Walkman.

She snuggled underneath the layers of clothes and blankets. She felt Dalila's body rise and fall against her back. Then Nadja placed the headphones over her ears, closed her eyes and pressed Play.

July 7

GRAMMA WAVES HER hands in front of me, trying to get my attention. I'm irritated, but I remove an earbud.

"Yes, Gramma?"

"Zara, here. Eat this, please." She places a plate of eggs in my hands.

All she's been trying to get me to do since she and Vovo arrived last night is eat. But I guess it's better than being stalked by Aunt Evelyn. Gramma is more direct, a woman of action. A plate of food shoved in my face. A smoothie placed in my hand. A banana left next to my pillow. I think she feels guilty they couldn't get to us right away. They were on a cruise when the bombing happened and came as soon as they got back to Florida. She says food will make me feel better.

Food has nothing to do with how I feel.

"Gramma, I'm not hungry." I'm really not. Normally I eat an omelet or eggs over easy for breakfast. But these days, food seems like a hindrance, like I just don't have the energy for it. Everything tastes like metal, and my cheek and jaw are still sore when I try to chew. Plus, I've got another headache and I feel slightly nauseous.

But Gramma just sits next to me, watching.

I take a small bite, just to appease her, concentrating hard as I chew and swallow.

She smiles at me.

"See? Trust your gramma." She pats me on my shoulder. Normally she would be more affectionate, but since I stiffened under her first hug, it's like she doesn't know how to be around me. No one does. The only one who doesn't watch me all the time is Benny. Since he's just a kid, he doesn't really get everything that's happening. He doesn't act different. And he has no problem eating. Gramma watches him, and you can see the worry draw back from her face like a curtain. But when she looks at me, it slowly returns.

Vovo watches the news in the living room. I wish he would turn it off. The continuous footage and interviews and speculation make my head hurt even more.

The world has gone mad. There have been more and more incidents like the one Dad and I witnessed at the gas station happening all over. It's like the bombings have given people the justification they needed to act on fear and prejudice.

Right now Vovo is listening to a commentator explain how Muslims all over the world have had more casualties from these terrorist groups than anyone else. That in actuality these extremists have killed more Muslims than any other group. He changes the channel, and it's an update on the bombings.

"It's like 9/11 all over again," Vovo says.

Older people use 9/11 as a reference all the time, as if before 9/11, the world was a different place that has since been divided into before and after. I've only known a post-9/11 one. Which means I've known a world where the words *acts of terror, Muslim extremists, becoming radicalized, ISIS, genocide, insurgents* are all part of my vocabulary. It's just never hit so close to home. I've never been personally affected.

It's like I'm in some constant state of nightmare, always wondering when I'll wake up. When things'll go back to normal, when I won't fear just falling asleep.

"Jim, turn that off," Gramma says to Vovo. He does and then they both turn to look at me, waiting, while Benny keeps eating. I stand there, feeling awkward and exposed. I don't know what they want me to say, to do.

Finally Gramma speaks. "Your dad mentioned you started taking a photography class. Maybe you could show Vovo some of your pictures?"

"Yes," says Vovo. "I'd love to see some."

"Me too!" says Benny.

But I don't know how to tell them that ever since the bombing my camera feels like a cold, foreign device, not the usual extension of myself. That I haven't taken a photo since my self-portrait in the bathroom. That the scariest part is I haven't even wanted to.

Something inside me is broken.

"Maybe later," I say, and look back down at my plate. Push my eggs around. Benny is almost finished with his.

"Zara took pictures of me scooting and playing dress-up the other day," he says. "It was silly." He smiles at me.

I start to smile back, but a thought flies in. *Is my camera still in my room?* I don't actually know. It's weird that I don't know where my camera is. I always know where my camera is.

"Zara?" Gramma is looking at me expectantly.

"What?"

"I said I can make you a dropped egg on toast next time."

"Oh, sorry. I didn't hear you."

She gives me a weak smile. "It's what I always made the kids when they weren't feeling well. Good for the stomach."

"Okay. Sounds good," I tell her, though I don't know how that'll help me. I don't have the flu. I'm not sick. Or maybe I am? My stomach hasn't felt the same since the attack. It's always tied up in knots, anxious, like it's waiting for something bad to happen.

"After we go to the hospital, I thought I'd go to church to light a candle for your mother. Would you like to come with me?"

"Yes!" Benny says.

I wonder how Dad would feel about him seeing Mom in her condition.

"Zara?"

I think about her offer. I had felt peace in the chapel, with that guy Joseph, but I don't feel like being around people right now. "Um, I'm pretty tired. I think I might try to lie down for a bit."

"Zara, you scared me last night," Benny says next to me. His plate is empty, so Gramma puts some toast with jam on it. He takes a bite.

"What do you mean? Why?"

"I heard you screaming in your sleep like Mom."

My heart stops. "No I didn't."

"Yes, you did. Just like her."

A cold chill runs along my spine. I get up from the table.

"But, Zara, you haven't touched your food," Gramma says.

I keep walking, almost running, down the hall to the bath-room. Inside, I remove the bandage and stare at my pale, jacked-up face in the mirror. Part of my cheek is beginning to scab over, but I still look like me even with the damage. I'm nothing like her. But I suddenly feel a wave of nausea and throw up. The stitches in my back pull with each convulsion, until my stomach is empty.

I take a shower to clear my head. Get dressed. Even though I don't want to be around people, I need to get out of the house. I ride with Gramma, Vovo and Benny to the hospital.

We enter Mom's room. We stand and look at her and try not to look at her. Gramma holds Mom's hand and says a prayer. Silently, I say one too—the same one I've been saying whenever I visit my mom. Benny holds my hand. He seems afraid to go near Mom.

He pulls on my shirt, and I bend down to catch his whisper.

"She doesn't look like she's sleeping," he says to me. "She looks dead."

The comment shocks me, but I don't let it show. I try to swal-low past the rising lump in my throat.

"She's just in a deep sleep," I say. "Her brain is healing." But Benny's right—Mom looks so far away from us. What if she never comes back?

After just ten minutes, Gramma escorts Benny out into the hallway. She doesn't think he should see his mother *that* way.

Vovo and I stay in Mom's room. Both of us silent as we wait for Dad. When he comes in, he gives us both hugs. Mom's doctor also enters and explains what's going on, which is basically nothing. Her condition hasn't changed. She's still in limbo. Dad lies and says it's going to be okay.

I stare at Mom and feel just as much fear as Benny.

On the way home, we stop at the Catholic church we go to with Dad on holidays. Gramma lights a candle. She has us kneel on the kneelers to pray for Mom. I say the same prayer as before and watch the flame. Benny says a loud "Amen!" when he's finished. But even he is quiet on the ride home.

I look out the window. Nothing has changed in the landscape, yet everything in the world has changed.

Nothing has changed with Gramma either, who feeds me again as soon as she possibly can. But the meat loaf and corn morph into body parts on the plate. And I cannot eat them. I don't want to eat ever again.

After dinner, Audrey comes over. She gives me a hug, and I try not to wince. My arms hang at my side. Her eyes search my face, and I see them register the damage to my cheek. I'm trying to let it breathe, like Dad said, but I feel super exposed.

I'm anxious to get the attention off me, so I show her my mom's box. She quietly looks at each of the items, now displayed on my bed. She plays with the prayer beads in one hand.

"These are pretty," she says, holding them up to her neck.

She's not careful with them. It bothers me the way she holds them, much too casual about their significance.

"They're prayer beads."

"I know."

"They're, like, sacred or something." I take the beads out of her hand and put them back inside the box.

If Audrey is offended, or notices that I am, she doesn't show it. "Your mom looks so young," she says, now focusing on the photo of Mom and Marko. "Look at her hair."

"That was the style."

"She was beautiful. And this guy, whoever he is. A cutie too."

I agree with her on both counts.

"How crazy is it that your mom has this secret life."

"Well, I don't know if it's really a *secret* secret. My dad knows. She's just never told me anything."

"No, but I mean, all these things. Secrets from her past. Old photos and letters and stuff. It's like something out of a movie."

I give her a look.

"Oh, come on, Zara, I just mean it's even got *me* curious. Like, I want to know the story. Don't you? Maybe I can help you."

"How?"

"I can search for this guy. Marko."

"What, like, you're just going to Google his name?"

"For starters."

We quickly learn that Marko is a popular name in the Balkans. Narrowing down the search by adding *Bosnian War* next to it and *Višegrad* doesn't really help us either. Instead, a bunch of articles pop up, and Audrey reads through one of them.

"I had no idea . . ." she starts to say. "They turned a spa into a rape camp?"

I'm exhausted after only a few minutes. I close the laptop.

"Can we do something else? This is giving me a headache," I tell Audrey.

"You should lie down," she says, looking at me with concern now.

"Yeah, probably." But I don't want to lie down. I want to push her out the door.

Audrey reaches out and touches my arm. The gesture is meant to comfort, obviously, but I'm irritated. I shake her hand off me.

This time she can tell I'm upset, and she doesn't reach out again. "Your mom is going to be okay," she says. "Soon you'll be complaining about her like usual and we'll be walking into our first day of senior year."

"Yeah, well, you don't know that," I snap.

Audrey looks down at her lap. "I didn't mean—"

"I'm just getting really tired of people saying that everything will be okay. That's all my dad says, and it's not fucking true. Sometimes things are not okay and they'll never be okay. Like people get beat up at a gas station or killed and blown up, and you can't just tell their families that it's all going to be fine." I feel my anger flare with each word. Suddenly I want to throw something across the room. "You have no idea what it was like, and what it's like now. I mean, there were severed arms and legs and guts. I still smell it. I smell the blood and the burning. So just . . . stop saying it'll be okay. All right?"

"I'm sorry," Audrey says. Her eyes are full of tears. "You're right. I can't possibly understand. I don't even know what to say."

I press my temples with my fingers. I take a deep breath and let it out slowly.

"I think I just need to sleep," I finally tell her.

She stands up, and the bed shifts with the lack of weight.

"Okay. I should go."

I don't try to stop her. I can't even get up from my bed.

"Call me if you need anything," she says.

I can't form a response, so she opens and shuts the door behind her.

I hear her walk down the hallway. I hear the front door creak open, then close.

I lean my forehead into my hands. Audrey was just trying to be a good friend, and I had to go and yell at her. Part of me wants to call her right away and tell her to come back and spend the night. But my phone is over on the dresser. I can see it from where I'm sitting, but it feels so far away. The thought of having to walk over there is too much right now. Instead, I curl up on my bed and let myself cry.

The next day, I spend pretty much the entire day drifting in and out of sleep in my room, in the dark, with a cool, wet cloth on my head. The fact that I'm using Mom's migraine remedy is not lost on me. She hasn't gotten one of her headaches in a while, but she used to get them frequently when I was a kid. A really bad one could put her out of commission for a whole day.

I don't know if I screamed out in my sleep last night, but I definitely remember having a nightmare. I couldn't get to Benny. He was screaming for me, but I was trapped. My leg was caught underneath something. I couldn't breathe. Now, as much as my head hurts, as much as it hurts to keep my eyes open, I won't let myself sleep.

At some point in the afternoon, when Gramma and Vovo are out with Benny, I take Mom's prayer beads from her box and put them on. I know there's no magic in them. They're just beads. But throughout the day my fingers keep returning to them, and I catch myself whispering, "Please, help me," through dry lips. I wonder if God is listening.

By the time it's evening and Dad has returned from working and visiting Mom, I'm feeling a bit better, but I still stay in my room.

My door opens. "Z, how are you feeling?" Dad asks when he enters.

The open doorway casts the bright hallway light on my face, and I cover my eyes with my arm. The cloth I've been using falls to the floor.

Dad walks over to my bed and puts his hand on my forehead.

"Tired," I mumble. And when I say it, I suddenly feel it, even though I've been lying in bed all day.

"No fever," he says. "Let me check your back."

I moan, but roll over.

"No infection. Good. Gramma says you haven't left your room all day. Headache?"

"Migraine."

He doesn't say anything, but he doesn't leave either. I can feel him assessing the patient. Thinking through the best course of action.

"Come on. Let's go for a walk. Stars are gorgeous tonight."

"Dad—"

"Doctor's orders."

I groan and sit up. I feel dizzy. Dad reaches to help me, but I wave his hand away.

"I got it," I say, and follow him out of my room.

We've started walking down the hallway when Benny comes racing up to us. "Can I come?" he asks.

"Just me and Z this time, buddy. But I'll come and read you a story when we get back."

Benny sulks, but immediately perks up when Vovo challenges him to an ice cream sundae making contest.

Outside, the warm summer air hits my face, and my cheek tingles.

"Isn't this nice?" Dad asks once we're half a block away from our house.

"Mm-hmm," I say. It is, but each step feels incredibly heavy.

We walk a few more paces, and then Dad says, "I'm worried about you, Z."

I loaf along next to him, quiet. I'm surprised he's even had time to think about me or notice how I'm doing. Lately almost all of his energy has been devoted to Mom.

We leave our cul-de-sac, and the woods meet us on the other side of the street. We walk parallel to them. Tonight, they feel large and menacing.

"I noticed you haven't been taking pictures. You don't want to make plans with friends. I know what's going on with Mom has us all scared, but I want to make sure you know you aren't alone. You can talk to me. I'm here for you."

He doesn't get it. It's not just Mom. I feel broken too. I raise my hand to the throbbing that's now returned behind my right eye.

"Talk to me, Z," he says.

"It's just this headache."

"Do you feel nauseous too?"

"Yeah."

"I can give you something for that when we get back to the house."

We keep walking. I try to relax. The stars are full and hang heavy in the black sky. *It's the same sky,* I think. At least that hasn't changed.

We pass our usual turnaround point, and I realize he's going to make me walk until I start talking. So finally, I do. "It's just . . . I feel like everything's off . . . like I don't know how to be myself anymore."

He nods. "Well, maybe you should do something that'll make you feel normal. Like try just carrying around your camera, even if you don't feel like taking pictures."

Dad's always trying to fix things. It's part of being a surgeon, I guess. Wanting to help and heal are hardwired into who he is. But sometimes I just need him to listen before he goes right to the solution. I'm not even sure what's going on with me can be solved so easily.

But I want him to be right; I want to feel normal. So I say, "Okay. I'll try."

He takes my hand, and we head back toward the house. He's satisfied with my response. I want to tell him to stay home tomorrow, that Benny needs him, that *I* need him. But I know he needs something else. He needs me to be okay. He needs to think he's fixed me so he can go back to focusing on Mom.

I don't say anything more.

We walk along in silence; I lean into him like I have so many times before. My body a perfect fit alongside his.

July 9

IT'S SATURDAY, THE second week of class with Mr. Singh. The first time I've held my camera, taken it anywhere, in almost a week. I set it on the desk and try to hide in the back of the room, but it's impossible. I've got this huge wound on my face, and even with the bandage on, they can tell I've been through something awful. They must know that I was *there*. That I was a *victim of a terrorist attack*. Their eyes keep darting to my face. I hear their unspoken questions. Did it hurt? Did I see anything? How do I feel?

How do *I feel?*

Dad encouraged me to attend the class like I would have before the attack. Since Mom's condition hasn't changed and he doesn't know when it will, he figures I should do normal things. As if those even exist anymore.

Being in this class, ignoring all the silent questions and sideways looks, is not normal.

Dread creeps along my spine, and my stitches start to tingle. I feel myself begin to sweat. The doorway looks like it's narrowing. I take a breath and touch the prayer beads around my neck. There's something in the wearing and feel of them that comforts me a bit. I eye the door again, remind myself I can leave anytime I want to.

Mr. Singh acts like there is nothing strange about me. He treats me like I'm any other photography student, and for that I'm grateful.

We have a discussion about the rule of thirds. Well, the rest of the class talks, and I listen. I have to work extra hard to pay attention, which is weird for me. Normally I'm very focused. But I keep getting distracted by the tiny dust mites that float in a shard of light as they come in from the window. Mr. Singh shows a couple of photos, explaining how the rule works. How where we position our subjects will affect the mood and the story we're trying to tell.

"Okay. I'd love to hear from each of you what ideas you have for your story sequence. It's okay if you haven't decided yet, but I think we'd all benefit from hearing from each other. Let's start with you." He points to someone in the front row, and I'm relieved again to be sitting in the back.

The first student has this cool idea of taking photos of people right as they are given good news or as they finish opening a present. She's calling it *Surprised by Joy*. Of course Mr. Singh loves it.

I don't even remember what my plan was. It seems like years ago. Something about Benny? I sink in my seat, feeling stupid, and feeling pain too, because the seat back presses against me.

I hear Dad's voice in my head—something he's always told me. *Someone else's success doesn't have to be your failure.*

Sometimes, it does, I respond.

The more people share, the more I realize my idea sucks. The more I realize that taking this class right now sucks too. I don't even know why I came. When class ends, I wait in my seat until everyone has left. Then I pick up my camera for the first time since I set it on my desk, and I approach Mr. Singh like I would a sore tooth—slowly and afraid that I'm going to feel some sharp pain.

"Mr. Singh?"

He looks up at me from his desk. "Yes, Zara?"

"Um, I don't think I'm going to be able to keep taking this class."

"Oh?" he says, and just stares at me like he's waiting for me to continue.

What, does he need me to spell the whole thing out?

"Yeah, it's just not really the best timing. You know"—I point to my face—"with everything that's going on. It's probably better for me not to waste your time and mine."

He leans forward in his seat.

"I have a friend who documented every phase of his partner's cancer. Everything. He was obsessed with remembering all of it. His pictures were his way of saying good-bye, and they became a kind of love letter. Yes, they were sad and painful, but they were also lovely and true and hopeful. And they preserved something forever that he knew couldn't possibly last. Sometimes our art is the only way out of the dark."

I can feel myself staring at him, but I don't know how to respond.

"I'll see you next class," he says. It's not a question. He goes back to writing in a notebook.

I back away, completely at a loss.

Before I'm out the door, he calls to me, "Just start taking pictures, Zara. Start with what you know how to do."

I nod once, and then I'm gone.

I head straight to the hospital. I'm actually a little hungry after class, so I get a protein bar out of the first-floor vending machine. Gramma would be so proud.

Up in Mom's room, I study her. The usual worry lines around her eyes and mouth have disappeared in this deep sleep. Her natural eyebrows are so light, but I can already see them beginning to grow in. She has twenty-three freckles. I don't think I've ever looked at my mom as much as I have this past week.

Wait.

Was it really only a week ago? Less—six days? It already feels like a year. So much has changed. The way she lies there so still and peaceful, something cracks through, and I tumble into memory.

I'm a little girl, and we're in some field.

No, that's not right—we're in the backyard. It's night. The stars are out. So are the fireflies. They blink on and off like tiny traffic signals. There's music coming from inside the house. And I'm cold, so I snuggle into Mom's side. I can tell she's crying, and this makes me feel scared, like I've upset her somehow. I want to comfort her, but I don't know how. I try to get as close to her as I possibly can.

I tell her, "Mom, I love you as big as the sky." I point to the stars. This is something a teacher has read to us, I think—a story about a mother and daughter, and it stayed with me because that's how I wanted to be with her. But even then, I kind of knew that something was wrong; there was this distance between us. We weren't like the mothers and daughters I saw in picture books. There was a part of herself she kept from me.

Mom reaches her hand up next to mine and says, "I love you bigger." Then she laughs and tickles me, and I laugh. She laughs at my laugh, and her laugh is so loud, and suddenly we are in the book. We are the main characters.

I haven't heard Mom laugh like that in a long time.

Now we're in a different kind of story.

It's a story I wouldn't have chosen for either of us. Because *I love you*s have been quiet for a long time here. Here there is maiming and pain and things that I don't know how we can come back from. I want to believe that our story will end well, but sitting with her, coma stricken, it's hard to see beyond the now. And each breath in, every moment of silence just reminds me of all the ways we aren't close. Of all that we've already lost.

I think of the others. The people who lost limbs. Those who died. Why did I survive? Why did Benny? Or my mom? Nothing makes sense anymore.

I think about what Dad said. Just do something that makes me feel like my old self. I think of what Mr. Singh said about his friend who photo-documented his partner's battle with cancer. How he told me to start with what I know how to do. My camera still feels awkward in my hands, my fingers less certain than before. But maybe I can give it a shot.

I bring the viewfinder up to my eye and take my mom's picture, zooming in on where they shaved her head and operated. The staples make her look like something out of a science fiction novel. They look painful. I wonder how she'll feel when—*if*—she wakes.

If.

So many unknowns. But suddenly, I know I can't stay here looking at my mom for one more minute.

I leave her room and walk quickly with my head down, taking deep breaths, until I get to the elevator.

"Hey, girl from the chapel," someone says when the door opens.

"Oh, hey," I say.

He steps out, and instead of getting inside, I stand there awkwardly. The elevator door closes. I miss my chance to escape.

"Zara," I say. He clearly doesn't remember my name. Now that I'm getting a good look at him, he's actually really cute. I notice he's holding the same journal he had with him the other day. His black tee has a huge white question mark in the middle. I brush my hair over my cheek to cover the bandage on the side of my face.

"That's right," he says, and puts his hand on his chest. "Joseph."

I nod and push the button again. Now I have to wait for the elevator to come back up.

"Where are you going?" he asks.

"Oh, I'm just leaving."

"How's your mom?"

"The same." *Just watch the numbers, and you'll be fine.* Better yet, change the subject.

"How's your grandmother?" I ask. She's sick with something. I can't remember if he told me what it is or not.

"She's actually perking up."

"That's good." I push the button for the elevator again. *Why is it taking so long?*

"Yeah. Just on my way to see her, actually, so I should probably go." He begins to walk away, but then stops and turns. "How good are you?"

"Excuse me?"

He points to my camera, slung across my shoulder. "At photography. That looks like a professional's. Are you good?"

I shrug. "Pretty good."

He walks back toward me. "Can I see?"

The elevator is stuck on floor three. "Um, okay. I guess." He looks over my shoulder as I scroll back, quickly skipping over the recent photo of my mom plus the one I took of my back, to find the shots that I took at Baker's Beach the other night.

But the farmers market photos assault me first. The ones from just after the bombing. The frenzy, the hazy pictures of people running. Dust everywhere. Bodies on the ground. My mom's feet poking out from underneath the rubble. A little girl sitting, crying in the middle of it all. The back of a man digging.

"Wow," Joseph says over my shoulder.

My hands are shaking a little. I don't even remember taking those photos. I keep moving through them, unable to stop myself. Back and back, to the tomatoes. The vendor. My mom's blurry profile.

Before.

I lower my camera. I think I'm going to be sick.

Joseph gives me a look of concern, and I can't stand here another moment.

"I have to go." Quickly, I move away from the elevator and speed up as I reach the stairs.

"Wait."

I stop, turn back around.

"Do you think . . ." Joseph says, then he puts his hand on the back of his head and leans the other one against the wall. "Could you take a picture of me and my grandmother?"

I stare at him.

"I don't have any good ones with her, I mean professional quality—just from my phone. It's her birthday this week, and there's nothing really that I can buy her. But I know she'd love a picture of the two of us. And I can totally pay you for it."

"You don't have to pay me," I say, touched that he would want to take a picture with his grandmother.

"So you'll do it?"

An anxious feeling rises in my chest, something that I didn't have before the bombing. I think of what Dad, and Mr. Singh, said again. Just take some pictures. I suck in my breath.

"Sure," I say.

"Okay, great. Come on."

"Now?"

But he's already down the hall.

When we enter room 572, the little old lady lying in the bed perks right up at the sight of Joseph.

"*Bonjou*, my Joseph," she says.

"*Bonjou*, Grann," he says, and bends down, kissing each of her cheeks. "Are you well today?"

She touches his face with her open palm. "*Kon si, kon sa.* Did you bring me something?" Her head tilts to the side, and her eyes are playful when they meet mine.

He reaches into his pocket and hands her what look like candies.

She smiles and opens one and pops it right into her mouth.

Joseph turns to me. "She needs her caramel fix. Grann, this is my new friend, Zara."

"Hello," I say from the foot of her bed.

She nods in greeting, her mouth still chewing the candy. Joseph places the rest of the pieces underneath her pillow, as if they are in some kind of conspiracy and need to hide the evidence.

I study some of the photographs she has by her bed. Family members, I assume. Joseph is in one with a couple that could be his mom and dad.

"Zara," she says, finally working through the sticky caramel. "That's a lovely name. What does it mean?" She wipes her mouth with a small napkin.

I smile and the bandage on my cheek pulls. "Blossoming flower."

His grandmother nods. "The name suits you."

It doesn't suit me at all, especially now. But it's a cool name. I've never met another Zara. So I tell her thanks.

"How do you know my Joseph?"

"Zara and I met the other day at the chapel," Joseph says. "Her mother is here. But Zara's also a photographer."

I used to be a photographer. What if I've lost my eye? My ability to see the moments?

"I asked her to take our picture together. That way you can always have a special shot of just you and your favorite grandson with you."

She chuckles and points her finger at Joseph. "You are my most political."

I take another breath and give in to Dad and Mr. Singh's advice. I point my camera in their direction, trying to capture them in a candid moment. But Joseph stops me.

"Not here. I was thinking we could walk to the garden. What do you think, Grann? You up for a walk?"

"Yes. These old bones need to get out of here before they forget how to do it."

I leave the room while Joseph helps her out of bed and fetches her walker.

We move at a snail's pace down the hall, his grandmother in between the two of us. She shuffles, a little hunched at the shoulders. A red, orange and white flowered scarf covers her head. Even though she's old, she's the type of woman you can tell was once very beautiful. Her deep brown skin is not cracked with age. Her brown eyes are large. She's wearing a yellow pajama top with yellow and orange and green flowered pants. She's decked out with jewelry—small gold hoops in her ears, necklaces and gold bracelets that she pushes up every now and again. Nothing like my gramma.

Because it's another hot day outside, I position Joseph and his grandmother in the shade, underneath a tree. But I don't like the shadows the leaves are casting across their faces. However, I also don't want them to be in direct sunlight. It'll be too harsh.

I have Joseph stand next to his grandmother, his arm protective around her shoulder. She only comes up to the middle of his chest. I hit the shutter once. The click is louder than I remember it being, but I try to stay in the moment. I press it again. And again.

"You going to tell us when to smile?" he asks.

"Oh, yes." I pretend like I haven't already been snapping photos.

"Wait," she says. "I don't have my lips on."

"Grann, you don't need it. You're beautiful."

She removes a tube of lipstick from her pants pocket and stains her lips a cherry red before smacking them together. "Ready now," she says.

"Okay. Joseph, why don't you sit on this bench with . . ." I realize I don't know her name.

"Name's Flora, *chérie*."

"Flora," I say.

They sit and face me, a little stiff.

"Just act like you're having a conversation. Like I'm not even here," I say.

They turn toward each other and start talking. It doesn't take long for them to settle into a comfortable mode. I don't see many people with such an age gap who have this kind of ease with each other, related or not. I love my grandparents, even though

Gramma does annoy me sometimes, but we don't speak like this.

Joseph and Flora are beautiful together. I move around them and take more photos. It feels good to escape into the moment.

"How about over there?" I say, asking them to move next to a patch of red roses. The color matches Flora's scarf, and I take some pictures with just her next to them. She reminds me of an old movie star or singer. Maybe like a Bessie Smith. One of Dad's old-time favorites.

"So many photographs," Flora says. "How many do you want, Joseph?"

"She's the professional," he says, deferring to me.

"Sometimes we need to take many to find the perfect one."

"How about one with just Joseph? I don't need to be looking at myself."

There's a brick wall, and I ask Joseph to stand in front of it. It's the perfect backdrop. He holds his hands at his sides and stares at me. I zoom in and see how clear and intense his gaze is and am startled. His brown eyes are striking. I suddenly feel nervous.

"Okay, give me something different. Not as serious," I say.

He crosses his eyes and sticks out his tongue.

I laugh. "No, I mean with your stance. You can loosen up a little."

He puts his hands in the pockets of his jeans, leans against the wall and smiles. *Click.*

"Make sure you get my best side," he says, and turns to the left. And then to the right. His jawline is defined with high cheekbones. He could actually do modeling work. Something about the way he is loving the camera, and the way the camera loves him, tells me that he already knows this.

I grin. He is totally playing me right now.

"I think that's good," I say.

"Good, because all this work is making me thirsty," Joseph says playfully. "You want a drink, Grann? Zara?"

We both respond yes, and he enters the hospital to get us something.

"How did we do?" Flora asks.

I sit down on the bench next to Flora and show her some of the photos. Careful this time not to go too far back.

"These are all very good," she says.

"They'll be better after I edit them. But I can send them to Joseph and then he can decide which ones he wants to print out."

"You are very talented."

"Thank you," I say, and smile. It feels good to please her.

"So, Joseph said you're here visiting your mother? Why is she in the hospital?"

It's still hard for me to put what happened into words. It's hard to tell the story. Because it's not like I'm just telling it; I'm reliving it. But there's something about Flora that makes it easy to open up, and as I tell her about the morning at the farmers market, she takes my hand in both of hers. I'm uncomfortable at first, but her hands are lined and soothing and steady, as if they have carried a great deal in them. So I give her some more to carry. I tell her what I remember.

"*Mwen regret sa*, Zara." She rubs my hand. "People do such terrible things to one another. It's a wonder how we survive any of it. I'll tell you, none of us come out of it unscarred. When I was a little girl, I saw incredible suffering in my country at the hands of our own government. Not just poverty, but corruption and murder. We were terrified that we'd be killed in our beds. This terrorism is just proof of the sickness of the world."

I don't know what to say, so I just let her massage my hand. It feels good, even if her words don't, and soon my body is a bit more relaxed.

"But you know what I have learned?"

"What's that?" I ask.

"Love is the most powerful force in the universe. Love will guide you on the course of your life. Love has freed me from letting them win. I don't know why this happened to you and your family. There is no why. But I know this to be true." She leans in and places her hand on my chest. "There's more inside here than you realize."

I stare at the ground, afraid I'll start to cry if I look at her.

"I will pray for your mother." She motions to the prayer beads at my neck.

"Thank you. She's not very religious." But I rub my fingers across the beads.

"That's okay. Bondye's not interested in religion. He's interested in people."

Joseph returns with water bottles for each of us. I gladly take one and drink as if I haven't had water in days.

"I think I should go back to my room now, Joseph," Flora says.

"Of course." Joseph helps her stand and places her hands,

strong enough to steady my own just moments ago, on the rims of the walker.

The idea of going back inside the dreary hospital right now upsets me. "I think I'll stay here," I say.

Joseph nods.

"Okay. *Orevwa,* Zara," Flora says with a wide smile.

"*Orevwa,*" I say.

"May we meet again. *Si Bondye vie.*"

"That means if God is willing," Joseph translates for me.

"*Si Bondye vie,*" I whisper as he leads her away.

MRS. VINKOVIĆ'S HOUSE smelled like old potatoes. Light from the cracks in the curtains hit the thin layer of dust particles dancing in the air. Nadja crept along the wooden floor, so as not to disturb anything. Which was silly, she knew; there was no one there. Only dust and the thin shards of light that always found their way in.

She ran her finger along the top of the kitchen counter, making a worm track. It didn't take long for dust to cover what once was living. Two weeks? Maybe three? And it was already as if someone hadn't lived there in a long time. Any sweets would be long gone by now. The neighbors had already ransacked the cupboards and taken anything else that could be put to use, including the piano. It had been cut up and used for firewood. All that remained now were the ivory and black keys, which lay in a pile on the floor like extracted teeth.

Nadja picked one up, wondering what note it had been, and placed it in her pocket. Outside, she heard the shelling start up again. She dropped to the ground and pressed her back against the wall, drew her knees to her chest.

She started counting. The shelling lasted to number twenty-eight, fading as she continued past thirty.

When she felt it was safe, she stood back up and went to check out the bedroom. It was undisturbed. Maybe people thought this was where Mrs. Vinković still remained and didn't want to touch it. Nadja knew her own ghosts only came in her dreams and nightmares. She would love for them to visit during the day. Then she could speak with them, ask them to never leave her.

There was a bowl on the floor for a cat. She wondered where the woman's cat had gone. If someone had eaten it. Or if, realizing its owner had not returned, the cat had left. Gone looking for food.

Nadja walked through the hallway, where pictures and artwork once hung. Now only nails marked the walls. She picked at a spot where the pale-orange-striped wallpaper was starting to give way, and tore a large strip off. It felt good to tear it, so she did it again and again until she had uncovered another layer of wallpaper. This one was an ugly lime green with flowers.

Creak.

The sound came from upstairs. The attic. *The cat,* she thought, and she found the door in the ceiling. She pulled it open and climbed up into the space.

It was dark and dusty. She sneezed.

When her eyes adjusted to the dark, she peered around the room. Nadja's eyes met another's, but it was not a cat. It was a woman.

Nadja's heart raced. She backed away from the eyes and down the stairs, closing the attic door above her.

As she stepped back into the hallway, the front door burst open.

"Hey!" a man yelled at her. He grabbed her arm and pulled her to the kitchen.

"Got her!" he said.

Two other men came into the room. Their eyes searched her face.

"Not her," the one with a brown beard said.

Nadja kept both hands on the table, clasped together, so they would not shake. She tried not to let them see her terror. She tried not to remember the last time a group of men burst into a home.

"What are you doing here?"

"I . . . I knew this woman. I was just looking, seeing what was left."

"Have you seen anyone else?"

"No."

"Damn." The one questioning her pounded the table with his fist.

"She can't be far," said the other man. "It's only a mile from the line. She could have made her way."

"How?"

"The roofs?"

"Jumping from roof to roof? She's a sniper, not Spider-Man."

The brown-bearded man looked up and noticed the door to the attic. "What is up there?" he pointed his gun to the ceiling, where Nadja had climbed down.

Nadja pictured the scared eyes in her mind.

"Nothing but a dusty room." She held up her dirty hands to show him.

He pointed a finger at Nadja. "Do you have family?"

"Yes, a block over and down the street."

"You should go home."

The three men looked through the cupboards and swore, having come up with nothing. They left through the front door. At the window, Nadja watched them enter the next house. Across the street, another small group of men was doing the same.

She waited until she was certain that the men were a couple of homes away before she crept to the door of the attic.

She trembled as she climbed the stairs. She peeked inside, blinking and letting her eyes adjust to the dark. She saw them again, the human eyes in the far corner.

"What's your name?" Nadja whispered.

"Jela."

"I'm Nadja."

"Are they gone?"

"Yes."

Nadja joined the woman in hiding and sat with her legs crossed on the floor. The woman was huddled in a far corner behind an old lamp and a stack of books. Her brown hair was pulled back into a ponytail. She wore a green flak jacket and jeans. If you just glanced at her, maybe you'd think she could be a boy, a small one.

They continued to whisper as if the men could come back any minute.

"Are you really a sniper?"

Instead of answering the question, the woman asked, "You from Sarajevo?"

"No," Nadja said.

"Me neither. I visited once before, though. My parents took us all over. Even up to the bobsleigh and luge track on Trebević mountain. You ever been up there?"

Nadja shook her head no.

"You can see the whole city." The woman said it like she wished she were there now.

"The Serbs have it now," Nadja said.

"Yes, they do." Jela paused. "How old are you?"

"Eighteen." But that wasn't right. She had been eighteen for too long. "No, nineteen. You?"

"Twenty-two. Before this, I was in my third year at university in Banja Luka. I was going to be a physical therapist. Sports medicine."

"I've never been to Banja Luka."

"You should go. It's very beautiful. From my house, I could see our river, the Vrbas. We have tall weeping willows along the banks, just like the name suggests. As a girl, I used to swing on their branches. If you like to go river rafting, we have the best places."

"I grew up next to the Drina, but there are no rapids. We have a bridge. We have willows too." Nadja didn't tell her that she also swung from branches.

"That bridge from the huge book that they force us to read in school. By Ivo something, right?"

Nadja nodded. Growing up in Višegrad, their main claim to fame was a writer who won the Nobel Prize, Ivo Andrić. The house he grew up in was preserved near the bank of the Drina close to the entrance of the bridge. The only reason tourists came was because of that book and the bridge.

"*The Bridge Over the Drina*."

"That was a boring book," Jela said.

Nadja smiled. She kind of thought the same, though it was cool seeing her little town in a book and learning about the history. They had a copy of it in their house growing up. She wondered if it was still on the shelf.

"Took forever for me to get through," Jela said. "Though I'm not much of a reader. Are you?"

"Sometimes."

Jela motioned to the pile of books next to her. "You should take some of these, then. If not for reading, for kindling. Most are covered in mold anyway."

Nadja didn't make a move for the books. A long rifle lay on the ground that she hadn't noticed in the beginning. A reminder of more than just the physical divide between them. But if Jela was going to kill her, wouldn't she have done it already?

They didn't say anything for some time. Nadja wondered how long Jela had been hiding in the attic.

Finally, Nadja spoke again. "It is late," she said, though she didn't know what time it was. "I should get home."

Her mouth was dry. She licked her lips, feeling the rough patch at the corner of her mouth that was a recurring canker sore. Ramiza said she needed more vitamin C.

"I only have one more year left," Jela said. "Then I'll have my degree. I'll probably go to Germany. That's where my sister and her husband are. I'll learn how to be a good German."

"I'm going to America," Nadja said. She hadn't told anyone this except for Marko, back in another time and another place. Until this moment, Nadja had forgotten that had been the plan. It took everything she had not to think about the past, just to focus on surviving. But now she decided. She would go too. She would get out of here, never look back. "With my friend." Dalila wanted out too.

"McDonald's and Madonna," Jela said.

Nadja nodded. "I'll become an American and forget this place."

"That's a good plan."

Jela pulled her legs up to her chest. A sign that she was going to stay put for a while.

"Bye, Nadja, the American."

"Bye, Jela, the German."

Nadja backed away from the woman, never taking her eyes off her. She stepped backward down the steps, her head sinking as though underwater.

A week later, Nadja heard that they'd captured Jela. After torturing her for information about the Serbs, they had let Jela go. But in the middle of the day, they forced her to walk toward the Miljacka River. Once Jela stepped on the Latinska Bridge, a sniper's bullet blasted through her skull, knocking her body into the river. Nadja wondered if the waters would carry her home to her beloved Banja Luka. If the willows along the banks would weep for her.

Or if they would remain quiet like Nadja, having no more tears to give.

AFTER JOSEPH AND his grandmother leave, I stay on the bench outside the hospital for a little while. The humidity isn't as bad today, and even if it was, anything is better than being inside the hospital. I breathe deeply and look at a few of the photos of Joseph and Flora. There are many to choose from. Both of them are so photogenic. I love the one where they're holding hands and looking at each other. Maybe I could even use this one for my single-frame story, since Mr. Singh's not going to let me off the hook.

There's something about Flora's eyes. I'm curious now about her. She mentioned having gone through terrible things in Haiti. I wonder what happened. I pause on a photo of Joseph leaning against the wall. I wonder what his full story is.

My phone buzzes with a text.

Where r u?

It's Audrey. My heart sinks with guilt. I haven't spoken to her since I was kind of a jerk. Truth is I've been avoiding her. I don't know how to be around her.

Hospital

Where?

On a bench in the garden.

Ok. Coming

?

She doesn't respond.

Five minutes later, Audrey walks toward me.

"Hey," she says, and plops down next to me. She hands me a Red Vine from the small pack she's carrying. I accept it as the peace offering it is. She knows they're my favorite. Though I should probably be the one asking for forgiveness.

We sit quietly, the sides of our arms pressed up against each other, chewing our candy, and suddenly things feel a little bit okay.

"What're you doing here?" I ask after I've eaten four Red Vines.

"Thought I'd come and support you."

I give her a half smile. "Thanks," I say. The blob of emotion that I've been stuffing down deep rises up into my throat.

"Also, I wanted to see Christine. Have you been yet?"

"Oh, um, no . . . I haven't really had the time."

All I have is time. I wonder if Audrey recognizes my excuse for the lie that it is. Even so, she knows that Christine is more her friend than mine. We're more like acquaintances who share Audrey. It's not that she's mean, just a little standoffish and hard to get to know. To be honest, I haven't really thought of Christine at all, which is probably worse than trying to avoid her. I forgot that she was here too, that she was injured. The guilt spreads like a rash on my skin.

Then something else clicks.

"Wait, she's here? I didn't . . . I mean, I just assumed she was home," I say. It's been almost a week since the bombing, so I'm surprised to learn she wasn't already discharged, like me.

Audrey opens her eyes wide. "You didn't hear?"

"What?"

"Zara, she lost her arm."

I stare at Audrey, but I can no longer hear what she's saying. I see her lips moving, so I know she's still talking, but all I hear is static, white noise. Like I still have residual hearing loss from the bombing. Even though a full medical examination revealed that I had no damage other than bruising and contusions. Nothing at all like Christine.

I have no words.

I shake my head to clear out the din, and I hear Audrey say, "It's horrible." She focuses on the ground.

Normally I would ask Audrey to clarify, to tell me everything. But all I see are body parts, the man's leg I crawled over. How when I stepped on it, it felt like something both dead and alive. The severed hand I saw in a closed fist, was that Christine's? Had she been standing anywhere near me?

"She's been working toward her tennis career since even before

I knew her, like, since she was five. And now . . . I just feel so terrible for her," Audrey says.

"Yeah," I say. Suddenly my feelings about Christine seem so small and petty. They're the feelings of a horrible person.

"Want to come with me to see her?"

No. I do not.

"Of course," I say.

It's easy to spot Christine's room. Her family spills out into the hallway: grandparents, her mom, probably some aunts and uncles. I feel awkward about intruding.

I really don't want to do this.

"Maybe we should come back later," I say to Audrey. She grabs my hand and pulls me along.

When Christine's mom spies us, she smiles and hugs Audrey first, then me. "Thank you for coming. Christine will be happy to see you." She lowers her voice. "She really needs her friends right now."

Christine's mom says good-bye to the others in the hallway, thanking them for coming, she'll let them know what she needs, and so on. Then she ushers us into the small hospital room, where there are tons of flowers and cards. A gray-and-yellow balloon already losing some of its helium hangs halfway in the air in the corner by the window. Christine sits up in the bed when she sees us. Her short black hair is pulled back from her face in a couple of clips. The left side of her face is bruised as if she was hit across her cheek and jawbone. Like me.

"Hi," Audrey says, and walks over to give Christine a gentle hug.

"Hey, Christine," I say.

"Hi." Christine smiles at us.

I avoid looking directly at her right arm, but in my periphery, I can see it's bandaged and appears shorter than her left.

"How are you?" Audrey asks.

Christine shrugs and tears fill her eyes. "Well, I've moved past the stage one anger into stage two, feeling sorry for yourself."

"How much longer are you in here?"

"I actually get to go home today."

"That's great!" Audrey says a little too brightly.

"Yeah. Spending a week in the hospital sucks. The best part is I'll finally get out of this gown."

The gown is the same as I wore, what my mom's wearing now. Standard light-blue hospital chic.

I stand there next to Audrey, who sits on the bed.

"Zara." Christine turns to me, as if noticing I'm there for the first time. "How is your mom?"

"She's still in a coma. But my dad is hopeful, so—"

"And how are you doing?"

"I'm fine. This"—I refer to my cheek—"will heal, I guess. A few stitches on my back . . . Fortunately I didn't . . ." I'm about to say *get really hurt*, but it seems insensitive and stupid in front of the girl who just lost her arm, so I stop midsentence.

Christine's mom pokes her head in and says, "Audrey, can I talk to you for a minute?"

"Sure." Audrey exits the room, leaving me and Christine alone. My eyes keep darting to her arm. Just like people have been doing to me, with my face. I guess it's impossible not to.

After a moment I can speak again. She knows what it was like, being there. It feels okay to ask. "Does it hurt?"

"You know what's crazy—I don't remember it hurting when it happened. They say I was in shock. Now I'm on tons of meds, so I'm not sure what it's going to feel like when I'm off them." She extends her good arm and flexes her hand. "It's true, though, you know, what they say about that phantom limb stuff. At first, I literally had no idea that it was already gone. And even after the surgery, I felt like it was still there at first. I still kind of do. It aches." She rubs the end of her bandaged arm. "Does your cheek hurt?"

I shrug. "It's okay. It looks worse now than it actually feels."

She nods. "Can I see your back?"

I hesitate. I've only shown the doctors and Dad. Not even Audrey has asked this of me. But there's something in Christine's eyes, something that says she needs to see that I suffered too. That even though I still have my arm, I've also been maimed. That she isn't the only one. So I turn and slowly lift up my shirt.

"That looks like a lot of stitches."

"Sixty-seven."

I lower my shirt.

"Painful, isn't it?"

"Yes."

"Where were you standing when it went off?" she asks.

I've been asked this question many times. Shouldn't the answer come easier by now? A moment later, I remember.

"Over by the candy, you know, the saltwater taffy and licorice. You?"

"We were on the other end, just leaving. Actually, I'm the one who wanted to wait in line for a juice. My mom wanted to go."

"We must have just missed each other." Though I wonder, if I had seen Christine, whether I would have called out to get her attention.

"If we weren't still there waiting, we would have gotten out of there. We would have been in the car, driving home."

I'm quiet. I can't speak to another person's feelings because I've got enough of my own to deal with.

"I didn't even like it," she says.

"What?"

"The juice. It was a green one. Something you're supposed to get because it's all healthy, but what I really wanted was the shake."

I nod. "Their shakes are the best."

Christine's eyes well up with tears. "Now I'm a freak. Who's going to want to date a girl without an arm? Travis hasn't even come to visit me."

Travis, her boyfriend for a few months toward the end of this past school year. They broke up not too long ago. I knew him from the beach. His family had a bathhouse one aisle down from us. We grew up seeing each other most summers.

"He's probably just scared," I say.

"Yeah. Because I'm a freak."

"No, because he doesn't know what to say. It's the same with me. No one knows what to say to me about what happened to my mom and me except they're sorry. My grandparents, Audrey, Natasha, Sibyl, even my dad . . . they keep searching for the right words. As if the right words will make everything all better. If there even *are* any right words to say."

"Still, he could have at least called. How does he think *I* feel? Does he think *I'm* not scared?" She lies back on the pillow and stares at the ceiling. "So much time and work, for years, all for nothing. Wasted."

I sit next to her and offer her the only thing I can. I listen.

"You know, last year, I really started to hate playing tennis. I even told my parents that I wanted to quit. Oh, that set them off. They couldn't believe it. I was so good. So dedicated. How could I give up when everything, all the sacrifice, was just starting to pay off? Blah. Blah. Blah. But I didn't enjoy it anymore. I guess I got what I wanted. I can't play like this, obviously. But now I want it back." The tears stream down her face. "I just want to play tennis."

If I had lost my arm, would I still be able to take photos? It would be difficult, but I could probably learn how, adjust over time. It's more like, what if I went blind? That would be horrible. To never be able to take or see a picture, or see anything, ever again. I wouldn't even know how to process the world.

I place my hand on Christine's leg. "It's horrible," I say.

"Thanks," she says. "For not trying to make me feel better."

"I could try to make you feel worse?"

She laughs.

I smile.

"Can you sleep?" I ask.

"They've got me so drugged with painkillers that I'm sleeping like a baby. Why? You having trouble sleeping?"

"Benny heard me cry out in the middle of the night once. I didn't even know until he told me the next morning. But since then, lately, I've been having nightmares. It's like all these really graphic, gruesome memories from the bombing just pour into my head, and I can't stop them."

"Wow. I don't remember anything about the explosion. When I woke up, I was already here. Do you remember anything?"

"Yeah. More than I'd like, actually," I say. "It was . . . unreal." I try to find the words. "There was this booming sound and then I was thrown. I couldn't hear anything at first. But I could see people screaming. It was really scary. Like the worst horror imaginable."

"Wow," Christine said. "I keep trying to remember. The doctor said that it could come back or it may never, but not to be too hard on myself." She looks down.

I nod.

"You still taking pictures?" she asks.

"Kind of," I say. "Not as often. It's weird, but I haven't really wanted to. It doesn't feel as important as before." I shrug. "But I'm trying."

She considers this. "Could you take one of me?"

"Really? Um . . ." The question shocks and confounds me. My injuries are way less noticeable, and I still wouldn't want my picture taken.

"I know it probably sounds weird, but I don't want to forget this experience. I mean, it can't ever be this bad again, right? So maybe, if I can look back on this time in my life, actually physically look back on it, then when things get hard in the future, I'll have a visual reminder that they could always be worse. And that they have actually gotten much better."

It reminds me a little of what Mr. Singh said about his friend documenting his partner's battle with cancer.

Sometimes our art is the only way out of the dark.

I swallow past the lump in my throat and smile. "Sure. Happy to."

Christine slowly unwraps the elastic bandage covering her amputated arm. "The doctor is supposed to change this anyway." She unwinds the outer wrap. The skin is raw and red, and she is completely exposed. It's very hard to look at, but Christine is so brave, I just start clicking.

"It's weird," she says. "I guess you and I have something to bond over now that's not about Audrey."

When I'm done, we look at the photos together, and she chooses the one she thinks best captures what she's feeling. I tell her I'll upload it and send it to her.

"Thanks for coming to see me," she says.

"My pleasure," I say. And I mean it.

Audrey returns to the room a few minutes later and sits on the bed. We hang out with Christine until her doctor enters the room and examines her arm. Audrey and I leave to give her privacy and head for the cafeteria. We order ice cream bars and sit at one of the tables.

"What did Christine's mom want?" I ask.

"She asked me about organizing people to come visit Christine when she gets home so that she won't be alone so much. Kind of like those food registries after someone has a baby."

"That probably is a good idea, even if she fights it at first."

"Why would she fight it?" Audrey asks.

"She may not want to see so many people." I set my camera down on the seat next to me and take a bite of the bar. Chocolate and vanilla together.

"This is amazing," I say.

"Mm-hmm."

We're quiet for a few minutes. But I can tell Audrey is just biding her time, waiting to ask me something.

"So, Zara, how are you doing?"

I finish chewing. "I'm good." Talking with Christine, taking her picture, has actually made me feel a little better. I didn't have to try and explain. She's dealing with something so much worse than my own physical pain, but we understand each other in ways that Audrey will never get.

"I'm being serious. I don't want you to feel like you're going through this alone."

I shrug. "I have my grandparents and Benny." Dad practically lives at the hospital, but I know he's going through a lot too, and he's trying. If I really needed him, I know he would be there for me.

"That's not the same thing. And you tend to isolate yourself when you're going through something."

"I do not."

"Yeah, you do. Remember when you and Mike broke up? You didn't talk to me for a whole week."

"You're exaggerating." But I know she's not.

"Or when you didn't get into that photography program last year? I think that was even longer."

Audrey may have a point. "Sometimes I just need time to process, that's all."

"Okay, but just . . . please don't shut me out, all right?" she asks, and then takes a bite of her ice cream.

I'm about to object again, but I can't. She's right. I do shut her out when things get hard. It's not personal. I shut everyone out. I don't know why. Survival mechanism, I guess. It's easier to avoid than deal; don't get too close. Now that I think about it, Mom is the same way. I wonder if I learned it from her.

"Look, I know that I'm not one hundred percent," I say. "Not even fifty percent. It's going to take time. Seeing Christine like that . . . that was tough."

"For me too. I kept staring at her arm."

"I just kept thinking that that could have been me, lying in the bed with an amputated limb. I got off easy. I haven't lost any-thing." The word "yet" hangs in the air and hovers there—like my mother's life—as though it could dart in either direction. "I just don't want her to give up."

"Christine is tough. She'll make it through."

"Yeah," I agree, though I wasn't referring to Christine.

"Hey, you're wearing the prayer beads."

My hand flies up to them. "Oh, yeah." Since I put them on the day I had that terrible migraine, I've just kept wearing them. They're comforting somehow. And they remind me to pray for Mom. It feels right to pray for her.

"That's good. Have you found Marko yet?"

"No. I haven't done any looking since you were over." I kind of regret showing Audrey the box. Mom doesn't even know *I've* seen it yet. How would she feel if she knew I'd shared her private things with someone else? Suddenly, it doesn't even feel right to be talking about it. "I should go," I say, popping the last of the bar in my mouth and putting my camera strap over my shoulder. I've already been gone too long. "Check in on Mom."

As we stand to leave, I hear my name being called.

"Zara!"

I turn to see Joseph walking toward Audrey and me.

"Glad I found you," he says when he reaches us.

"Hey, Joseph."

"Hey, I forgot to give you my number," he says.

"Oh, right. Sorry." I take out my phone.

"What's yours? I'll just text you."

I tell him, and he types it into his phone.

"I'm Audrey," Audrey says.

"Joseph. Nice to meet you."

Audrey is smiling all goofy and wide.

"So, you guys know each other how?"

"Oh, we met in the chapel," Joseph says. "Zara took some photos for me."

"She's a *great* photographer," Audrey says, and looks back and forth from me to Joseph.

"Yes, she is."

"Really good. Like gallery-good one day."

"Thanks, Audrey," I say, pinching her arm.

"You go to school together?" Joseph asks.

"Since sixth grade. Where do you go?"

Joseph hesitates, but says, "I'm homeschooled. Well, technically I was. I just graduated. This is kind of my gap year."

I don't think I've met anyone who's been homeschooled before. But I'm surprised he already graduated. I thought we were the same age.

"Gap year?" Audrey says.

"Yeah, you know, when people take a year off from high school before college? It's more common in Europe than America, I suppose."

"Are you from Europe?" Audrey asks.

"Nope. Boston. My mom's from Ireland, though. For her gap year, she backpacked across Europe. Right now I'm exploring religion and faith a bit, asking the big questions and stuff. Figuring it out."

"Joseph's grandmother is in the hospital. That's why he's here," I say.

"I hope she gets better," says Audrey.

"Thanks. She really enjoyed meeting you, Zara."

Out of the corner of my eyes, I can see Audrey staring at me, and she's no longer even trying to conceal her what-have-you-been-keeping-from-me expression.

"Well, we need to go," I say, backing away from Joseph and pulling Audrey with me.

"Right. See you." Joseph lifts his hand in a wave and walks back the way he came.

When he's barely out of earshot, Audrey turns to me, smug. "Now I see why you've been so busy."

"Oh, stop it."

She nudges me with her elbow. "Spill it."

"What? He's just a nice guy visiting his sick grandma in the hospital."

"Yeah. A nice *hot* guy."

"He's relatively attractive," I admit.

"Relatively? He's got those eyes that bore right through your soul." She touches her chest. "I was getting nervous just talking to him." She giggles, and I can't help but laugh too.

Pretty soon we're laughing so hard, walking down the hallway, past the reception desk, that I need to lean against a wall by the elevators for support. Even though it pulls at the wound on my cheek and across my back too, it feels really good to laugh.

My phone buzzes with a text. It's Dad.

Where are you? Mom's awake

1994
Spring
Sarajevo
BiH

"THE WORLD IS shit," Dalila said while expelling a plume of smoke into the already hazy air. "No one in the West cares. Big American nothing. They are busy watching TV and getting fat eating while we are dying like animals in the street. They can all go shit on themselves." The words were Amir's, stolen from one of his typical rants. Dalila selected only the leanest and most provocative for the room.

The older boys watched her with amused, hungry eyes. Dalila seemed to grow bolder under their gaze. However, when their eyes roamed over Nadja, the boys shifted, scattered like rabbits. The boys were not welcome there.

"We're fucked," Dalila concluded.

One of the boys said something under his breath, and the rest laughed. Even though Nadja didn't hear it, she knew it was vulgar. Dalila laughed along with them and drank from a large bottle of Sarajevsko that they passed around.

Nadja put on her headphones, pressed Play and walked away. Dalila could fend for herself. Nadja sifted through the people who stood in small clusters like stone altars. What else was there to do? Hang out. Smoke. Drink if anyone could scrounge up something. Pair up. Soon someone would play music. Then there would be dancing. Nadja used to like dancing. But that was before. She didn't dance now.

She was bored with the scene and wanted to leave, but she didn't want to make Dalila mad. Since Nadja had arrived in Sarajevo, Dalila had become a good friend, her only friend. In the beginning, when Nadja couldn't get out of bed and didn't talk to anyone, Dalila had read romance novels to her. As Nadja's hair started to grow out, Dalila would brush it and give it more of a style. She held Nadja's hand the first time she ventured outside. She never asked why Nadja always wore the headphones around her neck. Sometimes Nadja cried at night, and when she woke from one of her recurring nightmares, Dalila woke too, comforting Nadja. Gradually, it was Dalila who coaxed Nadja out of the darkness. For that Nadja owed her. So she would stand watch on nights like this and let her friend drink and cuss and maybe make out with a boy.

One boy suddenly appeared next to Nadja. She ignored him like she did all the boys. But out of the corner of her eye, Nadja sized him up, noting where she could do the most damage if she needed to. She decided she'd go for the throat. It was open. The shirt collar unbuttoned. His Adam's apple small and unassuming. One chop with her hand followed by a face palm to the nose should do it. Faris had showed her how. He had showed all the women in the family how to do it. How to use a gun. How to go for the eyes. How to survive.

Nadja was good at surviving.

But the boy just stood there like he didn't know what to do

with himself either. Like he didn't want to be there. He wasn't much taller than her, and he was maybe just as skinny. His clothes were baggy like hers, so it was hard to tell what was flesh and what was cloth. There was a faint trace of brown hair on his upper lip. His cheek displayed a small constellation of acne. He held half of a fresh cigarette in his hand. His fingernails were bitten down and dirty. His black boots were scuffed on the tops. The cuffs of his too-long jeans folded over. He reminded her of Jusuf, a boy she'd grown up with who always had a football with him.

The tape stopped. Nadja took out the cassette and turned it over.

"What're you listening to?" the boy asked. His voice was so soft, she barely heard it over the noise.

She handed him her headphones. He put them on, and she pressed Play. He closed his eyes. The first song was "Nothing Compares 2 U" by Sinéad O'Connor. He listened to it the whole way through.

When it was done, he wiped his eyes and handed her back the headphones.

"Thanks," he said, and walked away.

Dalila threw up on the walk home.

"I'm sorry," she said.

"It's okay." Nadja patted her back while Dalila threw up again. "Done?" she asked after a few moments.

"I think so," Dalila said, her voice a strained, weak imitation of what it usually was.

Nadja helped her to her feet and put her arm around Dalila's neck. They walked slowly, stumbling up the steep hill.

The gunfire echoed in the night sky, but Nadja was too busy with Dalila to try and hide from the sound.

"Don't ever let me do that again," Dalila said.

Dalila had taken a cup of some drink that she said tasted like battery acid.

"Well, why'd you drink it?"

"Nothing else to do around here. Oh, no." She leaned over and threw up again. This time some of the puke landed on the tops of Nadja's boots.

"It's probably because you don't have much in you to begin with. And you're, like, forty kilos."

"The war diet," Dalila said when she was done, and laughed. "When this war is over, I am going to eat everything, and I don't care how big I get. In fact, I am going to get fat. I will work on it."

"What will you eat first?" Nadja asked.

Dalila was quiet, thinking.

"*Tulumba* first, then *rahat lokum*, then ice cream, then halva."

"Oh, you'll make yourself sick."

"No. No. It'll be heaven. What will you eat?"

"Maybe *burek*," said Nadja.

"*Burek!* That's not dessert."

"No, but I miss meat. It'll be like a dessert to eat meat again." Nadja imagined the smell of the sausages cooking on a grill, and her stomach growled.

"Yeah, you're right. *Burek's* the first thing we eat when this war is over."

"The first thing. And maybe peaches," Nadja said. Peaches were her favorite.

Dalila stopped and put her hands on Nadja's shoulders. "Peaches? I forgot about those." Her eyes were intense and wide, kind of crazed. Maybe because of the drunkenness.

"And strawberries," Nadja said. Those were a luxury.

"Strawberries."

"And blueberries."

"Blueberries."

"And apples."

"Apples."

Dalila let go of Nadja, and they continued walking, with Nadja bringing up all kinds of fruits and Dalila repeating them. The rhythm helping both girls up the street.

"I wish the neighbors hadn't cut down their tree," Dalila said. "They used to have the thickest, juiciest peaches every year. When we were sure they weren't home, we'd climb the fence and steal them."

Nadja didn't remind Dalila that they weren't in her old house. They were in the new one. The one they had stolen from the family that disappeared. The neighbors and the tree were long gone.

"Did they mind?" Nadja asked.

"How could they? They'd let them drop to the ground and rot. I'd even eat one of those rotting peaches now."

They reached the house and sat on the pavement, away from the basement window.

"I feel eighty years old. Look," Dalila said, and ran her fingers through her hair. There was a small clump in her hand. "This started happening."

She began to cry.

Normally Dalila was the strong one, but this drink had made her weak. Nadja made Dalila lie down and put her head in her lap. Nadja stroked her friend's hair, careful to be gentle so no more would come out. She absorbed each cry into her own body and added them to all the others already there. It was okay—Nadja was a deep well.

"Now watch, our ovaries are going to freeze," Dalila said.

Nadja burst out laughing. She hadn't heard anyone say that in a long time. She shifted her bottom on the concrete slab—the supposed cause of the freezing.

"It doesn't matter," Dalila said. "I probably won't get to use them anyway." And she started crying again.

"Watermelon," Nadja whispered. "And not cut up, but scooped up into those small balls arranged all cute on a plate, and next to it, some gelato."

"I forgot about watermelon." Dalila burped. The smell almost made Nadja gag. "I'm sorry."

"Shhh." Nadja hummed an old song and patted Dalila's head.

"I shouldn't say it, but I'm glad you're here," Dalila said. "You're the only good thing to come from this fucking war."

Nadja didn't answer, because her thoughts escaped to where they weren't supposed to go. Far away, 120 kilometers maybe. To an old house up on the hill. By a green river. Near an ancient bridge. In a bed that needed a new mattress. She remembered a woman held her once. Ran her cool hands through her long brown hair. Sang the same song that Nadja hummed now.

She remembered.

July 9

EVERYONE ASKS QUESTIONS.

They ask about Mom's reflexes, her brain, how she can be "awake" yet not really "all there." How much longer until she starts speaking? What is she looking at? Can she hear us? But all the questions really add up to this: Will she be okay?

Right now she doesn't look okay.

Mom's doctor does his best to answer; he tells us she suffered extreme head trauma and the only thing to do now is wait. As if we haven't been waiting long enough already.

Standing a little off to the side, I watch her. Benny is next to me. Mom's eyes are open and looking up at the ceiling. They seem to be focused there. Even from my angle, I see her irises shake like small green-and-black bees, trapped and darting back and forth inside a windowpane.

It's like she doesn't even know we're here. She seems alien. Not herself.

It's more disturbing than her being in a coma.

I shift my camera from one shoulder to the other, the weight of it suddenly too much to bear. I make no move to document this moment. I don't want to remember her like this.

When the doctor leaves, Dad tries to explain about Mom's condition a bit more, but as he does, her left hand starts jerking with tiny spasms. Dad holds it as he talks. He massages it. But I can still see the hand shake underneath his steady grasp.

Benny holds my hand. He stands a little behind me.

"What about lingering brain damage?" Gramma asks.

"Again, the chances are . . ." Dad starts, but he stops. Sighs. "We just don't know."

"Why is she staring like that?" I ask. "I thought she'd be more alert, like what they show on TV."

"It's not really like that," Dad says. "Sometimes coming out of a coma takes a while. Like the doctor said, her brain has experienced severe trauma, and we won't know the extent of it until . . . we know."

He places his hand on her face, and I wait for a moment of recognition from her.

It doesn't come.

Her eyes stay glued to the ceiling. I look up to see what has caught her stare, but there's only the light.

"She is progressing, though," Dad continues. "She's coming out of the coma. And believe me, after a week, this is a good thing. Dr. Yang is the best in the country. Our staff will start working with Mom on her reflexes, doing some physical therapy. It can be hard on the family to see the patient like this, but it really is all normal."

There is nothing at all normal about this.

Not in seeing Mom awake but far from alert, or listening to Dad talk about her so formally. Like we're someone else's family and not his own.

I stare at "the patient." Her eyebrows need plucking. I want to cry. This isn't what's supposed to happen. Mom is supposed to wake up from her coma and get better. We're supposed to get better together.

Dad sits down in the chair next to Mom's bed. "It's important as you visit with her that you touch her. Talk to her. Here, come closer, Benny, Z. It's okay."

Benny slowly pulls himself away from me. He climbs up on Dad's lap and holds Mom's shaking hand.

"Hi, Mom," says Benny, nervous.

"Z?" Dad reaches his free hand out to me, but I can't move.

I shake my head and back away until I'm pressed against the wall. Pain shoots through my whole body. I want to cry out from it and from the deeper hurt that Mom's lost to us forever. That this shell of herself is all there is. All there will ever be. This broken body and brain. Her stare terrifies me. This emptiness is all that's left.

"Zara?" Gramma says.

"I'm sorry," I say, and rush out of the room.

**1994
Spring
Sarajevo
BiH**

NADJA WANDERED INTO the hospital like a wounded cat, wrapping her body as close to the walls and edges as she could. Part of it was because she was a little frightened to be there. So many injured people. So much crying. And she also knew that this time of day was the worst for shelling. Amir had told them. He had told them that the enemy, the bastards, purposely targeted patients and civilians.

Nadja didn't know what section or floor of the hospital Amir worked on, though she knew that everyone from the top floors had been transferred to the lower levels because of the shelling. Much of the upper part of the building had been destroyed, riddled with bullets. She slowly crept through the hallways, past people lying in beds and cots. Most of them were injured. Nadja wondered where the regular sick were. Quietly, she approached a woman at a desk.

"Oh, you scared me, girl!" the woman said after turning around and seeing Nadja at her side. "Can I help you?"

"Amir," Nadja whispered. "He works here."

Her forehead crinkled. "Don't know him. Is he a doctor?"

"Anesthesiologist."

Just then a man came into the building carrying a woman. She was bleeding from the arm. "Help me, please!"

The woman behind the desk went over to him and directed him to the only free bed in the hallway—a couple of feet away from her desk.

"Sniper," the man said. "In her shoulder. She's lost a lot of blood. I had to carry her all the way up here."

"Are you her husband?"

"No, no. I don't know her."

The woman's legs were all scratched up on one side as if, when she fell, she slid across the asphalt. Nadja could make out the small bits of asphalt and rock lodged inside. The woman moaned and moaned. Nadja wanted to cover her ears to make it stop.

No one was coming right away for her. All the doctors were tending to other patients. A nurse came and tried to soothe the woman and examine the wound. It was not life-threatening, so she would have to wait. The man seemed uncertain about whether to leave her there or not.

"You're going to be okay now. We are safe," he said, but she grasped his arm and wouldn't let go. So he stayed with her.

Nadja backed away, sick from the noise and the blood, and turned down another hallway. She bent over in pain and breathed deeply, as if controlling her breath could control the pain. She felt the need to pee again, like she had been feeling for days, but she didn't want to. She knew it would burn, causing a fire between her legs.

Nadja lowered herself to the ground and sat as close to the wall as she could, drawing her feet up underneath her. This position sometimes gave her some relief from the pain. She'd been ashamed to tell Ramiza about it, even Dalila. When she left the basement and went upstairs to use the restroom, that's when she saw the blood in her urine. She walked out the door and immediately headed for the hospital, ignoring the danger she might face.

To the left of her, a guy lay in a white bed. He had an IV drip connected to him. He was asleep.

Nadja closed her eyes and rested her head on her knees. She counted to ten, wanting to distract herself from the dull pain in her lower abdomen.

"Hey," the man said.

Startled, Nadja raised her head to see him looking at her.

"Sorry, I can move." She thought maybe she was disturbing him. But she didn't make an attempt to relocate. She was in too much pain.

"What's wrong with you?" he asked.

"I don't know," she whispered. "What happened to you?"

"Grenade. Didn't even see it coming. Bastards. They are going to amputate my leg."

Nadja looked away from him. She did not know what to say. She was in pain but still had her legs. She was ashamed for being grateful for this. She pressed the ball of her hand into her lower abdomen as if that would help.

The guy kept talking. "My grandfather lost two fingers on his left hand in World War II. I always stared at it, played with the scar tissue when I was a kid. But even with three fingers, he could still load a rifle in five seconds. He's in Banja Luka. Haven't heard from him in months. I hope he got out."

She remembered Jela was from Banja Luka. Nadja had heard about terrible things happening there. But terrible things were happening everywhere.

"I shot a rifle once," Nadja said.

"Just once?"

"Well, a couple times. With my dad. We went hunting."

"You remember how to do it?"

"Yes."

"Good. What's your dad do now?"

She pictured the last time she saw her father. He had his arm around Benjamin's shoulders. He was saying something, but she couldn't hear him.

"He is a teacher," she said. "Math."

"I was terrible in math," the man said.

"Me too." Her father used to help her at the kitchen table with word problems. He never minded how long it took, never reacted to her tears. He kept a steady hand on her back as he glanced over her shoulder at the page. *Nadja. Nadja. You will get it. You are smart. It will come.*

"This won't last forever," the man said. "Keep up your studies. As soon as the war ends, I'm gone. This place isn't my home anymore. Sarajevo is not Sarajevo." He turned his head away from her and closed his eyes.

Where was her home? Nadja couldn't get her mind around the idea that she wouldn't always live this way. What would life look like when the war ended? Would she live with Dalila's family? Would everyone just get together and say they were sorry and then stop shooting one another? Would she go to America?

Apply to university in Sarajevo? Try to go back to Višegrad? She had no home to return to, just broken things inside an empty house. Her bed left unmade. Tape player. Couches. Chairs. Dishes all stacked, coated with dust in the cupboards. She imagined another family occupied the space now, much like the home she lived in. She knew someone else slept in her brother's bed. Someone else used the stove and the sink. They sat down at the table. Ran their fingers across the grooves in the wood, making new grooves.

The tips of her own fingers tingled.

"Look," the man said. "If you are in pain, you should tell someone. It is a long wait here, but you need to say something. No one will stop for you. I'm tired now. They've got me on good drugs. The best thing about this place. Good drugs."

"Okay," Nadja said. "Thanks."

He didn't speak to her again, but his eyes were open. She listened to make sure he was still breathing. The man looked at the ceiling. She wondered what he stared at. Maybe it was the yellow water stain that spread from a corner like spilled juice. Or the blocks of broken plaster and cracks.

Nadja started counting again. The screaming began when she got to seventeen. Nadja wanted to tell the woman to be quiet. She decided if she were to get shot, she would not scream. She would not make a sound. She would be like she was now, silent and strong, like a large willow tree near the river.

Others came and told the man it was time. They wheeled his bed into a room. Nadja could see inside because there was no door. Two men in white doctor coats and a nurse swarmed around the man, preparing him for his surgery. She wondered if Amir would come and knock him out.

He didn't.

A nurse stayed with the man, by his head. She spoke to him while the doctors at his leg turned on a saw. A loud saw. He was awake and talking. They cut off his leg while he was conscious. He didn't cry out. Nadja tried to close her ears to the sound, but she heard the saw, heard the pitch of its machinery change as it went first through flesh, then tendons, then bone.

She shook in the corner.

I am a willow. I bend in the wind. My roots run deep. I am ancient. I am all living things. I am calm. I am strong. I am a willow.

Nadja couldn't ignore the feeling any longer. She needed to use the restroom again. Now. She forced herself up and wandered; her fingers trailed along the dirty wall.

She found a bathroom and squatted. Barely any pee trickled out, but it burned again. Terribly.

When she came out, she found another nurse. This one took the temperature of an old man sitting in a chair. Nadja waited until she was done.

"I think I'm dying," she whispered.

There was no private room to conduct the exam, but the nurse took her behind a sheet that had been raised like a wall dividing patients. Only women were in this room. Nadja explained her symptoms, and the nurse asked her a series of questions. *Was Nadja currently sexually active?* Blank stare. No. *Had she been sexually active in the past?*

Nadja let herself slip into memory.

. . . . .

She reached up to brush the hair from Marko's eyes. And then they were kissing. She couldn't stop touching him. He pressed her hard against the stone wall, kissing her like he was starving and she was the only food in days. They slid to the ground. And then it was all earth and flesh. Her legs wrapped around his. She was consumed, and so was he. They burned so bright that when the voices came, they were almost upon them, they jumped up, running away from the river, all the way through the dark, knowing streets, laughing and falling all over themselves because they were in love and alive. They were really alive.

"No," she said to the nurse.

When was her last period? She couldn't remember. Dalila called it another benefit of the war diet.

"You are not dying," the nurse said.

"I'm not?"

"No, it sounds like you have a urinary tract infection. Normally I would send your urine in for analysis to verify, but now . . ." Her hand gestured to the hallway, where there were too many patients waiting. "I will send you home with some antibiotics that should knock it out."

The nurse left and returned with two different medications.

"This will help you right now." She handed Nadja one of the bottles. "Some ibuprofen. And I want you to take one of these as well." She gave Nadja the second one. "Two times a day for seven days. If you are not feeling better by the third day, come back in. Are your parents here?"

"No." She told the nurse about Amir and how he worked there.

"Okay, let me see if I can find this Amir. Come with me."

Nadja followed the nurse to a small room where she was told to wait. She didn't feel better yet, but she was happy to know that she didn't have anything too serious. And then she felt guilty because she was happy that she was alive.

In the corner there was a stack of magazines and books. Nadja pulled at one from the middle, almost knocking a bunch to the floor. She smelled the pages, looking for something familiar, but there was only dust. She sneezed. She opened to the first page and ran her fingers along the thin paper. She didn't read it. She just looked at the pictures.

"Nadja?" Amir bent down close in front of her. His eyes tired from a long shift. She showed him the bottles of pills. He held out his hand for hers and pulled her up. He put his arm around her. She was up to his shoulder. He patted her and told her it would be okay.

He was shorter than her father, so her body didn't know how to fit against his at first. But the longer they walked, the more she settled. She leaned into him, comforted by his strength. The whole way home he held her up. He did not limp. He did not stumble.

THE DRIVE HOME is quiet. Gramma and Vovo ride back to the house in their own car. It's just me and Dad and Benny. But not even Benny speaks. I glance at him in the rearview mirror. He's staring out the backseat window. Is he okay? He doesn't seem okay. How could he be? How could anyone? Is he making any more drawings? I wonder if his pictures are his way of dealing. Maybe I should try drawing.

"Zara," Dad says, "I think maybe you need to talk to someone. A counselor or a therapist, maybe."

No one said anything when I froze in Mom's room. When I stood there, paralyzed, against the wall, then fled. Now this.

"I'm fine, Dad. I was just a little freaked out. From your text, I thought . . . I thought she'd be *awake* awake. I didn't know she'd be doing that thing with her eyes."

Dad takes a deep breath in and then out through clenched teeth, making a soft whistling sound. This is something he does when he's stressed. I get a good side look at him. His face is more lined than I've ever seen. He looks ten years older.

"That's my fault. I'm sorry I didn't prepare you guys. I'm sorry you even have to experience seeing Mom like this."

It's not entirely Dad's fault, but I don't say anything.

"How about you, Benny? How did you feel, seeing Mom?"

"Scared," he says softly.

"It's okay to be a little scared. But the way her body is beginning to respond is a good sign."

"Will she be able to talk again?" he asks.

"Yep."

"And stand and walk and do all the things she used to?"

Dad nods, but he's not fooling me. He can't promise any of that.

He can't promise anything.

"Benny, maybe you and Zara can talk to someone about what you're thinking and feeling about Mom. I have a friend at the hospital who helps people after they go through trauma."

"What's trauma?" Benny says.

"Trauma is when something bad happens to you. And sometimes it can make you feel scared or upset, but sometimes it can also make your body feel bad. It's good to talk about it so that your body doesn't carry it like stress."

"Does trauma give you bad dreams?"

"It can. Are you having bad dreams?"

"No, but Zara is."

"Is that true?" Dad asks.

"I had one dream," I lie. "And you would too if you experienced what I—what *we*—did."

That shuts him up. We're almost home when Dad says, "I think I should make an appointment with Dr. Rivera."

"I'm already speaking to a chaplain," I tell him, which is not entirely untrue. Joseph is like a chaplain with all his religious talk.

"Really?" Dad says.

"Yeah, I'll be fine."

"Still, Vanessa is very good," Dad says. "I'd like you to meet with her. Just once. Then you can decide if you'd like to continue or not."

"Can we focus on my body instead? My cheek really itches, so does my back," I say, partly to change the subject. "What am I supposed to do about that?"

In the mirror, I peel back the bandage a bit and see patches of my skin are still red and raw. I scratch all along the sides of my wound, like I'm maneuvering along the borders of a small country.

"That's good. It means you're healing. Try not to scratch it, though."

"Impossible," I say.

He points to my camera on my lap. "You're taking pictures again? How does that feel?"

I shrug. "Trying. Weird, I guess. But maybe a little better," I say.

Dad nods, and we sit in silence the rest of the ride.

When I go to sleep I have the nightmare again, but there's more to it this time. I'm at the farmers market. I see Mom walking ahead. There are a bunch of people around me. And suddenly everyone's screaming. A man crawls, holding his insides together with one hand. I press on toward Mom. I want to reach out and grab her, but I realize I'm holding Benny in my arms. He's looking up at me with wide eyes. Terrified. Then Mom turns to look at us. There's blood oozing from her eyes and mouth.

I wake up in a sweat. My heart racing. My hands gripping the sheets.

My door opens and I prepare to attack whoever comes through, but it's just Benny. He stares at me for a moment before stumbling to my bed. He doesn't wait for an invitation.

I'm still awake an hour later when I hear the steady rhythm of his sleeping breath next to me.

IN THE MORNING, Dad suggests that Benny and I stay home. I overhear him telling Gramma and Vovo that he thinks it would be good for me to have a break from the hospital. He'll call with any updates on Mom's condition. You know, in the event she miraculously regains her speech, range of motion, normal bodily functions and consciousness.

I don't bother arguing.

A little while later, I get a text from a number I don't recognize.

> Hey, how are you doing? let me know when the photo is ready . . .

Joseph. It's only been a day, dude. But I text him a thumbs-up emoji.

> This is Joseph btw

> Lol. Got it

I haven't had the chance to get to the pictures yet.

I tell my grandparents that I'm going to work on some photos. Gramma smiles too widely. Her cheeks puff up like they're lopsided balloons.

"All right, Zara. Just let us know if you need anything. We'll be right here. I may take Benny to the park later if you want to come."

"I'm good," I say. "Thanks."

In my room, I download all my photos to my computer. I pick out the top ten shots of Joseph and Flora and touch them up, though there's not much to alter. The story their photos tell is clear. They love each other. I text Joseph the three I think are best.

It feels good to be doing something normal for a change. I've missed editing photos. I've missed creating.

I work on a photo of Christine a bit too. It's much harder, but I know it's important to her that she has this memory.

When I'm done with that, I scroll back until the pictures from the day of the bombing stare up at me. The series begins with the ones I took of the fruits and vegetables. I wasn't ready to look at these when I stumbled across them with Joseph. I don't know if I'm ready now. But I scan through them, slowly—looking for what? I'm not sure—taking deep breaths as I go.

I think about Mr. Singh and the idea of story, and I wonder if there's anything in the images that can tell me what's happening. Is there anything here that lets me know how this story will end? What's the inciting incident? The drama? Anything to suggest that someone has planted bombs? But there's nothing sinister I can see that reveals the devastation yet to come.

Where are you, Mr. Bomber? Did you stay to watch? How close were you to me? Did you see my face? How did you choose where to place the bomb? Did you think I'd make a good target?

Most of the photos captured the same images and elements. I study the faces in the background, looking for anything suspicious. Who are the main characters? The vendor who sold us the strawberries smiles just a little left of center. My focus had been on the berries, but he's also there. What happened to him?

Mom's side profile as she handles the fruit. There's also Benny, looking kind of wishful. He's staring at something in the distance. On the right of the frames are people walking and shopping. It looks like a typical morning at a farmers market.

But then the pictures shift dramatically to the few that I took afterward. All of these photos have a haze to them. The air is full of dust and smoke. I didn't realize how thick it was. I could use one of these for Mr. Singh's class. They tell a story for sure. The one that shows the kid crying in the background. Or the other that gives a view of one whole end where the market used to be, but is now empty. There are a few of people mid-run and two bodies on the ground and debris all over. I stare at one, trying to see if there's anything I can learn.

Then I come to the photo I don't really want to look at, but I know I have to—the one of my mom's feet poking out of the wreckage. I pause. Then I zoom in. One yellow shoe. One foot bare.

That's the one for Mr. Singh's class. My single-frame story. I mark it to begin editing later.

In the end, I have about thirty photos or so from that morning. I wonder if they would be helpful to the people investigating the bombing. I think of the terrible interview I had with those officers and the card one of them gave me.

Dad said not to talk to them again without his permission, so I'll ask him about it later. He'll know what to do with the photos.

I close my laptop. Now what?

I take out Mom's box from where I've stashed it underneath my bed and sift through the items again. The money. The letters. The photos. The comic. The teddy bear. This has become my ritual.

I stare at the photo of Mom with the bridge in the background. What's the story here?

The girl is out in early gray morning. The river is dark and a little menacing in the background. Maybe something lurks underneath the waters. It's the setup for a good horror movie.

She's the focal point of the picture. The bridge and the river are a little blurred around her. Mr. Singh would probably say the blur is good *bokeh*, a pleasing out-of-focus effect. I turn it over and read the name and date for the hundredth time. *Nadja '92. Love Marko.*

I pick up one of the letters. Since it looks like it's going to be a while before Mom can translate them, if she's ever able to read and write again, I'll have to find another way to read them. I search online for a company that offers translation services of documents from Bosnian to English. I scan the letters, find a manila envelope in Dad's office and put the documents in the mail.

In a few days I'll have answers, whether I'm ready for them or not.

A text comes in from Audrey.

Get ready

I send her a confused emoji face.

We're coming to get you.

I pile into the backseat of Natasha's car next to Audrey, my camera in my lap. Sibyl sits in the front seat. They've decided we need to go out and celebrate two things—my mom waking from her coma and Audrey's last night in town before leaving for her dad's. My friends look beautiful with their leggings and jeans and sleeveless tops and lip gloss and long hair. I feel like I don't belong, even with Audrey's help and some makeup.

"Beautiful," she said when she stepped back to examine her work. But no foundation in the world can cover up the big white bandage on my face. I don't think I'll ever feel beautiful again.

Benny waves to me from the doorway of the house. For a moment, I think maybe I should stay with him, but Natasha pulls away from the curb and the windows are down and the wind blows and my hair is flying all around my face and the music is loud and the girls are singing at the top of their lungs, and I can pretend there never was a bomb, there never was a hospital, that my mom is home, waiting for me, so instead I sing too, until my throat is scraped raw.

Downtown Providence is always hopping in the summer. It's

normally a college town during the year, but the summer is when all ages come out to play. There's restaurant after restaurant. Live music. Most summers I spend a fair amount of time here in the evenings. But now it's different. I've barely been out in public since the attack.

Natasha finds a parking spot, and we get out and just start walking. Sibyl points to a bunch of people dancing to some big band music in the small lot alongside an Italian restaurant. Right out in the open. They look like they're having so much fun. Like they don't know that at any second some guy could come along with a bomb and blow them all up.

I try to shake the thoughts out of my head, but they're stubborn. They stick.

I look over my shoulder, suddenly wary. Clusters of people walk around. Everything seems okay. But is it? I force myself to stay present, to stay in this moment, and then Audrey grabs my hand and pulls me along.

Even before I see the flames burning on the surface of the river that flows through the middle of downtown Providence, I can smell the wood smoke of WaterFire. The flames dotting the river like small torches. My family and I go every year to the first full lighting night, which is usually at the end of May. This year we walked around and got food from one of the trucks. I feel their missing presences lingering now like ghosts.

We find a spot by the rail and lean over, watch as the flames dance on the water. It is beautiful and eerie. The little boat with the volunteers who tend to the fire rows past us. People cheer, and the volunteers wave like they're part of a small-town parade.

After about ten minutes, we leave the rail and start walking, passing street performers.

"Hey, Z, take my picture," Sibyl says, and poses for me.

The last time I took pictures of my friends, the world was a different place. But something about all of us being together, tonight, makes me say okay.

Click.

Natasha and Audrey join her.

Click. Click.

We've done this a million times. We're just hanging out. Being silly. Being us. Being me. It feels so good. I get inspired and start positioning shots.

"Over here," I say, and point to the spot I want all three of them to stand.

Afterward, we crowd around my viewfinder, laughing at most of the shots.

"Ooh," Natasha says. "Send me that one."

The girls take their turns claiming the pictures they want.

"Let's go eat," Sibyl says.

I feel hungry, like I could eat a huge meal.

"Yeah. Let's go eat," I echo.

We find a restaurant and decide to sit outside. But as the server leads us to our table, the section where all the street vendors are set up catches my view, and I suddenly feel woozy. There are rows upon rows of white tent tops, exactly like the farmers market.

I can't move.

My mouth is dry, and I'm sweating. All these people. Milling about. Talking. Laughing. Eating. Completely unaware of the danger they're in.

My eyes dart around.

Why is that guy just standing there? What's he carrying in his backpack? Who's he talking to on the phone?

"Zara, what's wrong?" Audrey says. All three of them have stopped and are looking at me.

My fingers are on my face. Suddenly everyone around us turns. They are staring. They're all *staring* at me. I pull my fingers away, and they're wet. Is it raining? No, there is blood seeping out the bottom of my bandage. I hold my face and run. I run and run and run.

July 10

MY BACK BURNS. The fire climbs up toward my face. But I'm safe in the backseat of Natasha's car. Safe from all the people. The girls are quiet as they keep glancing at me. They're afraid of me.

I'm afraid of me.

I dab the blood from my face with the tissue Natasha gave me, careful not to cause any more damage. It still hurts from where I scratched at it earlier. I didn't even know I was hurting myself. That's how messed up I am.

My whole body is sore, as if it's just been steamrolled. I lean forward. Audrey holds my hand. She was the one who found me curled up, hands over my ears, hiding against the side of some building. I was crying, and then she was too. Natasha and Sibyl stood there frozen and worried, not knowing how to help.

Natasha turns the radio on, rescuing all of us from the silence.

The burn on my back has faded, and now it just itches. How much longer will these stitches be in? It has already been a week—more than a week.

It feels like they've been holding me together for years.

I start to cry. Again.

"It's okay, Zara," Audrey says next to me. She makes me lay my head on her shoulder. She holds me.

But it isn't. I'm not a person who cries. At least, I didn't used to be. Now it feels like tears are always hovering at the top of my throat, and I have to force them down or let them out.

Before, I didn't even cry when Mike broke up with me. And it wasn't a mutual thing, even though that's what I told people, including Audrey. He told me that he liked me, but he just didn't think it was working.

"Don't get me wrong," he said. "You're awesome. And I've really liked getting to know you, but I don't think it should be this hard. People either click or they don't. And you've kind of got a lot of walls."

"I don't have walls," I said.

He gave me a sideways look that, in the past, I had found charming and cute. But in that moment it made me want to reach across the table, grab him by the neck and slam his face down.

"Everyone has walls," I tried again. *Don't they?*

"Let me put it this way," he said. "I feel like I'm always playing offense and you're playing defense."

I picked all the olives off my slice of pizza. Mike always ordered olives, even though he knew I didn't like them.

"I get it," I said. "I know what you mean. I've kind of been feeling the same way."

"Really? We can still be friends, right?" He smiled. Cocked his head to the side.

"Right," I said.

I watched him eat his pizza while mine got cold on the plate.

We remained friends. Distant friends. And when he started seeing someone just a month later, it was okay. I was over him by then.

The worst part of all of it was that Mike was kind of right. I do have problems letting people in. But it's not my fault. Mom is the one who taught me to be like this. Hard to get to know. Walled up. Too difficult for a boyfriend to want to scale. She's the one with the silence. The one who has kept parts of herself locked away for years.

Except I have this one memory.

Last year, Audrey and I had a bit of a blowup over something that seems stupid now, but at the time it was epic. I asked Audrey to come over and hang out, but she said she couldn't because her mom needed her to do something. Then later I saw pictures of her and Christine online. They'd gone to the movies and didn't invite me. Audrey had lied to me. Obviously, I was hurt. I didn't talk to her for over a week.

By the start of the second week, Audrey came to my house, but I wouldn't see her. Mom told her I wasn't feeling well. A few moments later, Mom knocked on my door with a small tray of Turkish coffee in two small cups. There was also a stuffed Totoro doll on the tray. She set the tray down on my desk.

She handed me the stuffed animal.

"Audrey brought this by for you."

I tossed him on my bed. Audrey and I had been going through Miyazaki films. Our favorite was *My Neighbor Totoro*. He was this huge gray mystical animal that a girl found in the forest. We loved him. But looking at him next to my pillow, he seemed kind of small and insignificant as he stared and held on to his tiny umbrella.

Mom sat in my small green armchair, and I sat on my bed. We sipped coffee, and she asked what I was working on. I showed her the photos I took of Natasha and Sibyl at the mall. We had walked around asking random strangers to pose with us. It was fun, but not as fun as it could have been, because the whole time I was thinking about how it would've been better with Audrey. Sibyl and Natasha just didn't have the same intuition that Audrey did. She normally went along with any crazy photo session I devised.

"That's a cute animal," Mom said, nodding to Totoro, who lay on his back, staring up at the ceiling, just like he did in the movie.

"Whatever," I said.

Then Mom told me a story. "You know, I was once in a fight with my friend Uma. We argued about a game. She said I cheated, and I didn't, but she wouldn't believe me. She told everyone I was a cheater. So we stopped being friends. I was angry, but after a while, my anger faded. I didn't know why I was so angry. I just missed her. But it was too late. I didn't know how to bridge the waters between us. And then she walked by me one day at school and asked if I wanted to work together on our homework." Mom shrugged. "I said yes."

She drank her coffee.

"So what happened?" I asked

"We were friends again."

"Then how come I haven't heard you mention her name before?"

Mom's eyes darkened over the edge of her cup. "It was a long time ago."

"Well, this isn't over a stupid game," I said. "And Audrey knows what she did."

I turned my attention to my computer screen then. I didn't want to talk to her. I wanted to be mad because I felt like it was justified, like anger gave me a strength to fight the loneliness and hurt I felt.

Mom placed her empty cup down on the tray and stood up.

"You will regret cutting people out. It takes a stronger person to let others in," she said, and she walked out of the room.

Mom's words now ring through my head, and I can't deny the irony. In that moment, she was trying to be kind and reach out. She was trying to help me, trying to warn me. And instead of meeting her halfway, I ignored her. I treated her just like she treated me when she was hurt.

Maybe *I'm* the reason we're not close.

And suddenly, I'm angry at her all over again. I don't want to be this way.

I think of Mom. Lying in her hospital bed. Twitching. Her eyes betraying her state of mind. What if I never get the chance to know her? Never get the chance to let her know me?

Tears sting my cheek.

Natasha parks in front of my house.

"Can we just wait a little?" I say.

Of course.

Sure.

Absolutely.

The four of us sit there in the car looking out our respective windows. The air is thick, humid, not even a breeze. I make us wait until my heart calms down, until I'm breathing regular again.

When I'm ready, they walk me up to the door. We walk inside, and my dad says hello, but I keep going, head straight to my room. I hear my friends talking to him, but I don't stop until I reach my bed. I collapse into it. My fingers find the prayer beads around my neck.

"Help me," I whisper. I say the words again and again until they rise like an incantation and I drift off to sleep.

THE NEXT MORNING my phone buzzes with a text, waking me up. My head throbs.

> Grann loves the pictures. Come to the hospital?

I look at the time. It's only eight. And then a bunch of texts come in one after the other.

> I mean when you want to
> Here all day
> No rush
> She wants to thank you in person

I close my eyes and try to get back to sleep, but my back itches and my head aches.

The phone buzzes again. Does he ever stop?

> And thank you from me too
> I didn't tell you that.
> Sorry.

I sigh.

Welcome

And now I'm awake. I groan and remove the covers, stepping slowly, carefully out of bed and down the hallway.

"Morning, Zara," Vovo says to me when I stumble into the kitchen. "Coffee?" he asks.

"Sure, thanks."

He pours me a cup from the pot.

"Where is everyone?"

"Your grandmother is on a walk with Benny, and I believe your dad is here somewhere. Maybe still asleep."

"Oh." I take a sip of the coffee. "This is good. Thank you."

Vovo is reading the paper, like an actual newspaper. He removes the entertainment section and hands it to me.

"I didn't sleep well," he says. "Pillow's too hard."

"Me neither."

He doesn't ask me how I'm doing. He doesn't stare at me. Even though my bandage is off. He treats me the same way he always has. And I settle more comfortably into my seat.

We're reading quietly when Dad enters.

"Zara, how are you feeling this morning?"

"Fine," I say. I don't look up. I wish he'd quit asking me that. I'm reading this article about a woman who is motorcycling around the world. I wonder if I could just take off like that. Escape from everything.

I feel his eyes on me, so finally, I give in and meet them. He's got dark circles.

"Your cheek looks like it's healing okay. Any headache?"

"A little bit. Not a migraine, though."

He rummages through a cabinet and gives me some ibuprofen. "Take two of these."

"Are you leaving soon?" I ask.

"Yes."

"Okay," I stand up. "I can get ready quick."

"You want to come?"

"Yes."

"Are you sure? After last night, I thought maybe—"

"I'm fine, Dad," I say with more conviction than I feel.

Mom stares at me. I can't tell if she's really seeing me or if she's just changed focus from the ceiling. Her eyes never leave my face, though. She is not able to speak yet, or have much range of motion, but she seems more aware. I sit in the chair next to her bed, feeling awkward. It's just us because Dad is working. The hall outside is so quiet, it's almost eerie. But I stay because I'm trying. Because I want to try.

I clear my throat, but "Hi, Mom" comes out thin, like crinkled paper.

I keep going. "I want you to know that Benny and I are doing okay. It's been hard . . ." I feel my eyes water, look away. "But we're going to be okay. And so are you. The doctor is really hopeful." I touch her hand and look back at her eyes, which rest squarely on my face. "And I'm sorry for shutting you out. I'm sorry for a lot of things, really. So you have to get better. Please. Get better."

Mom's nurse comes in then to check on her vitals. But the

way Mom's looking at me, you'd think she and I were the only ones in the room.

"Hello, Nadja," the nurse says. "You're looking beautiful today. How are you feeling?"

Nothing from Mom. Can she understand what we're saying?

"Well, you are looking better each day. Yep. Each day. One step at a time. And, Zara, you seem to be healing well."

I nod as it dawns on me that Mom has been here long enough for the staff to know her loved ones' names.

"It's good that you're here," the nurse says. "That you're talking to her. It can really help."

The nurse leaves, and Mom finally closes her eyes. I wait until I think she's asleep and then I stand up slowly, careful not to disturb her. Her eyes remain closed. I lean over and give her a kiss on her forehead. My fingers grasp the beads around my neck, asking God to heal her. I leave her room and head to Flora's.

"Knock, knock," I say to announce my presence. I peek my head into the hospital room.

"Zara," Flora says from her bed.

"Hey." Joseph puts down the book he's reading and stands up from the chair.

"Hi," I say.

He stands there awkwardly, like he's uncertain of how to greet me. Then he waves and shoves his hands into his pockets and smiles goofy at me, almost like he's nervous.

Suddenly, I'm fully aware of how good he looks and of how I look with my messed-up, bandaged face.

Flora holds her hands up to me, so I go over to her. She gives me a kiss on both cheeks, careful to avoid the spot that's injured.

"The pictures are beautiful. You made me look like a movie star," she says.

"You're very pretty. I didn't do anything at all."

"That's very sweet, Zara. Now, why don't you take my Joseph to get something to eat. He shouldn't be spending all his time with an old woman."

"Grann—"

"I'm tired. Go on."

He bends and kisses her and follows me out of the room.

"We don't have to hang out," Joseph says. "I know you're probably here visiting your mom."

"I am. I went to check in on her before coming here."

We stop a couple of rooms down the hallway, both of us unsure where to go.

"Want to get something to eat?" he asks. His voice cracks a little.

Am I actually making him nervous? The thought gives me confidence, until I remember I have a huge scab forming on my face. He's probably just being nice.

"You don't have to hang out with me," I say, giving him an out. "I can, you know, go back and see my mom."

"Oh, yeah. We don't have to."

We both stand there looking everywhere but at each other. I should have known he was just feeling sorry for me.

"So—" I start to say.

"Look," he says, "I don't want to keep you from your mom,

but I *am* pretty hungry, and I love my grann, but you know, there's only so much we can talk about. It'd be cool to hang out with someone more my age, you know, like you. And why not? We're both here now. And just standing here, doing nothing. So let's go get some food."

He says all this in an awkward rush. His hand on the back of his head, which is now cocked to the side.

"Okay," I say. "The Au Bon Pain?"

He lets out a big breath like he's been holding it. "Sounds good." He motions for me to lead the way.

We take the elevator down to the first floor.

At the counter, I order a coffee.

"That's it?" he says. "Come on, let me get you something else."

"No, I'm okay, really."

He gives me a look like he doesn't believe me. "You can't have any of my food."

"Good. I wasn't planning on it," I say.

"Great, because just so we're clear, you can't play the I'm-not-hungry card and then pick at my sandwich or something."

I laugh. "Oh, my gosh, are you kidding me?"

"I've seen the move before."

I hold up my hand. "Don't worry. I'm not going to eat your food."

"But you really should eat something."

"Seriously? You're worse than my gramma," I joke. "Fine." I scan the menu. "I'll take the parfait."

"Good choice."

Joseph orders for us. I take out my money, but he tells me he's got it. And then suddenly *I'm* nervous. Like I'm on a date. But we're in a hospital, so this is definitely not a date. We get our food and sit down at one of the empty tables.

"How's your question writing going?" I nod to the journal he has on him.

He opens it up to a page and reads. "Why do some people live a life of little tragedy and others great suffering?"

"Wow. You get right to it."

"Only the best questions go in here."

"But isn't all life suffering, according to your Buddhists?"

"Yes, but the degree of difference can be huge."

"What do you mean? Like some people suffer more than others?"

"Look at a nation like Haiti. There is great poverty there, nothing like here in the States. Something like eighty thousand people still live in tents in the dirt with no plumbing or water since Hurricane Katrina, years ago, not to mention the other hurricanes they've had to endure since then. But that isn't even as bad as when my grann grew up under Papa Doc and then his son Baby Doc."

He says the names like I should recognize them, like they are notorious gangsters. I suddenly feel like I'm ignorant about most things that have happened in other countries. The only time I've even remotely heard of Haiti is when bad things happen with the weather.

"I'm sorry, I don't know much about Haiti," I say.

"Yeah, you and most people. Papa Doc and Baby Doc were

terrible dictators. Murdered people for nothing. Stole husbands and sons away in the middle of the night. Kept the people in poverty and suffering. Did you know Haiti is the only state ever founded through a successful slave revolution? They rose up against the French."

I shake my head. I didn't.

"That's pretty significant, don't you think? The American history books give it two sentences. It was close to the same time of the US revolution, but the US went here." He raises his hand upward. "And Haiti went here." He lowers his hand. "I'm not going to give you a history lesson, don't worry. But it is a country that's struggling. Many people don't have jobs, and without jobs, they don't see a future."

"Have you been to Haiti?"

He nods. "Two years ago. And now Grann wants to go back."

"Does she still have family there?"

"Yeah, but that's not the reason. She wants to die in her country. I try to tell her that she is an American now, but she says she will always be Haitian first."

It's a sad thought, but I get it. "That makes sense."

Joseph frowns, staring at his cup. I hope I haven't offended him.

"So I think about this," he says, and looks up at me, his eyes full of intensity. "I have known very little suffering in my life, even though I've certainly caused it for others."

He's caused people to suffer? I make a mental note to ask him about that later.

"But Grann, she knew suffering firsthand. She lost children.

She went hungry. She and my grandfather came here to better their lives. And yeah, my father worked really hard to become the man he is, but he didn't know the suffering that Grann did. He never went to bed hungry. Same thing for my mom. She's got a whole other history, being Irish and growing up in Ireland. I have a nice home, a mother and father, clothes, sports, everything . . . But if Grann had stayed in Haiti, I could be living in one of those tents right now. Sometimes I think, why me? I'm no different than them. Why was I spared?"

"Yeah, I know what you mean. I wonder that too—about myself. If I had been standing a little closer to where the bomb went off, it could have been me trapped under a vendor stall, or my severed limbs on the pavement, not someone else's. I could have died. What sense does that make?"

Joseph just shakes his head. There is no answer.

"So, is that what you're doing now?" I ask him. "Trying to figure it out?"

"Maybe. In a way."

"Well, when you find the answer, let me know," I say dryly. But I also feel for him. He seems a little tortured, like there's something he's wrestling with beyond faith.

I'm about to ask him when he says, "Buddha says that the purpose in life is to find your purpose and to give your whole heart and soul to it."

"So what happens if you can't find your purpose?"

"Well, I don't know if it means, like, you're supposed to do just one particular thing, like you're supposed to be a mechanic or a dietitian."

"Or a photographer," I say.

"Or a photographer," he echoes. "Though you've got a gift. Your pictures could really help people if you wanted them to. Have you thought about what you'll do with it?"

"I used to, but . . ." I shrug and stir my yogurt.

"But . . . ? What was the 'used to'?"

"I used to look at pictures and remember the smells and the feel. Like I was transported. I could remember the emotion, the energy, the way I felt when I took the photo, all of it. Like I was traveling through time. It was the only thing I could picture doing with my life."

"That's awesome," Joseph says. "So what changed?"

"What changed?" I pause. "*Everything* changed. Ever since the bombing . . . I just feel different. Off. Scared and nervous when I used to just go for it. I mean, I used to take photos constantly. I had this 365 project where I took one photo a day—of anything, really—and I'd share it online with this group of other young photographers and we'd critique each other's work. Now I've hardly taken any photos since the attack. I've tried, a little, but it's like I don't have the vision I used to. Like I've lost my edge or something. I'm not even sure who I am anymore." I shrug. "I don't know. It's hard to explain. Everything just feels so hard."

He nods. "It can be good to do the things that scare us sometimes. That's what my grandmother says. Maybe the point is to push through and do it anyway."

I think about that for a moment, and wonder what my mother would say. My mother, who hates having her picture taken, who hates that I'm a photographer. Who was never interested in, and hardly ever asked me about, my pictures.

Thinking about it all makes my headache return.

"So what about you?" I ask.

"Me?"

"Yeah, what's your purpose? And what was that part about causing people suffering? You kind of threw that in there."

His eyes darken, but he smiles.

"My dad tells me that I have a purpose and it's big. That God wouldn't have spared me from a life of poverty if I didn't. But his family made the choice to move to America so they could have a better, non-poverty-stricken future. My dad's view seems to be a privileged one. It implies my purpose is more important than others'. Or at least that people in severe poverty and those leading what we might consider small lives don't matter as much. I don't think he believes that, but it's a question of value. Why should one life have value over another? Aren't all lives of value? Of the same worth?"

He stops. "That's a good question." He writes in his journal.

"It is a good question," I say. I notice he didn't really answer either of mine, but I let it go for now. "A follow-up might be something like, how is it so easy for some to judge the value of another's life and decide whether or not it matters? How do some people just decide that only some lives deserve to be lived?"

He nods. "Two very good questions." He writes them down.

I think about the bomber. Did he know he could do it? Destroy so many lives?

"I wonder whether I could do it."

"Do what?" Joseph asks.

"I wonder if there could be a scenario where I felt like I didn't have a choice and like I had to kill someone. I wonder if I could do it, if I had to."

He stares at me a long time before answering. Audrey is right about his eyes. They're big and brown, and it feels like he's looking all the way through me.

Finally Joseph says, "I'm going through all these scenarios in my head. Like, what if my mom and sister are being tortured? Yeah, I could kill someone for doing that, I think. I don't really know, though."

I nod. "I don't know either. But I keep having this dream. I'm walking in the farmers market, and I'm looking at all the faces. People just pass me by like they're on a slow-moving walkway, like at the airport. And I notice everything. How people are buying fruit. How moms are holding their kids' hands. How dads are pushing strollers. How kids are running to find the candy vendor. And then I see him. He's up ahead. He's wearing a backpack. He keeps walking, and I speed up. When I catch him, I turn him around. His face and head are covered in black. He looks just like those ISIS fighters on TV. I've got a knife, just a small one. And I raise my hand to do it, but he shows me he's wearing a bomb. I look around and start screaming at everyone to run. But there's nothing I can do. The explosion always happens. Even if I kill him. I still see . . . I still see the bodies. I still smell the burning. Even now I can smell it."

I stare at a small ant that crawls across the table. Joseph is quiet.

"My dad thinks I should get some counseling," I say.

"Counseling can be good."

"I told him I'm already speaking to a hospital chaplain."

"Which one? I think I've met two of them."

I smile. "His name's Joseph."

He nods and smiles back in realization. "Right. Well, I've never been called that before. Many other things, but not a chaplain." He laughs. "Talking does help, though."

"I get that, in theory. But I don't know. It's just . . . I've never . . ." My hand touches the side of my face. "It's like I'm damaged now. I don't know how to move forward with anyone or anything. And I feel like . . . I feel like I'm drowning because . . . or maybe it's just that I'm lost . . . it's like a part of me is gone and I don't know how to get back to myself. And I just keep thinking that if my mom never recovers, for the rest of my life, I'll always be missing something, no matter how much time goes by." The words flop around in my brain and don't even make sense anymore. Like there are spaces now, gaps that are too large—too terrible—to cross.

Joseph reaches over and takes my hand. I stare at it. Part of me wants to take it back, but it feels good to be touched in such a caring, unexpected way. Even when the tears come and fall on his hands, he stays there, steady, like he's sat and grieved with me a thousand times.

1994
Spring
Sarajevo
BiH

NADJA SEARCHED FOR the word. She should have known it, but her memory had gaps and holes in it now, as if someone had gone inside her head with a large rake.

"Quick, he's going to leave," Dalila said.

There. She found it and cursed herself for being so slow. It was actually so similar to the one in Bosnian.

"Chocolate?"

The UN man shook his head. "No chocolate."

"Just candy, then," Dalila said. "What's the word for candy?"

Nadja said the word, but the man had already disappeared inside the cavity of the white truck. Kids were beginning to gather around, calling out to him, asking for treats, cigarettes, some Coca-Cola. Some spoke in Bosnian, most in broken English. Nadja held the Bosnian-English dictionary close to her chest, worried some kid might try to steal it. It was the most valuable book the family owned. Most of the UN officers spoke English, so that was the language of currency. Nadja had studied it in school for years, but speaking it was tiring. Her tongue flopped around like a beached whale when she tried to make the sounds.

The man turned around and looked surprised at the group

that had formed. He smiled and gave Dalila the small package.

"I'm sorry," he said. "It's all I have."

His accent was different from the Americans', but Nadja could still make out the English words. He was probably French.

Dalila and Nadja stepped away from the others and Dalila revealed what was in the package: two MRE bars, a can of sardines, a can of meat and the jackpot—two lollipops and a pack of cinnamon gum. Careful that none of the other kids were watching them, Nadja and Dalila opened the lollipops and popped them in their mouths.

"Wow," Dalila said, and closed her eyes. She leaned against a building and savored the treat. "Strawberry. What's yours?"

"Lime."

"Switch?"

The girls exchanged lollipops. They smiled and traded back again.

"The best," Dalila said. "The Smurf really came through today." They called the UN guys Smurfs because of their blue helmets. "Want to see what we can get for the gum and the sardines?"

Nadja nodded; it was the more responsible thing to do for the family, even though she really didn't want to part with the gum.

They made their way cautiously down toward Baščaršija, where there was a market. They hardly ever went to the market because, first of all, it was too dangerous, and secondly, they didn't usually have money or things to trade. But today was a beautiful day, sunny and warm but not hot. And they had something to trade.

Nadja and Dalila walked up and down the crowded aisles, amazed at what was being sold. There were tomatoes and greens and fruit. They didn't look as good as the vegetables Nadja's mom had sometimes grown in their small garden, but they looked edible. And that's all that mattered.

After thirty minutes, it was clear: everything was too expensive, and no one wanted the typical UN sardines. In the end, they traded the gum for five potatoes and three tomatoes.

"We didn't even get one piece," Nadja said about the gum, feeling the weight of the potatoes in her bag.

"No, but Mom will be happy with the food. Imagine her face when she sees how big the tomatoes are."

Nadja ducked her head, ashamed at her greed.

They walked quickly through the cobblestoned streets, heads down until they turned right and headed back up to their neighborhood. At any minute, the shelling might begin.

When they entered the house, they heard the TV and rushed into the living room. Ramiza had the news on, but gave in to their pleading for a channel change when she saw the potatoes.

"I'm not even going to ask how you got these. I'll make *kljukuša*," she said. "We still have some powdered milk left. That'll have to do." She handed the remote to Dalila and went into the kitchen to start grating the potatoes.

The girls sat on the floor and watched the movie *Pretty Woman*. They didn't care what movie it was, just that they were watching one and it was American.

An hour later, Ramiza gave them the potato cakes hot out of the oven and joined them. After that, they watched *The Simpsons*.

The power lasted for a glorious three hours and fifteen minutes.

When it was over, the girls climbed to the roof and hung out the window. They had the best view of Sarajevo from the attic and the roof. They played the game that Dalila invented because tonight the sky was on fire all throughout the hills that surrounded the valley their city lay in. It was like the enemy was making up for being so quiet and peaceful during the day.

Tonight, the fighting looked the worst toward Dobrinja, an area of Sarajevo caught in the middle of the crossfire. First came the flash and then the rumble. They counted the seconds in between. The game was to decide what type of weapon was being employed based on the timing, the type of light and the sound. Nadja was better at the game, able to tell the difference between a shoulder-launched missile and one from the tanks.

"I'm going to California when this is over," Dalila said about halfway through. Her voice pouty, full of the fact that Nadja was winning. Nadja always won.

"Just like that?"

"Yeah. I'm going to Beverly Hills and getting Levi's and boots."

"You're going to be a prostitute?" Nadja knew she was referring to one of the scenes from the movie they'd just watched. The one where the snobby boutique women wouldn't sell to Julia Roberts's character because she was a hooker.

Dalila pushed her. "No, but I will go into a store like that. They will all wait on me. Give me champagne, cigarettes, chocolate. I will buy whatever I want."

"With what money?" Nadja asked.

"I'll marry a rich American. One of the reporters." Dalila referred to the reporters who stayed at the Holiday Inn. The ones who flocked to the war to document, who asked the same questions over and over as if repeating would give understanding to this senseless fighting.

"They don't seem so rich."

"Only one has to be my ticket out. What do you think of the guy who talked to us last week? He was cute."

"He was old. At least thirty-five."

Dalila shrugged. "Thirty-five isn't so old."

"He was also married." Nadja held up her hand and pointed to her finger. "The ring."

"Again, just a passage to America. I can leave him when we get there."

"Okay, you can have your fantasy life," said Nadja.

"Oh, and you don't want to go to America? You want to live here?"

There was nothing in Sarajevo for Nadja. "No." America would get them both.

"You will see." Dalila stared off in the distance. "This can't last forever."

Nadja spied the glow just past the cemetery. She pointed.

The girls counted in unison.

"One. Two. Three. Four . . ."

I GO BACK to the hospital, again, this time for a look at how my back is coming along. The swelling has gone down, so I'm hoping the stitches can be removed today.

"This looks good, Zara," the nurse tells me.

"So, today?"

"Yep. Most of the cuts weren't too deep, so I can do it right now, if you like."

"Yeah. Sure. Thanks."

"I'll be right back."

She leaves, and I adjust the papery shirt so that it's covering the front of me a little better. When she returns, I lie down on my stomach. I feel her get to work.

Snip. Tug. Pull.

It doesn't hurt as much as it feels totally weird.

"You're healing nicely," she says. "Now, it'll still be a little raw. Have you been using the A and E ointment?"

"Yes. Sometimes my brother helps me with the spots I can't reach when my dad isn't home."

"Good. No wonder you're recovering so quickly."

"I thought a week was a long time for stitches."

"Not at all. And since yours cover a larger area, up to two weeks is the norm. You don't want to leave sutures in too long, or else severe scarring can occur."

She helps me sit up.

"Scarring, huh?"

She looks at me with kindness. "Even with removing these on time, there will be a scar, but you won't know what it'll look like until it matures. And of course, putting the balm on it and continuing to be careful with your movements for a little while will help."

"Okay. Thank you. Oh, um, one more thing." I feel weird asking her, but I need to. "Can you take my picture?" I want to see my back more clearly. Document how it's healing. Christine seemed to think this kind of thing could help her in some way. Maybe it could help me too.

"Um, yeah, sure. If you'd like."

I hand the nurse my camera and turn around, facing away.

"You can take a couple," I say, and she does.

After she leaves the room and I've put my shirt back on, I look at the pictures. There are three jagged raised red lines that cross my back. I don't look so much like a freak because the stitches are out. But I don't look like I used to. Forget wearing a bikini again.

I don't know if I ever will.

Back in Mom's room, it's a little cold, so I cover her with the extra blanket I find. I sit in a chair close to the window, bathed in shafts of light. Her eyes open. Her pupils take a moment to adjust. They look around the room, not stopping and settling until they spy me.

"Hi, Mom," I say.

I'm not sure if she recognizes me, so I get up and walk over to her. "It's me, Zara. How are you feeling?"

She doesn't respond, but I keep talking to her, like the nurse said I should.

"Gramma and Vovo are still here. Everyone's pulling for you."

Her eyes are clear. They lock on me with an intense hunger, more focused than last time. And then her hand moves toward mine.

"Mom," I say, "that's so good! You moved your hand."

I hold it, firmly but gently. There are tears now, welling up in her eyes and starting to drip down her face. I wipe them away with my free hand.

"It's okay, Mom. You're going to be okay."

I text Dad and tell him to come right away.

Her mouth moves, but I can't hear what she's saying, so I bend close.

"I'm sorry," she whispers.

Her words are slurred and then her face is blurry because now I'm crying too. I can't help it.

"No, Mom. Don't be sorry. I'm sorry."

"Zara." It's all she's able to say. And though it comes out more like Sara, I've never been so relieved to hear her say my name.

My grandparents and Benny and Aunt Evelyn come to the hospital, and we spend the day with Mom. She cries again when she sees Benny.

It's difficult seeing her try to talk. Her words are slurred, almost as if she's had a stroke. And what little she's speaking is more Bosnian than English—the accent she's tried to hide for years now out in the open.

Dad is so happy. He says that each day, she'll get stronger. Each day she'll come back to us a little more. Bit by bit.

I'm so relieved Mom is awake, but I feel nervous around her too. A little uncertain of how to act, because this is completely new ground. I stand at the edge of her bed, smiling when she looks at me. Her eyes seem to go in and out of focus. Does she notice I'm wearing her prayer beads?

My phone buzzes with a text.

What're you up to later?

It's Joseph.

                                                              This.

I send him a picture of my family in the hospital room.

She's awake! Amazing!

                    Thanks. Not sure yet. What are you up to?

I wanted to see if you wanted to go to
Shakespeare in the park with me

I don't understand the question, so I send him a question mark.

Shakespeare in the park.

What's that?

Shakespeare performed in the park.
Haha.
A Midsummer Night's Dream

Oh, he's serious.

When?

Later, like 6

I ask Dad if it's okay, and he nods. I probably could have asked him for a thousand dollars and he would have agreed.

Sure

I'll pick you up at your house.
Just send me your address.

We stay with Mom until early afternoon, when she begins to get tired. Dad suggests we let her sleep. The mood on the ride home is one of sober relief. It looks like it's going to be a long way back for Mom, but we're all just glad that she's here.

At home, I head straight to my room to get ready for my date with Joseph.

July 12

"WOW, SO YOU really meant a park," I say as Joseph pulls his dad's car along the side of the road next to a small park in downtown Providence.

"Yep. You've never been to one of these?"

"No. But after you said it, I did remember a teacher in ninth grade talking about it. I didn't know it was still a thing."

I get out of the car, but then I hesitate. There is a large group of people already on the grass, sitting in chairs and on blankets. Joseph pulls two small beach chairs and a blanket out of the trunk. He starts to walk in, but I'm not ready to follow. When he turns and sees that I'm still standing by the car, he stops.

"Everything okay?"

"Um, yeah, it's just . . . the crowd." I really don't want to freak out on him like I did with my friends.

Joseph walks back to me and sets the stuff down on the ground.

"We can leave if you want."

I take a breath. "No." I have to be able to be out in public with people. I can't live my life in fear.

He leans against the car, next to me, and we watch as people mingle, set up their seats. Some are having a little picnic before the show.

One more deep breath. "Let's do it," I say. "But it might be good to have an escape plan. Just in case."

"Okay. How about we find a spot that's close to the car and not in the middle," he says. "That way if you want to leave, we'll have clear access."

I nod. "That sounds good." And the space is pretty open. Since the park is in the middle of the city, if anything did happen, I'm sure response time would be quick.

I scan for buildings that can fall, but all I can find is a small stage and scattered trees.

"Ready?" Joseph asks.

I play with the beads at my neck and try to push the fear away. "Yeah," I say, and walk in.

We find a spot along the edge of the crowd with the car in our line of sight. Joseph opens up a red blanket and lays it down before setting up the chairs. I sit down and take off my flip-flops, stretch out my legs in front of me.

"Be right back," he says. He runs down to the stage and speaks with someone behind a table. Joseph looks like he could be one of the actors—handsome and compelling even from a distance. He's wearing jeans and a formfitting gray T-shirt, and clearly he must work out. I wonder if he plays sports or what he likes on his pizza or what his favorite movie is. It occurs to me that I hardly know anything about him except that he's kind, which is important and, right now, feels like enough.

I scan the crowd for anyone I know, but no one looks familiar.

No one looks suspicious either. I try and calm my heart. I tell myself that it's okay. I'll be okay.

Just then, one of the female performers comes out from the side of the stage and rushes at Joseph from behind. He turns and picks her up. She's beautiful, black and petite with long black hair down her back, the other half up with a crown of flowers. He holds her in front of him, and she twirls a little to show off her beautiful white gown with a purple sash.

My cheeks feel hot, especially the scraped-up one. They're either good friends or together. Not that it's my business, but I'm hoping it's the first. Because taking me to his girlfriend's production and not even telling me is just rude.

Joseph bounds back through the crowd and plops a program down in my lap. It's got the title of tonight's production on the front with a full close-up of the beautiful girl he was just hanging all over a few moments ago.

"She's pretty," I say.

"Yeah. Don't tell her that."

"Um, how do you know her?" I ask.

"She's my sister, Cassandra."

"Your sister?" I immediately feel stupid.

"She's studying theater at Brown. Tonight she's Hermia, and that's very important, according to her. I'll introduce you afterward."

"Are your parents here too?" I ask, hoping that they aren't, because having to meet his sister is one thing. His parents would be something else entirely. I don't want to meet them like this. Scarface and all.

"No, they're coming tomorrow night and then we're headed down to Dorchester for a couple of days. Hey, you okay?"

"Yeah, of course." But I feel so exposed. I open the program and bury myself in reading it, thankful to have something to do other than try to make small talk with Joseph.

I study the headshots in the program and read a little about the play in a short synopsis, but it already sounds complicated. Lots of gender disguises and names to keep track of.

"Have you seen this before?" I ask.

"Nope." Joseph opens a bag of chips. He offers me one.

"Thanks," I say. Salt and vinegar. "My favorite."

"Mine too."

He smiles and I smile back, but look away. Joseph has a habit of making me nervous.

"All I know is there's some love triangle, mistaken identities, fighting, lots of monologues, your basic Shakespeare," he says.

"Any witches?" I ask.

He thinks for a minute, midchew.

"Actually, no. Fairies in this one."

"When I was little, I used to pretend fireflies were actually tiny fairies. I'd chase them around my yard during the summer, you know, catch them in a glass jar. I remember this one time I made them a little house out of twigs and leaves with a bed and . . ." I falter because he's lying down on his side watching me like I'm the most interesting thing here. It's unnerving.

"And?" he asks.

"And, well, this is kind of gross. But I gave them dead bees as pets."

"How'd you collect dead bees?"

"I'd spray bug killer on them."

I sound ridiculous. I push three chips in my mouth so I'll stop talking.

"Awesome," he says, and laughs.

Then an actor steps onto the stage. "Ladies and gentlemen, we are about to begin. Please take your seats. We ask that there be no flash photography during the show, but afterward, our actors will be available for close-ups and selfies. And now we present to you *A Midsummer Night's Dream*."

We all clap, and the play begins.

"If you get cold," Joseph whispers, his breath suddenly near my ear, "I brought this." He points to a green-and-blue-checkered blanket folded next to him.

"Thanks," I say. I do have goose bumps, but I'm not at all cold.

His sister walks out onstage. Joseph is immediately rapt with attention, and pretty soon I am too. Cassandra is wonderful and funny as a young woman in love. From what I can make of it, and having read the synopsis, it seems like she is in love with Lysander, but she's supposed to marry Demetrius. And if she doesn't marry Demetrius, she will be either killed or sent to a convent. When her dad tells her this, some of the people in the crowd gasp, making us laugh. Being a woman back in the day was no joke.

As the play goes on, there's all this drama and a play within the play. There's fairy mischief and potions and a forest. Then Hermia thinks that Lysander has fallen in love with her friend Helena because Helena is tall. It's so silly. But it makes me laugh. And it feels so good to just be out, having fun, doing something new.

The actors do an incredible job of making the action and comedy accessible to the audience. Through their motions and how they say the words, it's not too tricky to understand old Shakespearean English.

It's a long play, but it's really good, surprisingly good. I can't wait to tell Audrey about it. She'll want all the details about Joseph. He's been nothing but a gentleman. But for me, the real victory is that I've been able to be in a large crowd without freaking out. This is progress.

After the play is over, we pick up the blanket and chairs and wait around to meet Cassandra.

When she emerges from backstage, she smiles wide and brings me in for a hug. I try not to wince as her hands wrap around my back.

"Hi, Zara. It's so nice to meet you. I'm really glad you came."

"Me too. I loved it," I tell her. And it's true. "I've never been to one of these."

"They're the best. Free. Outside. Fun time with friends. Though getting Joseph here is always tough," she says.

"You were great, Cassandra, really," Joseph says.

"Yeah, really incredible," I say.

"Thank you."

"I only noticed one line fudge," he says with a teasing smile.

"Shut up," she says. "Although I did almost trip."

Both of them laugh, and I smile.

"Okay, I don't want to keep your fan base waiting too long,"

Joseph says, referring to the small line of people waiting to speak with her.

Cassandra smiles and slaps his shoulder. "Thanks for coming, guys. Zara, maybe I'll see you again?"

I nod and feel my cheeks flush. For a brief moment, I'm thankful one is bandaged.

"Bye." She waves us off and speaks to a woman who gushes about her performance.

Joseph turns to me. "It's still kind of early. Want to get something to drink?"

I check the time. It's not even ten yet. "Sure."

We pack up the car and walk downtown. But Joseph stops a few blocks in, in front of a new coffee shop.

"Have you been here yet?"

"Nope."

"Pretty good. Standard."

He opens the door for me, and we get in line.

"So what did you actually think of the play?" he asks me.

"It was cool. I mean I didn't catch everything, but the actors were so good and funny. I didn't expect it to be so funny."

"Me neither," he says. "The last one I saw her in was *Hamlet*, and that one had no laughs. Or if it did, I don't remember. Lots of talking about death and mothers."

Death and mothers. Why does it always come back to that? I wonder what Mom is up to now. Is she alone in her room? Asleep? Staring up at the ceiling? What's she thinking about? Is she relieved to be awake, or afraid that she won't fully recover? That she has lost a part of herself?

I feel Joseph stiffen next to me, so I glance at him. He's fidgeting with his hands and staring at the ground. I'm about to ask him if he's okay when I notice an older couple who just ordered is standing off to the side and staring at him. The man puts his arm around the woman's shoulders and turns her away. But she looks back over her shoulder at us. Joseph looks at her, and she stares at him. Hard.

"Do you know—" But I don't get to finish.

"Hey, you know what, there's a better place I forgot about."

And then he leaves the line, speeding out the front door. I have to run to catch up to him a little ways down the street.

I want to ask him what's going on, but his hands are shoved in his pockets and he's walking so fast. He eventually turns around the corner and rests his back against a brick building. He takes out his phone and texts someone. Then he looks up at me and even though it's dark, I can see his eyes are watery.

"I'm sorry, I forgot that I have to do something. Do you mind if we just go home?"

"No, not at all," I say. But I'm a little weirded out by his behavior. "Is everything okay?"

"Yeah, fine," he says, but we both know he's lying.

As he drives me home, he's strangely quiet. The only side I know of Joseph is a talkative, vivacious one. I try to make a little small talk, but he just answers with one-word responses. So I stop and look out the window the rest of the drive. When we pull up to my house, I see my gramma pull back the curtains from the living room. Joseph idles in the driveway.

"Thanks," I say. I point to the well-lit room. "Gramma's up and waiting."

I grab the handle on the door and am about to ask him again if everything is okay, but before I can, he just says, "I'll see you later."

"Okay. Bye," I say.

The tires tear out of the gravel by the time I'm halfway to my door. I turn around and watch him drive off, wondering what the heck happened.

1994
Spring
Sarajevo
BiH

AFTER A COUPLE of days of no bombing, it had started up again one Sehur, during Ramadan, before the day of fasting began. Since then, the enemy had shelled relentlessly all month long. Nadja and the family huddled together deep underground in their basement. They passed the time by playing cards, smoking, listening to Amir's radio when it worked, reading the same books and magazines they had already read, and making up stories. Only at night would they peek out of the hole, like gophers, their heads darting around as if trying to spy the snakes or eagles before they swooped down upon them.

The call to prayer that rang out across the city five times a day sounded more passionate than ever, even though the mosques were targeted and many had been destroyed. The song was rebellious against the rhythm of guns and bombs. Their devotion to God and each other would not be hindered by war and hate.

When people risked going out, they would greet each other in passing.

"*Esselamu alejkum,*" they would say. *Peace be upon you.* An expression as old as the Ottoman Empire. A tradition that started hundreds of years ago. That had survived other wars.

This was always met with "*Alejkumu selam.*"

And upon you, peace.

Ramadan wasn't observed by the family in the traditional sense, but because food rations were delayed and often unpredictable, it was as if they had joined a city-wide fast. Dalila didn't understand how fasting and hunger brought her closer to God. She argued about it with Faris one night. He said the only way to God was through hunger.

"It gets your focus off yourself. It makes you realize you are mortal, with a body."

"I knew I was mortal the first time I saw someone die. I don't need to understand that any more."

"Dalila, why so hard? What are you afraid of?"

"I'm not afraid of anything."

Nadja thought about how Dalila was afraid of not knowing love.

"Then you shouldn't be afraid to spend a couple of minutes listening to God. Read the Quran. Like it says, He is closer to us than our jugular vein. Maybe you'll like what He has to say."

She grunted. "God doesn't listen to us."

"Really?" Faris said. "Maybe you should stop yelling at Him and complaining. Stop talking, and you'll see."

"Why should I listen to Him?"

"Because He knows this isn't the end of the story."

Dalila rolled her eyes. "When did you become such a believer?"

Faris shrugged.

"Enough," Ramiza said. "Let's not spoil our last moments together."

Nadja watched Faris put on his green camouflage coat just as the morning prayer announcing Eid, the holy day marking the end of Ramadan, rose like a fog outside the window. Faris was leaving again, called back to the front line—an abandoned rubble of an old apartment complex built in Tito's times. Nadja knew the enemy he fought was only some fifty meters away in the hills dotted with homes exactly like the one they were in now—two storied and red roofed.

Nadja grabbed his weapon—a rifle, solid, heavy in her hands. She wondered how such a small gun could fight against the large weapons that she knew by sound and light.

"No, like this," Faris said, and motioned for her to come to him. "Like this." He positioned her alongside him. Repositioned the gun in her hand. Showed her where and how to hold the gun. Where to look through. Such a small, narrow and intimate view. The range precise.

Ramiza had trimmed Faris's hair close on the sides and in the back. He had shaved. Nadja thought he looked like he was going on a date.

They all drank lentil coffee and then went outside to send Faris off.

"Happy Eid!" a neighbor called as they walked by.

"Happy Eid!" Ramiza called back.

Nadja didn't feel so happy, but when another greeted her traditionally with, "*Bajram šerif mubarek olsun,*" she responded with "*Allah razi olsun.*"

May God bless you.

But Faris was leaving. This clouded everything. Even the celebrations to come.

Growing up, Nadja's family observed the end of Ramadan by going house to house wishing their neighbors well. Her mother made baklava like every other mother. They exchanged gifts. Restaurants were packed with everyone eating and dancing, breaking the end of the fast.

This year Nadja and the family had started celebrating Eid the night before, because Amir was working at the hospital today, and because Faris wouldn't be home over the next three days for prayers and festivities. Ramiza and Amir had given gifts to all the kids. To Faris they gave things he could use on the front, like a new sweater and boots that had been mended by a cobbler in town. Nadja, as usual, had no gifts to give.

Faris gave everyone one last hug and then slung his rifle over one shoulder, the small duffel bag over the other. As he walked down the street away from them, Nadja remembered she did have something to give.

She ran down to Faris.

"What is it, Nadja?" he said to her when she got to him.

"Here," she said. She lifted the headphones from around her neck and gave them to him along with the Walkman. "If you can get some new batteries, this may be good to listen to when you have to be awake all night."

He looked at her in surprise.

"But this is your music."

She gave him a hug.

"Okay. I'll keep it safe," he said, patting her back. He took the gift and put it in his duffel bag.

"You're a good friend," he said, and smiled. "Make sure Dalila doesn't get into any trouble while I'm gone."

Nadja watched him walk a bit before she turned away.

"It's okay if you like my brother," Dalila said later when they were digging up dirt along the side of the house. Ramiza had learned how to use cut-up potatoes and let them sprout. The girls were planting them. Hopefully it would mean that they would be harvesting potatoes in a couple of months.

"He has a girlfriend," said Nadja.

"Mirela?" Dalila grunted. "How long do you think that's going to last?"

Nadja knelt in the dirt, knowing exactly what to do. Her hands dug and scooped out the earth, moving it here and there. The motion was both comforting and familiar. There had been other gardens. Many seasons of digging and churning and watering and harvesting.

Nadja dropped the small potato piece into the hole. She knew what to whisper to seeds so that they would grow: she whispered the words that came from somewhere inside. She hummed the song. The song another woman used to sing. A woman with brown hair and eyes, and whom Nadja resembled. Nadja could see her still, wearing a yellow scarf in her hair as she worked. The garden was big and full of tomatoes, peppers, squash, all the things that Nadja used to complain about having to eat.

"It's not like we have much choice now, anyway," Dalila said. "When this war is over, I'm going to go out, pick some guy and make out with him. I don't even care who. Just that he brushes his teeth." She laughed as she patted the dirt.

Too hard. Too hard. Nadja heard the woman's voice in her head. *Soft, like this.* Her hands packed the dirt over the bud softly, cupping it with her hands.

"So," Dalila pressed. "Do you like him?"

"He . . ." Nadja wanted to say that he was nice to her, that he made her feel like it was all going to be okay. That she felt . . . safe with him. "He bought me batteries."

"Yeah. But I see the way he watches you. I think he likes you. I'm just saying if you like him back, don't think it's weird or anything. You can get married and then we would really be sisters."

Nadja hummed as she worked; there was something else bursting from one of the boxes she had stuffed inside herself. The one close to her heart, just behind it, pressing against her back.

"I have someone," she whispered.

Dalila stopped digging. "You do?"

"I . . . he . . . he is waiting for me," Nadja lied, and bent over, glad she wasn't standing. The force of the memory of him almost made her cry out. She felt the box opening, no matter how hard she tried to press the lid back down. She imagined herself standing on it, using all her strength and weight, but she was only a feather. She was all pale, fragile bone, no marrow, no flesh. The box had no more patience for her struggle. It needed to open.

And then Marko was there. He was sitting beside her. He was touching her hair. Her hair that had grown out and was now down to her shoulders, and so thin. Darker too. He whispered her name. He brought his hands down upon hers in the dirt.

His were so clean and strong. She tried to take hers away. But his hands were there now, and they pulled her to him.

She allowed herself to lean against him. To let him hold her as she cried. She gave in to his smell and touch.

"Marko," she whispered.

"It's okay. I'm here," he said.

Nadja saw his eyes. The fear. The love. The worry. All just before the darkness. The deep, deep darkness that took her away from him. That took her away from everything. That didn't kill her but made her survive. She cried because she hated him for it. She cried because she loved him for it.

"Marko," she said again, his name a wound tearing and mending over and over.

Dalila held Nadja and rocked her a little, as if she were a small child.

"It's okay. You can let me in," Dalila said, and she stroked Nadja's hair again and again.

Two weeks later, one of the men from the neighborhood who fought on the front lines came and asked to speak with Amir and Ramiza. Nadja excused herself from the family room, went outside and then descended into the basement. The cries reached her before she hit the bottom step. Above, she heard Ramiza wail, followed by a thump of something falling to the floor. She could make out Dalila's crying next. Only Amir was silent. She listened for him, but nothing came through the thin floor.

He had always been so much braver than the rest of them.

Nadja stayed down below in the dark. She sat on her bedding

and reached for her headphones, forgetting for a moment that they were gone. Forgetting they were somewhere with Faris. She wondered if he was wearing them when he died. Did he find batteries? If so, what song was his last one? Did the music somehow distract him and that was what ended up getting him killed?

Nadja remembered the feel of the rifle in her hand. A toy compared to the weapons of the enemy, he had said.

She wondered what type of weapon it was that killed Faris.

She bet if she had been there, she would have been able to tell.

Nadja slipped his name through the crack of the box inside of her, the one that had opened in the garden, and sealed it shut once again.

HEY

The text comes just before midnight. I'm still awake, laptop open. Trying to work on a couple of pictures to bring in to Mr. Singh's class. Mom's old photos are sprawled on my bed. The small teddy from her box propped up next to Totoro at the foot.

Sorry for earlier

I'm about to text *Yeah that was weird*, but I decide to go with a less combative response.

No sorries needed

Can't sleep

Me neither

Looks like I'm not the only one who has dreams they want to avoid. I wait a little to see if Joseph's going to explain, but he doesn't. A couple minutes pass.

What're you doing tomorrow? I text.

Nothing.

Want to come somewhere with me?

Yes

July 14

AS SOON AS the wheels of the car turn down the road and hit the part where they're covered with sand, I begin to relax. There's something about that soft, soothing sound.

I roll down the window and let the breeze hit my face. Even under the bandage, my cheek tingles slightly, but it feels good. I breathe in the seawater air.

"You like this place," Joseph says as we pass the mobile homes that are now inhabited by the summer residents but will be vacant come winter.

"No." I smile. "I love this place."

We pull up to the two guys at the gate. I recognize Johnny right away. The other guy I don't know. I show them my ID. Johnny waves me through.

Joseph finds an empty parking spot.

"So this is how the rich live," Joseph says when he gets out of the car. He surveys the wooden bathhouse structures and the ocean.

I cringe a little. "Well, it's not like it's our own beach house or anything. It's just a closet to store things, really."

"No." He stretches. "Just your own private beach. I've been

over to Horseneck, though. That's on the other side of this, right?"

"Yeah, over there." I point. I place my camera bag on my shoulder.

I bypass going to our little bathhouse. There's nothing I need there anyway. And his comment about rich people has me a little self-conscious. It's not like he's suffering. Didn't he say his dad worked hard for his success?

"So, where to?" he asks.

"This way," I say. "Watch the grass and horseflies. Their bites kill." I lead him up the small hill and into the dunes.

I find a spot that I like. I just have to start. Like Joseph said, maybe the point is to push through. To do the things that scare us most.

I lift my camera to my face and begin taking some photos. I drop down on the ground to get the perfect blade of grass. I don't know if there's a story here, but it kind of doesn't matter. I'm just having some fun. Trying to stay in the moment. There's nowhere else that I feel more at ease than here. It's so open. No crowds. No threat. I'm safe.

"How far do these dunes go?"

"Not sure," I say from behind my camera.

I take a picture of Joseph. "Wait, can you move a little to the left? Don't look at me, pretend you're staring at something over there."

He puts his hands on his hips and stands like he's Peter Pan or something.

I laugh. "Not like that. Try not to pose."

He drops his hands and watches the water in the distance. Then he turns his face and looks directly at me.

Click. Click.

I start walking again and keep taking photos. Joseph trails behind me. He's quiet, which allows me to just be in my head and get the shots I want. I'm grateful that he's not talking my ear off or anything. It's like he's read my mind and knows what I need. Or maybe he feels bad about the way he acted after the play.

I look at the ocean in the distance; the colors of the sky are just beginning to shift. The sun won't set for a little while still, but the late-afternoon hue hovers over the water like a thick haze. I feel at peace. It's that magic time when people are packing up, going home to make dinner.

Even though it's not crazy hot, I'm a little sweaty from walking up and down the dunes. My shirt sticks to my back, and when I move, it irritates my wounds.

I stop and peel my shirt free. "Ouch."

"What's wrong?" Joseph asks, concern in his eyes.

"It's just from the bombing. Some shrapnel cut up my back. It's much better than it was, but it's still pretty sensitive and my T-shirt was kind of sticking to it. Nothing serious, though."

"Can I help you?" He reaches out his hand as if he needs to steady me or something.

"No, I'm okay," I say, and turn away from him.

I look at the pictures I've taken so far. They're nothing special. I pause a little on one of Joseph. Maybe that one is special, but I'm not going to share that story with the rest of the class. Besides, I have no idea what the story even is.

The silence between us isn't uncomfortable, but I want to know why he was so weird the other night.

"So, you want to talk about anything?" I'm purposefully vague, hoping he'll want to open up.

He watches the water.

"Okay. I guess some things are off the table."

I start walking again, lift my camera and shoot some photos. Joseph follows me for a long time, carrying a now-uncomfortable silence with him. Whatever it is that he's dealing with, he is definitely not over it and not ready to talk about it.

After a few more minutes, I'm about to suggest we just go back to the car when he says, "Last year, my best friend, Sebastian, and I ditched school. We hung out and started being stupid. We drank and got all loopy and were goofing off. Jumping off walls and stuff. You know, just seeing how high and far we could go. We'd done it before, but sober."

I slow down and wait for Joseph so that we're now walking side by side in the sand.

"We took turns daring each other. There was this ledge. It wasn't that high. Maybe like fifteen feet. I went first and made it. Then it was his turn. I turned around and saw him jump, but he didn't have the distance. I could tell as soon as he leapt. He tried to grab on to the side of the building after he already jumped. But he fell and hit the concrete. He died instantly."

I want to reach out, touch Joseph, hold him, something, but I don't. I just keep walking. I don't know what to say.

"Those were his parents the other night. At the coffee shop. I haven't seen them since the hospital. I tried to write them a letter, tell them how sorry I was. I never sent it. They . . ." He shakes his head. "I get it. They lost their son. I couldn't face anyone after that. I didn't leave the house for weeks. It was my fault. Anyway, that's when my mom started homeschooling me."

"Wait, how is any of that your fault?"

"I'm the one who suggested we ditch, started us drinking. I know if we hadn't, Seb would have made that jump. He would have made it. He always made it."

I place my hand on his arm. "I'm really sorry about your friend. Thank you for telling me. But you can't blame yourself."

Joseph stops, faces the water down below us.

"I miss him. You would have liked him. He was funny and smart and could imitate almost anyone. He always made people feel at ease."

"He sounds like a great friend."

"He was." Joseph sniffs and wipes his eyes. "So, that's when I started looking for answers. But I've only come up with more questions. I still don't know why Seb died and I didn't."

I understand his searching now. It's been a kind of penance. The need to make his life count for something. He feels guilty just for living. I feel that way too.

I shift and my shirt rubs against my back again. I should just take my shirt off. Run naked across the beach. That would be a good story. Zara Machado finally loses it. Everyone could see my scars. I'd have nothing to hide. Then I get an idea.

"Can you do something for me?" I ask Joseph.

"What?"

I hand him my camera. "You know how to work one of these?"

He fumbles with it and locates the button. "Just push this, right?"

"Well, yes, but here—this is how you zoom, and this is how you alter focus." I take him through a mini lesson in the basics.

"I need you to take my photo."

He raises the camera and points it at me.

"No, not like that."

I turn around and very carefully lift up my shirt so that it exposes my back. I'm not wearing a bra. The strap on the back would chafe too much. I look over my shoulder at Joseph, and he's already taking pictures. I turn away from him then and watch the ocean as his fingers press the button over and over.

After a minute or two, I pull my shirt down. When I face Joseph again, he clears his throat, looks away. Then he hands the camera back to me.

"I think I got a few good ones."

I'm already looking through them. "Not bad," I say. There's one where he's zoomed in to just my torso and the light surrounds me. There are a few that I can work with. "Thanks."

We walk down to the water's edge and alongside it, letting our feet get wet. Piping plovers run ahead of us, dipping their beaks into the sand, looking for insects. Joseph carries my sandals so that I can step farther into the water and take pictures whenever I want.

I'm not sure if he's leading me or I'm leading him, but we zigzag up the coastline. It's calm and peaceful here; the sky is about to become a mosaic of color above and around us, like we're in the largest chapel. And he doesn't even mention my scars.

IT'S BEEN A couple days since my afternoon at the beach with Joseph, and Mom is doing much better. She's talking more. Moving. Eating real food. Her speech is still slurred and mostly Bosnian. But she's improving.

I haven't had the bad dream in a while. It's almost like we're getting better together.

This morning when I go to visit her, I watch the nurse help her stand. Her legs shake, so it isn't for long, but she does it. She even takes two steps.

"Good job, Mom," I say.

Her head shakes in agitation. The nurse helps her back into bed and then leaves us alone. I try to help pull the covers back over her, but Mom waves me away with her good hand, the one she seems to have the most range of motion with. I feel the sting of rejection instantly, and I fight the tears that well up. But Mom doesn't fight hers. She lets out a sob of frustration.

I sit down next to her, take a tissue from the box on the bedside table and wipe her tears for her.

After a few moments, she looks at my neck and says, "*Tespih.*"

I touch the prayer beads. This is the first time she's seemed to notice I'm wearing them. I wonder if it upsets her, if she's upset that I found her box.

She says the word again. "*Tespih.*"

I'm not sure what it means, and I don't get the chance to ask because Mom closes her eyes as if it has all been too much. I stay for a little while and pray for her, for us. Before I leave, I remove the prayer beads from around my neck and place them on the bedside table.

Later, I have my third photography class. Mr. Singh is very moved by the single-frame story of my mom's feet sticking out of the rubble. During my critique, he gives me tips about how I could make it stronger. I'm learning so much that I'm glad he made me stick with it.

At the end of class, Mr. Singh mentions the *Narrative* exhibit again. Many students have already made the trip down to Boston. It sounds so amazing that I really want to go. For the first time in a long time, things don't feel completely hopeless. It gives me a bit of courage.

"Dad?" I ask later that night.

"Yeah." He's sitting at the dining room table with Gramma and Benny, playing a game of cards.

"Can you come here for a sec? I want to show you something." He joins me in the kitchen. I turn on the screen of my camera and show him the photos from just after the bombing.

"You took these?" he asks.

I nod. I know it must be hard for him to see evidence of what we went through. "Do you think we should send them to the police? You know, just in case there's something here that could help?"

He lets out a breath. "Yeah. Yeah, I guess it couldn't hurt. Thank you for showing me. Why don't you email me the photos, and I'll take care of it."

"Sure."

Dad gives my shoulder a squeeze and walks back into the dining room to resume the game. I feel a bit relieved, but I have something else on my mind.

"Dad?"

"Yeah?" he says as he picks up a card.

"I need to go to Boston for a photography exhibit."

"Um, okay," he says. "When?"

"Tomorrow."

"Oh. I don't know if anyone can take you." He draws a card from the pile, eyes focused on his hand.

"It's okay. I thought I could just take the train."

That gets his full attention. He looks up at me, and I see Gramma's eyebrows rise behind her cards.

"Ooh, can I go too?" says my brother.

"Oh, sorry, Benny. It's for my class."

He sinks a little in his chair, pouting.

"I don't know, Z. That's pretty far to go by yourself," Dad says.

"I've done it plenty of times."

"Yes, but that was before . . ."

He wants to say before I was a victim of a terrorist attack. Before, when I could handle being in public places without question.

Things have definitely changed, but I can do this.

"I'll have my phone on all the time. I'll check in. I think it would be good for me. I'm not saying I'm not nervous, but I really want to go. I need to see this exhibit." I can't stop living just because some terrible thing might happen. I need to keep going, push through.

Vovo surprises me by chiming in from the living room. "I can drop her off in the morning."

"Thanks, Vovo," I call back.

Dad examines my face. He sees something there that makes him nod and say, "Okay."

"Anyone want some coffee?" Gramma asks.

"I'll make it," I say.

I grind some fresh beans and pull out the *džezva*. I haven't had proper Turkish coffee in a while.

Gramma doesn't say anything, just gives those eyes to Dad again.

July 17

IN THE MORNING, Vovo waits with me for the train. I tell him that he can go, but he doesn't. He gives me a hug before I board.

"Proud of you," he whispers.

I feel a tiny bit of anxiety as he walks away, but I fight through it.

My bandage is off too. I still feel a little more secure with it on, but today is about stepping outside my comfort zone. And since it's been two weeks, it's technically safe now to leave my cheek uncovered. Dad says once my wounds are fully healed, we can decide what steps to take. If I'll need any additional treatment. For now, I get on the train. I tell myself that no one is staring at me. That no one notices the thick scabs on my face. I find my seat and, finally, breathe. This was the hardest part. Making the decision to go. Taking those first steps. The rest will be easier.

Boston is my favorite city. It's not like I've done extensive traveling, but as far as the cities I've been to go, Boston is hands down the best. I love the feel of it. The style. The architecture. It's beautiful, and even though it's not too far from home, I want to come here for school, I think.

For years I've been planning to study photography, but I don't have my whole future planned out like some people I know. Audrey is going to community college first. She says it's to save money. *I* think it's because she doesn't want to leave her mom. And look at Christine. Her whole life had been about tennis. In one moment, that's gone. I wonder what she'll do now.

Either way, I know plenty of people who plan to stay put. I've just never seen myself as one of them. Rhode Island is too small. I need to find some new stories.

I raise my camera and take a picture through the train window as we cross a bridge. The image is blurry but cool, kind of like a gray smudge of water.

Everything ok?

Dad.

Perfect

I settle into my seat, put on my headphones, and enjoy the ride.

The exhibit is off Newbury Street, which is this upscale, very pretty and very touristy section of Boston. Trees line the street in perfect equidistant marks. Stores have little black fences and gates. There's greenery everywhere, small patches of perfectly manicured grass and flowers and bushes. It's sunny and hot out but, thankfully, not too humid. Small white puffs of cloud decorate the sky. There are a lot of people walking around. It makes me nervous, but I press through it. And if I have to, I'll stop. I remind myself that I'm not in a hurry, that I can take my time.

Redbrick brownstones line both sides of the street. I pass a number of cool places as I go; there are plenty of opportunities here to enjoy great art. There's shops and cute restaurants with tables set outdoors too. I contemplate sitting at a café before hitting up the gallery, but I kind of want to get started.

I find the gallery easily, and as soon as I enter, I notice the large framed photographs lining the walls. Already I feel a sense of home. I remove my notebook for class from my bag and approach the *Narrative* exhibit like an anthropologist.

I begin in front of a portrait of a child with dark hair and eyes, a narrow face and thin lips. He looks Spanish, maybe; I'm not sure. The picture is just an intimate and up-close look at him. Nothing special about it, except maybe the gaze, which is very personal. The next photo is a middle-aged woman wearing a dark blue hijab. Her face is round and full, with heart-shaped lips. Wrinkles spread from the corners of her eyes, and dark circles form underneath. The next photo is an Asian man with freckles dotting his upper cheeks. He's laughing like the photo was taken right after a joke was told.

I savor each picture, examine each detail.

The only things shown are the heads from the neck up. The background of each photo is white. The faces tell the whole story. I love how stark they are yet full of emotion. I wonder how the photographer was able to capture so much in each one. I take some notes. What kind of lighting and makeup did the photographer use, if any? I peer as close as I can, my nose inches away from the photographs.

"Quite intimate," the woman behind the desk says to me. "Isn't it?"

I hadn't noticed her when I entered, so her question startles me a bit.

"Yes," I say. Though it's more soul piercing, I think.

"Anything I can help you with?"

"Um, no. I'm just here for a class."

"Oh." She perks up. "What class is that?"

"I study with Allen Singh in Providence. He suggested we come and see this exhibit."

"Oh yes, Allen Singh. We curated a show of his a couple years ago. What a wonderful photographer."

"Yes," I say. Now that she realizes I'm legit, hopefully she'll stop watching me like a hawk and leave me alone.

I move on to a portrait of a group of black women in a hair salon.

"Are all these photographers local?"

"No. Most of them are international, actually. The one you're looking at is a Zambian photographer. I believe he's from Lusaka."

The photo wants me to focus on the woman in the chair. She's clearly the center, as she's laughing at something said, possibly by the stylist. But there's so much to take in. There are three women in chairs, getting their hair done. One woman has hers wrapped up in a towel. There's a stylist with long braids standing behind the laughing woman. And I spy a pair of eyes in the corner. There's a little boy crouching beneath a sink. He's staring at me, holding some kind of pastry, wearing cutoff shorts and a striped shirt. His mouth has some jelly on the sides, or maybe it's chocolate. He looks like he's been caught by the photographer. His smile says, *Shhh, please don't tell.* And just like that the story has shifted. Maybe the focus is not the woman in the chair, but this boy.

I glance over my shoulder to make sure the gallery woman isn't watching me, and I quickly take a picture. I don't know if they allow photos in the exhibit, but it's worth the risk.

I get a text. The woman clears her throat. I turn the volume off.

Hey what're you doing?

It's Joseph.

At a gallery

Cool. Where

Boston

Where?

I send him the name of the gallery. I wonder if he knows where it is. If he's been here before.

How long?

Couple hours at least

I slowly peruse the rest of the gallery. Each wall features a different artist's work and a different method. Most of the photos show people. Some are of land- and cityscapes. The occasional animal.

One of my favorites is this photo series of a group of children, all different ages and ethnicities. They're playing tug-of-war in the middle of a park in a city. I'm not sure where exactly, but the park is half grass, half dirt. When I look closer, I see it's actually an old baseball field, not really a park at all. The thick rope is really a bunch of rags tied together. The children's legs are streaked with dirt. But their faces are great. Some are concentrating so hard, like the little girl near the front of the line. Others have their heads thrown back and are laughing. One child has fallen in the back. The next shot shows one side is winning. Feet have moved, slipped. A couple more kids have gone down. The third photo is of the victory. One team has their hands thrown up in the air, and I can almost hear the excited screams. The other side has fallen in the dirt. A bigger kid at the end lies on his back, hands covering his face.

Clever. It's a documentation of a single moment. But it works so well because of the setting and the number of people in the photo. I wonder what the effect would be if it were only two people instead of, say—I count the children—twenty-one?

I continue through each section of the gallery. I feel both overwhelmed and inspired by the work here. Overwhelmed because I wonder if I'll ever be as good as these photographers.

And inspired because of all the amazing pieces and new ideas I want to try out later. It feels so, so good to be in this creative space. To *want* to be here.

I round the corner, and my eyes are immediately pulled to the wall at the far end. It's covered in what almost look like Polaroid photos. The magnitude of the piece is astounding. It's just picture after overlapping picture featuring a single person in each—some of the shots are black-and-white, some are color. They are taken against all kinds of backdrops—nature, rooms, buildings. The effect is almost as if I'm looking at a huge missing persons board. But more like the kind that people put up themselves at a memorial site. It's a collective memory. There are so many. So many lives. So many individuals, yet all telling the same story. *I was here.*

The title of the piece is *Lost.*

My legs are tired from standing, so I shift from one to the other. I look around and notice that I'm still alone. No one has entered the gallery since I came in. Sad. People are really missing out.

I sit on the ground and place my camera next to me. This also allows me to study the lower section better.

There's a photo three rows up from the bottom. Over to the left. It catches my eye because I've seen that bridge somewhere before. There's a girl with long brown hair standing in front of it, smiling into the camera. And in a flash, I realize I've come face-to-face with my mom.

1994
Summer
Sarajevo
BiH

Dear Mama,

*Yesterday there was some strange ceasefire. People
crawled out of their homes like rodents plaguing a
desolate graveyard, not a once beautiful city. All the
stories Dad used to tell of his school days in Sarajevo
seem like a fantasy. He couldn't be talking about this
place. This place was never beautiful.*

*But in the frenzy of freedom, a group of us went
to the Miljacka River that runs through Sarajevo.
Normally we wouldn't go because we would be
shot on sight. Today the boys stripped to just their
underwear and dove off the Latinska Bridge. It's
their famous bridge here. The one where someone
was shot and WWI began. How come our histories
are always connected to war?*

*The locals speak of the bridge with pride, but it is
like a puny version of our beautiful bridge back*

*home. I stood on it, fully clothed. Don't worry,
Mama, I wouldn't embarrass you with immodesty. I
stared down at the dirty gray river, which is nothing
like the beautiful green Drina.*

*I watched the kids swimming. Dalila—you would
like her; she is the opposite of me, fun, charming,
outspoken—she floated on her back, calling out for
me to join.*

*The wind picked up while I stood there watching,
sending a memory rushing through me. Do you
remember the time when we went fishing, just me
and you? I don't know where Dad and Benjamin
were. We only caught one fish, and it was so tiny.
It flapped around in the belly of our boat. Its gills
gasped, working for air. I didn't want to touch it, so
you laughed and scooped it up easily. You removed
the hook, unfazed by the blood, the cut of its scales.
You held it up to me and asked if I wanted to kiss
it before you released it again. I grimaced in horror,
squeamish at the idea.*

*You laughed. You laughed so hard you dropped the
fish and then I screamed and jumped up. And the
boat rocked and in my trying to avoid the fish, I
slipped and fell overboard. And you were laughing
and laughing, but I got so mad. I wouldn't take your*

extended hand. I struggled on my own. When I got
back into the boat, I pouted. You tried to get me to
laugh with you. But I sulked the whole way home.

Today I stood on a bridge and heard your laugh.
I had forgotten how you loved to laugh. And I so
desperately regret that I didn't laugh with you that
day.

Love,
Nadja

Nadja didn't like the feeling of regret. She didn't like indulging in memories either. Writing to her mother relieved her of some of the pain she felt, but nothing could repair her entirely. It didn't help to remember. It didn't help to remember that day with her mother. It didn't help to remember the bridge back home, how Marko made her pose for picture after picture in front of it that one day. How she'd laughed as he did.

She could hardly remember how to laugh now.

"EXCUSE ME," THE woman says behind me. "Are you okay?"

I'm sitting cross-legged in front of the mural of faces. I think I've been sitting this way for a while. I have no idea what time it is. I'm sure I should be getting back soon, but I'm afraid that if I move, she will vanish. Just disappear from the wall. Maybe she's only a figment of my imagination. But I keep turning my head one way and then the next, and each time I come back, she's still there. Still pinned to the wall.

Lost.

"Did one photographer put all of these together?" I ask.

She nods. "A French photographer named Klema."

How on Earth did a French photographer get my mother's picture?

"Are you sure?" I ask her.

"Yes."

"Okay. It's just that . . ." I point to the wall and then to the picture that has my full attention. "That woman is my mother."

The woman bends close to peer at the photo. "Really?" she says, surprised.

"The photo was taken over twenty years ago in Bosnia. Do

you think the French photographer took it? Or do you think maybe he found it?"

"This is an exhibit created by Klema, but I don't believe all the pictures were taken by him." The woman straightens. "It's more of a collaboration. I'm not sure of his process. I do know that all of the photos show people before and after war and hardship."

"I thought the photographer of mine was a guy named Marko. I have a copy of it too. His name is on the back—"

"Here, let me help you up." She extends her hand, and I take it. "I can't have you sitting on the floor."

I notice there are others in the gallery now.

"Come," the woman says.

I follow her to the desk, and she motions for me to sit in a chair. She could lead me anywhere, and I would follow. It's like I'm in a daze.

"I can make a few phone calls, see what I can find out. Would you like some water?"

"Yes, please."

She bends down and pulls out a water bottle from underneath her desk and gives it to me.

Another woman asks her a question about purchasing one of the pieces, and she's off to help her. Meanwhile I sit and try to absorb what is happening. What are the odds that I would find my mom's picture up on the wall in this gallery? It doesn't make any sense. I look around, suddenly worried this is some joke. I wait for someone to pop out and surprise me. But nothing happens.

"Okay." The woman returns to me when she's finished

helping the couple. "Why don't you write down your contact information. This might take me some time. I have to first contact Klema's publicist."

I stare at her.

"I mean, you're welcome to wait, but it could take time. A few days. A week. Maybe longer."

"Oh." I can feel my face fall, and my cheek aches. I feel exposed.

She pushes the paper toward me. I write down my full name and number and even my address.

Outside the gallery, I glance up and down the street, not sure which way I should go. I feel lost. Someone may as well take my picture and tack it up on the wall.

I pick one direction. No reason. It's only because I have to move.

Up ahead, someone waves. He must have me confused with someone else. Until he gets closer and I see it's—

"Joseph?"

"Hey," he says.

"You found me," I say. Tears come to my eyes.

He laughs. "It wasn't that hard. You told me where you'd be."

"How'd you get here?" I ask.

He tilts his head to the side. "I told you I'd be in Dorchester, remember? That's where my family's from. Not too far from here. I took the T."

"Oh, right." I don't remember, but I don't care. I'm just glad he's here.

"You hungry?"

Suddenly I am ravenous. I remember my face. But if Joseph

notices I'm not wearing my bandage, he doesn't say anything. "Yes," I say, "starving."

"Come on, let's get some food."

We grab some sandwiches and then go to the Common and sit on a bench that overlooks the water with the swan boats. The gardens are to the left of us. We eat and people watch.

"So, what's going on?" he asks.

I tell him about the exhibit with my mom's picture on the wall. I tell him about the box I found. I tell him everything.

After a long moment of watching the geese in the water, Joseph says, "You know this can't all be coincidence, right?"

"I don't know what to think."

"Check it out." He brings his legs up on the bench and faces me. "You survive a terrorist attack, find that box of your mom's and a photo you've never seen, take a photography class that gives you an assignment that leads you to an exhibit with that exact photograph? Not to mention meeting me, a guy from Boston who can show you around afterward."

"Don't tell me you believe in destiny or fate or something. Or, like, the universe is conspiring on my behalf."

"Nope."

"Good," I say. I'm not in the mood for a trite explanation. Though what he said makes me wonder: what is the probability that all those things would happen?

"The universe has nothing to do with it, because the universe doesn't care about you," he says. "The universe is a cold, dark place. It's not a person. It's not alive."

I wait for him to continue, but he doesn't. "All right, then. If it's not coincidence, what is it?" I ask.

He takes a breath. "It's love."

"Love?" I roll my eyes. "Joseph—"

He holds up his hand. "When you saw that photo on the wall—what did you feel?"

"Shock."

"Yeah, but when the shock wore off?"

"I . . . I felt like crying," I admit.

"Why?"

"Because . . ." I shake my head. It's hard to put words to.

"Come on." He nudges the side of my arm.

I take a bite of my sandwich, stalling. I let my eyes follow two little kids chasing each other. "It felt like someone had put it there just for me. It felt like a gift." I turn to him. "That's weird, right?"

He smiles. "No."

We watch the swan boats for a few moments.

"There is one thing I know to be true," he continues. "Across every religion I've studied, even though each one believes differently about God, in some way or other, nearly every religion connects God with love. And if the best definition of God is love and love made everything—the universe, the oceans, all the animals and plants, you and me—then love guides and connects everything."

"That doesn't sound very Buddhist of you."

"Well, I forgot to tell you. I'm no longer studying Buddhism."

"Oh, now you're studying another religion?"

"I don't know." He shrugs. "I haven't really committed yet. Though I'm leaning toward Jesus. Out of everyone, he got the love thing."

I wonder if Joseph is right. This does seem too intentional to be random. But there's something strange about how he jumps from question to question, one religion to the next. And it doesn't seem to be giving him peace. Then all of a sudden, I understand.

"Can I say something?" I ask Joseph.

"Sure."

"I think you're hiding."

He looks at me strangely. "What're you talking about?"

"What you told me at the beach about Seb, that was terrible. A terrible accident. But you can't just go from religion to religion looking for answers to explain away why something tragic happened. Looking for some kind of penance. You need to face his parents."

He turns away from me.

"Talk to them. Ask for their forgiveness and then forgive yourself. And then live. Live out the truth you're learning. You already know more than most people. But what good is all that knowledge if you don't use it? If you don't take what you learn and use it to change your life?"

He turns back to me and just stares, a little openmouthed. Then he stands up and walks away.

Shit. I must have really pissed him off. And I feel a little bad about it, but not really. If he can spout all of his wisdom at me, then I can speak some truth back at him.

I'm not sure if I should follow him, so I decide to stay on the bench. Less than a minute later, Joseph turns around and walks back. He stops right in front of me. I look up at him.

"I was going to tell you to back off, that you have no idea what you're talking about. But . . ." He shrugs. "You're right." He holds out his hand, and I take it. He pulls me up. And then he hugs me. It only hurts a little.

He releases me quickly, and I stand there, awkward. The air between us has changed drastically, and suddenly, I'm not sure how to act around him, what to say.

"So, this is kind of close to where you grew up?" I ask, looking around the Common.

"Pretty close, yeah. You ever been to Dorchester?"

"No, never have."

"You're not missing much. Typical Boston neighborhood. Markets. Parks. Big Haitian community, which is probably why my grandparents moved there. My parents moved us to Providence when I was in sixth grade. But I still have family here. We were at my aunt's today."

"Cool," I say. "My parents met around here. I think it was in Cambridge? My dad went to med school at BU."

"Good school. My mom did her undergrad there. Were you born here too?"

"No, in Providence. They left Boston right after they got married, and I came along nine months later. Well, eight months, actually."

"So you're one of those *love* children."

The way he says it makes me laugh.

"Pretty much. I wonder, though . . . if she felt like she had to marry my dad because of me. Like she didn't have a choice."

"Even if she didn't, does it matter?"

"I don't know . . ." Only the fact that it might explain the distance between us. How she feels that I screwed up her life. Me the unwanted child that she suddenly had to care for. That narrative makes sense in my head. It explains our disconnect. I was never wanted to begin with.

I change my answer. "Yes."

Joseph offers to drive me home, and I accept. Instead of talking, we listen to music, and it's nice to be able to sit in comfortable silence with someone. I spend most of the ride looking out the window, thinking about everything. Mom. The picture in the gallery. My life and the world in general, and whether I'll ever get back to feeling completely safe and secure in my own skin and community.

Gramma opens the front door as soon as we pull into the driveway. Before I say anything, Joseph is already out of the car and walking up to introduce himself.

"Hello," he says. "I'm Joseph, a friend of Zara's. You must be her grandmother."

She shakes his extended hand. "Yes. Nice to meet you, Joseph," Gramma says. "I thought you were taking the train, Zara?"

"Yes, but I ran into Joseph, and he offered me a ride back."

"Thank you, Joseph. Would you like to come inside for some lemonade?"

"No, ma'am, I need to get going. But thank you." And then

he kind of bows, which makes me want to laugh. "I'll see you later, Zara." He backs away toward his car.

"Later," I say.

Gramma watches him. "What a pleasant young man. Good manners," she says, holding the door open for me. "And handsome."

I turn my head back to look at her, and she laughs and scoots me inside.

"Where's Dad?" I ask.

"Working. How was the gallery?"

"It was good," I say. But I keep the part about the picture to myself.

"Good," she says. "And the train ride?"

"Nice." She waits for more, so I add, "I felt nervous being around so many people at first, but I didn't freak out or anything. I put my headphones on, listened to music. No one seemed to notice my face. And the exhibit was exactly what I needed."

She smiles wide.

Benny runs into the living room with Vovo trailing behind him.

"Zara. You're home!"

He speeds past me and grabs a package by the door. "You got a package."

My eyes widen.

"It came this morning," Gramma says.

"What is it?" Benny asks.

"Oh, just some photography magazines," I say.

I ruffle his hair as I take the package from him and head

straight to my room. I close the door behind me. My heart races, and my back tingles. The package is heavy. I sit on my bed and open it. The original documents are there, but now there are also fresh, white pages of English too.

I take a deep breath and start reading.

AFTER FARIS DIED, Amir often stared at Dalila and Nadja as if he was trying to solve a difficult problem. His eyes had a faraway look. His brow, jagged creases, as if someone had carved them. At night, Ramiza tried to iron them out with her hands as she massaged his head. But they always returned in the morning.

He came home one day from the hospital and announced that they were leaving. The war had taken his only son; it would not take his daughters. Nadja wanted to correct him. She had a father. She had a mother. She had a brother.

The girls packed one bag each, mainly stuffed with a change of clothes, underwear, some photos and their identification papers.

Afterward, Nadja and Dalila stood shoulder to shoulder on the side of the house. Dalila took a puff of the cigarette and exhaled as she passed it to Nadja.

Dalila was quiet, which meant something was wrong, but Nadja didn't ask her. She just smoked.

After a while, Nadja felt the weight of Dalila's body lean against her.

"I know all I talk about is leaving, but now that it's really here . . ." Dalila stared ahead. "Where will we go? Sarajevo is home."

Nadja had left home years ago. Her real family long gone. Now as she stood on the precipice of another departure, she felt like this would be how her life always was. That she would always leave and never find. The wound of her displacement so deep, home was now unknowable to her.

"Sarajevo has never been home," she said.

They smoked some more. The cigarette eventually a small stub between them. But it was as if the very word, the concept of home, evoked something in Nadja—something she had worked hard all these years at forgetting. In that moment, her mind betrayed her. With the reality of leaving again upon Nadja, the memory of when she was forced to leave Višegrad swelled inside. And like a rushing river, memory picked the lock and forced itself free.

She stood in the street unable to move. The old green truck carrying her dad and brother like they were livestock bumped and swerved as it disappeared down the narrow street. People around her whimpered. Somewhere, far or close, she couldn't tell, there were gunshots.

The truck, she thought. *I have to follow the truck.*

But her legs wouldn't listen. They had grown deep roots in seconds.

Nadja's mom grabbed her arm with an iron grip, ripping her feet from the earth. Nadja stumbled as if she had forgotten how to walk. Back into the house her mother dragged her, on limp legs. Nadja fell in a heap near the door. She watched her mom lock it behind them and close all of the curtains on the windows.

In the darkness, her mom looked around frantically for something, throwing everything her hands touched to the ground, but she couldn't find it. That was when she started screaming. She screamed like Nadja had never heard and waved her arms all around until she hugged them to her body, as if she were trying to keep herself from exploding.

Nadja crawled to the couch, afraid for probably the first time in her life. Her limbs were tingly with pins and needles, the terror making its way down her spine as she watched her mother sit and stare off somewhere in the distance.

Nadja heated water. She made tea for the two of them and had to hold the cup for her mother to drink it. After a couple of sips, she came back to herself and looked at Nadja as if she'd just realized that Nadja was there.

"It will be all right. It will be all right," her mom kept saying as she rocked back and forth.

Nadja prayed to God to protect them, to keep her father and brother safe. She held on to her mother, something she hadn't really done since she was little.

Nadja's mother got up from the couch and began to clean. She started with the kitchen. She took out a broom and began sweeping everything broken into a corner. Nadja helped her without having to be asked. She picked up an overturned chair. She put the drawers of cupboards back together, restacked papers. Everything the Serbs had destroyed, they righted.

Nadja could not get her mind around what was happening. Even though they'd had to flee and return a couple of weeks ago and she'd heard reports about killings and war in Croatia and seen news coverage, she had never truly believed they were in real danger. Things were happening in some other place, some other time, to some other people. The absence in the house—the absence of her dad and brother—was just from some nightmare; she thought maybe she simply needed to lie down, go to sleep and wake up, and they would be there again.

But the silence in the house. It haunted her.

Nadja peeked through the curtains when her mother wasn't looking. There was no one outside. No one walking. It was as if everyone were asleep or dead.

That night she slept with her mother in her parents' bed. The two of them cried out at different parts of the night. Nadja kept seeing her brother's scared face. The body in the street. All the men being taken away.

Her neighbor Mr. Imamović had a wonderful flower garden that he would let Nadja pick from. He was in his sixties, married. He was a grandfather. What threat could he have been? She hadn't known well the woman they shot, only by sight. How could they just kill people? How was that legal? They were not soldiers. Where was the JNA? What had her father and brother done? What had they done?

Some time later, Nadja woke to the sound of deep thunder. At first she thought there was a storm coming. She peeked out the window and saw a clear sky. The neighborhood was still empty. No one was out walking. The homes all had the curtains closed like theirs. Since they lived up in the hills, most of the homes had a view of the town's beloved bridge. From her angle, Nadja could see the bridge below had trucks on it and soldiers. The river glowed emerald where the sunlight hit. The gunfire came next. It wasn't consistent. Sometimes it happened all at once, lasting a minute or two. Sometimes it was one lone shot.

Her mother woke next to her.

Each time they heard the gunfire, Nadja and her mother would huddle together and wait, listen for what was to come after. The not knowing what was going on was almost worse than the knowing. Nadja's mind went to all kinds of dark places. She already imagined her father and brother dead in the street like the old woman, shot between the eyes.

They ate some bread, cheese and the last of the hard-boiled eggs in the dark. The radio said nothing about what was happening. The phone line crackled, dead.

Nadja watched her mother wash her face and neck with a cloth, put on her best makeup. She zipped up her A-line navy blue skirt and tucked in her pretty white blouse with blue and green flowers.

"I am going to get information," she said, bending to put on navy heels. "Stay here. Do not go outside. Do not let anyone in."

"Can't I come with you?" Nadja asked. She felt a cold tingling at the base of her spine at the thought of being left alone.

"No. If they can just come and take our men and children away . . ." She grabbed Nadja's shoulders and stared into her face. "You must stay and hide. Listen to me. Do not go out. Do not open the door. No matter what. I will bring your brother and father home."

Nadja smelled lavender on her mother's neck as they hugged.

Then her mother stuck her head out the side of the door and looked both ways before she snuck away.

Time passed so slowly, as if it were unconcerned with what was happening. Minutes became hours that became days. Nadja lost herself in it. Couldn't be sure how time moved. Or maybe this was how time always behaved?

Nadja busied herself by looking out different windows of the house, peering through a tiny sliver drawn from a curtain. Cars slept. The town was deserted. Occasionally she heard the gunshots. But again, they seemed far away, like in a dream.

The rapid knock at the door startled Nadja from her place at the kitchen window. It was the one spot that gave her the greatest access to the street. She crept on hands and knees across the wooden floor to the base of the door. She put her ear up against it. The knock came again.

"Nadja?" A woman's voice, strained. "Nadja?"

Her mother had said not to open the door, but she was going crazy. And something in the way this woman said her name sounded familiar.

Nadja unlocked the latch, and Mrs. Hrženjak, a friend of her mother's, shoved herself inside. Nadja shut the door after her.

"I saw your mother," Mrs. Hrženjak panted.

"Where?"

"She . . . the soldiers have her. They are not letting her go. She went to Vuk Karadžić, the school where they've taken the men. She was brought inside. There are screams coming from there. Oh, there are screams." She put her hands over her ears.

Nadja grabbed ahold of Mrs. Hrženjak and shook her. "What do you mean she's at the school? What do you mean?"

But Mrs. Hrženjak cried, and Nadja's blood froze.

"Liar! Why do you say such things?"

"Nadja. Listen. Here." She took some pastries and cans and an apple out of her pocket. "This is what I could grab in the short time." She placed the food in Nadja's hands. "Take it."

Nadja backed away from her. The food dropped to the floor. The apple rolled, revealing a brown spot.

"You have to leave. It is . . . The world has gone mad." Her eyes darted around the room. "Do you have any money? Anything valuable to trade?"

Nadja watched the woman look through drawers. Watched another's hands on her mother's jewelry—jewelry that the soldiers had missed. She held up a silver necklace, the one with the heart and the petals inside.

"This would work."

"Put that down."

"Child, I'm trying to help you," Mrs. Hrženjak said.

"Not the necklace."

Nadja held out her hand for it. Mrs. Hrženjak dropped it into her palm. Nadja placed the necklace around her own neck.

"Collect what you can. Anything. Stay hidden," Mrs. Hrženjak said. "I'll come and check on you in a couple of days. I wish I could do more, but they are—they are moving so fast. I fear even coming here . . . but Maja was my friend. You know this, Nadja." Her eyes were wide and pleading. "You know that I would never want anything to happen to her. You know that I don't support this. You know that . . ." She started crying again.

Suddenly Nadja hated her.

"Get out of here." Nadja opened the door.

"Listen to me, Nadja—the mountains. Flee to the mountains!"

Nadja pushed her out and locked the door again. Why were they bringing men to the primary school? What did she mean, there was screaming? Nadja steeled herself against tears. This was not a time for crying. Or running. Her mother had said to stay, but what if Mrs. Hrženjak was right? What if they had Nadja's whole family? What were they going to do to them?

Nadja went to the kitchen and put the goods from Mrs. Hrženjak on the counter. She made a quick assessment of her food situation. The cupboard contained dozens of cans of vegetables and beans and tomatoes. A couple jugs of water that her father had stocked up recently were on the floor next to the refrigerator. There was a small pile of wood still. If she rationed, she had enough to wait it out for a week, maybe even more.

A week was an eternity. Nadja couldn't imagine this lasting more than a week. In a couple of days, everything would be sorted out. Her parents and brother would be returned. Apologies would be made.

Thunder and rumbles sounded in the distance.

Pop. Pop. Pop. Pop.

All day Nadja went from room to room and looked out the window. She was careful not to be seen by anyone. At one point some soldiers stopped their truck on the street. She heard the brakes squeal and the tires. They kicked a man out of the vehicle and drove off. He lay in a heap. Soon a woman ran out of her house and helped him to his feet. The side of his face bled from a wound. His clothes were ripped. He held his side with one of his arms.

The situation sickened Nadja.

The waiting, the not knowing, all rose to a crescendo. A symphony of terror and fear played on repeat in the darkness of her house and mind. How would she not go mad?

Nadja slept in her parents' bed again that night. She tried to ignore the sounds that came. The yelling. The doors. The crashing.

Tap. Tap.

She heard the sound and traced it to her bedroom window.

Again. *Tap. Tap.*

Marko?

Nadja crawled to her window and peered down to see him. He brought a finger to his lips. She opened the window, and he climbed inside. He crashed into her and held her so tightly she couldn't breathe.

"Are you hurt?" he said, pulling away from her. His eyes scanned her face, her neck, her body, looking for any and all injuries.

"No," she said. "But my family." She choked on a sob. "They came and took my father and brother away."

"When?"

"Two days ago. My mother went to find out where they had been taken, but she has not come back. She told me not to leave the house. A neighbor told me they have taken her too. They are at the school."

"Come away from the window."

They lay down in her bed and faced each other. He kissed her and told her that he was scared.

"Everyone is crazy. Paramilitaries are driving all Muslims out. My father says we must fight for our people and rid the land of Muslims because this is Serb land. This group, the Avengers, they are . . . They beat and torture the men. But they aren't even asking them anything." He stopped. "They are just killing people," he whispered.

Nadja saw the man's head open like a melon on the street. She saw her father and brother forced into the truck. She gave in to her fear and began to cry.

"Do you think they are torturing my family?"

"No," Marko said, but he wouldn't look her in the eyes. "No, your family will be safe. Your dad is respected. A teacher. Why would they harm him?"

Marko rolled onto his back. Nadja lay her head on his shoulder and crossed her arm over his chest.

"I have heard a plan. You will not believe it. I did not, but they will do it. I have seen . . ." His voice cracked. "They will round up the women. Young ones. Pretty. Put them in the spa."

Nadja had been to the spa before. It was a tranquil place to have beauty and massage treatments just outside of town. But the way Marko talked about it now, she knew it was no longer a place for beauty. Nadja did not ask Marko why they would want the women.

"I will not let them take you," he said. "You understand."

"Yes," she whispered.

"I will get you out of here. I will find a way."

· · · · ·

Nadja pulled her hair back into a ponytail, and with the large blue-handled scissors first, she cut off the length in one lob. She then grabbed hold of sections and cut them one by one. Even with her hair the shortest she had ever had it, above her ears, she still looked too much like a girl. Too pretty to be a boy.

She found her dad's razor in the bathroom. She set it on number two and buzzed the sides and front. Marko helped her with the back.

He stood next to Nadja as she stared at her reflection.

"Good," he said. "You look like a boy."

Nadja looked nothing like herself.

She looked like death.

July 17

AS I READ the last lines, my heart breaks. I sit in stunned silence, the light slowly fading from my room. I get up and turn on a lamp and note how the darkness cannot occupy the same space as the light.

I've always known my mother survived a war, but her words give me a glimpse into her heart and the suffering she's had to endure. I see now that because of what she went through, she is broken and scarred in ways that I am not. But I also know that I carry my own scars, my own brokenness. And if we continue to live and act from this place of hurt, there will never be healing.

I read her words again. Absorb all their pain and longing.

How would I feel if I'd been through what she has? Would I be able to come back from such things?

I need to see her. To tell her that I get it. That she might not be able to love me the way that I want, that she may never be able to let me in. But that I can choose to love her anyway, even if I get nothing in return.

It's late when I leave for the hospital. I write Dad a note telling him where I'm going and that I'll be back soon. I take Mom's car.

"Mom," I whisper.

She opens her eyes.

My eyes well with tears.

"Zara," she says, alarmed.

"I'm okay," I say, wiping my eyes. "Sorry, I didn't mean to scare you. Just glad you're doing better."

"Still in *bolnica*." She shifts in the hospital bed.

We are alone in the room. I notice she's holding the prayer beads.

"Can I do your hair today? And maybe some makeup?"

She starts to wave the idea away, but I grab her hand.

"Please, Mom. Let me do this for you."

I brush Mom's hair as gently as I can, working around the staples and the part where they shaved. She closes her eyes as I apply some blush and draw her brows in her usual medium brown. I add mascara. For the first time since Mom's been in the hospital, she looks more like herself.

"Done," I say. I hold up my phone to her like a mirror.

Her eyes linger on where they operated. And now it is her turn to have tears.

"It's okay, Mom," I say. "The hair will come back. No one will see. Look, I had to be stitched up too."

I turn around and lift up my shirt to show her my back. I feel her fingers touch the wound.

"See how it's healing." I pull down my shirt and face her. "My cheek too."

"*Zao mi je, Zara,*" she says. "Didn't protect you."

"Mom. There's no way you could have. It was an attack."

She stares at me and then through me to some place in the past. "Like before. All over again." Her fingers squeeze the beads.

I wait for her to say more, but she doesn't.

I take a pile of photos out of my bag. "Hey, I brought some pictures for you."

It's difficult for her to hold all of them, so I sit next to her on the bed and pass them to her one at a time. Many are of Benny and me as kids. She has trouble remembering who people are and what we were doing. I walk her through each picture, helping to restore the memory, the story of us.

I give her my favorite picture, the one where she's at the beach with Dad. The one where she's smiling with her head thrown back, mid-laugh.

"*Bio je to dobar dan,*" she says. "Was a good day."

"Yeah? Why?"

Her eyes well up, and she says, "You move for first time."

I stare down at the picture. So many times I've looked at her in the photograph. I've tried to guess at what made her so happy. I never guessed that it was me. That she was already pregnant with me.

I wipe my eyes again. When did I become such a crier? When I look over at Mom, she is crying again too.

"Mom, your prayer beads . . ."

She looks down at her hands, and something in her face changes. Like she's just now realized what it means that she has them, that I left them for her. She looks back up at me, then turns away for a moment, and I brace myself for her anger or indifference. But she doesn't say anything.

"I'm sorry. I didn't mean to pry. It was right after the bombing, and I was looking for . . . I don't know. Something of you I could hold on to, I guess. It seems like a really special box."

She lies there, still quiet, looking down and touching each bead, one by one.

I take another risk. "Maybe I can bring it to you?"

I don't tell her that I've already had the pages of her letters translated. I'm scared that'll make her angry, like I've overstepped a boundary. I could explain that I thought she might die and I just needed to know. But it feels like we're making progress. I don't want to mess that up. So there's no way I can tell her about the picture of her I found at the Boston exhibit either.

She closes her eyes and soon drifts back to sleep.

I stare at the photo of her and Dad in my hands. Study her face, the joy, the light in her eyes, and try to let it sink in that all of that's for me.

July 20

EACH DAY MOM gets stronger, escaping from the deep dark place she'd been in. Her mind is still a little fuzzy at times, but her English is getting better. Dad says it's because of my time with her. I tell him about the box of hers I found. He tells me she shared it with him long ago. But he was just as surprised as I was about the picture at the gallery. I'm still waiting for the woman to get back to me on that. It's only been a couple of days, but it feels like forever.

We take turns sitting and being with Mom. Even Benny stays for longer chunks of time now, since seeing him makes Mom so happy.

I'm sitting at her bedside when she asks me about the prayer beads. I'm surprised at how much I miss them. How often my hands still search for them when I feel the need to pray. The rhythm and ritual and peace they gave me. Maybe I'll buy my own.

"Where did you find?" Mom says, touching them with her strong hand.

"The box," I say, "remember? I found it in your room?" Has she forgotten our conversation about me finding it?

I watch her face for a moment of recognition, and she nods ever so slightly.

"I brought it for you. Would you like to see?"

I place the box on her bed next to her good arm.

Her eyes widen as she touches the outside of it gently, but her hands have trouble with the ribbon—lingering effects from the coma, in addition to her slippery memory. On her good days, she can sit up and talk and practice moving her legs. On her bad days, she needs someone to help her use a spoon. Today is in between.

"Here, let me get that. It's tricky." I untie the ribbon for her.

She looks inside and is quiet for some time.

"I wrote these during the war." She holds up one of the letters addressed to Marko, her hand with the IV line in it shaking.

I wait for her to say more, but she doesn't. She's off somewhere, remembering.

"Long time ago . . ."

"Do you think you could maybe tell me about some of it? Like maybe, this . . . Who are these people in the picture?"

"This is my mother, my father and my brother, Benjamin." She giggles, taking me aback. "This day I was so mad. *Vidiš? Moje lice izgleda kao da sam pojela limun.*" She puckers her lips and scowls like the girl in the photo.

"Why? Where were you?"

"I wanted to be with Marko, but my dad wanted the family together."

"Who was Marko?"

"My boyfriend."

"And this one?" I ask. It's the one of just her, on the bridge.

"Marko. He was always trying to get me to pose. The bridge is beautiful, yes?"

"Yes." But I've read the letters; I know what happened on that bridge. How can Mom still find it beautiful?

"I was seventeen."

"My age."

"Really?" She looks at me, trying to find something.

I stiffen. I know her mind is far from healed. Is it possible that she doesn't recognize me? Could she think she's been talking to a friend all this time?

"*Zar je proslo toliko godina?*"

"What, Mom?"

"How'd I get so old?"

She looks back at the photograph of her teenage self.

"This was my last best day in Višegrad. This was before my life ended."

"What were you doing?"

"Posing for Marko. As usual. He was like you. Good photographer."

I sit up a little straighter on the seat next to her bed. It's the first time Mom has acknowledged me being a photographer, let alone a good one.

"Always clicking, clicking the camera. He wanted to be professional, like you. You remind me so much of him. The way you are with your camera. How you see the world."

My breath catches as though the wind has been knocked out of me, and suddenly, something else comes into focus. All this time, I thought Mom didn't support my photography, my dreams of becoming a photographer. I had no reason to think there was more to the story. I realize now that maybe in some way, she still connects it to Marko. Like it's a trigger for sadness that she only knows how to express in anger. It doesn't make her behavior right, but it gives me an understanding and something more, deeper, instead of just hurt.

Mom keeps talking. "That night we hung out on the steps with some friends until the old women yelled at us to be quiet." She smiles and closes her eyes. "There was music. We danced in the street. He was a good dancer."

I can't imagine my mom dancing.

"Sounds like a great day," I say.

"Yes."

Mom hands the picture back to me. I wonder what she would think if she knew it was in some exhibit in Boston. Would she be happy or angry? Before the bombing, I would have guessed angry, but now I'm not so sure. Maybe I should call the woman at the gallery again. Leave another message along with the other two I've already left.

"I'm tired, Zara."

"Okay, Mom. I'll let you sleep."

I listen to her breathing as she drifts off to sleep. I wonder what she dreams now.

"God," I say, reaching out to touch the beads still in her hand, "keep the bad dreams away."

That night, I call Joseph. We talk for almost an hour about everything and nothing. I'm beginning to learn his speech patterns.

How his voice rises and falls. How he holds his breath a little before speaking sometimes. How he asks me questions and makes me feel like he really wants to know me.

I go to sleep with the same prayer I said for Mom, and for the first time in a while, I don't fear the dreams that may come.

July 21

THE NEXT DAY, after I spend some time with Benny in the morning, I ride with Dad to the hospital and try to continue my conversation with Mom.

"What was it like growing up in Višegrad?" I ask.

Mom shrugs. "We were regular teenagers. In the summers we swam in the river. We went to cafés at night. We got dressed up and had dances. We had sports. I loved my town."

"Did you have a best friend?"

"Uma," she says. "She was like your Audrey. We were always together. She was really good at sewing and designing clothes. My mom taught her how to make jewelry."

"Your mom made jewelry?" I ask.

She points to the necklace with the heart from the box. "This is one of her pieces." I remove it and place it in her open hand. The other hand is closed. She'll need physical therapy to help her be able to unclench her fist on her own. "Mama was the best jewelry maker in eastern Bosnia."

I continue to ask Mom questions, prodding her along. She doesn't need much. It's like a dam has been broken. I learn about her brother, Benjamin, how he loved superheroes and swimming and soccer. He sounds a lot like Benny, except for the soccer part. My grandfather, a math teacher in the high school, who was well respected. He taught her how to shoot and fish. I learn that my grandmother had small hands and loved birds.

"I used to play piano," Mom said.

"Really?" I've never seen Mom play piano in my life, even though we have one. I took lessons when I was little.

"Yes. I was going to study music in Sarajevo. But then . . . the war."

There's another question I've been dying to ask. "Mom, were you in love with Marko?"

Mom takes the prayer beads in her good hand. She avoids my eyes. And I regret asking her. I've pushed too far.

"I was, yes." She looks up toward the ceiling, stares at something I can't see. "It was so long ago now."

I stare at the picture of him and Mom together. I feel like crying. He was so young, so full of promise. So was she.

"Can you tell me about the war, Mom?"

"It's . . . it's very difficult," she says, and lowers her eyes.

I'm quiet next to her, listening to the sound of the beads rolling between her fingers. Waiting.

And then she lifts her head. Her eyes vibrant, the color of mine. "What do you want to know?"

"Everything," I say.

1994
Summer
Sarajevo
BiH

EVERYONE WAS ASLEEP, except for Nadja. In the morning they would leave Sarajevo, possibly forever. The family was anxious, even Dalila, at what the next steps would be for them. But Nadja didn't feel the same. Everything had already been taken from her. Lying there awake, Nadja wondered why her ghosts had all chosen now to revisit her. Maybe it was because she was about to begin another life, and they wanted to be sure she'd take them with her. So they sat with her all night, feeding her the memories she had tried so hard to forget.

Just two years ago in Višegrad, Marko left without waking Nadja. She had felt him stir next to her, run his fingers lightly across her cheek, kiss her softly on the forehead. She had heard him walk across the floor, put on his shoes and go out the window. She'd pretended to be asleep.

He left her a note on her desk.

Stay indoors. I will be back when I have a plan. I love you. Marko.

Nadja walked to Benjamin's room. His bed was made. She opened a notebook on his dresser. Page after page of his drawings. She hugged the book to her chest.

She touched a family photo on the wall. The four of them—with her parents sitting in the middle and the children on both sides. All four of them smiled. Nadja's mom had hated her own permed hair, but the photo session had already been scheduled. Her father had a mustache. Nadja was twelve. Benjamin was six.

Nadja left and stood in the living room. She waited. She went to the kitchen. Stood with her hand on the counter. She found peanut butter. She didn't put wood in the oven. She didn't light any candles. She didn't do any of these things for fear that someone might smell or see and come looking for the origin. Besides, there was enough light seeping in through unknowable cracks.

Instead, this is what Nadja did: she walked from room to room and stood. Each time she hoped maybe she had missed something. That maybe her father would be sitting at his desk in the corner. Maybe her brother would be drawing in his book. Maybe her mother would be leaning against the counter, making a list of what she needed to get at the store. But there were no maybes.

She inhabited a home full of ghosts.

She tried to read. She tried to rest. She tried to clean. But mostly she tried not to think about what might be happening. She pushed away what Marko had said, dismissing his words and sending them off like little puffs of smoke.

When it got dark outside, Nadja still didn't light any candles. She sat in the darkness, naming each shadow so she wouldn't fear it. She played a game like she used to with Uma when they were kids. They would lie on their backs and call the clouds into shape. She would point and say, "Lily," and the cloud would transform into the flower. Uma would say, "Car," and the cloud would shift again.

Nadja said, "Rabbit," to an especially large shadow cast against the closet door. It shrank down into a little rabbit like the ones that lived in the grass and hills and came out at dusk. Like the ones she used to try to catch.

Nadja heard some commotion outside. Gunfire. Shouts. She huddled against the wall of her parents' bedroom. It was the room farthest away from the front door. Or maybe she should be in the basement, she thought. But the basement was cold and stank, and in the end hadn't saved them earlier, so why should it now?

There was the opening and shutting of a door and then a vehicle driving by. She heard the faint sound of music. An accordion played a happy dance song.

Nadja listened for a while to all the night sounds, taking no comfort in any of them.

When the tap came at her window again, Nadja was ready.

She tossed her bag that contained some clothes, photos, her old stuffed bear and Benjamin's sketchbook to Marko and climbed out the window. He went first, making sure no one was around. He put his finger to his lips, telling her not to talk, but he didn't need to do that. She didn't dare speak; she was terrified of everything the darkness threatened to expose.

Marko led her through the deserted streets. The lights were off in every home. In the distance, she saw the ends of cigarettes bouncing in the air, a group of men huddled together. She and Marko avoided them.

Down by the water, Nadja saw soldiers on the bridge.

Marko led her past the famous writer's house and down the side, following a small footpath along the water. The sound of squealing brakes made them stop and duck down behind the bushes. A truck parked at the start of the bridge, only about fifty meters from where they hid. Soldiers ordered the people standing in the truck bed out. They yelled at them to move and waved guns.

The soldiers lined them up against the stone rail of the bridge. Even in the darkness, Nadja recognized her father right away. He was tall and stood out amongst the others. Her mother and her brother were on either side of him. It had been two days since she had seen them all. She began to rise, but Marko pulled her back down next to him. Nadja heard the voices then. They were pleading with the soldiers. Her father's voice.

"Please, what have we done? What is our crime? Let my wife and son go. They have done nothing."

The whole town seemed to be holding its breath from the banks up into the hills, both sides of the river listening.

Then, in reply, one soldier raised his gun and began shooting.

From her spot in the bushes, Nadja saw her father's body fall, slumped over the rail. Her mother and brother fell in a heap to where she couldn't see them. One woman screamed and screamed. A soldier slit her neck with his knife, silencing her. Marko's hand covered Nadja's mouth so she wouldn't scream out too. He made her turn away from the bridge, but she could hear the bodies. The splash they made as they were pushed over the rail and into the Drina.

Twelve splashes. Twelve bodies. Three Nadja had known.

Nadja shook and thrashed underneath Marko. Marko had to use the weight of his entire body to hold her down. She started crying and moaning.

"Please, Nadja. Please, shhh," Marko said. "They will hear you."

At that threat, Nadja stopped. She looked at Marko and nodded, and he released her mouth. He had tears in his eyes as they waited until the truck left, then Marko helped Nadja back up. They kept moving away from the bridge.

Nadja followed Marko, moving only because of her primal desire to stay alive, simply because she was a living being. Otherwise she would have stopped. She would have dropped, already dead. Her body next to her father's and mother's and brother's.

"We cross here," Marko whispered.

Marko waded into the river, pulling Nadja along behind him. The water was freezing, and Nadja struggled. The numbness she now felt outside matched her insides.

Marko wrapped his arm around her stomach and swam for the two of them. Their heads barely poking above the water. He had always been a good swimmer. He was on the swim team and competed every year in the huge swimming competitions held in the city. He even traveled to other cities. Nadja would watch him, marvel at how strong he was. At how he could swim for hours and never tire.

The current was strong. Nadja felt Marko strain against it. She wanted to tell him that it was okay. That he could let her go. She could join her family underneath in the deep, drifting down the swift waters.

She began to see them next to her. Her father floated on his back. His eyes were closed. His face pale in the moonlight. Her mother was there too. Her beautiful brown hair fanned out from her head, floating on top of the water like a fairy. Her brother came next. His eyes open because he loved the night sky. He told her that in his comic, his hero had defeated all the Serbs. His hero had swooped down upon the bridge and blasted them all with lasers that came from his fingers. He had been meticulous, splitting the soldiers in two, cutting off heads and freeing them all. How wonderful it was out tonight, he said to her as he floated by. He wondered why she was swimming. She should just float along. It was so easy to just lie there and let the current take you.

Nadja tried to touch them, the bodies, but her hands found only darkness, liquid. It was thick and smelled like rust and death. She began to panic and slipped under. The blood water, heavy and sticking to her, dragging her down. She felt hands on her, and she tried to break free from them, but they were strong.

Marko's hands pulled her up and pushed her toward the bank. She climbed out of the river, coughing because of the water she had swallowed. She threw up on the small pebbles that dug into her palms and knees. Marko patted her back. "You all right? We have to walk a little more."

"The blood. I can't get the taste of blood out of my mouth."

He stared at her with worry, but he helped her to her feet and led her into the woods. At the base of a large tree, he said, "I'll be back. Wait for me."

Nadja clung to him, not wanting him to leave her alone.

"It's okay. I have to see if he's here." And with that, he ran off.

Nadja leaned against the thick tree. Her teeth chattered, and she shook, and though she should have felt cold, she wasn't. She held her knees to her chest and tried not to think of her family. She tried not to think of poor Benjamin.

She heard rustling and was glad that Marko was back. She never wanted to be alone again. She stood up and went to the sound, but it was not Marko. It was the green-fatigued back of a soldier. She froze when she saw him, but it was too late; he'd heard her.

She bolted, running she didn't know where, because she didn't really know where she was, but still she ran. The leaves stirring and breaking beneath her.

"Hey!" the man said, and chased after her.

He was upon her quickly. She was no match for his speed. He grabbed her by the arm and spun her around to face him.

"Where are you going?" he asked, but she wouldn't answer him or look him in the face.

"What's your name?"

When she didn't answer, he grabbed her head and forced her to look up at him.

"Name?"

"Nadja," she said. Her voice cracked like the old forest floor underfoot as she realized her mistake too late. She'd shaved her head for nothing. She'd given her real name by accident.

"A girl?" He pulled tighter. "Surname."

She gave him a fake name, hoping that hearing a Croat one would appease him.

"Croats, Muslims, you all smell the same." He kneed her in the gut. She doubled over in pain. He punched her in the face, and she fell to the ground. Her body contracted into a fetal position without her even telling it to. He kicked her. The taste of blood came into her mouth. This time it was her own.

"You want me to kill you?" he said.

She didn't answer him. She couldn't. But if she could have, she would have said yes.

He pulled her up and turned her over. With one hand, he pressed her face into the dirt. The leaves were broken pieces of glass cutting into her cheek. She heard him doing something behind her, fumbling. She didn't know. She caught a glimpse of light floating. And then another. And another. Tiny orbs. Fireflies. Early for this time of year. Their light made her think of her mother because of how beautiful she looked in the shiny earrings Nadja had made her for Eid this year. Small gold hoop earrings with green beads. Nadja had surprised her. Her mother had beamed with pride at the skill.

Had she worn the earrings when she went to look for her father and brother? What had her father been wearing? Nadja couldn't remember. Something he normally taught in? That black button-down with his trademark tie? Benjamin had on his favorite shirt, the one with the Superman emblem.

Huh, she thought as she felt her pants being pulled and tugged down over her bottom and scrunched up at her ankles. She'd just realized they took Benjamin before he had a chance to put on any shoes. She'd have to go home and get him his shoes. How could he walk around outside without his shoes? He would ruin the bottoms of his feet. Get sick. She had to find a way to bring him his shoes.

A cracking thud, like a bat hitting a gourd, sounded. Something heavy slumped on top of her. Nadja was still thinking about Benjamin's shoes as the body rolled off her and landed at her side. She was picked up. Her name said over and over. Hands cupped her face. She stared into Marko's eyes. They were dark and wet with tears. He hugged her to him.

Marko? Nadja thought. *How did he get here?*

The soldier lay facedown in the dirt beside them, unmoving.

Marko pulled Nadja's pants back up, gently. He wiped away the blood from her nose and mouth with his shirt. He examined the cuts to her face.

"Nothing broken," he declared, but she did not believe him.

Everything was broken.

Nadja winced when he helped her stand. She bent over and threw up, which made it even worse for the pain in her side. It hurt so bad, even to breathe.

Marko swore and kicked the solder twice, stomped on his face. He reached into the soldier's boot and pulled out a knife. He then took the rifle and pistol from him as well. He aimed the gun at the soldier's head. His hand shook. He was crying.

Marko lowered the gun and stuffed it in the back of his jeans. He picked up Nadja like she was a small child and carried her the rest of the way.

Later, Nadja was forced to take a few sips from a water bottle held to her lips. A woman washed her face with a wet rag and kept whispering soft murmurs to her, like she was her mother. Nadja became confused. She didn't know where she was and pictured her mother there with her and clung to the woman, crying.

After a few moments, another voice said, "Now. Quickly."

Dark figures moved around her. Marko picked her up and placed her in the trunk of a car.

"I love you," Marko said. "I'm sorry, but this is the only way through. It will be dark, but you can breathe. You are safe in here. Try to sleep. I will see you soon."

Even though he kissed her softly, it hurt and stung as his sweat and tears met the cuts on her face. He put headphones on her ears and placed a Walkman in her hands. "Close your eyes. Listen to this. Think of me." He pressed Play and shut the trunk.

Nadja felt the car start and move along the bumpy dirt road. She listened to a love song. She didn't need to close her eyes because the black was river deep. She let the music and the darkness wash over her, swallowing her up.

She never saw Marko again.

IT'S BEEN FOUR days since I brought Mom her box. Since then, I've learned that after Marko helped my mom find passage to Sarajevo, he was killed. She didn't find out until years later that he'd been shot, that he never made it out of Višegrad.

I've learned about my grandparents. How Mom used to do fashion shows with her friend Uma, how her brother, my uncle, liked to draw. Of course some things are still too hard for her to talk about, but I can see she's trying. She's slowly regaining more and more command of her speech, too, and beginning physical therapy.

We're sitting and talking in her hospital room when my phone buzzes.

"Hello?"

"Hello, may I please speak with Zara Machado?"

"Yes. This is she."

"Hi, this is Rosa, from Gallery 57."

My heart stops. "Oh, hi," I say.

"So, I made some calls, and I was able to track down the source of that photo you expressed interest in. You're never going to believe this, but your source is actually in Manhattan. I didn't feel that it was appropriate to give out your information. But I have a phone number if you would like it."

"Okay, yeah, let me . . ." I look around for something to take down the name and number with. "Just a second." I grab a napkin left on a tray of food and a pen from the bedside table. "Ready."

I take down the number and notice Mom beginning to doze off.

"Thank you so much," I say quietly.

"You're welcome."

I sit there for a while watching my mom sleep, napkin in hand.

"I'll be back, Mom," I tell her, just in case she can hear me.

I find my way to the hospital garden, where I can have a private conversation.

I dial the number and hold the phone gently to my cheek. My breaths come quicker with each ring.

"Hello?" a woman answers.

"Hello. Um, this is Zara Machado. I got your number from this woman who works at a gallery in Boston, and well, I know this is going to sound a little strange, but I recognized a photo of yours in an exhibit by Klema. The one of the girl by the bridge in Višegrad. Um, I'm her daughter. I was told that you were the one who actually donated the picture."

Silence on the other end.

"Hello?" I say again. "I'm sorry, is this—"

"Is this really Nadja's daughter?" the woman asks before I can even finish.

"Yes," I say.

And she begins to cry.

DALILA IS SHORTER than me. Her brown hair is as straight as a blade of grass over at Baker's Beach. Her lips are red, and she paints her eyebrows in smooth brown arches like my mom's. She's dressed in all black—black T-shirt, black jeans and black boots.

I pass the original photo across the table toward her. We're sitting outside a coffee shop in Providence.

"I found it in a box, packed away at the top of her closet," I say.

She breathes deeply. "I used to see Nadja looking at photos late at night when she thought I was sleeping. She'd hold them and sometimes cry." Dalila's eyes water. "My friend Klema, the artist who put the exhibit together, asked me if I had any photos from the war, and he was especially drawn to Nadja's. I made a copy of it for him. Marko loved to take her picture, and there were a couple of her in this one pose. She gave me the photo one night so I would remember her. That was when she thought she was dying from an infection."

"An infection?"

She shakes her head. "It ended up being nothing to worry about."

"Were you close?"

The woman takes a sip of her coffee before saying, "We were inseparable during the war. When your mother came to us from her village in eastern Bosnia, she was mute. Her head was shaved so close there were nicks in her scalp. She was dirty and had cuts across her arms from the barbed wire she had crawled under to cross at the airport. I was scared of her. I thought, 'What could have happened to her?' But my mother and father said that she was my sister now. I only had a brother, but I always wanted a sister. So I helped to feed her the rice and little food we had. I helped bathe her. Gradually she got better."

I lean forward, her words feeding a hunger inside.

"Mom never talks about it—the war. Until a few days ago, I didn't even know anything about her time in Višegrad before the war either."

"That sounds like your mother. It was her way of coping. Everyone does what they have to do to survive and then you have to live with it. I do not fault her for this. We all dealt with our displacement differently. Some needed to cut ties completely, while others have clung so tight to their Bosnian identity. Your mother was not a clinger."

"Are you . . . I mean, do you cope the same way?"

"Not now. Now I can talk about it without falling apart. But at first, yes. After the war, no one wanted to talk about it. It was like everyone wanted to just go back to living a normal life. But what is normal after such a thing? After neighbor turns on neighbor. After you lose a brother. You stare into the heart of humanity and see a darkness." She smokes. "But there is also a light. And this light chases away the dark. There were many people who helped us. And then when my family eventually came to the States, I remember all of the people who reached out and befriended us, who helped me with English and helped me find a job. It was not easy, but I made good friends."

But something she says confuses me. "Did you come to the States with my mom?"

"I did, yes."

"So then why hasn't Mom ever mentioned you and your family before?"

Dalila leans back, turns her head to the left and lets out a long plume of smoke. She turns and looks at me.

"I think for Nadja, being around my family was what saved her in Sarajevo, but in the States, she needed to start completely over. At first I was very hurt. I didn't understand why she wanted to leave us. We resettled in Chicago because my father had a cousin already there who could vouch for us. Nadja came with us, but then she wanted to go to school in Boston. She had read about the city and became obsessed with going. It was difficult for my parents to let her. For me too. But now I am not angry. I have my own kids and husband. It is a good life. I am happy."

Dalila says she's happy, but it seems like a sad happy. Maybe it's because I'm asking her to talk about the past.

"When was the last time you saw my mom?" I ask.

"Almost twenty years ago. Just after she left Chicago. I wanted to stay in touch, and your mother knew how to reach me, but I never heard from her again after that."

"Wow," I say. I guess my mom has always used silence—used

distance—to protect herself from pain. I have no words. I'm just so grateful that finally, through everything, Mom and I have found a way to talk to each other. I start to tear up.

"How is Nadja now?" Dalila asks.

I take a deep breath. I explained to Dalila when we spoke on the phone that we had been in the terrorist attack in Rhode Island. She insisted on coming up from Manhattan the next day. Dad thought it might be good for Mom too. That given all we've been through, a connection to her past might bring more healing and comfort than harm.

"She's getting better," I say. "But she's not fully recovered."

Dalila nods. "I was hoping that I could see her. What do you think?"

An hour later, I'm in Mom's hospital room. This time I'm not alone.

"Mom?" I say as I approach her bed. "Mom, there's someone here to see you."

She slowly opens her eyes.

"You have a visitor, if that's okay."

"Okay," she says.

"You can come in." I speak in the direction of the door to Mom's room.

Mom's eyes open wide in recognition and then surprise as her past walks in.

At first she can't speak. Then, finally, "Dalila?"

Dalila moves toward Mom and sits on her bed.

"Yes, Nadja. I'm here."

Mom smiles and begins to cry as Dalila leans in and kisses her on both cheeks.

"Dalila." Mom says her name again. They speak softly in Bosnian, words meeting and overlapping and becoming laughter.

I stand back watching and am filled with gratitude. Because here is a beautiful picture of love. I remember what Joseph said about love connecting everything, about how love wanted me to find the picture. About love taking something evil and making it good, making it a conduit for healing.

And I suddenly understand something. It's not that the attack needed to happen. Who can explain such a thing? Who can find or understand the reason for suffering? It's more like love would find a way, no matter what happened. Through the good, through the most heinous of acts, love is the greatest weapon against the darkness. Love is always working, always reaching out to find us in the dark and bring us into the light.

I smile and make a mental note to text Joseph. Maybe he was right. And maybe it's not really about religion. Maybe God is love.

I watch Dalila hold Mom's hand and take in this moment as the room swells with this truth and this love, this perfect, simple love.

I take their picture.

I take photo after photo so I'll never forget how this feels.

July 25

THE CHAPEL IS empty except for Joseph. He's sitting straight backed, perfect posture, hands resting on his knees. I enter and sit in the seat next to him. He opens his eyes, notices me and takes out one of the earbuds he's wearing. He gives it to me, then goes back to his position.

A man with a British accent tells me to breathe in through my nose for a count of four and then breathe out through my mouth for a count of four. Joseph's eyes are closed, so I close mine and start to count. I follow the man's instructions, which are to think about the highest point of a mountain, to climb my way to the top and imagine what I see. Feel the wind and the sunshine.

I peek to see if Joseph still has his eyes closed, because a mountain, really? But he does, and his face is so relaxed. I blow out some breath and try to imagine the mountain. And the sun. And the wind. Then the voice tells me to feel the sunlight at the top of my head, the energy of it, and let it begin to travel from my head, to my face, to my shoulders. The voice tells me to let the light scan my body. To bring my awareness to what my body is feeling. And not to judge what I'm thinking or feeling. Just to be aware of what I'm experiencing.

Without warning, the image flies in and I see my mother's naked foot poking out from underneath the rubble.

I open my eyes. My heart's racing. I'm not ready to fully experience that morning again.

The voice tells me to let thoughts and images come into my mind and then to let them go. Just observe them. Let the warmth of the sun hit them. I try to calm myself by taking deep breaths. And since Joseph is still, I try again and close my eyes.

The voice tells me to focus on my breath. To count to ten and then, when I get to ten, to start over. To just keep breathing and think about my breath.

I sense Joseph move next to me, and I suddenly imagine him kissing me. The thought comes fast and makes me blush, which makes my cheek tingle. It distracts me and takes me out of my head because now I'm hyperaware of him next to me. The small hairs on my arm reach out toward his as if there's a magnetic field between us.

The voice tells me to take one last deep breath through my nose and then out through my mouth and then to open my eyes whenever I'm ready.

It takes me a couple of seconds before I am. When I do, it feels strange. I'm not sure if I'm imagining it, but I feel a bit lighter somehow. The mosaics in the room only add a sense of peace and tranquility.

"Well?" Joseph says.

"That was . . . interesting."

"Yeah."

"I mean, I couldn't really focus the whole time, but I can see it as being valuable."

"It takes time to get used to. At first, I could only go three minutes. You went almost five. That's amazing."

A woman enters the chapel, so we get up to talk somewhere else. I notice her eyes are puffy and red-rimmed like she's been crying. I try to send good vibes her way.

Outside the building, we find a place in the shade underneath a tree.

"Grann's getting out today," he tells me.

"Really? That's great."

"Yeah. She's done with this place, she says."

"That means she'll be okay, right?"

He shrugs. "She's still dying," he says, and looks down at the green grass. When he looks back up at me, his eyes are so sad and watery.

"I'm sorry, Joseph."

"Yeah." He puts his hands in the pockets of his jeans. "We're all going to die someday. There's no tragedy in living a long, full life."

"Death is so . . . weird."

He grunts.

"Remember when we first met?" I say it as if it were so long ago and not just a couple of weeks.

"Yeah." He sits, and I join him down in the grass, both of us cross-legged.

"So I've been thinking about what you said—about life and suffering," I say.

"Really," he says.

"Yeah. And if that were all it is—life equals suffering—that'd be pretty sad. Depressing, actually. But you know, you could look at suffering another way. It's more like how you grow and change through it. How you build resilience." I shrug. "Suffering isn't really meaningless, if you look at it that way. I mean, it sucks, don't get me wrong. If I could go back and not be at the farmers market that day, I would. I'm not some sadist. But at the same time, if that hadn't happened, then . . ."

"Then you wouldn't have met me?" he says playfully.

"Thank God for that," I joke, though he's not wrong, and he clearly knows how glad I am we met. "But there's also a deeper understanding and now a bridge to my mom that I didn't have before." I pick at the grass. "It's not easy. I'm still not sleeping all that well, and I'm anxious in crowds, and . . . it's . . . all a process. But it's part of me now. I have no choice but to use it, right? Not just the outside scars, but the ones inside too."

"There's this paraphrase of a quote of Rumi's that says something like, 'The wound is the place where the light enters you.'"

I think about that for a minute. Before, I might have been flippant about the quote, but today, I take out my phone and write it down. I want to remember it. Because I kind of get what that means now. My scars don't have to bring me shame. They can be the places where love, where God meets me too.

"Who's Rumi?"

"A Muslim mystic. I'll send you some of his stuff. I think you'll like it."

"Okay, yeah." I'm curious about what a Muslim mystic would

say, especially knowing more about my own history and family. "That'd be great."

Joseph smiles, but his brow quickly furrows like he's processing something. He takes a deep breath.

"So . . ." He exhales the word. "I'm going to Port-au-Prince."

"Where's that?"

"Haiti. Grann wants to."

"That's great. When?"

"In a few days."

"Nice. I hope you have a good trip." I want to add that when he comes back, we should hang out, but it sounds so lame in my head. Instead I say, "When do you come back?"

"Not sure. Dad's getting me a one-way ticket."

"Oh . . ." I can't hide my disappointment, and Joseph can tell.

"It's not like I'm moving for good or anything. I'm still going to apply to college for next fall. But for now, I'm just taking a year to figure things out."

"Right." I nod, like it's no big deal. "The whole gap year thing."

"Exactly."

But it sucks. We're both quiet for a moment.

"Zara, I keep running through that day with Seb. I can't stop thinking about what I could have done. How I should have stopped him. If I had just reached out. Or even before that. Like if I hadn't suggested we ditch. If we had just gone to school, or if—"

"If you weren't friends. If you'd never met. If you hadn't moved to Providence," I interrupt him. "If we hadn't gone to the farmers market. If Mom hadn't taken too long at every stand."

He looks at me.

"What happened to you is horrible. And I can't even imagine the pain in that, losing your best friend."

He stares at the ground.

"But you lived. And you've been searching for why. I don't know if you're going to find *why*," I say.

He looks up at me and shakes his head.

"I know." He smiles. "By the way, I talked to Seb's parents."

"You did? What happened?"

"It was terrible. His mom started crying. And she told me how she's spent so much energy hating me. How she's blamed me. But then she just pulled me in for a hug, and I cried too. She said she forgave me."

"That's so great, Joseph."

"Yeah. I'm still working on the forgiving myself part."

I nod. "That'll take time, just like everything," I say.

I think about Mom and me, and how forgiveness is part of our story too. How loving someone and being willing to offer forgiveness go hand in hand, and that it's not a one-time thing. I know things between my mom and me will never be perfect. But the next time she says something that triggers past hurt, maybe I'll be better able to make a choice not to let it take me on a downward spiral. Not to close myself off to her. I can make a choice to show her grace. Because Mom has a long journey ahead of her, and she's going to need all the support she can get. We both will.

"So . . . Haiti?" I say.

"Yeah. Grann is talking about all the places she wants to take me, like where she grew up, where my grandfather was born. I've heard all the stories, so it'll be cool to go and see where they happened. And maybe I can volunteer somewhere, make a difference. Go to the tent cities and work."

"That sounds amazing." I would love to be able to travel like that after I graduate. Maybe I will. Take a year off school. Just me and my camera. Follow wherever inspiration leads me.

But a year is a long time. "I'll miss you," I say.

I look down at the ground, suddenly afraid I'm going to cry, which makes me feel stupid.

Joseph leans forward and puts some of my hair behind my ear. I flinch because it's my bad cheek.

He holds my face with both of his hands and kisses me right on my ugly scabs. Then he kisses me on the other side.

"I'll miss you too," he says, and brushes his lips against mine.

1998
Summer
Boston, MA
USA

NADJA STEPPED ONTO the bridge. She was early, so she took her time. The day was beautiful. Not too hot yet. Though the weather report for tomorrow said it was going to be hot and humid, more typical for the time of year. She nodded to others as they passed, as was the custom here.

"Hello," she said to a girl close to her age.

"Hey," she said back.

"Hey," Nadja repeated softly when the girl was out of earshot. She practiced the short breathy clip of the word. Trying to match the accent. Her time in night classes had already given her much of what she needed with English. Thankfully, she knew the base of the language, the conjugation and syntax, having studied it for years at school. But she hadn't come to know the rhythm, the idiosyncrasies that every language possesses and that you only really get to know when living, immersed, in the culture.

Boston was different from Chicago, where she had first resettled with Dalila's family. The syncopation of the words. The inflection. Though both cities shared the affinity for fast speech and a body language that she also had to master reading. Nadja studied all the time. Watching how people said hello. How they said good-bye. How they stood and waited for a train. How they ate their meals. How they hugged without giving kisses. She wanted to assimilate as fast as she could. She didn't want to leave any trace of her being from Višegrad. As far as she was concerned, she was a girl without a country no longer. She would be American. Embrace all of it. It was too painful to look back, so she kept her gaze on the horizon.

When she got to the middle of the bridge, she leaned over to watch the water. It rushed much like it did during certain times of the day. But it wasn't the beautiful Drina. A memory came to her as she stood there. It had been a day just like this one. She had walked with her family across another bridge. A bridge they must have walked across hundreds of times, almost every day of her life.

But this particular memory she had forgotten. It had lodged itself somewhere between *never forget* and *never remember*. And now it assaulted her like memory often does. Without consent. Without regard for feelings. But today, maybe because her guard was down, because she was happy, or because she was on the cusp of another change, she allowed herself to indulge in it.

She hadn't wanted to be there. Something about wanting to go and hang out with Uma. But her parents had insisted that she go with them. They ate at a restaurant, a big deal for them because they rarely ate out, and took a walk where they ended up at the sofa—the seat in the middle of the bridge over the Drina. A group of college students were there—tourists—taking silly pictures of themselves.

Because of the students, Nadja was embarrassed that she

was with her family. The girls wore short shorts and one had a black AC/DC T-shirt on. Nadja had stared at them, unafraid to hide her fascination. With their beautiful long legs and hair and bodies. They were laughing and hugging and free. She wanted to be them. Instead, she was stuck with her embarrassing family.

Her father offered to take their picture. They stood up and got in super close. Smiled wide. How she couldn't wait to be one of them. To get out of this place. Be one of those sophisticated college girls from Sarajevo or Mostar or someplace she'd never even heard of.

Her father gave Benjamin some candy from his pocket, offering some to Nadja too, but she refused. She didn't want him thinking she was happy about anything having to do with this outing. The sunlight lit the Drina, giving the green a sparkle like it was a precious jewel.

Then she saw him. Marko stood a little off to the right, underneath the willow. He held up his hand in recognition. How did he know she would be here? She leaned over the bridge, and he mouthed, *Later?*

She nodded.

The girls offered to take the family's picture. They got together. Nadja's mom, then Benjamin, then Nadja, then her dad. Nadja smiled wide as the girl with the pretty hair and bracelets took her picture. She wasn't thinking of her family. She was thinking of Marko and how he made everything more bearable.

Today on this bridge, Nadja saw him when he was still a ways off. He held up his hand in greeting, and she waved back. She stayed where she was, watching him approach her. His gait revealed his confidence. He wore his standard T-shirt and jeans with a Red Sox baseball hat covering curly dark brown hair. He was everything she was not: confident, funny, easygoing, good with people. She still didn't understand what he saw in her. But in him, she saw a future. She saw a security that she desperately wanted.

And as he got closer, the baby inside moved. Nadja caught her breath. She still wasn't used to the feeling. It was just a tiny flutter. She brought her hand to rest on the right side. There it was again. A small butterfly kiss.

Wonder and fear filled her. This was not what her mother would have wanted. Getting pregnant before marriage. Her mother would have been ashamed. But her mother wasn't here. None of them were. We are all that's left, she told the baby growing within.

There was a time when Nadja, too, had wanted something different for herself.

She closed her eyes and saw his. Deep, dark, looking out at her from behind the camera, gazing down at her as they walked side by side, his arm around her shoulders, or his face inches from her in her bed. His eyes never leaving hers until the lid of the trunk came down. The smell of him, how he filled everything at one time. He had been everything.

Strange how now she couldn't even remember Marko's smell.

The baby moved again. Another small butterfly kiss along her right side.

When Paul found out about the baby, he asked her to marry him. Even though she loved him, she said no at first, not wanting his obligation. He said he loved her, and that this was the best thing to ever happen to him. He wanted her and their baby.

She had to squint a little to see him as the sun shifted and began its slow descent. His gaze never left her.

Paul is a good man, she thought. And she really did care for him. If her mother had met him, she would have approved, eventually. So would her father. Benjamin would have thought of him as an older brother.

Paul was almost within reach.

"Nadja!" he called.

This baby would change her life, give her something to live for. She would be a good mother. She would be like her own and teach her daughter how to be strong and fierce so she would survive in this world. She would know safety here in the States. She would be American, first and foremost, not anything that would bring her harm. And Paul, he would give Nadja love and protection. He would be a good father, a good husband. This was a good choice.

She embraced Paul, and he bent and kissed her.

"I missed you," he said.

"So did I," she said, and buried her face in his neck, taking in his smell. Today it was garlic and rosemary and antiseptic. He must have been cooking something after his rounds.

"Ready?" he asked.

"Ready," she said. And she took his hand. Let him lead her home.

August

I CHOOSE THE photos as if my life depends on it. Slowly. Deliberately, looking for the story in them. This is a story that I have come to learn, and I think it is one that you can only know through experience. I'm trying to give the viewers the perspective, but I know it won't be the same. They won't be able to physically feel how wounds are made, then repaired. How stitches are removed. The itch that is constant. The smell of the washcloth after you've cleaned the area.

They won't be able to touch and feel the raised, swollen skin. They won't know what it's like to speak to someone who is no longer the someone you thought you knew.

But I can tell them the story. I can tell our story through our scars. Of how there is pain and love in the healing.

I've chosen eight photos. I start with the blurred profile of my mom from the farmers market. Then the one of her feet sticking out from under the rubble. The next is my bandaged face in the mirror, followed by a picture of my back and three rows of stitches. One of Mom in a coma—a close-up of the back of her head where they shaved her and had to operate, and the staples they inserted. Another one of my back without the, the one Joseph took at the beach. I'm kind of cheating with that one, but the shot is beautiful with the soft light surrounding my body like a halo. There's a photo of me and Mom holding hands. The last one is a close-up selfie of us lying side by side in her hospital bed.

I show Dad the photos, pausing on the ones of my scars, of Mom's.

There are tears in his eyes. "Z, these are . . . really good. And it's not the quality, because of course you're talented. It's what they say that makes them so compelling. I know I'm biased, but these are some of your best work."

"Thanks, Dad."

He wipes his eyes. "You and your mom have gone through some horrible things, things no one should ever have to experience. But these photos show your strength too. I love this one of you both together."

"Me too."

He smiles.

"You think I should show them to Mom?"

He thinks for a moment. "Maybe not now, but yes. When she is stronger. I think she will love them."

"I hope Mr. Singh likes them."

"He's a fool if he doesn't."

Mr. Singh isn't a fool. The next day in class, he takes my photos and says that he wants to enter them into some contest. He praises me for my bravery at revealing our scars and for not exploiting them. He uses my series as an example to the class, going through the photos one by one and asking if they can tell what techniques I'm using in each and what effect they have.

"So," he asks us, "what's the story here?"

The students throw out different answers.

"We all have scars?"

"Scars alter us in more than appearance; they make us something more, and we connect to others because of them. They don't diminish our lives, but make them richer somehow."

"She and her mom have both been through trauma, and it's the trauma that now bonds them together."

"It's okay to let others know the bad things that have happened to us. And when we reveal those pasts, or those scars, that's how we become close to one another. That's how we grow and heal."

"Scars can be hot," says this guy three rows down, who usually gives snarky comments. He's referring to the beach shot.

I blush. Everyone laughs.

"Zara, can you tell us about the story you wanted to tell?"

I think about the story, what I survived, what Mom survived, and suddenly I'm overwhelmed by it. I stare at the photos. How ugly my back looks. I really tried to bring out the pain in that one. And part of me still feels sad—no, not sad, angry—that I had to go through what I did. But another part of me is proud of myself. Because I survived. And I'm still surviving. I had no idea the amount of strength that I had inside myself.

I think of my mom, how much strength and courage she's had to carry within her every day just to face life head-on like she did after what she went through. And I'm part of this story now too. One of resilience and survival, but also one of . . .

"Love," I say. "It's a story of love."

Mr. Singh nods. "Love is the greatest story we can tell."

Late August

TODAY I GO to Baker's with Audrey. Our last day before school begins. We lay our towels down on the sand. She takes off her shorts and shirt. Her body golden brown from all the lazy days in the Arizona sun. I have on board shorts with a bikini top underneath a yellow T-shirt. As I remove my T-shirt, the cool air hits my back, making my scars tingle.

I look around, wondering if people are staring. But no one is. I reach into my bag for the sunscreen. Dad told me to make sure to cover myself in it, especially my face and back, and reapply more often than I usually would. I start to spray it on the places I can reach.

"Here, let me get your back," Audrey says.

I hand her the sunscreen, and she sprays a steady stream all up and down. It burns a little, but nothing I can't handle.

"Thanks," I say. "Does it look that bad?"

"No."

"Liar."

"It looks like it's healing," she says. "Which isn't bad."

We sit down, and she asks me which magazine I want to start with. I pick *Vogue*. She starts with *People*. Her mom subscribes to all the best magazines.

For lunch, we eat two quahogs and drink Cherry Coke. We talk about our schedules. So far we have three classes together. We plan to make that four by switching to a baking class. Our justification is that we need a no worry or drama class. And since both of us have no idea how to cook, it seems like a good idea. My dad will be thrilled.

We hang out all day, up to the start of the magic hour. The one where the sun is just going down and there's the in-between sky. I take a couple of pictures of the horizon. The light is bluish white against the ocean. I breathe in deep through my nose and let the air out slowly through my mouth.

I touch the new set of prayer beads around my neck, the ones I bought a few days ago.

"Thank you," I whisper to God, who always finds me in the sunsets.

After Audrey drops me off, I hang out with Benny and Mom outside on the porch. Benny plays with a huge pile of Legos strewn on a white bedsheet. Dad is working late, so I order us a pizza. Mom is writing in our journal. We decided to try something that our therapist recommended. We are both seeing the colleague Dad recommended, Dr. Rivera, who specializes in family and trauma counseling. Because some of what we've experienced is too hard for face-to-face communication, she suggested we write each other. In the journal, we can ask questions and answer whichever ones we want to. Mom and I are the only ones allowed to read what's inside. It's our safe space. Our chance to share and understand our story.

I carry the scars of my story like Mom carries hers. But because we are mother and daughter, we also carry them for each other. Dr. Rivera told us that some studies now show that trauma can actually change your DNA. You aren't just altered on the outside or emotionally, but you're forever changed on the inside as well.

What's even crazier is that parents can pass that DNA on to their children. Those children carry inside of them the scarred DNA. I'm not sure what that means exactly, except to say that it doesn't just affect the victim; trauma can affect a lineage.

I think about my lineage. I don't know much about my great-grandparents on either side. Vovo's parents are from Fall River, Massachusetts, his grandparents from Portugal. My gramma's family came from England, Canada and maybe France? My mom's parents and grandparents came from eastern Bosnia. Before that? I'm not sure. But I've absorbed all of them. For better or for worse.

At the table with Mom, I read and reread the postcard Joseph sent me. The picture on the front is a map of Haiti. He has circled the spot where he's living. On the back he's written, *Zara, I am truly home here. I'm even learning Creole. Here's something for you—mwen sonje ou.* Yesterday I looked up the Creole words. *I miss you.*

Mom asks about the postcard, and instead of hiding it from her, I pass it her way. She reads it and pushes it back across the table to me.

"You're his *draga*. This is what we call it."

I roll the word over in my head.

"What does *draga* mean?"

"Sweetheart."

I blush, remembering Joseph's lips on mine. The way he held me at his good-bye. The way he smiled before he left.

I show Mom the photos of Joseph and Flora, but not my favorite one—the one at the beach when he didn't think I was looking. I stare at his profile, remember the texture of his shirt as our arms brushed up against each other when we walked, feel the wet sand between my toes. I smell the salty air. Hear the sound of the waves hitting the shore. But mostly I remember how I feel when I'm next to him, like I am safe and warm and loved.

That memory I keep to myself.

Dad comes home and joins us on the porch a little while later.

"Look! They're back!" Benny yells, and points into the yard. He runs inside the house, darting out after a few moments, a clear glass jar in his hands.

"Fireflies!"

We haven't seen a lot of them this summer. For some reason, fireflies are disappearing, kind of like the bees. I've heard it has something to do with light pollution or pesticides. But I think it's more mysterious than that. I think it's because they're hiding, waiting for just the right moments. We only have to be watching.

It takes a few moments for me to see the tiny bobbing light in the dark. Once my eyes focus, I see another and another.

"There are so many," I say.

"I know. Help me catch them!" he says.

"As long as we release them when we're done."

"Yes! Yes!"

I run into the house and find another jar in the cupboard. In seconds, I join him back outside.

"Quick! There's one behind you!" Benny yells and chases after the light.

I watch him jumping around like a crazy person and laugh. Mom and Dad laugh, too, from their spot on the porch.

And then everything goes dark.

"Where'd they go?" Benny asks, turning this way and that. The jar hangs limp in his hands.

"Benny, shhh," I tell him. "If you just stand still and wait, you'll see them all. They will come to you. Here, watch."

He walks over and stands by my side.

We scan the dark.

"Where are they?" Benny asks.

"Give it a couple more seconds," I say.

"But—"

Then the lights blink all around us like we are inside a large constellation, our own private universe.

"Wow," he whispers.

I glance back at Mom. She's smiling. And I know if someone took a picture of us, they would feel how beautiful this moment is.

"Yeah. Wow," I say.

And I let the light in.

Author's Note

The first time I met a Bosnian refugee was the fall of 1995. I had joined a domestic peace corps (AmeriCorps) and was stationed at Catholic Charities Immigration and Refugee Services in Boston, Massachusetts. I had heard sound bites over the years in college about the war in Bosnia, but I was so insulated. I remember on the news they called it a conflict, not a war. During my time at Catholic Charities, I met survivors and heard the horrors of what they had experienced—from brothers and fathers taken in the night never to be seen again, to being forced at gunpoint from their homes, living years under siege, dodging bullets, facing freezing temperatures and starvation. I felt anger and shame. While I'd been having an idyllic New England college experience, others were dying and suffering.

As I helped to resettle Bosnian refugees, I got to know many of them. We became friends. I hung out at cafés and listened to their stories, watched how steadily their hands rose as they smoked. (And, boy, could they smoke!) They were beautiful. They were kind, laughed easily, even though they had experienced great pain. I spent Easter in the home of a family and ate amazing food and painted beautiful eggs. I had never been to Bosnia, but I felt connected to the Bosnian people in a deep way. They made me feel like family.

In the spring of 2015, almost twenty years since, I traveled to Sarajevo and Višegrad, the cities mentioned in this book, looking for the story. I arrived with an open heart, a little fearful, not even sure of what I was doing. Again, I encountered such hospitality. I thought I might have to look far for signs of the past, but the bullet holes on the buildings as we rode in the taxi from the airport looked surprisingly fresh, almost preserved, as if time had stopped. And as I spoke with people, I realized the memories and wounds of the war were scabbed over, but it didn't take much of a prick to get the blood flowing again.

Besides traveling to Bosnia and Herzegovina, I also did an extensive amount of research for the chapters set in BiH. In addition, I am indebted to *The Body Keeps the Score*, a work about the effects of trauma on the psyche and the body. Any mistakes or inaccuracies are entirely my own.

This story is my attempt to pay tribute to all the Bosnian refugees I met. The experience changed my life. They challenged my worldview, my faith, and helped me grow in empathy toward others. Writing this story is also my act of coming alongside and bearing witness. This, I feel, we all must do.

Thank you,

Carrie Arcos

References

Books

Logavina Street: Life and Death in a Sarajevo Neighborhood by Barbara Demick, Kansas City, MO: Andrews and McMeel, 1996.

The River Runs Salt, Runs Sweet by Jasmina Dervisevic-Cesic, Eugene, OR: Panisphere, 1994.

Sarajevo Marlboro by Miljenko Jergović, translated by Stela Tomasević, NY: Penguin, 1997.

My War Gone By, I Miss It So by Anthony Loyd, NY: Grove Press, 1999.

Love Thy Neighbor: A Story of War by Peter Maass, NY: Vintage, 1997.

The Suitcase: Refugee Voices from Bosnia and Croatia edited by Julie Mertus, Jasmina Tesanovic, Habiba Metikos and Rada Boric, Berkeley, CA: University of California Press, 1997.

Goodbye Sarajevo by Atka Reid and Hana Schofield, London: Bloomsbury, 2011.

Safe Area Goražde: The War in Eastern Bosnia 1992–1995 by Joe Sacco, Seattle, WA: Fantagraphics Books, 2000.

The Body Keeps the Score: Brain, Mind, and Body in the Healing of Trauma by Bessel van der Kolk, MD. NY: Viking, 2014.

Films

For Those Who Can Tell No Tales

No Man's Land

Warriors

Welcome to Sarajevo

Glossary

Alejkumu selam—And upon you, peace.

Allah razi olsun—May Allah (God) bless you.

Bajram šerif mubarek olsun—Blessed celebration of Bajram (the end of Ramadan).

balaclava—Cloth headgear that only exposes part of the face, typically the eyes.

balije—A pejorative term used for Bosnian Muslims.

Baščaršija—Sarajevo's old bazaar and main tourist attraction, and the historical and cultural center of the city.

Bio je to dobar dan—It was a good day.

bokeh—A Japanese word used in photography for elements in the picture that are purposely blurred, or out of focus.

bolnica—Hospital.

Bondye—God (Haitian Creole).

bonjou—Hello (Haitian Creole).

Bosnia and Herzegovina—Commonly referred to as Bosnia or BiH, a country in southeastern Europe located on the Balkan Peninsula.

Bosniak—Another word for Bosnian Muslim.

burek—A meat-stuffed phyllo-dough pastry.

Četnik—A Serbian nationalist guerrilla force that formed during World War II. The term was revived during the early 1990s and used to describe various paramilitary groups that fought for the Bosnian Serb cause.

ćevapi—A grilled dish of five to ten small sausages, usually served with flatbread and chopped onions, sour cream, cheese and salt and pepper.

draga—Sweetheart or dear.

Drina—A 346-kilometer-long international river, which forms a large portion of the border between Bosnia and Herzegovina and Serbia. It is known for its beautiful emerald green color because of the limestone that it runs through.

džezva—Also called a *cezve*, a pot used to make Turkish coffee.

Eid (Eid-ul-Fitr)—The "Festival of the Breaking of the Fast"— Bosnian and Herzegovinian Muslims celebrate with a three-day holiday that marks the end of Ramadan. It involves celebrating with family, exchanging gifts, eating (especially baklava), visiting graves of loved ones and giving to charity. It is a holiday of forgiveness, fellowship, peace and gratitude toward Allah (God). Also referred to as Bajram.

Esselamu alejkum—Peace be upon you. A traditional expression of goodwill among Muslims.

heklanje—A crocheted doily.

imam—The person who leads prayers in a mosque.

Imovina Benjamin—Ne dirajte!—Property of Benjamin—Do not touch!

JNA—The Jugoslovenska Narodna Armija, or Yugoslav People's Army, which was the military of the Socialist Federal Republic of Yugoslavia.

Karadžić, Radovan—A Bosnian Serb politician who served as the President of Republika Srpska during the Bosnian War.

He was found guilty of genocide, war crimes and crimes against humanity.

kiflice—A type of biscuit.

kljukuša—A traditional Bosnian dish made of grated potatoes mixed with flour and water or milk, yogurt and cream, then baked.

kon si, kon sa—So-so (Haitian Creole).

kriminalci—Criminals.

lokumi—Sweet fried pastry.

orevwa—Good-bye (Haitian Creole).

Oslobođenje—Sarajevo's daily newspaper.

papci—Literally, "pig feet," a negative term used to describe people from the country or mountains who are uneducated, equivalent to hillbillies in English.

Pazi Snajper—Danger Sniper.

potkošulja—An undershirt.

rahat lokum—A sweet or dessert, also called Turkish Delight.

Ramadan—A holy month of fasting, the ninth month of the Islamic calendar, observed by Muslims all over the world.

Ramadan Bajram—See Eid.

silla—Seat or sofa.

tespih—Muslim prayer beads.

Tito—Josip Broz Tito (1892–1980), a statesman, communist leader, premier and president of Yugoslavia.

tulumba—A dessert; fried batter similar to churros, soaked in sugar syrup.

Užice Corps—A unit of the JNA that was active in eastern Bosnia.

Vidiš? Moje lice izgleda kao da sam pojela limun—See? My face looks like I've eaten a lemon.

Zao mi je—I'm sorry.

Zar je proslo toliko godina?—Has it been so many years?

Acknowledgments

I began writing this book during my residency at Hedgebrook, so I will start there. Thank you to the women I met and shared my life with during those weeks—the meals, the conversations, the walks. Thank you to Laurel Fantauzzo, who just happened to have a graphic novel about the Bosnian War and set in the same location of my story. I do not believe in coincidences. Thanks for the sign.

Thank you to Emily Morgan, who helped me see the world as a photographer.

Thank you to Kerry Sparks, my agent and friend. One of these days there will be time travel. Thank you for your support and commitment.

Thank you to Liza Kaplan. Your comments to me after reading the first draft still burn bright. I am so proud of this work we accomplished together. Thank you to Talia Benamy and Ana Deboo for your insight. To Kristie Radwilowicz for my amazing cover and to the whole team at Philomel.

Thank you to Mirela and Nuaim Hendricks for showing us Bosnian hospitality and your beautiful Sarajevo. I am so glad we met. Mirela, thank you for reading and giving me the courage to publish this novel. I admire you and know our paths were meant to cross.

Thank you to David and my kids, who continue to support me on this writing journey. I love you guys.